one
minute
later

Susan Lewis is the bestselling author of over forty books across the genres of family drama, thriller, suspense and crime. She is also the author of *Just One More Day* and *One Day at a Time*, the moving memoirs of her childhood in Bristol during the 1960s. Following periods of living in Los Angeles and the South of France, she currently lives in Gloucestershire with her husband, James, stepsons, Michael and Luke, and mischievous dogs, Coco and Lulu.

To find out more about Susan Lewis:

www.susanlewis.com
www.facebook.com/SusanLewisBooks
@susanlewisbooks

one
minute
later

Susan Lewis

HarperCollins*Publishers*

HarperCollins*Publishers* Ltd
The News Building
1 London Bridge Street
London SE1 9GF

www.harpercollins.co.uk

First published by HarperCollins*Publishers* 2019
4

A catalogue record for this book
is available from the British Library

ISBN: 978-0-00-828676-7

Typeset in Sabon LT Std by
Palimpsest Book Production Ltd, Falkirk, Stirlingshire

Printed and bound by CPI Group (UK) Ltd, Croydon CR0 4YY

MIX
Paper from
responsible sources
FSC C007454

This book is produced from independently certified FSC™ paper
to ensure responsible forest management.

For more information visit: www.harpercollins.co.uk/green

In loving memory of
Jim Lynskey
The bravest and most inspiring
young man I know

CHAPTER ONE
VIVIENNE

The day started out so well.

It was sunny, warm – a welcome bonus for what had so far been a rainy April – with misty slats of sunlight streaming through the partially open plantation shutters. The delicious aroma of fresh coffee and buttery croissants floated up from Max's café next door, enticing her further into the day.

Vivienne Shager stretched luxuriously, her taut, lithe body unravelling its impressive length from the contours of sleep as her mind made a happy reconnect with the world and what it had in store on this glorious work-free day.

It was hard to believe that four full weeks had passed since she and the GaLs – Girls at Law – had run – and completed – an entire marathon to raise funds for the charity Heads Together. So much had happened in that time – mostly work related – but she'd also had an irritating bug that kept coming and going, trying to lay her low, but never quite succeeding. However, she was feeling pretty good today, she soon realized. This was a huge relief, for she and the GaLs were planning some serious celebration of their fund-raising efforts. The day was exclusively theirs; partners, spouses,

1

offspring, parents, bosses and colleagues had been given notice that they'd have to manage without the key women in their lives from midday until said women were ready to tip in the direction of home.

For Vivi there was less of a problem on the family front, since she had no children and her partner, Greg, was going to Lord's for the day. Her mother fortunately didn't live anywhere close by. On the work front, her immediate boss, Trudy Mack-Silver, was one of the GaLs, so no difficulties there. This wasn't to say that Vivienne didn't have a mountain of work to get through; being a senior member of the in-house legal team at FAberlin Investments meant her desk and inbox were always crammed with issues needing urgent attention. Over time she'd learned how to prioritize the ceaseless flow of demands, though many of them saw her labouring late into the evenings and often over entire weekends. She didn't mind. She loved her job, and even liked many of the giant corporation's upper-management team. They could be tough, bad-tempered, inconsiderate and in some cases offensively sexist, but in times of crisis she watched closely, spoke confidently, and managed to learn a lot from those whose jobs she had in her sights.

'You give great kickback,' Trudy often told her following an intense negotiation or fiery confrontation. 'They respect you for it. It makes them listen and, provided you don't go wrong, you could be heading up the entire legal team by the time you're thirty.' Trudy didn't have a problem with this, because she had no such ambitions for herself. She was happy to stay at the level she'd already attained, since it allowed her time to be an at-home-most-evenings wife to Bruno, and available-for-school-runs mum to Nick and Dean.

The other important thing about today was the fact that it was Vivi's twenty-seventh birthday, another reason the GaLs – all graduates of LSE law school – had decided that this should be the marathon reunion day. Combining occasions was something they often did; being so busy with their careers it was the only way to make sure nothing got overlooked.

Throwing back the pale blue striped duvet, Vivi stood as tall as her willowy five foot nine inches allowed, arched her long back and gave a lazy side-to-side twist to stretch out her waist. Since ending the intense pre-marathon training her body had softened slightly, making it, according to Greg, more feminine and curvy, and way sexier. He had a thing about large women, which made his attraction to her a bit of a mystery, given how slender she was. However, they'd been seeing one another for several months, non-exclusively, so their friends weren't living in daily expectation of some significant news. A baby. A wedding. Or perhaps something as simple as moving in together.

Despite their casual relationship, Vivi had to admit that he was a bit of a dreamboat in his way, sporty, witty, fiercely intelligent and very well connected in the financial world, thanks to his gentrified family and their historic ties to the City. When he spoke it was immediately evident that he came from privileged pastures; however, Vivienne strongly doubted that he gave a single thought to the relative ordinariness of her own roots. He wasn't a snob, or not that she'd ever noticed. Nonetheless, she'd never taken him home to meet her family, who still lived in the hopelessly unsophisticated coastal town that Vivi had called home for the first eighteen years of her life.

She'd moved on since uni, had redefined her focus, and was part of another world that could hardly be more different from the simplicity of her early years. Not that *she* had changed in character, for she was still the same upbeat and optimistic Vivi that her beloved grandpa used to call Vivi-vacious. This nickname came from her love of life and people, especially him and NanaBella, which was what she used to call her grandma on account of her name being Bella. Vivi also adored her younger brother, nineteen-year-old Mark, and there was no doubt that she loved her mother with all her heart, and knew that her mother felt the same about her. However, their relationship was the most complicated and frustrating part of Vivienne's world, which was why she didn't often go home. She'd spent too many years trying to unlock the closed doors in her mother's heart and unravel the secrets Gina had never shared, and now all Vivienne wanted was to avoid the confusing and conflicting emotions she always came away with after spending time with her mother.

She wasn't giving any of this a single thought on this glorious spring morning, although she expected her mobile to ring at any minute bringing a dutiful happy birthday call from home. The postman would almost certainly deliver a card from her mother later, and a text would no doubt pop up at some point during the day saying something like *Hope you're having a fabulous day, but please don't have too much to drink.* There wouldn't be a present, because her mother had stopped buying them a few years ago, saying, 'I always get it wrong, so there doesn't seem any point in wasting my money. If you want something, just ask.'

That was Gina all over. In spite of being a glamorous and successful forty-six-year-old businesswoman with a good sense of humour and plenty of friends, she could be prosaically practical about things that called for frivolity or indulgence. (Although, Vivi reminded herself, their surprise trip to Venice a few years ago had proved her mother could be both imaginative and impulsive when she wanted to be.) However, it was true to say that Gina was usually awkward with celebrations, and as for showy declarations of feeling, well, that wasn't her at all. Actually, she was nothing if not a maddening set of contradictions, because she could be a lot of fun when she wanted to be, and when it came to throwing a party she didn't do things by half. Things had changed, however, since Gil, Vivi's stepfather and Mark's father, had left, just over nine years ago. Dear, wonderful Gil, who was still as much a part of their lives as if he'd never gone, except he didn't live with her mother any more – and if anyone could work out the bizarreness of that relationship they'd certainly have a better insight into Gina's mysterious psyche than Vivi had ever managed.

'Don't ask me,' NanaBella had lamented at the time of the break-up. 'I've never really understood your mother, you know that, and she could baffle the heck out of Grandpa when he was alive.'

'But you always loved her and stood by her,' Vivienne had pointed out, for it was true, her grandparents had always been there – for them all.

There was no NanaBella or Grandpa to stand by any of them now. Grandpa had succumbed to cancer when Vivi was six, and NanaBella had been the victim of a drunk driver four Easters ago while on her way into town.

That was another reason for Vivi to feel guilty about not going to see her mother more often. Gina had been devastated by the sudden loss of her beloved mother – they all had, including Gil. But trying to be supportive of Gina was like trying to hug a cactus. She couldn't accept love without becoming prickly and awkward; although she clearly wanted affection, she just didn't seem to know how to handle it.

What was that line about an enigma wrapped up in a mystery inside a riddle? Well, that was her mother, and even Gil, as besotted as he was with her, never tried to claim she was easy.

Reaching for her mobile as it rang, Vivi saw it was one of the GaLs and decided to let it go to messages. She simply had to go to the bathroom before speaking to anyone, and then she'd pop down to Max's for an Americano and pastry to fuel herself up for the day. If her mother called and didn't get an answer she'd assume Vivi was either out for a run, or at Greg's, or still asleep with the phone turned off. She wouldn't worry, because that was something Gina resolutely refused to do, in spite of the fact that the tight line between her beautiful eyes showed that she spent just about every moment of every day worrying about something.

Did she even realize that?

Vivi thought she probably did, but whatever was causing her anxiety – and maybe it was many things

– she guarded it jealously, as though letting go of a single hint of an issue would snap the strings inside her and everything would fall catastrophically apart.

Standing in front of the twin-mirrored bathroom cabinet with its frame of snowball lights and inbuilt heat pad, Vivi pulled a face at herself and stretched out her jaw. She must have slept awkwardly because her neck seemed achy, and the stiffness in her limbs told her that she ought to get back to some proper exercise soon. Still, at least she was breathing more easily this morning, so the bug she'd no doubt picked up on one of several flights she'd made in the past three weeks might finally be clearing.

She was, by anyone's standards, a strikingly lovely young woman. With almond-shaped eyes, blue as a summer sky, and a full, sloppy mouth (her description), she was so entrancing that her friends swore she could hypnotize at a hundred paces. Her complexion was smooth and olive, her cheekbones high, and her light brown hair was a wayward riot of waves that fell about her face and neck in a style all of its own.

Right now it was a tangled mess, and her still sleepy eyes were shadowed by the residue of last night's mascara.

Last night?

Oh, that was right; she'd been at the office until almost midnight, after returning from New York on the red-eye in the morning. It had been a flying visit to the Big Apple, quite literally: one meeting, followed by a dull dinner at Bobby Van's Steakhouse and an overnight stay at the Beekman.

After dragging some trackie bottoms on over her

pyjama shorts and a T-shirt over the camisole, she slipped her feet into an old pair of flip-flops and texted Max with her order. Before leaving she made a quick scan of her emails to be sure nothing earth-shattering had cropped up overnight and finding that nothing had, she went through to the spacious open-plan kitchen-cum-sitting room and gave a small sigh of pleasure to find it virtually drowning in sunlight.

She loved this apartment so much she could marry it. With its high, stuccoed ceilings, tall sash windows and wonderfully airy rooms – all two of them, plus full bathroom containing utility area – she simply couldn't bear to think of living anywhere else. It was certainly one of the reasons she and Greg hadn't considered moving in together. It wasn't big enough for two, and it would be crazy to make this their home when his riverfront duplex in Wapping was at least three times the size, and in real-estate terms far more desirable. Plus, he owned his place outright, thanks to his father, while her first-floor, street-view section of a Georgian town house close to Hollywood Road in Chelsea, was rented. It wasn't that she couldn't afford a mortgage, she was earning enough now to take on some hefty repayments, but the amount needed for a deposit in an area like this – in fact almost anywhere in London – was still out of her reach, largely thanks to her lavish lifestyle. Her friends had managed their down payments thanks to BoMaD – bank of Mum and Dad – but her mother could never have found a near six-figure sum without selling her own house or hairdressing salon, and even if she'd been prepared to do that (she wasn't), Vivi wouldn't have let her. However, her mother – refusing Gil's offer to step in – had practically emptied her savings account to help raise a deposit for the lease on this flat. Having viewed it with Vivi she'd understood right away why her daughter had fallen in love with it, so she'd been keen to make it happen. Since that time, just over four years ago, Vivi had repaid almost two-thirds of the amount, and by the end of the year her mother's account, thanks to the interest Vivi had added to the loan, was likely to be healthier than it had ever been.

Still feeling slightly stiff, she performed a couple more stretches, then grabbed her phone and wallet and let herself out of the flat into the black-and-white-tiled front hall where her upstairs neighbours had parked a bicycle and pushchair. There were also several paintings lining the walls, all done by the delightful and talented Maryanna, who paced about the large attic studio like a trapped cat in the grip of an artistic frenzy. Though her canvases were as indecipherable as they were confrontational (Maryanna's word), Vivienne had long ago decided that she loved them. She owned two, but had left them in the hall for others in the building and their visitors to enjoy as they came and went.

The large black front door with its colourful stained-glass windows and shiny brass letter box was as grand as any Regency house could boast, as was the Doric-columned portico with its ornamental box hedges in tall granite pots. Slender black railings edged the steps down to the pavement, where they turned at right angles to each side to provide a barrier between passers-by and the void above the basement flats.

Max's was adjacent, with a handful of bistro tables

spilling out of the wide-open bifold doors, its palm-strewn interior with plush leather banquettes and slouchy sofas cooled by the gentle spring breeze. In spite of it not yet being nine on a weekend morning, the place was already buzzing.

After collecting her order, free for the birthday girl, Max insisted, and bowing her thanks to the Greek regulars whom Max encouraged to join in a chorus of *charoumena genethlia*, Vivi ran back up to the flat accompanied by the musical sound of many text messages arriving.

Five so far. As she read them, still catching her breath after the sprint, she sipped her coffee and blinked away a spell of dizziness. Remembering she hadn't eaten since yesterday lunchtime, she tucked into her Danish and turned on the radio. Though she probably wouldn't listen to the news, it was second nature to have it on in the background, and when she'd had enough of it she'd do her usual thing of planting her phone in the speakers and scrolling to some favourite tunes.

More texts piled in, mostly from the GaLs: Trudy, Shaz, Saanvi, Sachi and Becky, all saying they couldn't wait to see her later. In came a surprise message from Michael (CEO of FAberlin) and then up popped one from Greg.

Have a great day. Can you do dinner with Carla and Seamus on Wednesday? Sushi?

She thought there might be a conflict, so making a mental note to check before getting back to him, she finished up her Danish and began a quick sort of the mail that had come through the door while she was in New York.

Work hard, play hard, that was her motto, and lately she'd been doing far too much of the former. Boy, was she ready to party today!

Realizing that her mother hadn't called yet, she was about to try her when the telepathic airwaves beat her to it. 'Hey, Mum,' she chirruped as she clicked on. 'You remembered!'

'Remembered what?' her mother countered.

'Ha ha. Are you treating us to a few days at a luxury spa for some M and D bonding, or should I expect a back brush for the shower to replace the one that broke?'

'Did it break? You didn't tell me. I can return it.'

'If I didn't know you were joking I'd think you were weird.'

'You think that anyway. So what are you doing today?'

'Meeting the GaLs for lunch at Beaufort House. We'll probably still be there at teatime.'

'Well try not to make a fool of yourself. Drink tends to do that to a person.'

Vivienne mimed *yadda yadda yadda* and smiled as she said, 'And what are you doing today?'

'Working, of course. You know Saturdays are my busiest day, and Jan left yesterday so there's no one to run reception. I'll be frazzled by the time we close, so lucky I'm not going out tonight.'

That wasn't unusual for her mother; she hadn't had much of a social life since her marriage had ended, although Gil still frequently drove the fifty or so miles from his home to take her to dinner. Strange, but Vivienne kept reminding herself that it was her mother's

11

life, not hers, so if Gina and Gil wanted a long-distance relationship with unspecified benefits it was their business, not hers.

'Are you seeing Greg today?' Gina asked.

'No, but we're supposed to be meeting some friends for lunch tomorrow. I might have to cancel, though. I've got so much on at the office . . .' She checked to see who an incoming text was from and said, 'Mum, sorry, I have to go. I'll call again later, OK?'

There was a brief silence, and Vivi wasn't sure whether her mother was hurt or annoyed, probably both. 'If you have time,' Gina replied. Her tone betrayed nothing more than a soft sigh that said she was used to being cut short, since it happened all the time. *And where did I get that from?* Vivi thought defensively as she rang off. Her mother had been cutting her short all her life.

The text was from Michelle, her best friend since they were five; Michelle who'd been like a sister to her until their lives had taken such different paths, Vivi to go off to London and uni, Michelle to stay in Kesterly, marry young and have a family. They'd remained in touch mostly through birthday cards and the occasional text, but in spite of Vivi being godmother to both Michelle's children they hardly ever saw one another now. There was a time when it would have broken Vivi's heart to think of them drifting apart, in a way it still did, but life, ambition, motherhood and all sorts of other demands meant they no longer had much in common.

Michelle never forgot Vivi's birthday, and Vivi desperately wished she could say the same, but more often than not she was late with a text, and later still with cards. She was generous with presents, though, especially for the children, and Michelle always sent photographs to show how delighted they were with the new toy or book or outrageously expensive designer wear.

Happy Birthday to you. Hope you have a fabulous day. We all send love. What are you planning? Are you even in the country?

Remembering she'd been in Dubai the last time she and Michelle were in touch, Vivi couldn't help wondering how interested her friend really was in her life. Probably not very, for Michelle had never been ambitious, caring little for the crazy kind of jet-set existence that was so totally at odds with the plodding and predictable world of Kesterly. But it was typical of Michelle to show an interest: kind, considerate, full of fun and mischief, she had a way of making a person feel valued and special even if they no longer shared girlhood dreams. What a gift that was. Vivi wished she had it, but every time she tried to focus more on matters outside work something would come up and everything else would be forgotten.

She texted back: *Tx for the happy birthday. You're amazing. In London. Seeing the GaLs at Beaufort House. Should be fun.* Had Michelle ever heard of Beaufort House? She'd know who the GaLs were, though she might not remember all their names. She was aware, of course, that they were Vivi's closest friends now, just as Sam, Michelle's husband, had become her closest friend.

What mattered was that they'd always been there for one another while growing up. Nothing would ever change that; Vivi just hoped a time would never

13

come when they lost touch completely, though she was aware that it easily could.

Kicking off her flip-flops, she was about to read her other texts when Michelle came through again. *Millie wants you to know that her little brother should be called Eeyore because he cries like a donkey.*

Vivi broke into a deep, throaty laugh, and for a few minutes they texted back and forth as though almost five-year-old Millie was sending the messages about her new pony and the present she and Mummy had sent to Vivi for her birthday that smelled lovely.

Ten minutes later Vivienne stepped into the shower and closed her eyes as a power-charged flow of warm water cascaded over her. She spun around, lifting her face to the jets, and put a hand to the wall as she swayed. She was thinking about her sweet little god-children, Millie and Ash, and what a pity it was that her own children (when she finally got round to having them, and that wasn't going to be any time soon) would be so much younger than them. And maybe, with her living in London and them way across the country in Kesterly-on-Sea, they wouldn't even really get to know one another. That felt sadder than sad, given how close she and Michelle had always been, but the only solution would be for her to meet and marry someone who wanted to live in Kesterly, which was never going to happen. Nor, considering Sam's business as a local builder and Michelle's own ties to Kesterly, were they ever likely to move to London.

By the time Vivi was ready to leave the flat she'd taken three more calls from various friends, and had managed to book herself a Shellac manicure for eight on Monday evening. She probably ought to make a hair appointment sometime soon, too, for the random whirl of waves clustered around her face and neck was in need of some taming.

Wearing ripped skinny jeans, a pair of flat strappy sandals and a waist-length leather jacket, she decided to walk to Beaufort House. The weather was too good to miss a moment of it, and capturing its buoyancy in her stride she seemed about to break into a dance as she started off down the street.

As she was turning into the Fulham Road her phone rang again, and seeing it was her half-brother, Mark, she swiftly clicked on. 'Hey you! What are you doing up so early?' she cried.

'My phone went off,' he grumbled. 'I was working until four this morning and I'm back on at five this evening, but no one cares about me.' A sport and exercise student at Birmingham Uni, he'd taken a job as a barman at Pitcher and Piano to provide himself with some spending money. His father, Gil, was covering the lion's share of his other expenses, including his rent and the small car he used to bomb around town. 'Happy birthday,' he said with a yawn.

'Thanks. So Mum called to remind you?'

'What do you think? Not that I'd forgotten, I just wouldn't have remembered until I woke up. So, are you back from New York?'

'Yesterday. Off to Singapore on Wednesday.' Of course. That was why she couldn't make a sushi dinner with Greg and the others. She'd better check her calendar to be sure she was up to speed with everything else. Waiting for an ambulance to cut its siren as it

15

pulled into Chelsea and Westminster A & E, she started across the road, saying, 'Any chance of you getting to London sometime soon? I feel as though I haven't seen you for ages.'

'Since Christmas,' he reminded her, 'but I get that you're missing me. It happens. I have to deal with it all the time.'

Laughing, she said, 'So how many hearts have you broken this week?'

'Lost count, but hey, who's taking care of mine?'

'That tough old thing? I think it can take care of itself.'

'Brutal. How's Greg? Are we ever going to meet him?'

'He's OK. Actually I haven't seen him since . . .' She tried to think. 'It's been too long. Did you get to the Six Nations match in the end?'

'You bet. The bloke's a genius. I already thanked him for the tickets, by the way.'

'Great. Did Gil go with you?'

'Sure. Then we drove all the way back to Kesterly to take Mum for dinner in case she was feeling left out.'

Vivienne had to laugh.

'Did she tell you she's taken up running?' Mark asked.

'You're kidding.'

'No, I went out with her while I was there. She's pretty fit, actually, but I guess that's no surprise when she goes to the gym quite regularly. Dad reckons the running thing is so she can run with you when you go home, or maybe she wants to do a marathon with you?'

And this, Vivienne was thinking, *is why my mother is so confusing. She doesn't mention anything about it*

16

*to me, but Gil is probably right, she'll have me in mind
on one level or another, because she always has – and
if not me then Mark, or Gil, then back to me . . .*

'Listen,' she said to Mark, 'I'll let you get some more
sleep before you have to go back on shift. Speak soon.
Love you.'

'Right back at you,' and he was gone.

She pressed on towards Beaufort Street, and checked
her phone to see if any more texts had arrived in the
last few minutes. Several had: more birthday messages
from friends and colleagues, also one from Gil, who
had no doubt also sent flowers, because he always did.

The only person she knew for a fact she wouldn't
get a call or anything else from on this, or any other
day, was her real father, because she never did.

Beaufort House was in the World's End part of Chelsea,
on the corner of Beaufort Street and the famous King's
Road. It was an area that Vivienne found as electrifying
as the City where she worked, though for entirely
different reasons. The buzz here was all about being
social, cosmopolitan, and fabulously multicultural. The
restaurants were as diverse as their deliciously exotic
ingredients, the fashions as outrageous as they were
expensive and the interior design shops as inspirational
as a genie's bottle full of crazy dreams. It could hardly be
more different from her home town with its unedifying
mix of tired terraces, fish-and-chip shops and donkey
rides. On the other hand, she was ready to concede that
Kesterly had its charms too, just not enough of them
to have kept her there past her eighteenth birthday,
when she'd launched herself with high excitement and

yes, some trepidation on London. Being in the capital had been her goal for as long as she could remember, so too had been studying hard and working her way into a high-powered job that would open doors to all kinds of other worlds, and make her feel as important and accomplished as she'd always longed to be.

It was happening every day, sometimes in small ways, other times in great significant bursts. The headiness of success was as intoxicating as the champagne she and her friends cracked to celebrate it while the satisfaction of knowing she'd bested a rival, or helped seal a long-fought-for merger, was perhaps the greatest kick of all. Though she wasn't particularly aware of how much everyone valued her as a colleague or friend, the way she was greeted as she entered the bustling, airy bar of Beaufort House made her swell with pride and pleasure.

'About bloody time!'

'Happy birthday!'

'Champagne's on you.'

'Someone get the goddess a glass.'

The other five GaLs were already there, grouped around their usual table next to the window, and as a flute was thrust into Vivienne's hand it seemed the entire room joined in a rousing chorus of 'Happy Birthday'.

It was exhilarating and hilarious as perfect strangers bowed or raised glasses, and a couple of bar staff shimmied about with more champagne.

As the fun died down and Vivienne sank laughing into the chair they'd reserved for her, she gasped and laughed again as Trudy pointed her to the pile of gifts at the end of the cushioned bench seat.

'All for you,' Trudy declared exultantly.

'All for one, one for all!' Sachi sang out, her engaging French accent resonating even in those few simple words.

Saanvi, whose stunning black hair and exquisite features made her as exotic as the Indian divinity she was named for, began passing the gifts along. Saanvi's much older husband ran a global macro hedge fund, where Saanvi had recently been promoted to head up the quantitative risk management team.

'How many carats did Greg manage?' Shaz, their Australian derivatives lawyer, wanted to know. Though Shaz mainly worked out of Frankfurt, she was back and forth to London all the time.

'I'm sure it'll be at least seven,' Vivienne shot back, causing another raucous uplift of glasses to toast the prediction.

They'd shared so much during their time at uni that sometimes it felt as though they hadn't had a life before. They never judged one another in negative ways; they did everything they could to support each other, because they understood who they were and what power their friendship gave them.

These GaLs were her family away from home, the rock that kept her safe and strong; the exclusive network that made everything possible.

'Are you in Singapore on Thursday?' Trudy wanted to know.

'I leave on Wednesday,' Vivi told her.

'Saanvi, did you hear that?' Trudy demanded. 'She is going to Singapore on Wednesday.'

'Brilliant,' Saanvi responded triumphantly. 'Email me your details and I'll make sure I'm on the same flight. Where are you staying?'

'I'm not sure yet,' Vivienne replied, 'but I'll put it in the email. Oh my God, what's this?' She pulled the softest, palest pink something from a satin-ribboned box with velveteen stripes and diamanté studs. 'Oh, you're kidding me. Myla silk pyjamas. I've always wanted a pair . . .'

Trudy threw out her hands. 'How on earth did I know that?' she demanded in amazement.

Vivienne pressed a hand to her chest as she laughed, then leaned forwards to embrace her friend. She coughed to try and clear the tightness in her lungs and sat down again to open more presents.

From Saanvi there were two tickets for a day full of treatments at the Thermes Marins spa in Monte Carlo. 'Oh wow!' Vivienne cried, completely blown away. 'We haven't been there since we graduated. This is amazing.'

'Open this one next,' Shaz insisted, pushing a small silver-wrapped packet into Vivienne's hand.

Vivienne's eyes widened with astonishment when she found more tickets, this time for a helicopter transfer from Nice to Monaco.

'And in this one,' Sachi told her, 'you will find a voucher for two return flights to Nice – and a little something else to go with it.'

The something else turned out to be a night at the Hotel de Paris.

'Now all you have to do,' Trudi pointed out, 'is decide which one of us you're going to take with you.'

'Oh for God's sake,' Vivienne protested. 'How on earth am I going to do that? Can't we get our diaries together and work out a time for us all to go?'

'Best idea I've heard all day,' Shaz concurred, refilling the glasses.

As Vivienne watched and joined in the bubbling excitement she pushed at her chest again, as though the pressure might disperse the ache. She really ought to eat something before downing the champagne, or she'd have another dizzy spell. She reached for a smoked salmon hors d'oeuvre and popped it into her mouth. Delicious, heavenly, so she tried another.

Shaz was asking her something, but for some reason Shaz's voice seemed to be coming through water. It bobbed back to the surface with sudden clarity as she said, 'Vivi! Are you all right?'

Vivienne laughed. 'Of course,' but the room was dipping away and lurching back as though she were on a ship in a storm, and when she tried to lift her glass she found she couldn't move her arm. Everything hurt, she realized, her whole body, and the pain was clenching so hard into her chest . . .

'*Vivienne!*' someone shouted. She thought it was Saanvi.

'Oh my God!' Hands were closing around her arms. 'She's fainting. Get her some air . . .'

Vivienne's face contorted as she tried to breathe. 'I don't . . . It's . . .' she gasped.

'Her lips are blue . . . Oh Jesus! Vivienne!'

'*Help!* Someone. We need help.'

Vivienne was still trying to breathe.

'Let me through. I'm a doctor, clear some space.'

A man's face came into view, blurred and dark and moving close.

'Call an ambulance,' he barked. 'Do it now. What's her name?'

'Vivienne.'

'Vivienne,' he said urgently. 'I'm going to lie you down . . .'

She was trying to listen, even to laugh, because this was funny wasn't it, or embarrassing . . . It couldn't be real, but it hurt so much . . .

'Deep breaths,' he was saying, moving her roughly to the floor. 'Come on Vivienne, you can do it. In, out. In, out.' His fist was banging into her chest.

She tried. In . . . The noise was awful. Rushing, ripping, breaking . . . 'Mum,' she murmured weakly.

'In, out.' The world was going black. He was still banging her chest . . . 'Stay with me,' he shouted angrily. 'Vivienne. *Stay with me.*'

CHAPTER TWO
SHELLEY

Summer 1984

It was a crackpot idea.

Everyone had said so.

Friends, families, even Shelley and Jack, whose plan it was, thought they were crazy, but hey ho, they'd gone ahead and done it anyway. Why not? They'd spent holidays at Deerwood Farm as far back as when they were knee-high to tadpoles, as Shelley's uncle Bob used to call them. They'd continued to come as teens, helping out in the barns, running wild and loving every animal as if it were a pet – and every mouthful of Aunt Sarah's home bakes as if they were the very best in the world, which they were.

Even when Jack and Shelley had started going further afield for their holidays they'd continued to count those halcyon summers at the farm amongst their happiest memories. The place was as special to them as any place could possibly be, for it was at Deerwood that their childhood friendship had blossomed during their teenage years into an embarrassed and fumbling romance, and was also where Jack, aged fourteen, had first asked Shelley to marry him. (He'd asked several times after that and she'd always readily accepted. It was just something they used to do every now and again for the sheer joy of it.) Jack even swore Deerwood was magical, and Shelley, whose aunt and uncle owned the farm, had earnestly assured him he was right.

Jack had grown up in the semi next door to Shelley on a shady, red-brick street in Ealing. They'd been best friends forever, so it was no surprise to anyone when they'd married as soon as their uni days were over. By then Jack was a qualified veterinary surgeon, and Shelley was already teaching at a West London primary.

With a little help from Jack's parents they'd scraped together a deposit for a two-bedroomed house in Brentford, and their first child, Hanna, was born a year after they moved in. Their second, Zoe, came along eighteen months later on the same day that Princess Diana gave birth to Prince William. They were happy, blessed, had little to complain about, with Jack's popularity as a vet growing and Shelley's role as a full-time mum keeping her occupied, if not entirely satisfied.

Then Uncle Bob died, four years after Aunt Sarah, and to Shelley and Jack's amazement it turned out that Deerwood Farm, together with Bob and Sarah's meagre savings, were now theirs.

'Why didn't Bob leave it to you?' Shelley asked her father, still reeling from the unexpectedness of it that was already turning into something that felt vaguely like excitement. 'You're his brother.'

'I'm no farmer,' her father chuckled, 'and Bob knew that.'

'Well you can hardly say that I am either,' Shelley pointed out. 'Or Jack.'

'Ah, but Bob knew you loved the place, and that's what would have mattered to him and Sarah. I'm sure she was behind the idea, and when Jack decided to become a vet it would have made up her mind. Having said that, there are no conditions attached to the inheritance. You can sell it if you like and use the money to get a bigger house, or put it aside for the girls' education.'

Jack and Shelley looked at one another, not needing words to know what the other was thinking, but not yet ready to confide those thoughts in anyone else.

Less than six months later they were in the depths of the rolling countryside, the proud new owners of a rambling, draughty, leaky farmhouse, several ramshackle barns, half a brick shed (the other half had collapsed like an old drunk into a pile of desolation around its own feet); seventy-five acres of untended fields with any number of streams passing merrily or sluggishly through them; ancient woods that Shelley and Jack remembered playing and camping in but were now filled with bindweed and brambles; and heaven only knew how many miles of unkempt hedgerows, rotting gates and clogged ditches. Added to this were five batty sheep of varying ages (breeds yet to be determined, four ewes and a vasectomized little runt of a ram); ten cheery hens very generous with the eggs, three Aylesbury ducks also generous with the eggs (so they were told, yet to see any); a hamster that they'd brought with them and an ageing border collie called Todger whom everyone instantly adored and who was swiftly renamed Dodger (soon to be known as Dodgy). There was also a lot of machinery they had yet to identify, an ancient tractor with a missing steering wheel, a broken trailer, a 1960s Land Rover with more miles on the clock than the clock had numbers, a few dozen bundles of very useful wire fencing, and enough furniture inside the house to keep an auctioneer busy for weeks.

By now Shelley and Jack were in their early thirties and had all the energy and belief in themselves – and each other – that was required to turn this place into a dream home, a thriving farm and an educational paradise for their girls. From the instant Hanna and Zoe arrived their eyes had glowed with excitement and wonder; the fact that there was another brother or sister on the way wasn't anywhere near as thrilling as the apparent imminent possibility of lambs. Yes, all four ewes were expecting, Giles, the next-door farmer and interim custodian of Deerwood, had informed them on arrival (and yes, there really was a farmer Giles in the area, although that was his first name), and if they wanted any help with the lambing he'd be happy to send someone over when the time came.

They readily accepted the kindness. Jack might be a qualified vet, but it had been a while since his work experience on a farm in Cheshire, so he was definitely open to a refresher course. And if the girls wanted to watch the miracle of birth then so they should, because they might be on duty next year, by which time they were likely to have a flock of thousands. Well, dozens – or at least twelve, depending on how things went.

'You are absolutely loving this, aren't you?' Shelley murmured one evening, gazing into Jack's midnight-blue eyes and feeling (strangely, given how long she'd loved him) how wonderful it was to love him. She was lying on her side – so large with her pregnancy by now that even rolling onto her back was an effort – and he was lying on his side looking at her.

'Aren't you?' he asked, smoothing damp tendrils of her fine sandy hair back from her face. It was late February and freezing outside, but for tonight at least the generator was working, making them so hot indoors that in a few minutes they might just take a moonlight stroll.

'Yes, I am,' she whispered. 'I really think we're going to be happy here.'

'I know it,' he murmured. 'I've been looking for a way of saying this since we arrived, and now I think I have it. The minute we turned in from the road, all the way along the drive to the farm, seeing the fields, the huge sky and humpback bridge, the cattle grids, trees, hedgerows, I felt as though we were fitting back into a place we'd only ever left temporarily. Then, when I saw the house, this house, sad and neglected, I thought, I swear this, I thought it gave a little sigh of relief when it realized it was us – and if you laugh I'll leave you.'

How could she not laugh, and at the same time not cry, because he'd just found a far better way of putting into words their return to Deerwood than she ever could. That was her husband all over, as romantic as a poet, as rash and tempestuous as the wind, and as attuned to his surroundings as the wildlife that shared every nook and cranny. And how lucky she was to have him as her lover; her rock; the father of her children, her best friend forever and now her partner in this mad, challenging and exhilarating new dream.

* * *

A week later things had moved on at such a pace at Deerwood that Shelley was struggling to keep track of it all. Builders, plumbers and electricians were assessing the cost of repairs and rebuilds; Jack had signed on with an urban veterinary practice for three days a week in order to ensure some sort of income; the girls were enrolled at a nursery school in the nearest village – six miles away – and Shelley was registered at a small health centre on the outskirts of the same village, where she'd had a long and enjoyable chat with the midwife about country living. She was due to give birth at the maternity unit of Kesterly Royal Infirmary – fifteen miles from the farm – sometime in the next two weeks.

Meantime, she and Jack were devouring all the books they could find on farming, sheep, land cultivation, understanding organics, slaughter, local markets; there was so much to learn that they'd probably never take it all in, but at least it was a start. With the support of their families, who'd descended to help out during this crucial period, they'd started to clear the cluttered farmyard of all the rusty paraphernalia, brambles and build-up of filth that had accumulated since Sarah's passing. Giles and a couple of his workers came to ferry the junk to the tip, or move usables to a storage trailer that they'd parked in a nearby field. Giles was happy to leave it there for as long as it was needed.

'Five quid a week,' he announced in his gruff West Country burr. His mischievous hazel eyes were round and fox-like, his grizzly grey beard trembled with his suppressed laughter. 'If it's all the same to you I'll take it off the rent I pay to put my cattle in your top fields.'

More than happy with the arrangement, Shelley made a note to find out how much rent he actually paid and for what number of acres, also whether it might be possible to interest him or any other neighbouring farmer in making further use of their thirty-odd hectares until they had need of them themselves. It would all add to their income, which stood at zero for the moment, but they still had the money Bob had left, and their savings (mostly earmarked for doing up the house and barns), and Jack's salary would soon kick in. She also needed to check out what government subsidies they might be entitled to, and any rules, ancient or modern, British or European, that they needed to obey.

So much to do and to learn, and not only about reviving a farm, waterproofing barns and birthing lambs, but how to manage without electricity and heating each time the ancient generator took a wheezing, groaning break from its efforts. With no idea when it might get a second wind, they'd already had the chimneys swept so each of the four hearths on the ground floor was filled with flaming logs, and since Jack had managed to start up the old Aga they'd found themselves with a haphazard supply of lukewarm water. Cooking was mostly done over the fires or on a spanking new portable gas stove that Jack's parents had brought with them, having been warned of the need. Quite what the electricity company was doing about restoring their supply was anyone's guess, but they certainly didn't seem to be in any hurry to get things sorted.

The girls were loving every aspect of their new existence, from having their aunt and uncle – Jack's brother and sister-in-law – along with both sets of grandparents camping out in three of the six bedrooms (they'd brought their own sleeping bags, pillows and hot-water bottles), to lighting candles to go up to bed like Wee Willie Winkie, to toasting their breakfast over rekindled fires in the morning. Best of all was collecting eggs from the henhouse, which they carefully carried back in cardboard boxes, watching their bounty with round-eyed awe in case one of them hatched. The impossibility of that had yet to be explained to them, and no doubt would be in the fullness of time – the wicked gleam in Jack's eye whenever the subject was mentioned told Shelley that he already had a story worked out.

It was midway through the afternoon of their ninth day at Deerwood that Shelley found herself standing alone at the centre of the still cluttered farmyard, hands pressing into the small of her back as she took a good long look at their new home, although of course it was anything but new. Set as it was against a backdrop of billowing clouds and the vast outstretched branches of a giant evergreen oak, it appeared as settled as the centuries that had passed since its foundations were dug, and as contented in its place as the hills on the far horizon. In spite of its shabby roofs with their missing tiles and broken gutters, and its crumbling grey stone walls and splintered window frames – not to mention the fortune it was going to cost to restore its dignity – she already loved the place with a passion, and knew that Jack did too.

They had no clear idea yet of how they were going to liven up the interior while carefully retaining its gentle and noble character, but it would include doubling the size of the kitchen, knocking two sitting rooms into one and installing at least three more bathrooms. She wanted the place to feel as happy with them as they did with it, as respected as it was cherished, and as proud as it deserved to be. She'd thought about engaging an interior designer, but it was a luxury they couldn't afford, and besides, it didn't feel right for an outsider to put his or her stamp on a home that was so intrinsically theirs. Somehow she was going to do this herself, using magazines for ideas and builders with skill and imagination for execution.

Meanwhile, they needed a temporary solution to the leaks and draughts, and a brand-new generator so they could quietly and tenderly release the old boy from its struggle to help them get settled.

'Back aching?' a voice behind her asked.

She turned to find her father coming out of the barn where he'd been watching over the pregnant ewes while the two grandmothers did a supermarket shop in town. Nathan and Katya, Jack's brother and sister-in-law, were out walking the land with the girls, nature spotting and gathering sticks for the fire. Jack was being a vet this afternoon, and Giles and his men who were so often around seemed absent for the moment.

Resting her head on her father's shoulder as he put an arm around her, she inhaled deeply the sweet scent of haylage that clung to his clothes. Giles had sent over the mix, because he knew their requirements long before they did and he was always willing to give supplies, advice and support (at a small charge).

'Don't tell me you're having second thoughts,' her father teased as he too drank in the farmhouse's serenity and soul-nourishment.

'Definitely not,' she replied. 'OK, I realize it's going to take years and a small fortune to get it into shape and that we'll probably never have any money to speak of, but we will have a home and what better one could we wish for than this?'

Her father squeezed her gently. 'Sarah knew what she was doing when she made sure this place went to you and Jack.'

Later that evening as they gathered round the old kitchen table with a fire roaring in the hearth and the Aga doing its stuttering best, Shelley's mother waited for dinner to be over before setting down a battered cardboard box. Keeping a hand on the lid she looked first at Shelley, then at Jack.

Shelley regarded her curiously, sensing that her full attention was required for this, whatever it was, and when Patty was satisfied all eyes were on her she carefully opened the box. 'I found these in the chest in our bedroom,' she explained, lifting out something heavy wrapped in limp and faded tissue paper. 'I reckon Bob must have put them away after Sarah went because they were painful for him to look at. Do you remember these?' she asked her husband.

Shelley winced at the clench of a Braxton Hicks contraction as everyone watched her mother unwrap two bronze statuettes, each about ten inches high, and set them facing each other on the table. They were exquisitely crafted, seeming to move with each other, hands outstretched, hips slightly turned, feet partly raised. The male was in a sharp, baggy suit, a trilby tipped back on his head, his arms raised in rhythm before he spun his partner into the dance. She was wearing a flapper dress, the fringes seeming to sway as she started the turn, the fingers of her right hand appearing to yearn for his touch. There exuded such a profound feeling of romance and togetherness that Shelley found her eyes going to Jack as his came to her.

'They were given to Sarah's grandparents as a wedding gift,' Shelley's mother told them. 'Sarah treasured them above anything. I think, I *know*, that she'd want you to display them again.'

Shelley smiled as Jack, the old romantic, got to his feet and hummed softly as he pulled her to hers.

'You're like the dancers coming to life,' Hanna declared, catching on delightedly.

Jack winked at her and moved Shelley into his arms, while her eyes returned to the bronzes. They felt special even beyond their probable value, and she knew that her mother felt it too. It was as though they had come straight from her aunt's heart, with love and gratitude for taking the place on. And they would always be here, a symbol of how important it was to move in step with one another, to love and dance and never forget how precious life was.

The visiting family had gone to stay in town tonight, taking a luxury B & B break from the hard floors and dripping ceilings of the east-wing bedrooms. Though Hanna and Zoe's room didn't leak, and had proper beds with feathery duvets and pillows, even a thin trail of heating, Jack and Shelley had thought it might be a nice treat for them to go too. However, there had been no moving them. Lambs were on the way and they knew very well that it would happen tonight if they weren't there.

They weren't wrong.

The first excited shout went up around 2 a.m., carrying through the wind like a bird, waking Jack and Shelley and setting them scrambling for matches to light the candles when the lamp switches clicked uselessly. It was Harry, Giles's second son, letting them know that one of the ewes had gone into labour.

'The girls,' Shelley panted, tugging on her voluminous jeans and one of Jack's sweaters.

'I'll get them,' he said, stuffing his feet into old trainers and rushing from the room.

'No, I will,' she insisted. 'You go and see if Harry needs help.'

The girls were already on the landing in nighties and slippers, and tugging on the coats they'd kept next to their beds for just this moment. 'We heard Harry,' Zoe shrieked eagerly. 'Are the lambs here?'

'About to be,' Jack promised, scooping her up. 'Come on, let's go and see.'

'Can I name him?' Hanna asked, running after them.

'If it's a girl,' Jack reminded her.

'I'm naming him if it's a boy,' Zoe said over his shoulder to make sure Hanna heard.

'What if it's twins?' Hanna asked. 'I hope it's twins. Daddy, you're going too fast, I can't see.'

'Climb on board,' he instructed, pausing for her to jump onto his back.

Shelley could just about make them out at the bottom of the stairs as she started down with a precariously balanced candle.

Jack was lighting a paraffin lamp. 'Is everyone OK?' he demanded as a weak amber glow lit the hall. 'Are you all here?'

'We're here,' the girls chorused.

'Me too,' Shelley called out.

He was at the door, tugging it open. A spirited wind hurled across the yard, pushing him back. He battled through it. The girls cowered into his neck, shielding their faces from the silvery spikes of rain.

From the front door Shelley shouted, 'Jack!'

Harry appeared at the barn door. 'Bit of trouble,' he shouted. 'Tried fishing it out myself, but you'd better come.'

'Jack!' Shelley yelled again.

'Is it going to be all right?' Zoe panicked.

'You won't let it die, will you, Daddy?' Hanna wailed.

'*Jack!*' Shelley all but screamed.

At last he caught her voice and turned round.

'My waters have broken,' she yelled above the storm.

His eyes rounded in the moonlight, as driving rain whipped into his face and gusts tore at his hair.

'We have to get to the lamb,' Hanna cried, digging in her heels to make him go faster.

Shelley watched them, clutching the door frame as the first contraction bit down hard.

Jack seemed frozen.

Harry shouted again.

Hanna was pointing to the barn and yelling.

Shelley gave a quick pant. Hers wouldn't be the first

baby born in a stable, she reminded herself, provided she could get there.

The next contraction clawed so harshly she slumped to her knees.

She looked up just in time to see Jack disappearing into the barn.

CHAPTER THREE
VIVIENNE

Present Day

This wasn't a place Vivi knew, or a feeling she recognized, or a sound she could identify through the strangeness of this elusive reality. *Thump, wheeze, thump, click, bleep.* On and on, never stopping, never changing: soft, loud, lilting, dropping . . . There was a fog, not in her eyes, yes, in her eyes, but in her head too, deep inside her brain, spreading all the way through her right out to the edges of her vision, circling brief moments of clarity in a dim, misty halo.

She blinked slowly, and felt a clutching sensation around her mouth. She thought she might be standing on the corner of the Fulham Road talking on the phone, waiting for an ambulance to pass.

The siren wailed into silence; voices rose and rippled across an invisible divide. Someone was speaking her name. 'Vivienne, can you hear me? Vivi. Vivienne.'

The fog closed in, colourless and opaque, and everything went quiet again as she floated back into darkness, away from the strange sounds and confusion of pain.

* * *

A while later Vivi's eyes flickered open again. She could see a vague, bluish light and blinked to try to focus on it. She felt dazzled and trapped, pinned inside a place she couldn't distinguish. She tried to make sense of the peculiar noises around her: heavy whispers; loud, desperate breaths. An unsteady hush was punctured by bleeps; grazed by a constant, low-pitched hum.

She moved her pupils to the edge of their sockets. She was lying down, that much was clear, and without trying she knew she couldn't get up. In the semi-darkness her gaze reached the long, loose limbs of someone sprawled on a chair. It was her brother, Mark. She'd been talking to him on the phone while on the corner of the Fulham Road. A siren shrilled as an ambulance went by . . .

Now Mark was here, beside her, his head and body slumped awkwardly as he slept. He seemed younger than his nineteen years, more like sixteen, although the stubble on his chin and shadows, like bruises, around his closed eyes aged him again.

There was someone beside him, in another chair. He was asleep too, his handsome yet grey face resting on one hand.

It was her stepfather, Gil, here to wish her happy birthday. He'd probably brought flowers. He always gave her flowers.

She tried to speak, but something was filling her mouth. She wanted to take it away, but her hand wouldn't move, weighed down by something she couldn't see. Her tongue was heavy and too weak to clear the blockage.

Confusion and fear descended on her, like clouds

gently bursting with the threat of more to come. This was a hospital, she realized. *She* was in hospital, but why? What had happened to her? She felt a sudden, desperate need for her mother, so powerful that she wanted to cry out for her, but her voice was a small, stifled moan inside the mask over her mouth.

Mark's eyes opened, and as he saw her watching him he sat forward so quickly he almost slipped from the chair.

'Vivi?' he croaked urgently. 'Oh God, Vivi,' and he started to cry. 'Dad,' he muttered over his shoulder. 'Dad!'

Gil woke with a start and shot to his feet almost before he knew what he was doing. He looked rumpled and afraid. 'Vivi, sweetie,' he murmured, coming forward. 'Oh, Vivi.'

A nurse suddenly swept into the room, summoned by only she knew what. She slipped in front of Mark and Gil, blocking them from Vivi's view, but her face was kind, her voice reassuring.

'I'll get your mother,' Gil said, and a moment later he was gone.

Mark stood silently watching the adjustment of tubes and patches, the checking of readings and making of notes on a tablet. The small, plump woman was calm and efficient, smiling as she smoothed the hair from Vivienne's forehead to inspect her eyes.

'Hello, Vivi Shager,' she whispered in a soft, accented voice. 'Nice to meet you.'

Vivi couldn't answer, wasn't even sure what she'd say if she could. It was hard to think, to register everything that was happening, to move beyond the terrible pain in her chest.

A face appeared beside the nurse, gaunt, pale and trying to be calm. As Vivi's eyes locked onto her mother's she felt safe for a moment, the way she had as a child when Gina had moved in to make everything all right, but then the feeling was gone again.

Gina's voice, her tone as she said, 'I'm here,' provided another brief lifeline, but Vivi didn't know how to grasp it.

Flashes of memory were showing themselves now – the brightness of sunshine in Beaufort House, friends' faces turning from laughter to confusion and horror; a stranger thumping her chest, sirens wailing – and as the stultifying reality of it overwhelmed her she closed her eyes again, trying to shut out the fear.

A week passed in frightening and painful stages; a slow and often doubtful return from a near-fatal myocardial infarction – in other words a major heart attack. Vivi had been told more than once that it was lucky a doctor had been at hand, *and* that she'd been so close to the hospital, because every second had counted.

Apparently she'd suffered two cardiac arrests in the ambulance, and had twice been brought back to life.

She had no memory of that short, frantic journey to A & E, although some residue of it seemed sometimes to filter into her dreams. What had come next, her arrival, the emergency treatment, also remained a blank, but she'd been told about the resuscitation efforts, the urgent transfer to a cardiac catheter lab, how her poor, struggling heart had collapsed into near-catastrophic failure.

She was in the High Dependency Unit now, having

been moved from Intensive Care two days ago, though she wasn't sure she could remember it happening. She remained weak and sometimes disoriented, as though she was tuning in and out of someone else's world. The monitors she was attached to registered her heart's functions, from its rhythm, to blood flow, to pressure, while the drainage tubes in her chest and bladder performed their unjolly, but necessary duties.

In more lucid moments she felt as though she'd been slammed by a speeding truck. It hurt to breathe, to move, even to think. In some ways thinking was the worst for it invariably took her to a place of panic, to a dark, unnatural world she might never now escape from.

People came and went: doctors, nurses, medical students, technicians, friends and colleagues. Everyone was trying to bolster her, to tell her how much better she seemed today, but she didn't feel better, and didn't know what to say to them.

She wasn't herself. She'd changed in ways she didn't yet understand; she just knew it had happened, not only in her heart, but in her head.

As her strength staged a tentative and unreliable return she was weighed daily and encouraged to eat and drink. Her heartbeat and blood pressure were held steady by the inotropic drugs being fed through the IV in her neck.

'I think we can remove the pacing wires tomorrow,' Arnie Novak, the cardiologist, had told her this morning. He was a nice man, Eastern European, she thought, but she couldn't tell which country, and she didn't like to ask. She hadn't said much to anyone since waking;

often she didn't have the strength to utter more than a few words, and just as often she wanted to hide away from what she might be told.

Now, hearing footsteps approaching, she knew intuitively that they were heading her way, and that they belonged to her mother. It was a kind of telepathy that made her feel secure and relieved, but other things welled up in her too, such as anger and resentment, things her mother didn't deserve. Breakfast was barely over and here was Gina, worried, frightened, and failing to understand why this had happened when they'd been told, twenty-seven years ago, following two-week-old Vivienne's arterial switch operation, that they had no more to fear, she could lead a normal life.

As far as Vivi was aware no one understood what had gone wrong, or, if they did they hadn't yet told her whether the serious episodes she'd just suffered were in any way connected to the congenital heart defect she'd been born with.

'How are you feeling?' her mother asked fondly, putting down the magazines she'd brought in and pressing a kiss to Vivi's forehead. Vivi caught the citrusy scent of her, light and fresh with the earthy warmth that came from her skin – as familiar as the sound of her voice and the movements of her hands.

How was she feeling?

'Fine,' Vivi replied. Her voice was stronger than a whisper now, but not as full as it should be. What was the point in telling the truth when there was nothing her mother could do to change things?

'No pain?'

Vivi shook her head. She didn't class the constant

42

hurting in her chest as pain any more; it was more of an ache that occasionally flared up into something hot and untameable until the drugs kicked in.

'How are you?' Vivienne asked. 'You look tired.'

Gina's blink made her seem slightly lost, as though she'd forgotten that she might matter, and Vivi felt a flood of love filling her struggling heart. Funny how emotions didn't hurt – or they did, but in a different way. They worried her too, in case they were causing undue strain, especially the negative ones. 'Did you sleep last night?' she asked.

Gina smiled. 'I did,' she said, but Vivi knew it wasn't true. 'You have a very comfortable bed.'

Thinking of her flat was as difficult as thinking of all other aspects of the life that was going on without her, and would continue to as if she'd died that day in Beaufort House. The world wouldn't wait for her, it simply wasn't possible, but she wasn't to worry, her boss had told her when he'd come to visit, she'd still have a job when she was strong enough to return.

No one had told her that was never going to happen, but they didn't have to, because on a deep and intractable level she knew it anyway.

Greg had come to see her, twice, but he'd seemed so awkward the last time that she'd almost asked him right then not to come again. His wide, baffled green eyes hadn't been able to hide the panic he felt, or the helplessness, or the shameful need to escape. She could tell he hated himself for it. It wasn't that he didn't care about her, she was sure he did, but he wasn't able to cope with her being anything other than the vibrant young woman he'd been dating. She'd decided to text him after he'd left. It would be easier that way, no pretence that things could be the same when she got out of here, no difficult goodbyes. She needed to be as pragmatic and brave about this as her mother was trying to be; as truthful and unemotional as the charts detailing her progress and mapping the way into her future.

She didn't feel brave or pragmatic, or like being truthful or detached; what she felt was shattered and terrified, a wreck of the person she really was – and beyond angry with the cruel fate that had put her here.

She would fight it; show it who was in charge. It wasn't going to win this battle and it might as well know it now. She'd find the weapons she needed, strength of body and spirit, indestructible determination of mind, belief in herself. Her dreams might lie in shattered pieces now, the debris of a collision with life's capricious and brutal plans, but she wasn't a puppet to be jerked about on the end of some random, intangible strings. She'd put everything back together and go on as she was before . . .

The flame of defiance was hard to keep alight when it was constantly assailed by fear; and when it sometimes took all her strength simply to summon the breath to speak.

'Where's Mark?' she asked her mother, her voice low, the words croaked with effort.

'I let him sleep on,' Gina replied, taking out a tissue to wipe something from Vivienne's cheek. A speck of breakfast? Maybe it was a tear. She felt like crying all the time, crying and crying as if somehow the flood would widen and deepen and carry her away from all this.

'I'm sure he'll be here as soon as he wakes up,' Gina added.

Vivienne remembered being told that he was sleeping on the sofa in her sitting room, the one she'd bought mostly for when he came to stay. She wished she could see him there. More than that, she wished he wasn't there, because then this might not be happening. 'He should be at uni,' she said.

'His exams haven't started yet and he wants to be close.' Gina drew a handful of white envelopes from her bag.

Vivienne looked at them and guessed they were get-well wishes from her mother's friends and clients.

Gina watched her uncertainly. 'Shall I put them away again?' she asked, clearly ready to do so.

Vivienne didn't know what to tell her, so she said, 'Where's Gil?'

'Still at the hotel, I think.'

Gil, her wonderful, loving stepfather who'd left her mother, and Vivienne still didn't know why. Or did she? For the moment she was struggling to get things straight in her head. She knew she'd asked many times, but had she ever been given an answer? 'Is it awkward for you?' she ventured.

Gina seemed puzzled, and Vivienne felt a stir of irritation. She'd apparently asked a question that didn't chime with reality, or her mother was pretending it didn't.

'Why would you say that?' Gina replied carefully.

'I don't know . . . I was . . . I'm glad he came.'

'Of course he came. He loves you very much, you surely can't doubt that.'

45

Vivienne loved him too, and had always wished he was her real father. Mark would be her real brother then, and they'd be a proper family with no divisions or secrets . . .

Gina gently curled her fingers round Vivienne's. 'Don't worry, my darling, your memory will piece everything together again soon,' she promised.

Vivienne nodded, but wondered how she would know if she was functioning normally when she couldn't be sure what normal was any more. 'Do you wish you'd tried harder to hang onto him?' she asked hoarsely.

Gina looked so vulnerable for a moment that Vivienne almost said sorry, but then Gina was covering her feelings with a smile as she said, 'It was all a long time ago . . .'

'Almost ten years,' Vivi put in, wanting to prove that she knew.

'Indeed. We've moved on since then . . .'

'*Why* did you let him go?'

Gina's gaze didn't waver as she said, 'Why are we having this conversation? It's hardly important . . .'

'You pushed him away. You always do that.'

Gina didn't answer and Vivi felt herself falling into a sinking, darkening sense of defeat, or exhaustion, or something she didn't really understand. She too wondered why they were having this conversation, when she felt sure they'd had it many times. Maybe it was because that bleak and difficult period when Gil left was easier to think about than the one they were entering into now. The one that she might not survive . . . Why was no one talking about that? Or maybe she'd been

46

told she wasn't going to make it and had blotted it from her mind.

'Would you like to sleep?' Gina asked gently.

Vivi realized her eyes were closed.

'I can stay, or I can go,' Gina said. 'Whichever you prefer.'

Vivi wanted her to stay, wanted her never to leave so she could somehow make this all right, but she said, 'You can go if you like.'

Gina settled herself into a chair and stayed.

There was a man standing at the gate, tall and fair-haired with his hands on his hips and a big smile on his face.

'There's my daddy,' Michelle whooped, and zooming off across the schoolyard she leapt straight into his arms, yelping and laughing as he spun her round and around.

'And how was your first day at school?' he asked, holding her aloft so he could see her sunny, freckly face, a small child's version of his own.

'It was really good,' she told him eagerly. 'My teacher is really nice, and I've got a locker all to myself.'

As he gasped in awe, five-year-old Vivienne watched, her eyes round and puzzled. This big, friendly man who was like a film star was Michelle's daddy!

'This is my best friend, Vivi,' Michelle declared, sliding out of her father's arms and grabbing Vivi's hand in a proud, proprietorial fashion. 'Vivi, this is my daddy.'

'Well hello, Vivi,' the tall man said, gazing down at Vivi with blue eyes that seemed to laugh and ask

questions all at the same time. 'That's a very pretty name you have there.'

'That's what I said,' Michelle told him. 'It's Vivienne, really. Our birthdays are nearly on the exact same day.'

Sounding impressed, he said to Vivi, 'So you were born on February 15th as well?'

Vivi shook her head. She felt shy of him, but she liked him too and wanted to say something to please him. 'I was born on April 15th,' she said proudly, hoping it might make him realize she was as special as her grandpa always said she was.

'See, the exact same day,' Michelle chipped in, 'just different months. So I will be six first, but it doesn't matter, because we don't care who's the oldest, do we?' she asked Vivi.

Vivi shook her head. It had been a whirlwind of a day, starting school, meeting Michelle, finding herself with a best friend for the first time ever, and now she didn't want it to end.

'Where's your mummy?' Michelle asked, looking around at the parents who were busily claiming their children.

'I don't know,' Vivi replied, looking around too. Part of her wished her mother wouldn't come so she could go home with Michelle and her daddy. Then her mother was there, pushing through the crowd, looking flustered and worried and then relieved when she spotted Vivi.

'There you are,' she gasped, stooping to pull Vivi into her arms. 'The bus didn't come so I had to walk. How did you like your first day?'

'Hello, I'm Michelle,' Michelle said, tapping Gina's arm. 'Me and Vivi are best friends.'

Gina broke into a delighted smile. 'That's lovely to hear,' she replied, seeming to mean it.

'This is my daddy. His name's Paul.'

Gina turned to the tall, fair-haired man, and Vivi hoped they would fall in love and get married.

'Hello, I'm Gina Shager,' her mother said, holding out a slender hand to shake his big, bony one. 'It's very nice to meet you.'

'We've met before,' he informed her, 'but I don't expect you remember me. My wife is one of your clients. I come to pick her up from time to time. Yvonne Markham.'

'Of course,' Gina said, her smile taking on more warmth. 'I do recognize you now.'

'Daddy, can Vivi and her mummy come for tea?' Michelle demanded. 'Please say yes.'

Laughing, he said, 'Maybe not today, sweetheart. We're going to see Grandma and Grandpa, remember?'

'Oh yes. Vivi lives with her grandparents, don't you, Vivi?' She said it with such admiration that Vivi immediately felt important and glad to say yes.

'Can I give you a lift somewhere?' Paul Markham offered, as they walked away from the school.

'Oh, that's very kind of you,' Gina replied, 'but there's a bus . . .'

'It wouldn't be any trouble,' he insisted. 'Are you going home, or back into town?'

'Home. I've closed the salon for the rest of the day.'

'Then if I'm not greatly mistaken you're heading for Westleigh Bay. Isn't that where you live?'

'How do you know that?' Vivi asked him, thinking he probably knew magic.

Twinkling, he said, 'Didn't Michelle tell you that I know everything?'

'He does,' Michelle asserted earnestly.

It wasn't until after Paul and Michelle had dropped them off that Vivi said to her mother, 'Do all daddies know everything?'

Ushering her along to the front door, Gina said, 'I'm sure he knows where we live because Michelle's mummy told him. Or maybe he knows Nana and Grandpa.'

Vivi felt a bit disappointed by that. 'I wish you could marry him,' she said glumly.

'Oh, Vivi, don't be silly,' and pushing open the door Gina shouted, 'Mum! Dad! Here comes our big girl after her first day at school. And you'll never guess what, she already has a best friend.'

As Vivienne let the memory drift away she was remembering how she'd wanted to be the one to tell NanaBella and Grandpa that she'd made a best friend that day. Then the thought was gone as she saw Michelle leaning over her, except it wasn't Michelle, it was a nurse showing concern with a smile that seemed to ask a question.

Was she waiting for an answer to something?

The nurse held up a mobile phone. 'You've lots of messages,' she said softly. 'Would you like to read them?'

Vivi wasn't sure what to say. It was hard to think straight, to know anything about what she did or didn't want, apart from this not to be happening.

She didn't want to connect with anyone's pity. She understood they were sorry, that everyone was anxious to come and see her, but there was nothing they could do and she didn't want them to try. It would only make everything worse.

Worse would be if they didn't care.

'I can read them to you if you like,' the nurse offered.

Vivi looked at her round, olive-skinned face with its deep brown eyes and pear-shaped birthmark covering one cheek. She should probably know her name, but for the moment she couldn't remember it, and realizing that, she felt tears sting her eyes. What was going to happen to her now? Who was she? Where was her mother?

She heard a voice and realized it was her own. 'Arnie Novak is coming to talk to us in the morning,' she said, naming the senior cardiologist. The nurse would already know this, but for some reason Vivi was feeling the need to say it. 'My mother won't admit it, but she's afraid it's going to be bad news.'

The nurse's tender eyes gave nothing away as she said, 'It's natural for her to feel worried, but . . .'

'I don't seem to be getting any better,' Vivi interrupted.

'You're stronger now than you were a week ago.'

Vivi didn't argue, because it was true. She closed her eyes and felt the relief of giving in to exhaustion – it was so much easier than trying to fight it.

When Vivi woke up again Mark was there, plugged into his iPhone, probably watching the latest episode of *Breaking Bad*. He'd told her, when she'd first asked, that he was getting into *The Walking Dead*.

'Good choice,' she'd croaked drily.

'I thought it was appropriate,' he'd grinned, knowing it would make her smile too. They'd always had an easy, teasing relationship in spite of their difference in ages. From the moment her mother had brought him home from the hospital, all big blue eyes and grasping fists, Vivi had loved having a brother, and nothing had ever happened to change that.

Now, realizing she was awake, he tugged out his earbuds and removed his feet from the edge of the bed. 'Hey, looking good,' he said admiringly, looking a lot better himself than he had over the past few days. He'd shaved and made an effort with a comb, and with his naturally moody eyes, strong jaw and drop-dead smile he surely had to be the fittest nineteen-year-old going. Not that she was biased.

'Where's Mum?' she asked.

'Downstairs in the coffee shop with a couple of your work friends. Do you want some water, or anything?'

'Water would be good.'

After sipping from the glass he passed her, she said, 'You don't have to hang around here, you know. I'm sure you've got better things to do . . .'

'Hey, we're only on season one of *Breaking Bad*. There are four more seasons to go after that.'

Lifting a hand she linked her fingers through his, careful not to dislodge the tube in hers. He was more man than boy now, almost six feet tall with toned biceps and broad shoulders, but he would always be her little brother. 'It's a good series,' she told him, grateful for the distraction it had provided during the endless hours they were spending here, in spite of how often she nodded off. She couldn't be entirely sure, but she suspected she was asleep more often than she was awake.

He shrugged. 'Everyone said it was fantastic, but I never got round to it until now.'

'Promise not to keep me here for the entire five seasons,' she said wryly.

'It's a deal. Let's aim for starting season two at home, yeah?'

Her eyes drifted at the mention of home. They both still referred to it as that, even though she'd left when she was eighteen and so had he. The only family they had in Kesterly these days was their mother, who'd moved back in with NanaBella after her marriage to Gil had ended. Gina now had the whole of number eight Bay Lane to herself, the last house of ten (there was now a 1A and 2A) past a private gate (always open) off the coast road. They were less than fifty metres from the towering coastal cliffs of Exmoor, with a back garden that climbed in wide, low layers up to a rocky ridge behind. Their front garden looked out over the circular turning space of the cul de sac to a wide stretch of sandy dunes that separated their house from the beach and constantly changing vista of the estuary beyond.

She and Mark still had their rooms at number eight, unchanged from the time they'd left, and always freshly made up in case they made a surprise return. All the neighbours they'd known while growing up had moved on now, having sold their desirable seafront properties to the London elite for use as holiday homes. Vivi had never understood why any of them would want a place in Kesterly-on-Sea when they surely could have afforded much more exotic locations on the south coast, or even in Europe. Never in a million years would she have chosen the dreary, depressing coastal town as a weekend or summer escape. She was a London girl through and through, she wanted colour, life . . .

She didn't realize her eyes had drifted closed until she heard Mark say to whoever had come in, 'I think she's asleep.'

'OK, I'll stay for a while in case she wakes up,' Gil murmured.

For the next few minutes Vivi drifted in and out of awareness, catching only parts of what was being said and who was saying it. However, it seemed Gil was going to be around for Arnie Novak's visit tomorrow, and her mother, who had returned, was sounding grateful for it. Gil was such a good man, so gentle and considerate. She'd always feel grateful to him, love him, for the differences he'd made to her life during the time he'd been in it – differences he still made, in his way. Mark was lucky to have him as a father. Gil would be there for his son if the news wasn't good tomorrow. He'd be there for Gina too if she'd allow it, but Vivi wasn't sure that she would.

'Why don't you have a daddy?' Michelle whispered.

'I do,' Vivi whispered back. She glanced at the bedroom door to make sure it was closed and no shadows were moving about in the cracks of light underneath. They were having a sleepover tonight, at her house, and she didn't want her mother to hear what they were saying.

'Then where is he?' Michelle asked.

Vivi hesitated. She'd never shared this secret with anyone, hadn't even admitted to herself out loud that she knew who her father was, but she thought she could trust Michelle. 'I can show you if you like,' she dared to suggest.

In the orangey glow from the nightlight Michelle looked excited and dreamlike, as though she was a kind of fairy whose very presence could make things come true.

'You'll have to be really quiet,' Vivi cautioned. 'I'm not supposed to know where he is, but I found him in my mum's room when she was outside in the garden.'

Bemused and seeming a little worried, Michelle crept on tiptoe after Vivi, out of the room and along the passage to the three stairs that led up to a door that was half open.

Vivi paused, listening for the sound of the TV downstairs. Her mum and NanaBella always watched Come Dancing *on Saturday nights, and from the sound of the music she could tell it had already started. That was good, because they wouldn't be able to hear anything else, not that she and Michelle were going to make a noise. Grandpa, she knew, was out at one of his card nights, so he wouldn't hear them either.*

'Better not turn the light on,' she whispered to Michelle as they crept into her mother's room, 'but the curtains aren't drawn yet, so we might be able to see.'

Michelle kept close behind as Vivi led the way round the high bed with four short posts and over to a chest of drawers with photographs of a baby on the top (Vivi), and a wooden-framed mirror that reflected an unlit chandelier hanging from the middle of the ceiling.

'Ssh,' Vivi murmured as she eased open the bottom drawer. 'He's in here.'

*Michelle was looking worried again. 'Is it a photo?'
she said faintly.*

*Vivi shook her head, and pushing aside a pile of
clothes she found what she was looking for and lifted
it out.*

*Michelle stared at the big round bundle. 'If it's his
head I don't want to see it,' she said earnestly.*

*'It's not his head,' Vivi assured her, and carefully
unwrapping the muslin shroud she revealed a heavy
bronze figure of a man in a hat and a baggy suit, with
arms outstretched and legs that seemed to be moving.
'This is him,' Vivi whispered, holding it so Michelle
could get a good look. 'I think it's why my mum always
watches* Come Dancing, *just in case he's on.'*

*Michelle was bewitched. 'Why does your mum keep
him wrapped up in a drawer?' she asked.*

'I don't know.'

'You should ask her.'

'I think she'd be cross if I did.'

*Seeming to understand that, Michelle continued to
gaze at the sculpture until Vivi wrapped it up again and
put it back in the drawer.*

Vivi was feeling strangely distanced from the life-saving
equipment around her, hardly hearing it, or even sensing
its attachments to her body, as she willed time to stop
or, better still, turn back. Her mother and Mark were
on one side of the bed, Michelle and Gil on the other
and the senior cardiac nurse plus two junior doctors
were grouped around the end, trying to look professional and compassionate. Dr Novak himself, with his
Slavic features and easy manner, was studying the tablet

he'd been handed on entering the room, assessing the latest reports of her progress and saying nothing yet.

Eventually he turned his attention to Vivienne and smiled in a way that made her feel fleetingly brave, even though she was racked with dread.

What was he going to say? Whatever it was she had to try to deal with it, even if it was bad.

As he came closer his grey eyes didn't move from hers, and for a bewildering moment it felt as though they were the only ones in the room. 'What I'm about to tell you is good news,' he began in his pleasantly accented voice, but before Vivienne could register relief he was saying, 'It probably won't seem like it at first, but once you've had time for it to sink in I think you'll agree that it is.'

Vivienne's eyes went to her mother. Gina apparently didn't understand either. She was clinging tightly to Mark's hand.

'You have presented us with an unusual situation,' Dr Novak informed her, 'because the sort of infarctions and arrests you've suffered are currently falling between two diagnoses. Please don't look so worried.' He smiled gently. 'I said unusual, not impossible, as both conditions are treatable, it's simply a question of going forward in the right way.'

This was sounding reasonable, not too frightening. Treatable was always good.

'. . . because of the damage the muscle – your heart – has suffered, and the complications that have arisen, I'm afraid your recovery isn't going in the way we'd hoped.' He put a hand over Vivienne's as though sensing the deepening of her fear, and wanting to hold her back from it. 'It's my professional opinion,' he said softly, 'that your heart isn't strong enough to give you much more than a year of life, and that life won't be like the one you've known up until now. This is why, with your permission, I'm going to recommend that you are assessed for a transplant.'

Vivienne heard a gasp, a small cry of shock, but she had no idea where it had come from. Maybe her; or maybe it was her mother. Her eyes were still on Dr Novak's, her fingers holding fast to his, as if letting go would cause her to spiral down into an abyss of such darkness and despair that she would never find her way back.

He began speaking again, saying more, much more, but none of it changed what he'd already said. The heart she had was so weak, so sick, that unless it was replaced, and soon, she was going to die.

CHAPTER FOUR
SHELLEY

Early Summer 1989

'. . . and *I'm* the one who has to name him, because he's going to be my pig, isn't he, Daddy?'

'He is indeed,' Jack cheerfully confirmed, while glancing in the rear-view mirror to where all three of his children were framed like a small family portrait – Hanna aged eight, Zoe seven next week, and four-year-old Josh, soon to be the proud owner of one small pig. Josh was a miniature version of his father; the same untameable dark hair, deep blue eyes and a smile that was as infectious as his laugh – apart from in his sisters' opinion, but he didn't worry too much about that.

Shelley checked the wing mirror on her door of the old Land Rover, making sure Jack's brother, Nathan, and his wife, Katya, were still in close pursuit. This was going to be Nate and Kat's first visit to the Dean Valley County Fair, and while the children were thrilled to have them along, their aunt and uncle's most important task today was to tow the trailer that would later carry home any new livestock they purchased, most importantly the piglet.

Behind the Land Rover was another trailer, this one

transporting Milady, the imperious, overweight and highly coiffed sheep that Zoe was entering into the children's Best in Show competition. Zoe had done most of the grooming herself – post shearing, which she'd watched closely with her inexpert eye to make sure a good job was done – and had only just stopped short of mascara and lipstick. She'd also persuaded Jack to join her for a camp-out in the barn last night to make sure no rival competitor tried to steal the potential prizewinner. (There had been no reports of rustling in their area, but someone had put the idea into Zoe's head and so all precautions had to be taken.)

'I'm going to call him Alan,' Josh announced for the twenty-eighth time, bouncing up and down between his sisters. His excited little face was as flushed and eager as it always was at the prospect of a newcomer to his personal menagerie. He'd been collecting, studying, doctoring, releasing and sometimes burying wildlife since he was old enough to know what it was, and his enthusiasm for all creatures great and small was only surpassed by his incredible, even instinctive understanding of their peculiar habits and needs.

'Everyone thinks Milady is going to win,' Zoe informed them confidently. 'Mummy, you remembered to bring the camera, didn't you?'

'I did,' Shelley assured her.

'Stop jerking about,' Hanna protested as Josh knocked into the cress sculpture she was holding. She'd grown it into the shape of a cookie monster over the past few weeks in preparation for the show, and Josh's life wasn't going to be a long one if he bumped it again. 'Daddy, did I tell you that Lydia Harris has made a horse with her cress, but it doesn't really look like one?'

'Yours does,' Josh informed her loyally.

'*It's not supposed to be a horse!*' she cried furiously. 'It's a monster, you idiot.'

'Well it looks like a horse to me,' he argued, 'a bit of a weird one, though.' After a beat he added, 'Actually if it doesn't frighten anyone I expect you will.'

Jack and Shelley choked back their laughter as Hanna thumped her brother, regarding her artistic endeavour with an unsteady mix of anxiety and pride as they jostled along the rutted track and into the field that was hosting vehicles for the show's tradesmen and competitors.

It was a hot June day with no more than a few wisps of clouds in the sky, and the sour, sweaty stench of livestock doing its best to overpower the perfumed cocktail of flowers, cakes and sizzling hot dogs that floated about between trees and stalls. This was the Raynor family's fifth show in a row (Josh's third), and each year they'd gone home with a small clutch of awards and souvenirs, assorted foodstuffs, several chickens, a couple of ducks, and many cases of locally brewed cider. Last year they'd snared a prize for the Scariest Scarecrow, which they'd modelled on Lord Dregg of Ninja Turtle fame and who, Shelley had secretly felt, bore an uncanny resemblance to their roguish neighbour, Giles. In fact, it was possible Giles had recognized himself, for she'd spotted him shooting baleful glances at the straw-stuffed effigy as though not entirely sure if he was being wound up or not.

Much had changed during the almost five years since

they'd taken over Deerwood. The farmhouse was now almost fully renovated, some of the outbuildings had undergone serious repair, and as of last week they'd become the proud owners of no less than twenty-seven ewes and six neutered rams. However, the greatest excitement since their arrival – next to Josh being born, of course – was the fact that Nate and Kat had decided to build a large, rambling stone cottage on the acre of land that Shelley and Jack had gifted them. It was set back from the main-road end of the mile-long track up to the farmhouse, barely visible to passers-by in spite of the delightful welcome gate cut into the hedge. Nate was now a firefighter with the Kesterly service, and Kat helped to run the local nursery school.

'Look at him,' Jack sighed, sliding an arm round Shelley as they strolled towards the entrance and Josh zoomed off to join a couple of friends he'd spotted. 'I haven't seen him this excited since . . . yesterday?'

Shelley had to laugh. 'Let's hope we find a pig,' she declared, 'or he's going to end up as disappointed as Steven.' Steven was Josh's pet lamb, a sorry little creature who'd apparently decided that he'd rather have a piglet as a friend than another lamb. They knew this because Josh had told them, and apparently Steven had told Josh. Steven had been helped into the world by Josh a few months ago, and was now a part-time resident of the farmhouse, along with Petunia, Zoe's three-and-a-half-legged lamb (grown into a sheep), who'd popped into the world on the same February night that Josh had made his own speedy debut.

Jack still enjoyed teasing Shelley about her horrified disbelief that he'd actually left her to give birth alone that night, when what he'd actually done was dash into the barn for the car, leaving Harry and the girls to deal with Milady's lazy efforts to rid herself of twins. Sadly the first one out had perished, causing many tears. However, happiness had been restored when Milady hadn't shown any interest in becoming a mother to the second arrival, so Zoe had taken on the role. Meantime, Jack was delivering Josh in the car halfway down the drive with the nearest phone box more than two miles away (if it was working and it usually wasn't); and since they were still on their own land there had been no chance of passing traffic to come to the rescue. In the end, with the newborn in Shelley's arms, he'd driven to hospital at breakneck speed in order to get mother and child separated, cleaned up and checked over. An hour later all three had been on their way home again.

Jack had felt very proud of himself that day, and Josh never tired of hearing the story of how his daddy had single-handedly brought him into the world, as though Jack were some sort of magician who didn't bother with rabbits and hats, because babies out of mummies was much more impressive, especially when that baby was him.

'Daddy!' Zoe shouted from somewhere. 'Milady's dragging me . . . Stop! I said *stop*! Daddy! Help!'

Laughing, Jack went to the rescue, and when he realized that Milady was trying to make a beeline for Roger, the ram who'd come to service the ewes these past two years, he was helpless with mirth as he tried to drag her back on track.

'It's not funny,' Zoe complained. 'She's naughty. You're a very bad girl, Milady. Dodgy should be here,' she told her father. 'He never takes any nonsense from her.' Dodgy was in fact Dodgy Two, who'd come to join them fresh from training, after the original Dodgy had gone to round up sheep angels earlier in the year. By then dear old Dodgy had lost all sense of time and purpose, often chasing in the small flock only minutes after Jack or Shelley had let them out, or circling hikers who came along the public footpath, as though they needed sorting out too. Jack had wept for days after sending the beloved old collie off to new pastures, and Shelley had been no comfort for she'd been beside herself too.

'We shouldn't be farmers,' she often declared, 'we love animals too much.' And we're not even close to making enough money to live on, she never added, for it didn't seem anywhere near as important as how happy they all were.

In truth, if it weren't for Jack's income from his three days a week as a vet, added to the small rent they received from Giles and other neighbours for thirty of their seventy-five acres, and the meagre government subsidies, they wouldn't be managing at all. Buying and selling sheep, rearing and grazing them, shearing them, and sending them for slaughter in September usually left them with a grand total of next to nothing at the end of each year. The bright side of that, of course, was that they never had to pay any tax.

Throughout the frenetic and frequently hilarious day full of morris dancing, showjumping, local bands playing, and assorted auctions, they shopped at the various food stalls, and stopped to chat with the many friends they'd made since moving to the area. By the end Milady had won runner-up at Best in Show, Hanna had howled in justified fury when some contemptible toff had stubbed a cigarette out on her cress creation, and Josh had struck a deal with Terry Yarwood, a local farmer, two piglets for the price of one. So now Steven would have Willy Wonka and Charlie Bucket to keep him company. No Alan in sight.

'We should call your dad on the way home,' Shelley said, as they piled children and animals back into cars and trailers. 'He'll be wanting to know what time to expect us.'

'If he's still out on the road selling eggs,' Jack replied, 'we won't get hold of him, but you're right, we should try.' Ever since Jack's mother had suddenly passed two years ago his father, David, had virtually moved in with them, which Shelley didn't mind at all. He was as helpful and easy-going as her own father, and it was a big relief to Jack and Nate to know that he wasn't grieving silently at home on his own in London. Moreover, his passion for growing vegetables was starting to come into its own, for they'd lately begun selling spring onions, cabbages and carrots along with eggs and home-made jams at the end of the drive. And if things carried on the way they were, David's green-fingered talents were likely to earn him an occasional stall at the Saturday farmers' market in Kesterly.

With everyone on board, Josh travelling with his aunt and uncle this time in order to be close to Wonka and Bucket, they set off down the track towards the main road where they stopped at the first phone box they found. Discovering they only had one 10p coin between them, Jack dialled the number and started the conversation with his father:

'Everything all right there? Quick, before the money runs out.'

'Just made myself a fortune of six pounds and forty-two p,' David replied cheerfully, 'and I was about to go and feed the chickens. What time shall I expect you?'

'In about an hour. Two piglets on board. Did the plumber come to find out why the water's not getting through to the sheep trough?'

'Yes, apparently there was a leak about ten yards out, but he's fixed it, so no bucket line tomorrow. Tell Shelley I thought I'd make a salad for tea that we can eat outside with the weather being so nice. The lettuces are lovely and crisp and the early-ripened tomatoes are as sweet as peaches. I made some bread, tell her, and I was thinking about baking a cake but then I thought you might have bought one.'

'Try six,' Jack responded wryly. 'We've also got a mountain of cheese, a ton of different pâtés, half a Wiltshire ham and that's just for starters. Nate wants to know if Perry's all right?' he added, referring to his brother's two-year-old son, who loved nothing more than being number one assistant to his grandpa.

'Fast asleep on the dog's sofa,' David replied. 'The dog's on the floor. Oh, before I forget, Giles came over. He seemed a bit worried about something. He wants you to call when you get back.'

'Did he mention what it was?' Jack asked curiously.

'No. I thought maybe he needed a vet, but that's not what he said.'

'OK, I'll try him now, and if I don't get an answer . . .' He broke off as the pips went and, remembering he didn't have any more coins, he pushed open the heavy door and returned to the car.

'Mm,' Shelley muttered after he told her that Giles wanted them to be in touch.

Jack glanced at her, puzzled, until, realizing she didn't want to say anything in front of the children, he put the car back in gear and started up a lively rendition of 'One Man Went to Mow' as they continued the drive home.

Something was wrong. He could feel it now; Shelley had just got there before him.

By the time they turned into the dirt track that wound through many fields and a bluebell wood to Deerwood Farm the girls were half asleep in the back, but Shelley still didn't voice her concerns about Giles's visit. Instead she kept them to herself, hoping she was wrong, and gazed around at their undulating patchwork of fields that stretched in both directions as far as the eye could see. Some were dotted with fat, woolly sheep and their fast-growing lambs, while many of the gates between hedges were wide open to allow them to roam freely. She and Jack had worked harder than they ever had since coming here, and she was more than happy to know that they would continue to. Even the winter months were fulfilling in their way, especially when the lambing season got going for there was something truly exhilarating about helping their ewes to bring new little creatures into the world. It seemed to bond the family even tighter together and make the daft and lovable flock even more a part of it as time passed.

Less enjoyable at that time of year was the pruning

of fruit trees and brambled hedgerows in freezing winds, and poring over accounts that never added up. However, there was always the roaring fire to come home to and gather around on stormy nights, and an endless number of games to play and movies to watch now they had a new VCR. (It had taken Jack almost a week to figure out how to connect it, and his normally mild temper had been tested many times since by the machine's refusal to obey the handbook.)

'Is that Giles's new Range Rover?' Shelley asked, as they crossed the humpback bridge at the end of the drive, and the farmhouse in all its summer glory came into view. Its many windows and doors had been carefully repaired, refitted and painted a gleaming white, while the centuries-old grey stone walls had been livened up by demossing and repointing. The old, Grade II listed roofs now lay snugly under the protection of the brand-new non-leaky red tiles that Jack and Nate had helped to lay. It was, in her opinion, a dream home that always seemed to smile when they came into view, as though wanting them to know how thrilled it was with the rose-covered porch they'd installed around the white front door, and the colourful beds Shelley was bringing on each side of it. The fact that it overlooked a scruffy, cluttered yard full of potholes, tractors and all sorts of rusted paraphernalia simply honoured its status as a farmhouse. As did the barns that faced it, and the creaking iron gates that opened into the fields.

'Yep, that looks like it,' Jack murmured, as they pulled up next to the Range Rover. 'Seems like he couldn't wait for us to ring.' There were several other cars around too, which wasn't a big surprise, for over the past three years Deerwood had gained a reputation for being a place where everyone was welcome. Hardly a day passed without someone dropping in, or ringing up to ask if they could come. Jack, with his irrepressible good humour and eagerness to listen and laugh at stories long and tall, was always at the centre of things, while Shelley kept the food and booze coming, or hit on someone for advice on whatever farm problem was bothering her that day.

As they came to a stop the children woke up and leapt out of the cars, ready to start unloading the squealing piglets and prize-winning Milady. Dodgy wasted no time in coming to help sort things out, and was ably assisted by Nate and Kat, while Jack and Shelley went into the house.

After the blazing sunlight outside, the flagstone entrance hall where a newly constructed oak staircase rose between the kitchen and family room seemed dark at first, but Shelley's eyes soon adjusted to find the place empty of people, but nevertheless welcoming. It was stuffed full of the charm and quirkiness that she loved. There was a brand-new Aga now, black, powerful and all-dominant in a vast inglenook fireplace where copper pots and pans hung from a thick wooden lintel that was almost as high as the ceiling. The battered rectory table at the centre of the room was, they'd been told at a local flea market, as old as the house, and had once belonged to a duke. As if they'd ever know if that were true, and as if they'd care. It suited them perfectly, as did all the other second-hand furniture scattered about the place that some would call antiques, but they considered new old friends. A magnificent triple-fronted beechwood sideboard that Shelley had found under a pile of junk in the main barn and lovingly restored stood against one wall. Its convenient surface had become resting places for various keys, animal treats, junk mail, stray jigsaw pieces, hair combs and even a couple of baby teeth. In pride of place, in a specially constructed niche above the sideboard, were the precious bronze figurines that belonged together as surely as if they were actually attached. Shelley often recalled the night she and Jack had first placed them there, almost reverently. Then they'd danced, romantically and effortlessly, to Nat King Cole's 'Unforgettable', as though they were continuing the fluidity of movement the sculptor had captured.

'That's my mum and dad,' Hanna would often say if anyone asked about the figures, and neither Jack nor Shelley corrected her, for in a way it did feel like them.

Hearing voices in the back garden, Shelley followed Jack out of the kitchen stable door onto the cracked and weedy stone patio where David was sharing a beer with Giles at a large wooden table under a dilapidated gazebo. There was still plenty of work to be done out here, but it didn't stop them enjoying the rambling garden with its ragged hedges and overgrown shrubs, or the pond at the far end (home to the ducks), and the various climbing frames, swings and slides for the kids.

'Everything all right?' Jack asked, grabbing a handful of sheep nuts as Steven and Petunia trotted from the shade of a weeping willow and across the lawn to greet him.

'I don't know,' Giles replied gravely. 'I've sent a couple of my lads to check up on it, but I'm still waiting to hear.' He nodded towards the walkie-talkie that would connect him to his farmhands as soon as they had some news to share.

'Is it travellers?' Shelley asked worriedly, realizing that the extra vehicles out front must belong to Giles's workers. 'I heard there were some in the area.'

Giles's eyes were steely. 'If it is then it's not the ones we know,' he replied gruffly, 'because no one's been in touch to ask which field they can use – and they're on your land, not mine. I went up there earlier, but no one was around. No caravans yet, but a dozen or more tents. I've sent a couple of the lads to check it out now, see if anyone's turned up yet and find out what it's all about.'

Unsettled by Giles's concern, Shelley was recalling the stories she'd heard about clashes with the Gypsy fraternity, the kind of damage to land and property they inflicted if crossed, the violence and threats to children and animals. 'If they don't turn out to be your regular travellers, is there anything we can do to make them leave?' she asked.

Giles tipped back his head and drained the bottle of beer. 'One step at a time,' he cautioned. 'For all we know it could be a bunch of hippies aiming to set up some New Age cult for nudists and nutters. But if they are pikeys of some sort we definitely don't want to start off by upsetting them.'

Shelley turned to Jack and felt another twist of unease when she saw the determined look on his face. She wanted to remind him that the top fields were a long way distant from the house – at least a mile and a half – so this unexpected settlement surely wasn't anything to get too worked up about, but he was already addressing Giles.

'Come on,' he said, putting down a beer he hadn't yet touched. 'Let's go take a look.'

Minutes after Jack and Giles had taken off on foot across the fields, heading for the ancient forest and beyond, the children came thundering in demanding food. Nate and Kat were close behind, a sleepy Perry in his mother's arms. Catching Shelley's worried expression, Nate glanced from her to his father.

'What's going on?' he wanted to know.

David nodded to where Jack and Giles were clambering over a stile at the far end of the nearest field, a trail of sheep trotting along in Jack's wake.

Clearly sensing he might be needed, Nate took off at a pace to catch up with them.

Kat's eyebrows were raised as she looked at Shelley. 'Later,' Shelley murmured, aware of the children watching them.

'Where's Daddy gone?' Josh demanded, unused to his father going anywhere on the farm without him.

'I want him to hang up Milady's rosette,' Zoe protested.

'You're all so mean,' Hanna snapped at them. 'Grandpa's made lemonade and you haven't even said thank you.'

At that the younger ones threw themselves at David, who took them inside for drinks and snacks before tea.

'What is it?' Kat prompted Shelley.

Shelley was still watching the men's retreating backs. 'I don't know,' she replied quietly, 'but I have such a horrible feeling about this that I wish I knew how to bring them back.'

By the time dusk started to settle over the fields there was still no sign of the men, and as Giles had left his walkie-talkie on the table, and neither Jack nor Nate had taken theirs, Shelley had no way to get hold of them. She rang Giles's wife, Cathy, but Cathy hadn't heard from them either, and she was just as worried, which wasn't like the usually sanguine Cathy at all.

In the end, unable to stand doing nothing, Shelley told Kat to stay with David and the children while she went down to the basement and took a key from a box on the topmost shelf of a wall cupboard. She used it to unlock the cabinet where Jack kept his shotgun. She'd never fired it in her life (nor had he, since learning how to handle it), but mindful of the premonition she'd had as the men had left, she needed something to bolster her courage if she was going out to look for them. Obviously she wouldn't shoot anyone, that wasn't her intention at all, but venturing out alone in the dark with nothing to help make a point, if necessary, didn't feel like a good way to go.

Twenty minutes later Shelley was in the Land Rover, driving gingerly through the narrow country lanes at the furthest perimeter of their land and keeping her eyes peeled for any signs of Jack and the others. The car's windows were open to let in some air, along with any number of insects to buzz around her face like the irritating pests they were.

The shotgun was on the passenger seat beside her.

She was close now to where their fields joined with Giles's, but there was no sign of anyone. The night was black; hedgerows and trees rolled in from the wings and disappeared again as the headlights passed by. A fox darted across the road in front of her and was gone almost before she hit the brakes.

Quite suddenly, the road flooded with light. A car came speeding towards her, headlights blazing; blinding her. She swerved frantically into a ditch, but needn't have worried – the other driver skidded into a hard left turn and disappeared through an open gate (that should have been closed), bumping and revving into one of their top fields. It was followed by another car, and another . . . She counted six in all, each with its headlamps blazing and music blaring.

Quickly backing up onto the road she killed her lights and edged forward in a low gear, her heart thudding and ears straining as she pulled in close to the hedge. The music had stopped, but she could see torch beams moving about wildly in the night air and then she heard the sound of voices, shouting, threatening. With an unsteady hand she reached for the gun, got out of the Land Rover and moved silently into the field.

The cars had been abandoned, some doors left open and interior lights still on. Ahead of them was an encampment of a dozen or more tents, all shapes and sizes. The voices were louder now, but she still couldn't see anyone, so she crept closer, keeping to the shadows and praying that no one would spot her. She didn't want to think about what would happen if they did; all sorts of scenarios were flitting into her head and none were good.

As she peered round the edge of a tent towards the commotion, her stomach gave a lurch of fear. A truly ugly scene was under way with Jack, Giles and Nate at the centre of it, yelling, waving fists and threatening violence if the travellers didn't move off *now*.

Except they weren't travellers, she realized, they were a bunch of drunk, arrogant youths who'd apparently set up camp in the field and were now showing off in front of their girlfriends, watching from the shadows, by refusing to budge.

Recognizing the ghastly Bleasdale twins from Dean Manor, Shelley moved closer still, and as one of the obnoxious oiks began yelling threats that could (or should in her opinion) get his head blown off, she raised the gun, pointed it straight at him and yelled, 'Get away from my husband or I'll shoot.'

To her dismay no one heard; so directing the gun skywards she pulled the trigger and almost came off her feet as the explosion tore through the night.

Everyone froze.

She took another step forward, aiming the gun at any yob who moved. She could hear voices muttering, 'What the fuck?' 'Madwoman' 'Get out of here.' Jack was gaping at her in astonishment, then ran swiftly to wrest the weapon from her trembling grasp before any real harm was done.

An even uglier scene immediately flared up, with Shelley joining in the yelling and no one seeming ready to give way, until a couple of Terry Yarwood's farmhands turned up with a trailer packed full of farm waste. As they dumped it over the tents Jack's party roared with laughter, while the Bleasdales and their fellow yobs began gagging and spluttering obscenities that could still be heard as they pressed the protesting girls back into the cars and disappeared into the night.

'What the hell were you thinking, bringing the gun?' Jack laughed, as he and Nate followed Shelley to the Land Rover.

'I was expecting travellers,' she reminded him. 'And you've been out here for so long.'

'We were waiting for them to show up,' he explained. 'We'd already guessed it was kids so we decided to have ourselves some sport.'

Rolling her eyes as if to say *men!* she returned to the driver's seat, while he stowed the shotgun in the boot and Nate climbed into the back.

'What are you going to do with all those tents?' she asked as Jack got in beside her.

He was grinning widely. 'That's a very good question,' he told her, 'and I do believe I have the answer.'

He said no more, but the following morning around seven o'clock he took off in the farm's forklift to meet up with Giles and Terry Yarwood in theirs. By eight they had shifted the stinking mass of an abandoned campsite over to Dean Manor's gates, where they dumped the lot before returning to the farmhouse for one of Shelley's scrumptious full English breakfasts.

It was just after ten when Sir Humphrey Bleasdale rang. 'I want that filth moved off my land,' he roared down the line at Jack.

'Speak to your sons, they're the owners,' Jack told him.

Shelley could almost hear Sir Humphrey gnashing his teeth like some pantomime villain. 'You don't know who you're dealing with, Raynor,' he growled, 'but mark my words, you're going to find out.'

In his usual insouciant way, Jack wished the old puffball a good day and put the phone down. It wasn't the first time Humphty Dumphty, as the kids called him, had threatened Jack, or Giles, or any of the other farmers who didn't pay obeisance to his superior status, and Shelley knew without doubt that it wouldn't be the last.

CHAPTER FIVE
VIVIENNE

Present Day

Kesterly didn't look any different from the way it always had as Gil drove them along the seafront in his silver Mercedes saloon. Vivienne hadn't expected it to, but familiar as it was, it *felt* different. Everything did. She guessed a time would come when she'd be able to put the strangeness, the chaos and darkness of her feelings into words, or some order of understanding, but for now all she could latch onto that didn't send her into panic was a bewildering sense of surrealism that made everything seem like an endless dream – or as though someone else had slipped into her skin to take over her life.

Her mother was beside Gil in the front of the car. Vivi sat behind with Mark, her head resting on the seat back as she gazed out at the calm blue sky and crazily glittering sea. The tourists were out in good numbers, to be expected on a sunny day in early summer, and in a vague, disconnected way she felt glad for them. At least their lives didn't appear to be in any sort of crisis.

As they drove on she took in those who were picnicking or napping on the grass verge between the four lanes of the Promenade; others filled the cafés spilling onto the pavements, and still others, not visible from the car, were no doubt baking themselves on the beach or paddling in the slushy waves.

Did they realize how important it was to cherish every minute of every day?

She was just learning the lesson herself, and still had a very long way to go.

Almost two months had passed since she'd gone from being a perfectly healthy person (or so she'd thought) to someone who was only alive thanks to tireless and dedicated expert care, and the massive cocktail of drugs she was now dependent on. Learning what life was going to be like for the foreseeable future – no more work, limited and careful exercise, constant assessments, pain management where needed, special diets: the list was endless – had been a shock she hadn't yet come to terms with, and she didn't feel confident that she ever would. This was nothing like the life she had planned for herself. She was an invalid now, someone who could only survive on medication and the hope of a new heart. It was as though she'd suddenly become old. The worst of it might have been the advice to refrain from physical intimacy until she was strong enough to cope with the strenuous nature of it, but since she didn't have a partner it was hardly an issue. And it was never going to be one, for what chance did she stand of ever finding anyone in Kesterly, or anywhere, who'd want to take on the hassle of a sick woman whose condition was only going to get worse, unless a miracle came along in the shape of someone dead so she could live?

The horror of that was too hard to think about, so she didn't.

While being assessed for a new heart she'd read stories online about those who'd managed to get their lives back on track after the transplant, and who'd even gone on to greater things. There was no reason, she'd been told, for her not to be one of their number. There was no guarantee that she would be, either, for in amongst the many upbeat stories had been just as many – more, even – telling a much sadder tale: waits that had gone on for years only to end in death; mad dashes to a transplant centre to find the donor heart wasn't suitable; post-operative immunosuppressive drugs causing cancer . . . The only good news in all this, as her mother saw it, was that she hadn't been rejected for transplant, which could have happened, since some people were too sick for the procedure. If she were one of their number she'd know for certain that she wasn't likely to make it beyond a few months. As it was, she probably wouldn't anyway.

Her mother had been there every day throughout the transplant assessment and the surgery, only a few days ago, to fit her with an ICD – implantable cardioverter defibrillator. There had been much discussion about going straight for a VAD – Ventricular Assist Device – and Vivi had prayed with all her might that it wouldn't happen. She'd read much about that too, the open-heart surgery to attach the pump to the left ventricle and aorta with drivelines connecting her heart, through the skin, to a controller and batteries that she'd have to take everywhere with her. Plenty had been written by those who had one about the pain of it, the fear of it stopping, and the dreadful things that sometimes happened if it did.

She'd wept with relief when the decision had been taken to hold the VAD in reserve for the time being.

Gina had shared the relief, but Vivi had turned away when her mother had broken into a smile. She was glad her mother was there, but she couldn't bear to see her clutching at straws that were little more than thin air. Nor did she want to see her fear and worry, nor how shattered and gaunt she looked as one setback was overcome, only to be replaced by another. This was obviously affecting her deeply, but there were times when Vivi had needed to wallow in her terrible, wrenching emotions alone. Surely running a marathon for such a deserving cause was a good thing, not something to be punished for, so why had it turned into this? It was small comfort – maybe no comfort at all – to be told that it would have happened sooner or later anyway. Her heart had been weakening for a long time without her knowing it, and now it was a virtually useless vessel of such pathetic performance that it could fail at any time. It was a pump that had run out of thrust, a muscle that was atrophying like a flower past its bloom.

This time next year, or maybe even before that, there would very likely be an empty space where she was now, just Mark in the back seat of the car, an empty chair at their table, a bedroom that would no longer be used, someone they wouldn't have to consider when they bought gifts and made plans. All that would exist of her would be the memories her friends and family shared, or maybe she'd be a ghost, moving amongst them unseen, unheard and unable to reach out and touch them.

'It's quite natural for you to be feeling blue and frightened right now,' the psychologist had told her before she'd left hospital. 'It's a lot to take in, but you'll find it becomes easier as you gain strength and your coping mechanism comes to the rescue.'

'What if none of it shows up?' she'd asked. 'No strength, no coping mechanism, no hope even?'

The psychologist hadn't seemed to doubt that it would all kick in at some point, and probably sooner than she expected. He'd then talked about the counselling that would be available any time Vivienne required it.

Reading reports from other heart patients, Vivi knew that the counselling promise wasn't one to rely on. There had been too many cuts to the NHS budget to guarantee anything, least of all treatment for mental health when the costs of her physical needs were running into many tens of thousands of pounds.

Why didn't they save the money and let her go now? What was the point of trying to keep her alive when they already knew they were going to lose the battle?

Vivi's eyes moved to her mother's blonde head. The little parting that had appeared at the crown made her seem vulnerable, as though she was the one who needed to be taken care of. What the worry of it all was doing to her mother kept agitating Vivi, upsetting her a lot, making her feel guilty and frustrated, even angry and resentful at times. She didn't want to concern herself with it, but as soon as Gina was out of sight Vivi's overwhelming relief at seeing her go was quickly smothered by an almost panicked, childlike need of her.

'What are you thinking about?' she sometimes wanted to ask, but afraid of the answer she stayed silent. She wondered how much pressure the turmoil of her own emotions was putting on her heart, if the quick flare-ups of bitterness and anger, followed by painful, anxious surges of love and guilt, were damaging it further. Maybe it would be better if she and her mother weren't together, and yet she couldn't bear to think of how much it would hurt Gina if she tried to shut her out. Worse would be attempting to manage without her – of course she couldn't – and all tied up in this terrible, tormenting tangle of feelings was the undeniable gratitude that she had a mother who cared. It wouldn't be true for everyone in her position; they might not have a wonderful stepfather either, or a brother who was doing his young man's best to navigate the thorny and explosive territory that existed between his mother and sister.

Wanting him to know how much she appreciated him being here today, Vivi reached for his hand and curled her fingers around his. His grip tightened, but she kept her gaze fixed on the passing hotels and town houses with their hanging flower baskets and wide-open windows, too tired to turn her head to look at him. Later, when she was feeling stronger and they were alone, she'd tell him that he didn't have to stay, that he *shouldn't* stay. His exams might be over, but the plans he'd made to travel through Italy with friends for the summer must go ahead. Just because she couldn't live a normal life any more was no reason for him to put his on hold. In fact, knowing he was out there making the best of everything the world had to offer would do far more for her than thinking of him wasting away at home.

Wasting away at home.

'Michelle should be waiting for us,' Gina said over her shoulder. 'She wanted to get a few things in and make sure everything was all right with the house before we got there.'

For the first time in her life Vivi felt no pleasure at the thought of seeing her oldest and probably dearest friend; she wasn't capable of feeling very much about anything right now. It was hard to imagine any kind of hope or enthusiasm swooping in to rescue her from the cloying, debilitating pessimism that was stifling her.

Rachel, the specialist cardiac nurse, had said, 'We're adding antidepressants to your medication . . .'

'No, please, not more pills . . .'

Rachel's hand went up. 'It'll be much harder for you to regain energy if you're feeling depressed. In fact it could be impossible, and that's not what we want. When it comes time for the transplant you'll need to be in as good shape as possible or it can't happen.' *When it comes time for the transplant.* It was good of Rachel to talk about it as if it were a foregone conclusion, when they both knew it wasn't. It was far more likely that a suitable donor wouldn't be found.

At this moment Vivi doubted she'd ever feel strong or happy again. She seemed even weaker than she had at the start of it all, but she realized that the sedation to implant an ICD probably still hadn't fully worn off. It was a nifty little device – that was how the cardiologist

had described it – that now sat just below her collar-
bone and was connected to her heart by a couple of
wires that had been threaded through a vein to their
destination. Its purpose was to monitor and record all
arrhythmic activity in her pitiful heart, and to deliver
a good electrical thump to get things going again
should they come to a stop.

Ingenious, even miraculous, considering that it also
allowed the dedicated cardiac team to monitor her
remotely. This meant they could check on her at any
time of the day or night – apparently it was going to
happen each night – via an Internet connection plugged
into the phone line next to her bed, and she wouldn't
even know it was happening. They'd be assessing
everything from her heart rate, to her blood pressure;
to the effect her medications were having on the heart's
struggling performance. She'd asked if they could
programme it to make her a cup of tea in the morning,
and they'd all dutifully laughed.

Anyway, it was quite possible she wouldn't be aware
of the device once she got used to the discomfort in her
shoulder, but if a major incident occurred she'd definitely
know it.

What a sobering, nightmarish thought that was;
she could be in the throes of an emergency CPR at any
minute, all carried out by the little gadget inside her.
Still, it was better than the alternative of letting the
heart try to fend for itself, when it clearly couldn't.
She'd been warned that the shock of the device going
off was likely to hurt – a lot – but only for seconds.
Like a donkey kick to the chest, she'd both read and
heard. It might also sap her strength and leave her

incapacitated for a while, but there again she might be able to continue as though it hadn't happened at all. She guessed she'd find out soon enough; she just hoped that the many emotional conflicts tearing around her depleted vital muscle right now wouldn't trigger an emergency all on their own.

It took no more than fifteen minutes to drive along the coast road past the marina, Ed and Kev's donkey sanctuary, then a wide and wild stretch of wasteland apparently about to be developed. Just after that they reached the narrow spur of Bay Lane that would be easy to miss for anyone who didn't know it was there, for the main road curved sharply away from the shore at that point to continue on to the lower reaches of Westleigh Heights. The Heights, as the area was more commonly known, was where Michelle's family had always lived. It was also where Vivi and Mark had lived during the time their mother had been married to Gil. After the break-up they'd returned to their grand-mother's house on Bay Lane.

Most of the properties on the lane, now used as holiday homes, were set back behind high wooden gates and protective laurel bushes. Number eight wasn't much different, except the gates were always open and the hedges were low enough to see across the lane to the dunes and estuary beyond. Gil pulled into the drive and came to a stop in front of the double-fronted Edwardian house where an Audi convertible was already parked. Gina's VW Beetle was presumably tucked away in the garage, and Vivi felt her spirits sink even lower as she remembered that she was no longer allowed to drive.

However, one look at Michelle's wonderful, freckly face as she came out of the house was a tonic she hadn't expected. The joy of seeing her, of realizing she was going to be there for her, was helping, if only for a few moments, to lift her from the misery she was in.

After hugging carefully and tearfully, Vivi gazed into Michelle's tender blue eyes and saw straight away that the bond they'd always shared was still there. They didn't need words to express it, they could both feel it and that was enough. There would be time later for talking, for trying to come to terms with what was happening and how they were going to cope. For now Vivi allowed Michelle to take her into the house, so glad she was there that it took her a moment to register the familiar scent of the place. It transported her back over many years, confusing her with emotions as all kinds of memories flashed up, and nostalgia closed in on her like the tide lapping the shore outside. The hallway was long and only just wide enough for the two friends to walk side by side past the old telephone table and coat hooks towards the foot of the carpeted stairs. They stopped at the threshold of the room NanaBella had always called her best room. It occupied the whole of the right side of the house with views out to the beach through the bay window at the front, and French doors to the garden at the back. The door to the left led to the kitchen-diner and family room for everyday use. NanaBella had entertained Gil in the best room when he was dating Gina, wanting to impress him and make him feel welcome as though he was someone very special, which he was.

Apparently her mother had asked Michelle to get the room ready for Vivi, and it was clear from the pillow arrangement, scented candles and new Smart TV beside the old-fashioned tiled fireplace that Michelle had done her best, but it wasn't what Vivi wanted.

'I'm not an invalid,' she growled, when she saw that the small double bed from the guest room had been set up in place of NanaBella's rosewood dining table. 'I can get up the stairs.' It might take her a while to achieve it, but she was determined to try.

'No one's saying you can't,' her mother replied evenly. 'I just thought it would be nice for you to have your own room for entertaining – and, well, it's a place you can call your own.'

Vivi said, 'So what are *you* going to do for a sitting room?'

Gina's eyes stayed on her, but her cheeks were flushed with colour, showing how upset and sorry she was that she'd apparently got it wrong. 'We have the one we've always used,' she reminded her.

Vivi decided not to protest any further because Gil, Mark and Michelle were clearly feeling embarrassed and sorry for Gina, and who could blame them?

'I expect the kettle's boiled by now,' Michelle said cheerfully. 'Let's go and have some tea.'

Vivi stayed where she was, looking around the large, rectangular room with its cream and yellow flowered wallpaper and NanaBella's mustard-colour three-piece suite. The sofa converted to a bed and had always been used when the house was full at Christmas or for birthdays – and now for when a dying daughter might have a visitor? It was so depressingly outdated, and so different from her wonderful flat in Chelsea that she wanted to sob. Aware that she might damage herself if she gave in to too much emotion, she put a hand to the implant in her shoulder, feeling its sharp edges through her skin, and let tears drop onto her cheeks. Her conscience was flooding her with beautiful, happy memories of times spent in this room when sparkling Christmas trees had filled the niche next to the fireplace, and when she'd helped NanaBella to set the table for all kinds of special occasions.

How could she be so ungrateful and mean about the room NanaBella had been so proud of? The room she'd apparently once helped her grandpa to wallpaper when she was three (no doubt causing havoc); where she used to practise her ballet for her mother and NanaBella, and where she'd watched NanaBella weep tears of joy as she'd taken a day-old Mark from Gil to cradle him in her arms.

Now her mother had turned this special place into hers, to try to make her life easier.

'OK?' Mark said softly, sliding an arm round her shoulder and putting a mug of tea into her hand.

'I will be,' she promised. She rested her head against him, inhaling the earthy, tangy smell that was so familiar and comforting it made her want to weep again. 'Have I upset her?' she asked, briefly closing her eyes.

'She'll get over it.'

Her gaze went to a sideboard where photographs of them both at various stages of their lives were displayed in silver and leather frames. There were several of their grandparents too, at their wedding, her christening,

Mark's first birthday party, but there was only one of their mother, with Vivi and Mark at Vivi's graduation.

There used to be one of Gina and Gil on their wedding day, but it had been taken down soon after they'd broken up and Gina had returned to live with her mother.

'I don't know why I feel so angry with her,' she said. 'It's like I'm blaming her for what's happening when it obviously isn't her fault.'

'I heard Dad telling her that it was natural to lash out at people you love when you're feeling afraid. She probably knew that already, but I think it helped her to hear it.'

Vivi felt sure it had.

Michelle appeared and drew her into a careful embrace.

'I won't break,' Vivi promised, relaxing into the feel of her, and wishing it could be just the two of them, though not wanting Mark to leave. Or Gil. Or her mother.

'You look tired,' Michelle told her.

Vivi's weary eyes managed a spark. 'If you're about to tell me to lie down then don't,' she warned, meaning it to sound like a mock rebuke, but it didn't quite come out that way.

'I wasn't,' Michelle assured her, apparently unfazed. 'It was just a comment. I'll trust you to know when you need to eat or sleep or pee or whatever you fancy. Mum's just texted to ask if you're feeling up to having dinner at her place tonight. All of you,' she added, looking at Mark.

Not wanting to admit that she wasn't up to it, while feeling grateful for the way Michelle and her family were drawing her back into the fold, Vivi looked round as Gil called out, 'Hey, son, can you give me a hand to bring this lot in?'

Realizing it was some of her belongings from the flat, Vivi's eyes went to Michelle's, knowing, because her mother had told her, that her friend had helped to pack them sometime over the last few days. She felt so useless and wretched that she didn't know what to say or do.

'We've arranged for a man with a van to bring your furniture,' Gil told her as he came along the hall with a heavy box. 'Once it's here we can get things looking a bit more like your kind of home.'

Unable to stop herself, Vivi looked down at the carpet with its yellow and black diamond design and in spite, or maybe because of how awful it was, she found herself wanting to laugh.

Gil followed her eyes, and Michelle said drily, 'I think it qualifies as retro.'

'Just what I was going to say,' Gil agreed.

Mark said, 'Remember, NanaBella was always going on about changing it.'

It was true, but the room was used so little they'd ended up forgetting about it, even after NanaBella had gone. Gina only used the other side of the house, which was much more up to date.

'Do you want me to take this stuff upstairs?' Mark asked. 'Or would you rather have it down here?'

Though Vivi had no idea what was in each of the holdalls or boxes, she remained determined that this wouldn't be her full-time base, so she said, 'Upstairs.'

'Are you sure?' her mother asked, coming out of the kitchen.

'Yes, I'm sure,' Vivi told her shortly.

Apparently not wanting to fight, but still keen to get her way, Gina said to Mark, 'Anything that needs to come down again can always be sorted out later.'

Vivi turned away, and Michelle put a steadying hand on her arm.

'If we're going to Yvonne's for dinner,' Gina said, 'then I think you should have a lie-down first.'

Vivi was tense to breaking. 'Do you?' she muttered.

She didn't have to see her mother's expression turn to one of awkwardness and regret as she picked up on her unrealized error, because she could feel it. It took a lot of effort for Vivi to raise her head and say, 'I'm sorry, you're right,' because of course her mother was, and she really didn't want to hurt her.

'I'll go on ahead to give Mum a hand,' Michelle said, breaking the tension. 'The kids are dying to see you, Vivi, but if you'd rather wait till tomorrow, Sam can always stay at home with them tonight.'

In spite of knowing she'd prefer to wait, Vivi said, 'I'll be fine by the time we get there, so I'd love to see them.' Life had to go on. She needed to find the strength to be normal.

After Michelle had gone Mark took himself off upstairs, and Gil remarked to no one in particular, 'Well, I guess I probably ought to be making a move.'

Vivi waited for her mother to protest, but Gina said, 'Thanks very much for driving us today. We couldn't have managed without you.'

Pulling Vivi into his arms, he spoke tenderly. 'Take care of yourself, sweetheart. You know where I am if you need me.'

'Thanks,' she mumbled, close to tears again. She desperately wanted him to stay, to carry on understanding her and her mother the way he always seemed to, but they weren't his responsibility any more. Her mother had seen to that.

As Gina walked outside with him Vivi watched from the window, wondering what they were saying and if they would kiss. They did, but briefly, dutifully almost, before Gil got into his car.

By the time her mother came back Vivi was perched on the edge of the sofa trying to get a sense of the ICD, and whether it was registering any rogue events in her heart to relay to the cardiac team later.

'Can I get you anything?' Gina offered.

Vivi looked at her as hard as she could as she said, 'Why do you do it?'

Gina flushed. 'Do what?'

'Why do you send him away when any fool can see that you want him to stay?'

Gina flinched. 'He's got someone else,' she replied.

This was the first Vivi had heard of someone else, and for a horrible moment it felt as though he was cheating on her mother, and on her. 'If it's serious,' she heard herself saying angrily, 'then you only have yourself to blame.'

Gina didn't argue, merely set about straightening up cushions that didn't need it at all.

There was so much more that Vivi wanted to say, or shout, or simply beg answers to, but it took all the energy she had left to say, 'Everything's different now, Mum, I hope you realize that. I intend to find out the truth before I die,' and knowing Gina understood exactly what she meant she turned away, not able to say any more for now.

Vivi had been awake for a while, remembering when Gil had come into their lives and bought a house only four doors away from Michelle's parents on Westleigh Heights.

He hadn't only done it for her so she could stay living close to Michelle, as she'd believed at the time, he'd done it for her mother and NanaBella, because NanaBella hadn't wanted Gina and Vivi to leave Kesterly either. So Gil had kept everyone together by renting out his home in Bath, relocating his consultancy business to Kesterly, and, best of all, he'd come most days to pick her up from school. That had shut everyone up about her not having a father, because they'd been able to see him, and so what if he wasn't a real dad? As Michelle used to say, 'That makes him even more special, because he chose you.'

Smiling at the sweet belief of that, Vivi opened her eyes, and wondered what time it was and, for a moment, where she was.

As everything came into focus she felt herself swirling back towards an abyss of despair. At the same time she was glad to be here, at home, no longer in hospital, and really she wouldn't want to be anywhere else, or with anyone else, while this was happening.

While this was happening.

That made it seem temporary; something simply to be got through until better days dawned. It was a good way to think of it, far better than the alternative of days becoming shorter and darker until there were no days at all.

She closed her eyes again, and tried to refocus, to think of the reasons to be grateful, and the many things she needed to do before time ran out. She realized there would be no bucket list for her – or not one that included daredevil stunts, long-haul flights or weeks of hot, passionate sex on a beach in the South Seas with a younger version of George Clooney. Her list would have to be far less ambitious – organizing her meditation programme would be a start. She also needed to see her GP, meet the specialist team at the local cardiac clinic who were taking over her interim care, and then she should make sure that the Kesterly ambulance service had been informed of the need to rush her to the transplant centre at a moment's notice should a new heart come up.

Feeling certain that the cardiac team had already done that, and if not her mother would have, she sighed shakily and tried to change her train of thought again. It did no good to torment herself with the deeply troubling issue of someone having to die in order for her to live. She wasn't even on the most urgent transplant list – she'd probably still be in hospital if she were – so it was hardly an immediate nightmare. Maybe she should spend her time feeling thankful that she wasn't too sick to receive a new heart, the way some people were. Nor was she having to cope with the life-saving horror of a VAD, or not until her condition worsened – which it would . . .

Don't think about it, she told herself forcefully. *For God's sake put it out of your mind or you might as well give up now.*

She needed to pick herself up, force herself forward

and do everything in her power to make things matter again – and something that really mattered, and always had, was finding her father.

That was what she needed to focus on now, and so she would.

CHAPTER SIX

SHELLEY

Midsummer 1989

The night was warm and still, richly scented by livestock and wet grass, and lit by a near full moon. Shelley was carrying a torch in one hand and a basket in the other, feeling not unlike a nocturnal Red Riding Hood as she traipsed through the small copse next to the riverbank on the far western edge of their land. Though the way was mostly clear, the darkness over the fields was faintly unnerving, as was the occasional glimpse of amber eyes watching her from the undergrowth, and the birds that suddenly fluttered or squawked in the trees. She felt sure a thousand ghosts were following her, and as for the big bad wolf who might eat Red Riding Hood all up . . .

Smiling as she thought of the girls squealing and ducking under the covers whenever Jack told them that story, she pushed aside a leggy bramble and trudged on through the silvery darkness.

At last she reached the riverbank and there, just where she'd expected to find it, was the home-made tent that Jack and Josh used for their moonlight vigils. Josh had been particularly excited about this one, for their mission tonight was to spot an otter, in spite of none having been seen in this county since the 1950s. However, Josh was determined to find one, and if he didn't, well, there would be lots of other things to spot instead.

Choking back a laugh as she found them fast asleep in their hideout with Jack leaning against a backrest and Josh lying across his lap, she quietly put down her basket and stood watching them, loving how peaceful and alike they were. Both had thick dark hair that curled and waved in no particular style, and when he was older Josh was clearly going to have his father's strong jaw and large nose.

She smiled as her precious boy opened his eyes and put a finger to his lips. He moved carefully away from his father and crawled out of the tent. 'Dad's asleep,' he whispered as he reached his mother. 'He's missed some really good stuff. I've seen everything.'

'An otter?' Shelley asked, sitting down next to him.

'No, but there was a hippopotamus.' Josh's eyes were round with awe, as though he truly believed it. 'It was enormous,' he confided. 'You should have seen it. It could have eaten us all up if it had spotted us.'

Shelley said gravely, 'Lucky it didn't.'

'Yes, very lucky. There was a deer with two fawns who came to have a drink,' he went on, still whispering. 'I was scared for them, but the hippo didn't see them.'

'Wow,' Shelley murmured. 'Where is it now, do you know?'

'I think it swam away, but it might still be somewhere, you never know.'

'Well, you'd better make sure it doesn't spot you.'

'I will. We're being very quiet.' He was digging into the basket now, bringing out apples and cake and two thick-cut sandwiches filled with cheese and pickle. 'I'll save one of these for Dad,' he said softly. 'He might be hungry when he wakes up. Oh! Did you hear that?'

'What?' Shelley whispered, all ears and intrigue. After all, it might be the hippo.

'It was an owl,' he told her. 'Ha! There it is again. I think it's the one that lives in our barn. I'll tell Dad about it when he wakes up.'

Shelley glanced over her shoulder, and seeing that Jack was watching them through narrowly opened eyes she had to swallow the surge of love that tightened her throat. Of course she'd known that he wouldn't fall asleep while they were out on vigil, but she also knew that it made Josh feel brave and adventurous to think that he was in charge of keeping them safe.

'You can go now if you like,' Josh told her, biting into his sandwich.

'OK, thanks,' she replied. 'There's some squash in the basket and a bar of chocolate. Don't let the hippo get Dad, will you?'

'No, don't worry, I won't.'

Hearing Jack turn a laugh into a snore, she pressed a kiss to Josh's forehead and obediently started back to the farmhouse.

A couple of days later Shelley was enjoying a rare few moments alone in the kitchen sorting through the mail, a small stack for her, one each for Jack and David, and another for issues requiring some sort of joint attention.

Opening an invitation to a friend's wedding, she

popped it onto her own pile as a reminder to RSVP with a definite yes – how long had it been since they were last in London? It seemed like another lifetime, another world, and actually it was. She made a mental note to ensure the event got marked up on the family calendar. This magnificent creation (the calendar, not the invitation) was half as tall and as wide as Jack, made by the children and hanging on its own space of wall in the kitchen. It was bordered in dried wild flowers, sketches of moles, rabbits, lambs and chickens; a Polaroid shot of Josh with his piglets, Wonka and Bucket; a photo of Hanna and Zoe under the weeping willow with Milady and Petunia; a blurred image of Jack and Shelley aboard Jack's new tractor, and another of David dressed up as Father Christmas.

There was no other calendar like it in the world. It was theirs and they loved it as if it were the beating heart of their family.

Checking the time, and satisfied she didn't yet have to drive Hanna back to the village for a piano lesson, or remind Josh that he was on lawn-cleaning duty today (meaning collection of sheep droppings), Shelley took another refreshing sip of iced lemonade and opened a handwritten envelope addressed to her and Jack. Guessing from the crest on the seal what this little missive was going to be about, she unfolded the single sheet and discovered that she wasn't wrong.

However, she was surprised, for the night of the tents, as they now called the inglorious fracas in the field with the Bleasdale twins and their yobby friends, followed by the dumping of all that was unsavoury at the manor's gates, was only two months behind them. So a request from Sir Humphrey to run the hunt across their land this coming winter seemed a bit rum.

She put it on Jack's pile with a smile. She knew already what he was going to say when he saw it, but as he enjoyed sounding off about the local hunt and those he truly objected to, she wasn't going to deprive him of this golden opportunity.

'Ma, where's Pop?' Hanna demanded, running in through the door with plaits flying out of their bands and a very Jack-like grin on her face. As a family they often read a book together in the evenings, and recently they'd become enchanted by H. E. Bates's *The Darling Buds of May*. Jack performed rather than read it, making it even more engaging, and exactly, the children insisted with unbridled delight, like them, for the story's Larkin family lived in a countrified Utopia just like Deerwood.

Ma Larkin, Shelley was often heard to protest, was nothing like her, since she wasn't fat, not even close, nor was she a saucy minx, at least not while the children were around. Jack, on the other hand, was more than happy to be compared to the rascally Pop Larkin, as he thought it was rather a good fit. Or, a 'perfick' fit, as Pop Larkin would say.

'The last time I saw Dad,' Shelley replied, checking the time again, 'he was baling hay in the bottom fields. We ought to be leaving in a few minutes. Have you seen Grandpa on your travels?'

'He's in the greenhouse,' Hanna informed her, going to write on the calendar in green crayon while crunching into a carrot. They each had their own colours for the calendar, although they did get mixed up from time to time, which could be hilarious when they discovered that Jack was down for Brownies at six, or David was going for a leg wax on Wednesday morning after dropping himself off at the town hall.

It was much later that evening, as a thunderstorm racketed about outside cracking apart the heavens and sending switch lightning across the fields, that the whole family was in the kitchen with the windows and stable door wide open to let in the cooling air. Having finished their current favourite, spaghetti bolognese with lashings of Parmesan on the top, the children were now tucking into second helpings of another of Grandpa's specials, plum crumble made with their very own fruit – picked by Josh and Perry, with fresh cream courtesy of Giles's dairy herd.

Full to bursting, Shelley kicked back to enjoy the last of Kat's home-made elderflower wine before starting the clearing up. She'd have help from Nate and Kat who'd brought Perry over for tea as they often did, while David, when he'd finished his own wine, would no doubt take off to inspect what havoc the storm had wreaked on his precious raised beds. Jack, she remembered, was planning to go out with Josh to try to put a dear little owlet back into the nest it had tumbled from. (Josh had tried to do it himself after discovering the owlet on one of his rambles, but he hadn't been able to climb high enough on his own.)

For the moment, Jack was flicking idly through the mail she'd sorted for him earlier, while chatting with Nate about their cricket team's fixture at the weekend. When he came to a stop she knew he'd reached the request from Sir Humphrey. His eyes came straight to hers, and the roguishness of his smile made her forgive him for calling her Ma Larkin when he'd come in for tea.

'Are you going to answer it?' she asked.

Nate regarded them questioningly.

Passing him the letter, Jack said, 'We'll send him our usual Oscar Wilde quote,' and Shelley laughed. '*The unspeakable in pursuit of the uneatable*', with Jack's usual addition of a blunt 'No', or 'Keep your bloody progeny orf my land', or 'Pick on someone your own size'.

'He'll no doubt do the same as he does every year,' Nate declared, handing the letter to Kat, 'clog up the roads around us with hunt vehicles, let the hounds loose in our garden before they set off, and leave us to clear up the shit.'

David said in a fatherly scold to his sons, 'They're such an unpleasant family, those Bleasdales, that I worry about the way you antagonize them.'

'So you want us to make friends with them?' Jack asked, clearly more intrigued by the idea than surprised.

'His wife, Jemmie, is adorable,' Shelley put in, 'so it's not the whole family. And their younger son – I forget his name – is quite different from those ghastly twins, or so they say, I've never met him myself. And their daughter, Fiona, is just like her mother.'

Nate's expression showed distaste. 'If the younger son is the hothead who blasted me off the road the other day in his souped-up sports car, and I'm sure he is, then I'm here to tell you that he's very much like the other males in his family.'

Letting it go, Shelley began clearing the table, while

Jack and Josh went to return the owlet to the nest it had fallen from and the others peeled away to various parts of the house. Finally, just before dusk, with the rescue mission complete and the children getting ready for bed, Shelley and Jack put on their wellies and wandered into the sparkling wet fields to watch the artful Dodgy rounding up his sheep. It was rare for them to manage some time together without the children running and yelling around them, demanding attention, falling out of trees, getting stuck in hedges, and generally shattering the peace. Now, being just the two of them, they let the sounds of nature wash over them as they walked hand in hand through buttercups and clover and felt at one with Deerwood and all the beauty – and challenges – it had brought to their lives. They gazed out at the distant earthworks of an old hilltop fort far away on the southern horizon, and on to the ancient forest that bordered their land to the east where it was said Bonnie Prince Charlie had once hidden from the Redcoats, and on to the undulating patchwork of fields that stretched out around them as far as the eye could see.

At a kissing gate they took a moment to honour its tradition, then turned back to check on Dodgy's progress, impressed and enchanted as always by how swiftly and efficiently he tended his flock.

'So what are you going to do about Bleasdale's letter?' Shelley asked, turning her eyes skywards to where a hot-air balloon was going over.

'Same as always,' he replied, waving out to the balloon's passengers. 'I'll send a polite note back explaining that if I want to get rid of a fox I'll shoot it, clean and quick. Same goes for deer and rabbits.'

Although she knew very well that as a vet, as well as a compassionate human being, the last thing he'd ever be into was the torturing and terrorizing of animals, she still felt a surge of pride every time he confirmed it. They might not be quite as daft or romantically soppy as Ma and Pop Larkin, but there was no doubt in her mind that they were every bit as much in love.

As the heat of August drained away into the cooler and shorter days of September, and their finances stopped adding up, Shelley began to notice a change in Jack. She understood that he was worried about how they were going to keep the farm going when their savings ran out, but there was more doubt or concern exercising him than that. She could sense it, even though he steadfastly denied it.

'We've always shared everything,' she reminded him one night after he'd returned from a late shift at the surgery and they sat down to enjoy a drink together.

'We still do,' he responded, 'unless you're hiding something from me.'

Though his tease made her smile, and she felt reassured by the way he added, 'We'll sort everything out with this place, I hope you know that,' she still couldn't rid herself of the feeling that something else was on his mind.

A few days later she cornered him in the barn. 'Something's going on between you and the Bleasdales,' she accused. 'Don't deny it, because I know when things aren't right with you.'

His deep blue eyes lit with surprise, and then laughter, as he dropped his pitchfork and used an old rag to wipe the sweat from his neck. 'I don't know why you think that,' he told her, 'but I want you to put it out of your mind, because I haven't heard anything from them since I let them know that we don't want the hunt on our land.'

'So what *is* going on with you?' she pressed. 'And please don't try to palm me off with how worried you are about our finances because . . .'

'That's not palming off,' he assured her, 'it's a reality. However, I have some news that might just help to turn things around.'

Intrigued, she waited for him to divulge it.

He shook his head. 'I don't think I should be the one to tell you,' he said mysteriously, 'but there is going to be a change around here if it all works out, that's for sure.'

Impatiently, she said, 'You can't just leave it there. I need to know what you're talking about.' Then, out of nowhere, she heard herself saying, 'Are you going to leave me? Is that what's going on?'

He gaped at her in profound astonishment.

'I'm sorry,' she tried to laugh, 'I've no idea where that came from. I guess . . . I've become paranoid about what's bothering you and you have to admit, we haven't made love very much lately.'

Appearing more stunned than ever, he swept her into his arms saying, 'Then I think we should put that to rights without any further delay,' and going to close the barn door, he carried her behind a giant stack of bundled hay and ordered her to take off her clothes.

Afterwards, still slightly breathless and laughing at how reckless and passionate they'd been, she plucked straw from her hair as she dressed and realized that she didn't feel edgy or even worried any more – which just went to prove that they really must relax this way more often.

They did again that night, in the kitchen after everyone had gone to bed, realizing that the risk factor worked rather well for them. When it was over, and they had rearranged their clothes, they stood for a while looking at the bronze dancers in their niche. 'They kind of ground me,' Jack confessed, kissing the top of Shelley's head, 'or maybe they remind me of how lucky we are.'

She nodded. 'I know what you mean.' It wasn't the first time she'd looked at the figurines and felt a kind of magic emanating from the movements that seemed so real, and she loved the fact that Jack felt it too.

'And now,' she said softly, 'you're going to tell me your news.'

CHAPTER SEVEN
VIVIENNE

Present Day

Vivienne had spent two entire days and nights at the cardiac clinic – fifty miles away from home – undergoing yet more echocardiograms, ECGs, CT scans, blood-pressure tests, ICD checks . . . There were so many she could hardly keep track of them all, nor did she feel anywhere near reconciling herself to the fact that this was what her life was all about now. She was resisting it in every bone of her body, even as her lungs struggled to take in air and her head filled with a numbing fog of fatigue. She knew she had to do better than this, that somehow she had to find a way to calm herself and her expectations, to accept that this really was happening and would go on happening until a donor heart was found – or until she died.

Of course the transplant centre had passed all the information they had to the clinic, but the new medical team had needed to carry out their own tests before taking full charge of her care. Her life was going to be a complex mix of drugs and tests, desperately trying to keep her heart going until a new heart became available.

She was going to be with this team now until . . . well, until fate stole someone else's life and gave her a second chance, or until it didn't.

Fortunately, the ordeal of being back in a hospital less than two weeks after she'd left one hadn't turned out to be quite as bad as she'd feared, though she was certainly relieved to be on her way home again.

Miraculously, given how weak she still felt, she was managing to stay awake through the journey and even take in the tranquil, billowing countryside they were passing through. The other miracle, that of still being alive, wasn't one she felt much like getting into yet. Instead she tried recalling the names of the new medical team, an exercise of memory as well as necessity. Saanvi Sharvelle, the senior cardiologist, a serious, softly spoken Canadian; Trey Dyer, the cardiac physiologist in charge of monitoring her ICD; Katie the arrhythmia nurse and several others whose names and duties would hopefully come back to her in the fullness of time. So many people, so much technology, effort and expertise involved to keep one small heart beating.

Her mother probably remembered them all.

She and Gina hadn't spoken much either on the way to the hospital, or since leaving. There was too much tension between them, too many fears, hopes, crushed dreams and new ones to try to fit into words that would either run out at key moments, or feel inadequate, or be painfully misconstrued. They were all being tested in ways they still didn't know how to handle. Yet at the same time they shared a comfort in each other's presence, in the other's unspoken but known love, that couldn't be provided by anyone else. They were close, too close, and yet so far apart that they seemed unable to find even gestures to help bridge the gap. It was easier when they didn't try, or when they had visitors at the house, such as Gil, who'd already made the drive from Bath three times in the past two weeks, or Michelle, who came every day. When others were around they didn't have to avoid one another, or feel guilty about their failures, or pretend they were coping when they weren't.

'But you are coping, and brilliantly,' Michelle had protested when Vivi had confided in her a few days ago. 'As usual, you're putting too many demands on yourself. You both are.'

This had been said on the morning her mother had finally returned to work, at Vivienne's insistence because having her mother around all the time was a reminder of how sickness, failure, and the shadow of death had taken over their lives. However, Gina hadn't been prepared to leave Vivi at home on her own. It was too soon, they hadn't learned to live with the ICD yet, much less what to do if it went off. It could happen at any time, and if it did someone needed to be there in case Vivienne fainted, or fell and hurt herself – or to call the paramedics if the proper rhythm wasn't restored.

Though Michelle's reassurance over the coping business had felt bolstering at the time, it was really still far too early for Vivienne to feel it was true. Staying alive was one thing, and of course not to be taken lightly, but coming to terms with her fears and limitations, with who she was now and what she could never be in the future, was another challenge altogether. She tried not to think about the lively, ambitious young lawyer who used to inhabit her skin; the Vivi who'd laughed loudly and easily and loved without thinking. To dwell on thoughts of how she'd pounded the pavements of Chelsea during early, misty mornings training for a marathon, had drunk champagne with friends in bars and nightclubs long into the night, and made mad dashes for business-class flights to New York or Hong Kong, did her no good at all. She'd hardly thought about the future then, she'd been far too busy embracing the thrills of growing success, throwing herself into meetings, negotiations, trials and tribunals as if nothing could matter more. She realized now that she'd believed in her own invincibility, her certain ability to reach whatever goals she set herself.

Those times, that person had gone, in the same way that people left when they died. There one minute, alive, noisy, vital Vivi-vacious, gone the next, leaving a sudden and shocking emptiness that no one was prepared for. In her case there had been no burial or cremation to mark her abrupt transition from one world to the next, nothing at all to effect the transformation of Vivienne the lawyer into Vivienne the terminal invalid, apart from a myocardial infarction, of course, and two cardiac arrests. And now here she was in limbo, living a life that could go nowhere unless someone with the same rare blood type as hers and a healthy heart of the right size and in good condition died in time to rescue her.

She'd never given much thought to donors before, of any sort; now she thought about them all the time and perversely kept fearing for their lives. Feeling her constant companion, tiredness, overtaking her again, she let her thoughts drift and sink into blessed oblivion.

Gil said, 'Don't worry, as soon as you're old enough you'll be able to give blood too.'

Vivienne, aged eight, skipped along beside him, thrilled to be going with him while he donated a whole pint of the very ordinary stuff that ran through his veins. That was how he'd described it, ordinary stuff, because almost everyone was in the same sort of group as he was, while she was in a very special category because most people didn't have the same sort as her, which meant that when she got older and was able to become a donor her blood would be very valuable indeed.

Gil was like that; he always made someone feel special – or stupid if they were being stupid, or very important if they did something clever or brave.

It was lovely having him as a dad. She'd liked it right from the start (apart from being a bit upset when he had taken her mum to Portugal on honeymoon and left her behind). She'd forgiven them as soon as they came back because she was so happy to see them, and as time went on she loved having him as a dad more and more. He was like Michelle's dad, only better, because he was hers. He was interested in everything she did, and he really did listen when she had something to say, she could tell because if she asked him anything about it later he always remembered and knew the right answer. He was funny too, and made her mum laugh in a way Vivienne had never seen her mum laugh before. And now her mum was having a *baby, which was going to be really lovely, especially if it was a boy. Vivienne didn't need a sister because she had Michelle.*

'Mum's going to come and pick us up when I've done my bit at the blood bank,' Gil told her, 'and then we'll go to the Seafront Café for lunch. Does that sound good?'

Vivienne told him that it did, but really she was a bit disappointed, because she liked having Gil all to herself. Then she immediately felt mean because she didn't want her mum to feel left out, not ever. So really, she was very pleased that her mum was coming too. Everything was always better when her mum was there, except sometimes it wasn't.

After a brief yet deep sleep, Vivienne was once again gazing out at the passing landscape of farms, country estates and rambling commons, thinking how beautiful yet remote it was, and so very far from London. It felt like a journey through a parallel universe, one that was taking as many years as minutes.

'I'd like to turn my hair blonde,' she suddenly announced, as though changing hair colour was something she did every day, or had been thinking about for a long time.

Gina glanced at her in surprise. 'You want to go blonde?' she said, as though needing to be clear.

Vivienne turned to her. 'You're blonde, and I'm your daughter, so I thought, why not be more like you?'

Gina looked uneasy.

Realizing she might have sounded sarcastic, Vivi quickly said, 'I always wanted to be blonde when I was little, like you. Now the urge has come back. Will you do it for me?' She didn't add, *while we still can* – there was no point, they both knew the other was thinking it.

After a moment that still felt tense, Gina said, 'Of course. If you're sure, but you have such pretty hair . . .'

'That might be even prettier if it was the same colour as yours.'

Gina swallowed, and Vivi wondered if she was thinking, *but you'll never be able to go anywhere to show it off.*

Gina said, 'I think it's a good idea. Having a different look might lift your spirits a little.'

Ashamed of having credited her mother with unworthy thoughts, and unsurprised by having her mind read, Vivienne said, 'You could be right. I mean, we need to do something to get me out of this slump. Not we, *me*. *I* need to do something, just in case *you* think I'm blaming you in some way.'

Gina's eyebrows rose. 'Why would I think that?' she asked quietly.

Because you always think that, Vivienne didn't say. She shrugged. 'You're my mother. Isn't everything your fault?'

The way Gina smiled made Vivienne smile too. She'd meant it as a joke, and for once they'd managed to share one without it springing barbs.

'I'll do it tomorrow, if you like,' Gina said, slowing up behind a tractor towing a heavy load.

Vivienne watched random strands of straw flying out of tightly bound bundles, taking little leaps for freedom with nowhere to go but down. 'Why don't we do it today?' she suggested.

Gina didn't seem certain. 'Aren't you tired?'

Vivienne might have argued if there had been any point, but the need to keep breathing, to detach from the brutal harshness of this new reality, was starting to overtake her. This was the most she'd done since being allowed home, and the effort it had required was indeed starting to close her down. Her eyelids were heavy, her mind was clogging as though a kind of glue was settling in, and her shoulders had started to sag.

She didn't sleep, but they continued in silence, passing the Ring o'Bells pub that a sixteen-year-old Vivienne had once been to on a date, and the Longfellow Timber Yard where Michelle's builder husband, Sam, came for supplies. The signs to far-flung villages and country stores went by in a blur, then they were skirting the edge of the ancient forest where legend had it that Bonnie Prince Charlie had once hidden from the Redcoats. Michelle's parents used to bring them here for picnics when it was sunny; it was the perfect place to play hide-and-seek, but scary too, because of how dark it was in places. They were sure it was haunted, which had added to the thrill.

They were still behind the tractor and its load, slowing almost to a stop as it turned off the road. She noticed a sign for Deerwood Farm and Shop, and a small clutch of unlikely-seeming teenagers with piercings and tattoos grouped behind a table with 'organic fruit and veg for sale' on a canopy-shaded table.

'Maybe we should take some home,' she said to her mother.

Gina's hands were tight on the wheel, her gaze so fixed on the road ahead that Vivi realized she wasn't listening, maybe hadn't even heard her, or spotted the stall.

'Shall we get some fruit?' she repeated.

'We don't have to get it here,' Gina replied stiffly. 'I don't want to stop.'

Though her mother's response seemed odd Vivi let it go; she didn't have the strength to argue, or even to check the mobile that began vibrating in her hand as they continued along the narrow road. She must check the phone, though, in case the transplant centre needed to get hold of her. Some chance of that this far into the wait! Or in case Trey, the cardiac physiologist, had detected some activity in her ICD overnight that she hadn't been aware of and needed attention, maybe clinical, or even surgical. There was a blue holdall in the boot of the car, packed ready for an emergency ambulance journey to a transplant centre . . . That little bag of hope had to go everywhere with her. She knew it wouldn't be long before she started tempting fate by leaving it at home.

She should check the phone. She was right: it wasn't a new heart.

She closed her eyes and wondered, exhaustedly, how it was possible to feel so crushed by disappointment at the same time as being flooded by relief. She didn't want a transplant, the mere thought of it terrified her, and yet not having one terrified her even more.

Gil was at the house when they got home, standing at the door ready to welcome them, and hastening to Vivi's side as he realized how depleted she was.

She didn't mind him helping her, his strong arm circling her waist in case her legs gave out. Her mother was behind, carrying in the bags and Vivienne's mobile, which had slipped to the floor of the car.

'Michelle rang,' Gina said, checking the phone.

Vivienne wasn't surprised that her mother had taken a look. She must have wondered, hoped – even dreaded in the same way Vivi had – that the call a few minutes ago had been the one they were praying for.

'I'm here,' Michelle announced, appearing in the doorway. Her eyes were shining in a half-concerned, half-mischievous way; her arms were full of grey satin cushions that she quickly passed to her husband, Sam, as he appeared behind her.

'I was calling to find out how far away you were,' Michelle said, going to Vivienne's other side and slipping a hand through her arm. 'How was it?'

'OK,' Vivi replied. 'This is a big welcoming committee.' She was looking at Sam and experiencing a surge of affection in amongst surprise and confusion. He should be at work; he usually was at this time of day. If she didn't already have a brother she knew she'd want Sam to fill the role, for around about the same time as he and Michelle had fallen for each other on sight, he and Vivi had experienced their own instant connection. His look wasn't suave or professional; he was more the sturdy, muscular type that gave off an air of capability and permanence and unfailing wicked humour – just about perfect for a builder, rugby player, husband and dad.

'We have a surprise for you,' Michelle confided. 'Don't worry if you're not feeling up to it, you just have to walk into it and lie down. It'll still be there when you wake up.'

Knowing from the taut, dry feeling in her face that her strain was showing, and feeling her eyes losing focus with tiredness, Vivi took a few quiet gasps of air as Gil handed her over to Sam, who put an arm gently around her. 'There's my girl,' he murmured, as though he was speaking to his five-year-old Millie.

As he took her the few steps along the hall and into the downstairs room that was now hers she hesitated, looked around and tried to make sense of it. It was as though she'd stepped out of time, or into a dream where the before and after had merged into new, but familiar images of both.

'We thought you'd like to have your things around you,' Sam said softly, 'so we got to work and made it happen.'

Her flat, her beloved London flat was here, in this room, from the washed-oak floorboards – he'd clearly laid them specially – to the huge ivory silk rug, the plush grey Toga sofa with matching armchair, and circular coffee table with opaque glass top and dandyish Louis Quinze legs. Gone was the sombre old dark wood dresser that had stood against the long wall for years, and in its place, between the curvaceous Design Italia floor lamps, was the chalky-white Long Island sideboard that she'd found at an antiques fair in Chelsea and paid a fortune to have restored. Even the photographs she'd always displayed around the flat were here, as were the vibrant abstracts by Maryanna.

She hardly knew what to say or do. She simply stood

looking at it, aware of a swamping sensation in her head, a distant conflict of emotions that turned to confusion, maybe alarm, as she saw that NanaBella's old dining table was no longer at the other end of the room. Instead, there was her ornate white French-style bed, complete with frost-blue Scandinavian linens and whimsical drifts of voile draped from the ceiling to complete it.

'We knew you didn't want to get rid of it all,' Michelle said, scattering the satin cushions over sofa and chairs, 'so Sam and I had the idea of creating a home from home.'

Vivienne swallowed drily. She was aware of the kindness, could feel it in every cell of her body, every vein that her blood was struggling to run through, but the words she needed stayed buried inside her.

'She should lie down for a while,' Gina said, and for once Vivienne was glad her mother had stepped in, because that was exactly what she needed.

A few hours later she was awake again, lying on her beautiful bed gazing up at the ornate patterns on the inside of the canopy, and feeling such a wrenching ache in her chest that she wasn't sure if it belonged to her physical heart or her emotions. Tears slid soundlessly from her eyes and dropped onto the pillows. She understood how much effort and planning had gone into transforming this room, and she was grateful to everyone who'd loved her enough to make it happen. But with every fibre of her being she wished they hadn't. It was just bringing it home to her that she was here now, to stay, and there could never be any going back.

Telling herself that she had to stop this, right now, she turned her head, to start getting up, but seeing the home monitor that her mother had apparently set up while she was sleeping she deflated. It was incredible really, that the ICD implanted in her shoulder could wirelessly transmit information to this device. In spite of how depressed it made her feel to know that she needed this amazing technology, she couldn't help being impressed by it, and grateful too, since it was playing a vital part in keeping her alive.

The other part, she knew, had to come from her. She really did need to find the will, the energy and determination to get through this, even beat it if she could, although she knew how impossible that was going to be without a new heart. Even so, didn't she owe it to herself, and to those she loved and who loved her, to make the time she had left as special and uplifting as she could?

Summoning her strength again, she swung her feet slowly to the floor and inhaled a deep, steadying breath. It took a moment for the dizziness to pass, a clearing of the senses that left her with a surprising but welcome feeling of calm. It was good to have her beloved flat around her, she told herself. It didn't have to feel frightening or wrong or anything negative at all unless she wanted it to.

Going to the bookshelves that filled the niche next to the new pale wood fireplace she ran her fingers lightly along the spines of her familiar friends. It felt comforting to have them here: a complete collection of Daphne du Maurier; a selection of Doris Lessing's short stories and novels; an assortment of quirky dictionaries and reference books; old travel guides; some spy thrillers; several box sets of DVDs; Jane Austen and the Brontës, Paul Theroux, Hilary Mantel, everything she'd treasured from her shelves in London was here.

Drifting over to the front window she folded back the plantation shutters – the trouble they'd gone to! – and looked out on a very different view to the one she'd had over a London street. As her eyes adjusted to the golden glow of a sunset she made out her mother and Gil sitting in deckchairs on the dunes with Michelle and Sam leaning against one another on a picnic rug. They looked so relaxed and settled, as though nothing was wrong in their world and all they had to do was drink a glass of wine and soak up the sweet balmy air at the end of a long and taxing day.

After a while she realized it was Mark sitting in the deckchair next to her mother, not Gil, and then she remembered that her brother had said he was coming home today. She liked the fact that he called this home, though she suspected he referred to Gil's house the same way.

She wondered where Gil was, and guessed he'd probably already driven back to Bath.

How did he feel? Banished? Unwanted? Glad to get away to his new girlfriend? She needed to ask Mark about that.

Minutes ticked on as she stood staring out at the bay, no longer seeing what was in front of her, but what had come out of her memory to remind her of three darkened figures in the same glow of sunlight many years ago, her mother and Gil with three-year-old

Mark between them. They were swinging him across the dunes, down to the beach and into the waves. Vivienne had been able to hear Mark's shrieks of delight, the roars of Gil's pretend monster and her mother's joyful laughter. She'd been about to run and join them, wearing the new swimsuit that she wanted to show off, but then they'd suddenly set off running to the rocks without realizing she was calling out to them.

She remembered slowing to a halt and the horrible stab of loneliness that had struck her, the bewildering, terrifying feeling that they were trying to get away from her, that she didn't matter any more. She remembered how the woman she was watching hadn't felt like her mother during those moments. She'd seemed like someone who had a separate family that she loved more than she loved Vivienne, and who made her happy in a way Vivienne never could.

So many frightened and nonsensical thoughts had jumbled themselves up in her eleven-year-old mind that day, in much the same way that they were managing to right now.

Forcing herself to let them go, she turned away from the window and looked around again at her belongings. They seemed, she thought, almost as baffled by being here as she was to see them. She wondered how they felt about their new home, as if it were even possible for them to feel. Did they mind being so far from London, exchanging the elegant setting of a Georgian town house for a less chic Edwardian detached; the distant roar of traffic for the gentle sough of waves? The metallic smell of diesel fumes, for the salty, invigorating tang of the sea? They fitted into the room quite well size-wise, perhaps a little more cramped than before, but the high sofa back provided a good divider between the two halves of the long room, while the sideboard seemed to join them like a bridge between past and present – or night and day, given their different functions. Were they looking forward to finding out who their new visitors might be in this part of the world? She tried to think of who might come that her long sofa and comfy chair hadn't hosted before. There was no one. She thought of the GaLs; how could she not? They cared about her, of course, and she knew they'd try to stay in touch, but she understood their lives, the speed of change, the pressures of their jobs, the unending demands from so many quarters. They were too busy to keep her at the front of their minds for long. And even if they did stay in touch, did she really want to hear about the world she'd known so well but could no longer be a part of?

She was gazing fixedly, though absently, at the sideboard when Michelle came in, pausing at the door to watch her, knowing that her presence had been sensed, holding the silence for a few moments more.

She wasn't surprised when Michelle said, 'I know what you're looking for, but I'm afraid it got broken in the move.'

Vivienne imagined the exquisite pyramid-shaped decanter, blazing with colours, that she'd brought back from Venice – Murano to be more precise – ten or more years ago, smashed into small pieces, no longer of any value, or of any use.

'You can have mine if you like,' Michelle offered. Michelle's was different, more of a pear shape and all shades of blue. Their mothers had taken them to Venice for a girls' break before their GCSEs, and had bought the decanters as mementos of a special time. Vivienne wouldn't dream of taking Michelle's, not only because she knew how much Michelle treasured it, but because she had no use at all for a decanter – and actually never had had.

'Shall I tell you what I think would look good there?' she said.

Michelle watched her, and her eyes began to widen with understanding as Vivi turned to her. After a beat Michelle asked, 'Do you know where it is?'

Vivi shook her head. 'I haven't seen it for years. I don't even know if she still has it.'

Michelle seemed anxious now, proving that she hadn't forgotten the first time Vivienne had asked her mother about the bronze male dancer, nor any of the times since, and like Vivi she wouldn't want any of the scenes repeated.

'Is he my father?' twelve-year-old Vivienne demanded hotly.

'Is who your father?' Gina's voice was terse and dismissive.

Vivienne flushed.

'What on earth are you talking about?' her mother snapped.

'I'm talking about the man that you keep in your

drawer.' Even as she said it Vivi felt miserably stupid. There couldn't be a man *in her mother's drawer*, so why had she said it? 'The statue,' she blurted, wishing she'd never started this now.

Her mother's eyes darkened with anger and something that Vivienne didn't understand. It frightened her, but made her defiant and determined to stand up for herself.

'Have you been snooping about my room?' her mother cried furiously. 'That's what horrible people do, I hope you know that. Horrible, sad, sneaky people go snooping about other people's rooms.'

Vivienne was so hurt, and incensed, that she raged, 'And horrible, nasty, sneaky mothers don't deserve to be loved, so I don't love you. I hate you, and I want my real dad to take me away, because I don't want to be here and I know you don't want me here.'

Her mother's exasperation was almost as scary as the way she spoke, cold and mocking, still angry and forceful. 'I wish to God you weren't so fanciful,' she snarled. 'Gil's your father. You love him and he loves you . . .'

'He's not my *real* father. He's Mark's, and I have a right to know who my real father is.'

Her mother stared at her in what looked like shock, or it might be fear, or fury, Vivienne couldn't tell. She was desperate to get away, because she didn't know how to argue with her when she was being like this.

'Who told you,' her mother asked, biting out the words, 'that you have a right to know who your father is?'

The answer was Michelle, but Vivi was never going to admit that, especially when she had no idea who'd told Michelle, or even what a right actually was.

'I hate you,' Vivi blurted. 'You're always mean to me, and it's not my fault that I don't have a dad, it's yours because you made him go away . . .'

'You have Gil,' her mother shouted angrily. 'Think how he'd feel if he knew you were saying all this. You are the luckiest girl in the world to have a dad like him. So why are you doing this, Vivienne? Tell me why Gil, who loves you, suddenly isn't good enough for you?'

Vivi hung her head in shame. She had no answer for that . . .

. . . And she didn't have an answer for it now – she only knew how deeply her mother had hurt her that day, how wretched and wrong she'd made her feel for something that shouldn't have been so complicated or fraught with emotion. She had a vague memory of four-year-old Mark coming to her room later and putting an arm around her as she cried. He'd said something about not minding sharing his dad, because he knew that his dad loved her very much and so did he.

For a long time after, Vivi had wondered if her mother secretly hated her, even wished she was dead. She became so worried about it and afraid that she'd ended up asking NanaBella if it were true, and the next thing she knew she was in her mother's arms.

'You're my precious angel,' her mother had wept, hugging her so hard it hurt. 'You're my little miracle who I nearly lost and I thank God every day that I didn't.'

At the time it was all Vivi had needed to hear. She'd felt safe again and happy. She didn't want to think any more about her real dad because it just upset everyone, and there was no point in that. So they hadn't mentioned him again until the next showdown, a few years later, which had ended in much the same way.

'She knows we have to have the conversation,' Vivi said quietly to Michelle. 'I'm not going to die without knowing who he is, and the sooner she understands that the sooner we can . . .' She was going to say *get on with our lives*, but that phrase didn't work so well for her any more.

Michelle was still looking worried. 'Just as long,' she said cautiously, 'as it doesn't turn into a repeat of what happened when you were eighteen, after Gil left, because frankly I'm not sure you could survive that again, not the way you are now.'

Vivi knew that was true. It had been terrible, wrenching, violent, even. Nevertheless, she insisted, 'I *need* to know who he is. Do you understand that?'

Michelle's eyes were tender as she nodded that of course she did.

'It has nothing to do with Gil and not loving him, because I always have and I always will. I just have to know why my mother's the way she is, because I'm sure it has something to do with my father . . .' Her gaze went back to Michelle's. 'Is it wrong to want to know him, and for him to know me before it's too late?'

Clearly as unsure of the answer as Vivi was, Michelle pulled her into an embrace. 'Whatever you want to do,' she said softly, 'you know I'll be there for you.'

CHAPTER EIGHT
SHELLEY

Autumn 1989

Many weeks had passed since Shelley had first experienced feelings of unease, and now they were back. She still wasn't able to put a finger on what was bothering her, could only say that it was like a premonition trying to take hold, though of what she had no idea. It just didn't feel good, and this morning as she crossed the cluttered farmyard to go and let out the sheep it was coming over her in waves, along with a damp, cloying mist rolling in from the fields. Dodgy was with her, as he always was first thing, but unusually for him he didn't seem as interested in urging his flock on their way as he did in watching her.

'What is it?' she asked him, glancing over to the chicken coop as one of the cockerels erupted in a raucous late start. 'Have you got a weird feeling too?'

Dodgy barked, turned a circle and put his muzzle into her hand.

She glanced over at the half-derelict barn, a great hiding place for man or beast if they were looking for one. Josh and Jack had installed a nesting box in its sturdier rafters and recently, to their great delight, a young kestrel had taken up residence. They'd waited, hidden, several nights in a row to watch it come and go, gliding silently, powerfully, past a vivid moon to and from the hunt, but there was no sign of it this morning.

Shelley felt a surge of love as she recalled Josh's excitement when he'd first discovered the bird. (Jack had found it really, but he was more than happy for Josh to claim the fame.) There was no creature big or small, furry, woolly, quilled or feathered that their adorable dynamo of a son didn't find endlessly fascinating and in need of caring for or studying.

She looked around again.

Nothing moved. There wasn't a sound or glimpse of movement that didn't belong to nature. She looked back at the farmhouse, half expecting to see someone on the way out, or watching her from a window, but there was no one.

Shrugging, she carried on to the main barn, tugged open the doors and was instantly greeted by an onrush of bleated affection.

By the time the sun burned off the dawn mist it was past ten o'clock, and she'd forgotten all about the peculiar unease that had bothered her earlier. So apparently had Dodgy, since he'd long ago returned from escorting their much-increased flock into the meadows, eager for his breakfast before the main event of the day got under way.

Since Jack's father, David, had decided to invest in Deerwood by more than doubling the number of their sheep – this was the good news Jack had finally broken following an intimate romp in the barn – the farm's finances hadn't exactly improved, it was still too early for that, but the potential for greater earnings had managed to raise their creditworthiness at the bank. Also, having so many more sheep meant that next year there could be three times as many lambs. A lot more work in the birthing sheds, of course, but with any luck it would result in some much-needed cash.

The first part of the process – impregnating the ewes – had yet to happen, and that little frenzy of animal passion was due to get underway today.

Shelley realized that for most other farms this was a natural, largely unremarkable part of the season, but Jack never had been able to resist turning an event into a celebration. It was what made being married to him so much fun, and living at Deerwood brought such a wealth of opportunities.

'Mum,' Zoe cried, coming up behind her as Shelley rinsed her hands under an outside tap, 'are they here yet?'

Knowing she was referring to the rams Jack and Josh had gone to collect from neighbouring farms, Shelley said, 'Should be any minute now.'

Their own rams, after being kept apart from the rest of the flock for the past few weeks, had already gone off to meet their servicing schedules (Shelley preferred euphemisms around the children), leaving only Pistol and Thunder, their teasers – vasectomized males – to strut and rut about the place to get the girls in the mood. This he-man stomp and romp that owed nothing at all to flirtation or finesse could be as hilarious to watch (for some, especially Jack and Nate) as it was effective in its purpose, for even the ewes that played hard to get by sitting on their plump woolly rumps at the moment of conquest couldn't resist this dynamic duo in the end.

So now, with the real-deal team about to arrive, and the warm-up acts in a pen for safety, the ewes were behaving like teenagers on a night out in Ibiza. Meanwhile Dodgy showed off his sheepdog manoeuvres to Bluebell the goat, who might have done a better job of appearing star-struck if Hanna hadn't just turned up to feed her.

As soon as Jack returned from his collection of ovine testosterone in the shape of two seriously macho rams, the whole family set about smothering the beasts' undersides in different-coloured chalk. This was how they'd later be able to tell which male had mounted which female, and to make sure that all ewes were covered. Then they let the four-legged lads loose and gathered to watch the start of the show.

It was bedlam, with sheep of both genders running around all over the place, the females keen to lead a merry dance, the males apparently up for the chase and their audience cheering them on. For a while it wasn't clear that anything of a reproductive nature was actually under way, but then one of the female Closewools emerged from the fray with a very definite grin on her face. (This was according to Jack, who insisted he could read all animal expressions – and it wasn't unlike Shelley's face when they'd . . . Shelley's daggered look cut the comparison short.)

'Yes!' he cried, punching the air, as though his horse – or sheep – had just come in first, which Shelley had to concede it apparently had. 'Let's hear it for Conker the Bonker.'

As everyone laughed and groaned, Josh exclaimed, 'That's not his name.'

'Dad, you're so silly,' Zoe declared, leaping onto his back and pretending to choke him.

After a few more shouts of 'Yes!', the cold started creeping through their wax jackets and scarves. Kat said, 'Who's for lunch at our place?'

As Perry was already taking off towards Tigger and Eeyore, his very own piglets who lived with Wonka and Bucket, it was a natural move to leave the very untantric sheep party to take its course and start back across the field.

'We're still going to see the pony this afternoon, aren't we, Dad?' Hanna reminded him in a voice that warned Jack woe betide him if he'd forgotten.

'Yes, yes, we have to,' Zoe cried, still riding on his back and hugging him hard enough to throttle him if he had made other plans. 'You promised, and if we don't buy him today someone else will.'

'He's going to be mine,' Hanna told her crossly, 'but you can help muck him out whenever you like. Will the stable be ready in time?' she asked her father.

'I want a donkey,' Josh suddenly declared.

'And me,' Perry clamoured excitedly, because he loved Josh and wanted to do everything Josh did. 'I had a ride on one when we went to the beach,' he announced. 'And you did, didn't you, Josh? Dad, can we go and ride on one again? Please, please, please.'

'I thought you wanted to see Dad's great big red fire engine,' Kat reminded him.

Shelley wasn't sure why that sounded smutty, it just did, and so she sniggered.

Apparently catching the same silly wavelength, Kat stifled a laugh too.

'What's so funny?' Hanna demanded, perplexed and annoyed because, as the eldest, she ought to understand even if the others didn't.

'Nothing,' Shelley tried to say, but she choked on another laugh as Jack shot her a ludicrous Conker the Bonker sort of look.

'They're being naughty,' Grandpa told them.

Hanna sighed, clearly bored by how childish everyone was. 'Mum,' she said, 'when you go into town later can you rent a video for us to watch tonight?'

'If we can agree on which one,' Shelley replied.

'And you should get some chocolate,' Josh piped up. 'We always have chocolate when we're watching a film.' This was often his favourite part, because having two older sisters meant his video choice usually went ignored.

The walk down the drive soon turned into a race, and as everyone disappeared around a curve in the track Shelley realized the eerie feeling she'd experienced that morning was stalking her again. She even turned around, as if someone might be there, someone she could snap at and order to go away. But whichever direction she looked in there was nothing to see but fields, hedgerows and cold blue sky.

After lunch everyone went their different ways – to look at a new pony for Hanna, or to dig a new vegetable patch, or visit the fire station. In Shelley and Kat's case they drove into town to order Abba outfits from the fancy dress shop for the Christmas cabaret at the pub. The song they'd chosen was 'Dancing Queen'. They could hardly wait to see Jack and Nate camping it up in all that fancy seventies gear, or the children beside themselves with embarrassment and hilarity.

Still laughing as they left the shop, they took off to the town hall for a secret meeting they deliberately hadn't mentioned to their husbands. Provided all went to plan they wanted it to be a surprise.

Jemmie Bleasdale, who'd organized the gathering, gave them a wave as she busied about the place with her trusty WI lieutenants, and by the time the seminar was ready to begin the room was full of curious, sceptical, and even slightly nervous female faces.

Computers were already revolutionizing the world, they were informed by the guest speaker, as if they didn't already know that. However, it was feared that women, especially those in rural areas, were going to be left behind if they didn't jump on board now.

By the end of the presentation Shelley and Kat had each ordered a home model, with colour monitors and a printer to share, and had also signed up for a six-week beginners' course starting in January.

'We're calling this Christmas presents to ourselves,' Shelley informed Jemmie Bleasdale when they went to thank her for arranging the talk. 'Jack already knows how to use one, of course, because they have one at the surgery, but I can see how useful it would be to have one at the farm.'

Jemmie was clearly thrilled to have been of help. 'I'm so glad you came,' she said warmly, hugging Shelley, then Kat. 'Us girls have to stay on top of things or those men will end up getting away with murder.'

'Don't they already?' Kat commented drily.

Though the words reminded them all of the tent fracas back in the summer, Jemmie showed no discomfort at her sons' unseemly behaviour, for her gentle face came alive with laughter, showing her almost childlike enthusiasm for everything, no matter what it was. It captivated everyone and made her most charities' first choice for patron. 'Oh, Bella dear, thanks for doing that,' she said to a slender woman with neat fair hair and a pixieish face who'd begun stacking chairs. 'Do you know Bella Shager?' she asked Shelley and Kat. 'She runs the tourist office here, and does a mighty good job of it, I can tell you.'

With an engaging smile, Bella came to shake hands. 'Lovely to meet you,' she said, and the warmth of her tone made it seem as though she really meant it.

Realizing this attractive woman was probably older than she at first appeared, Shelley replied, 'It's a pleasure to meet you too. I can imagine you have some stories to tell, working with tourists.'

As Bella laughed, Jemmie said, 'Bella's daughter, Gina, is in her second year at university studying computer science. Isn't that something to be proud of? A girl stepping into a man's world, and no doubt she'll outclass them all.'

With a shake of her head, Bella said, 'I'd like to think that'll happen, but I'm afraid she came home a couple of days ago and I'm still not sure why. Something's obviously upset her, but as yet I haven't managed to get to the bottom of it.'

Shelley smiled sympathetically. She had all the teenage hurdles to come; for now she could only wish Bella Shager good luck with Gina, since it was time for her and Kat to leave.

'She has a look about her,' Kat remarked as they headed back to the car, 'that makes you want to know her.'

'You mean Bella?' Shelley responded. 'Yes, you're right, she does.'

'You have it too,' Kat continued. 'So does Jemmie – and how that wonderful woman stays married to that odious oaf Humphrey, I'll never know. As big a mystery is how she's managed to produce a clutch of such boorish sons. It defies logic when she's an absolute angel.'

'We have to assume that there's a side to the Bleasdale males that only she sees,' Shelley responded, thinking this had to be true or it really would make no sense, and pulling a woolly hat over her hair to keep it from blowing about in the wind she cast a dubious look up at the sky. The temperature had dropped several degrees since they'd entered the town hall and darkness was already creeping in, making the prospect of getting home soon doubly desirable.

'I'm almost sorry Nate and I are going out tonight,' Kat grumbled as they reached Shelley's car. 'Sitting around your fire watching videos with the kids has much more appeal than a curry and quiz night at the Ring o'Bells, I can tell you.'

Shelley had to laugh. 'We've ended up renting *Top Gun* again,' she reminded her. 'I'm sure you won't mind giving that a miss.'

Kat rolled her eyes. 'Kids are a mystery, aren't they? They can watch the same film fifty-six times, recite the lines like they'd played all the parts, and still want to see it again.'

'If Hanna had got her way we'd be on our fiftieth viewing of *Ferris Bueller's Day Off*,' Shelley grimaced, 'so I suppose I can handle another go round with Tom Cruise.'

Since they were both keen Tom Cruise fans this certainly had more appeal than *Pirates*, which had been top of Josh's list, or *A Nightmare on Elm Street*, Jack and Nate's choice, which was never going to happen.

It was gone six by the time they drove into the farmyard to find everyone in the small barn gathered around Hanna's new pony, Madonna, smoothing her tenderly, feeding her, combing her mane and generally adoring her.

'Dad bought the saddle from the previous owners as well,' Hanna told her mother as Shelley approached, 'and he said we can go to the country store tomorrow to get me some new riding boots.'

'Where is Dad?' Shelley asked, taking a handful of fresh grass from Josh to feed to the pony.

'His pager went off so he had an emergency,' Josh told her, and upending a bucket he tried to climb onto Madonna's back.

Hanna was having none of that, but before a fight could break out Shelley scooped Josh into her arms and squeezed him too hard for him to break free. What a lovely feeling it was, holding his precious little body to hers.

'Ouch, you're hurting me,' he yelled, trying to escape. 'Put me down, put me down. Grandpa, help!' he cried as David came to let them know the fire was lit and a lovely beef casserole was ready to come out of the oven.

'I'm sleeping out here with Madonna tonight,' Hanna informed them.

'Don't be silly,' Shelley chided, 'it's far too cold and she'll be fine with Bluebell and Dodgy keeping an eye on things.'

It turned into a bit of a tussle – Hanna liked to have her own way – but eventually they all ended up inside with the doors shut tightly against the wind and a splendid log fire roaring up the chimney.

As usual Shelley fell asleep while watching the film and woke up to find Josh slumped against her, mouth wide open and chocolate smeared over his adorable face. There was no sign of Hanna and Zoe, but Shelley guessed they'd talked their grandfather into letting them go to say goodnight to Madonna.

'Where's Dad?' Josh yawned as he rewound the video ready to put it back in its box. He was the only one of the family who never seemed to have a problem operating the VCR, and Shelley had a feeling he was going to be a bit of a whizz on the computer when it came. He was like Jack in that way, with an unfussed, logical and often cavalier approach to life, meaning he was never afraid to tackle new things, whatever they might be.

'Where's Dad?' Hanna echoed, coming in through the door with the smell of a stable about her.

It was a good question. Shelley checked her watch,

and seeing it was past ten o'clock she sent a page asking him what time he expected to be back.

An hour later, with the children tucked up in bed and David in his room falling asleep to soft music, Shelley paged Jack again. It wasn't like him not to answer right away. However, if he was trying to save an animal in distress, or was at a farm with poor reception, or driving, he wouldn't be able to.

She was trying not to worry, but the dark feelings she'd had earlier in the day were back and no matter where she tried to put her thoughts, or what excuses she concocted for Jack's lateness, she couldn't quite escape them.

It was just before midnight when she heard his car rumbling into the farmyard, and by the time he came in the door she was ready to box his ears and fall on his neck in relief.

'I'm sorry,' he murmured, sounding as tired as he looked. He pulled her into his arms with a sigh. 'It's been a hell of a night. The RSPCA brought in half a dozen dogs they'd rescued from the Temple Fields Estate. You should have seen the state of the poor things. Two needed surgery and I ended up having to put one of them down.'

Understanding how hard it must have been for him, she said, 'Come on, you need a drink,' and taking him to the kitchen table she sat him down while she fixed them both a Scotch. 'I was worried,' she said, passing him a glass. 'Did your pager run out of battery?'

He checked it and nodded. 'Sorry, I should have rung anyway. Are the kids all right?'

'Fast asleep. We watched *Top Gun*.'

As he registered that he started to grin, and his eyes held to hers in a way that told her quite clearly what he was thinking.

She was ready with the line, and coming alive with the desire that didn't really need any words. '*Take me to bed or lose me forever*,' she murmured, giving her best impression of Meg Ryan as Carole.

And so that was what he did.

Shelley wasn't sure what woke her, or what time it was, but as she lay quietly in the darkness, Jack fast asleep beside her, she waited for whatever it was to happen again.

For long moments there was nothing to hear. The wind had dropped, she noticed, and it seemed all the animals were sleeping, since there were no sounds reaching her from the yard or barns.

If anything was wrong Dodgy would be barking, she reminded herself, and reassured by that she turned over and snuggled into Jack, ready to go back to sleep.

Then she heard it again.

Unable to discern what it was, she got quietly out of bed and tiptoed across the room. On the landing she stood still for a moment, trying to pick up the sound again.

Nothing.

She went to check on the children, found them fast asleep and the door to David's room closed, with no light showing beneath it.

She couldn't say why, exactly, but she still didn't feel that all was right with the house.

Then she saw Jack standing in their bedroom doorway.

141

'What are you doing?' he asked, keeping his voice low so not to wake anyone.

'I thought I heard something,' she murmured. She turned as she heard it again. A footstep? The muffled crunch of a movement? Her eyes shot to Jack's.

'Wait here,' he cautioned, and tightening the belt of his robe he went to the top of the stairs.

As she watched him descend Shelley found herself thinking of the gun, and wishing that they kept it next to their bed, not in the basement, locked in a cabinet, safe from the children.

Jack was halfway down and she moved to follow. It was so dark she could barely see him. She was just wondering why they didn't put on the light when everything suddenly went crazy.

Jack cried out as he fell. The thuds of his body hitting the stairs and the wall set Dodgy frantically barking outside.

'Jack!' she shouted, dashing down the stairs after him. 'Jack! Are you all right?'

All she could hear was Dodgy as he scratched wildly at the front door trying to get in.

The stairwell suddenly flooded with light. Hanna was on the landing.

Shelley stared at Jack in horror. He was crumpled so awkwardly at the foot of the stairs that something had to be broken. Then she noticed the trail of blood coming from his mouth and his eyes . . . *His eyes* . . . She threw herself onto him, frantically calling his name. 'Jack! Jack, answer me,' she begged, grabbing his hair. 'Please. Jack. Oh God . . .'

'Mum!' Hanna cried in panic.

'Call an ambulance!' Shelley yelled.

She was staring disbelievingly into Jack's face. His wide unblinking eyes weren't seeing her, she knew that, but they had to. She must make them. 'Jack,' she raged desperately. 'Jack, please, please don't do this.'

The ambulance took Jack's lifeless body away around five in the morning. The paramedics had tried to revive him, of course, but by the time they'd arrived it had been as evident to them as it had to Shelley that it was already too late. His head had hit the flagstones so hard that it had broken his neck and killed him outright.

It didn't seem real.

Nothing did.

Jack was dead.

She couldn't make herself accept it; wanted never to accept it.

A lot of people were in the house; most of them police, walking around checking doors and windows, making notes, asking questions.

Shelley was in the sitting room with the children huddled up against her. Kat brought tea; David sat slumped in a chair beside the fireplace, ashen, stunned, unable to speak.

Nate was dealing with things in the kitchen.

Shelley could hear a female voice and after a while realized it was Cathy, Giles's wife. Someone must have called them. They had so much else to be thinking about with all the rumours going round about BSE, and the fears lately that the disease could be transmitted to humans, but they'd come anyway.

She needed to move, to do something, but she didn't know what.

A doctor came and tried to coax her to go upstairs and lie down, but she couldn't leave the children.

Hanna got to her feet and started out of the room. 'Where are you going?' Shelley asked hoarsely, but Hanna didn't answer.

'I'll go after her,' Kat whispered.

Shelley let her.

Hours rolled past; or was it minutes?

The police were outside now, searching the garden and field beyond.

Shelley's thoughts were suddenly snagged by the Abba costumes she and Kat had ordered the day before. She couldn't seem to get it out of her mind. She was stuck in yesterday, when everything had been fun and Jack had . . .

She should page him. The urge was so great that she could barely stop herself going to the phone. It was what she always did when she was worried or afraid. Jack could calm her down, make everything all right.

She went outside into the growing dawn light with Josh and Zoe holding tightly onto her hands. She wasn't sure who was comforting whom. They watched Hanna walking with Dodgy and the sheep into the fields. The pony was with them, Kat close behind and Shelley felt herself starting to panic as they disappeared like ghosts into the misty beyond.

Two days had now passed since the terrible, senseless accident that had taken Jack's life. This was how everyone was viewing it, as an accident, but Shelley couldn't convince herself that it was. She was certain someone had been in the house that night, in spite of no evidence being found to prove it. They might not have pushed him down the stairs, but he wouldn't have been on them if she hadn't felt sure someone was there.

Was it her fault he was dead?

'You're sure nothing is missing?' the detective asked. His name was Rod Pullman; he was a young, sturdy type with fair hair, a round, pleasant face and a respectful manner. He'd come, he'd explained, because the officers who'd attended the scene on the night of Jack's death had reported the possibility of suspicious circumstances.

Shelley shook her head. 'No, nothing's missing,' she confirmed. Everything was where she and Jack had left it, their wallets, the cash they kept in a jug on the beam over the fireplace. The VCR and TV. They didn't have much else of any value.

'But you thought you heard someone?' he prompted.

She nodded. 'It was why I got up.'

'Could it have been one of the children?'

'No, I don't think so. They were asleep when I checked.'

'What sort of noise was it?'

'I couldn't really tell. It was so faint and . . . It was more a *feeling* I had that someone was in the house.'

'Did the dog bark?'

'Not then, no, but he must have heard Jack fall because he started barking then.' She fixed the detective with eyes that were raw with trauma.

'The dog was in the small barn, across the way. He might not have heard anything before . . .'

145

'Is there access to the back of the house without having to pass the barn?' he asked.

She shook her head. 'Not unless you come across the fields.'

She'd seen them checking the fields after she'd told them about her suspicions, but apparently nothing had been found to confirm them.

'Is there anyone you can think of who might have come here that night? For whatever reason?'

Her eyes went to Nate. He was rigid, stunned, clenching and unclenching his fists as he listened, and probably, like her, kept losing focus. She knew he was finding it impossible to accept that this had happened, that it wasn't all a huge mistake, or some kind of nightmare that would be over soon if only he could make himself wake up.

Pullman was waiting for an answer.

Nate haltingly explained what had happened on the night of the tents. He sounded bewildered and close to tears. The Bleasdales were the only family they had issues with in the area, he said, and Shelley added that they'd had no communication with the male contingent since the morning after the showdown, and that she considered Jemmie Bleasdale a friend.

'Jack didn't make enemies,' Nate told him. 'What happened with the Bleasdale twins was of their doing, not his.'

Pullman was noting things down. 'Is there any reason why they might have chosen your land to pitch their tents?' he asked Shelley.

'You'd have to ask them,' she replied, 'but maybe it had something to do with us not supporting the hunt.'

'Was your husband a saboteur?'

She shook her head. 'None of us is, but we don't agree with it.'

Pullman's eyes moved to Nate and back again. Shelley's mind was wandering again, going off to places that made no sense, had no connection at all to what was happening right here. The bonfire Jack and Josh had started building for 5 November needed to be finished. Nate and Perry were making the guy. It was her job to pick up the fireworks. Her parents had arrived two days ago. They were somewhere with the children now. She wondered how long they would stay. Certainly until after the funeral . . .

Funeral . . .

Panic and denial rose up to choke her, squeezing the breath from her lungs, the sanity from her mind. She wanted to scream Jack's name as loud as she could, over and over, wilder and wilder, until he came back just to make her stop, but she'd frighten the children and they were already frightened enough.

It would be better if they believed no one had been here.

There were no signs of a break-in; nothing was missing; she'd only imagined what she'd heard.

If there had been no one, then his fall would be her fault.

The day of the cremation was so bright and warm that it could have been the middle of summer. As Shelley gazed out across the fields she felt convinced that Jack had made it this way for them. He wouldn't want them to say goodbye under grey clouds or in driving rain.

He wouldn't want them to be cold either, so somehow he'd made the sun shine with a warmth unusual for late October. He was all around them, she could feel it as surely as if she were in his arms. He hadn't left them and he never would, because he was the heart of this family, the life and soul of the farm and the very centre of their world. It was how he would always be, and she was never going to have it any other way.

The question which would soon need to be answered was, could they manage the place without him? It was such a difficult and painful question that she couldn't allow herself to think about it today, and wasn't sure she ever could.

When they got to the crematorium she was surprised to see so many people, but she shouldn't have been. Jack had made friends as easily as he'd made her love him. He was an irresistible force; people were drawn to him in a way that she'd hardly ever seen with anyone else. So of course they'd be here today, gathering in this flower-filled chapel to say their sad and final goodbyes.

His favourite Eagles track played in the background as the celebrant waited for the pews to fill and overflow. Shelley was sitting at the front with the children and the rest of the family – and Dodgy, because Josh had wanted the dog to come too.

'Daddy loved him and he loved Daddy,' Josh had explained before they'd left, and no one had argued because it was true. Instead, Shelley had found a laugh as she'd said, 'I guess we're lucky you don't want to bring all the other animals too.'

'Maybe we should,' Josh said earnestly, and a tear trickled down his cheek.

The celebrant began. Shelley's mind went elsewhere, to the wildlife safari they'd been saving up for; to the Jackson Browne tickets Nate had for next month, to the fireworks for next week, and who was going to light them? She thought of the dogs Jack had tried to save the night he'd died, and the way he'd made love to her when he came home . . .

Her mind returned to the present, where the celebrant was speaking about Jack as if he'd known him. She didn't feel offended. It didn't warm her, either. She mostly felt numb, detached, and vaguely nauseous, probably thanks to the Scotch her father had pushed into her hand before they'd left the house.

She and Jack had never discussed what they wanted to happen when they died. Death wasn't something they'd thought about at all. This meant that the big decisions this past week had been left to her and Nate. She couldn't have got through any of it without her brother-in-law, and he said the same about her. They needed to be strong for one another, and for the rest of the family. It was their love for Jack that had always bound them together, and now it was saving them, and the others, from going under.

Nate delivered the eulogy, his voice cracking with grief, tears blinding his eyes. They were brave, meaningful words, telling the story of two boys growing up together, and how the younger, Nate, had always tried to best Jack at sports or studies and how Jack used to let him. 'Jack loved life more than anyone I've ever known,' he said hoarsely. 'That's what makes the suddenness of all this so hard to bear. If anyone deserved to live it was him. He was the best brother, son and husband that ever walked this earth, but most of all he was the best and proudest dad. Hanna, Zoe and Josh, we will do everything in our power to keep your father's memory alive for you and to share with you all our memories of him, so that you can carry them in your hearts as you go forward in your lives.'

As Josh climbed into Shelley's lap she felt herself starting to shake. Josh was so close to his father, they did almost everything together . . . How was he going to cope with this? Zoe sobbed against her, clinging to her arm. Shelley pressed a kiss to her hair and looked at Hanna, who was sitting straight-backed, ghostly pale and staring at nothing. Her pain was so brittle and raw that Shelley was sure if she touched her she would break into a thousand tiny pieces.

It was how Shelley felt, but she reminded herself that for the children's sake she must keep it together.

Outside, the congregation gathered quietly and sorrowfully before going back to the farm for a party. That was what Jack would have wanted, she and Nate had decided, a celebration of his life with music and lots of wine and maybe dancing. Not a mournful wake with everyone sitting around feeling morbid and sad over lukewarm cups of tea and a few dry-edged sand-wiches.

'Shelley, my dear. I'm so sorry for what you're going through.' It was Jemmie Bleasdale, taking Shelley's icy hands in hers and holding them tenderly. 'I've called a few times,' she said, 'but I don't want to intrude. I just want you to know that if there's anything I can do . . .'

Shelley was remembering what she and Nate had

told the police, and wondering if they'd visited the Bleasdales . . .

Sir Humphrey was taking her hands now. His face was grey, haggard and not at all as Shelley had seen him before. 'I know Jack and I had our differences,' he said gruffly, 'but I always . . .' He swallowed. 'He was a good man. One of the best. Like Jemmie said, if there's anything . . . You know where we are . . .'

Shelley's eyes moved to the twins. She felt suddenly hot and wanted to be sick, or somehow escape. Jemmie was saying, 'The boys flew back from New York yesterday. They've been there since the beginning of the month, but they wanted to come today to pay their respects. Felix, our youngest, is in Thailand.'

Shelley watched the boys' mouths as they spoke to her. They looked as awkward as any young men might in difficult situations, but she thought their condolences sounded as sincere as anyone else's.

They'd been in New York since the beginning of the month – Jemmie had gently made that clear. Felix was away too – so it couldn't have been any of them Shelley had heard that night.

She still wasn't sure she'd heard anyone.

When it came time to start back to the farm she stood beside the car waiting for the children to get in, and gazed absently across the gardens of remembrance. She wasn't expecting to see or feel anything, but she paused a moment as she spotted a young girl standing beside a red-brick wall, partly masked by the glare of sunlight. Shelley had no idea who she was, couldn't tell from this distance if she'd ever seen her before, but there was something about her, the tilt of her head, or perhaps the way she was staring at the funeral party, that made Shelley wonder about her.

'Do you know her?' she asked Nate.

Nate followed the direction of her gaze, but by then the girl was walking away.

CHAPTER NINE
VIVIENNE

Present Day

Vivienne was staring at her reflection in amazement, turning her head this way and that, spinning in the chair and holding up a hand mirror to get a good look at the back of her new hair. She'd never imagined that changing its colour could bring about such a startling transformation. It even seemed to be giving new light to her eyes and skin for they no longer appeared as dull as they had a few days ago. She realized the recent change in her medication was probably more responsible for that, since it had begun to improve both her energy and her spirits, but nevertheless . . .

She ruffled her silvery-blonde waves with her fingers, and watched the way they tumbled back into place, messier, but still lovely. Her hair had grown these past two months, and her mother had only tidied up the ends rather than take anything from the length. It had been the right decision; the style and colour flattered her so well that she could only wonder why she hadn't braved it before.

As she broke into a smile her audience started to

153

breathe – and laugh. In the salon with her was her mother; Michelle; Jade, the senior stylist; Holly, one of the juniors, and two regular clients who'd paused midway through having their hair washed and blow-dried.

Vivienne met her mother's eyes in the mirror and seeing how much pleasure it was giving her to feel she'd done something right for once, she got up to hug her.

She wasn't going to allow the negative, destructive part of herself to remind her of how shallow this was – *a new hairdo doesn't change anything; you're still going to die, so why don't you find something less selfish, more worthy to do with the time you have left?* That part of her had nothing of value to contribute today, when what she should really have been feeling was buoyed by the triumph of making it here this morning after spending four days in bed recovering from the strain of the hospital visit. She'd even managed to sit through the entire process of having her look changed without feeling the need to lie down. She wasn't even tired now, or breathless, or fogged by the side effects of a drug that had thankfully been removed from her daily cocktail. Instead, she was feeling something close to normal, she decided. OK, her heart might be failing, but that didn't mean she couldn't make the most of whatever life she had left should a donor not come along.

They all turned as the door opened and Mark, fresh from the surf in a black wet-suit and red crocs, stomped in, tearing out his earbuds as he ended a call. Seeing Vivi, his eyes widened as he treated her to a long, appreciative whistle. He even seemed about to sweep her up for a raucous swing-round, before remembering that might not be such a good idea. 'You look *smokin'*,' he told her, making everyone laugh. 'In fact, you look . . .' He stepped aside, eyed up his mother, then Vivi again and said, 'Yep, you definitely look like twins.'

'Don't be ridiculous,' Gina chided, as Vivi said, 'Spare me, I'm half her age.'

'You're well past that,' Gina retorted, eyes shining with laughter.

'OK, but *really*,' Vivi protested. 'Although I do look a lot more like you now. Just not forty-six.'

'Gina doesn't look that old either,' Michelle put in. 'In fact, you're such a hot pair of babes I think we should do something to celebrate.'

Holly, the junior, gamely called out, 'Shall I go and get some champagne?'

'My treat,' Vivi declared, reaching for her purse.

'Tea will be fine,' Gina cut in firmly, a reminder to them all that alcohol was out of the question for Vivi.

Vivi's cheeks flamed as she glared at her mother. 'Even if I can't have it that doesn't mean no one else can,' she said tightly.

'But you're the star of the show,' Gina pointed out, 'so there wouldn't be much . . .' She broke off as a yowl of pain suddenly erupted from a cubicle at the back of the salon.

'What the f . . . ?' Mark muttered, giving Vivi's shoulder a comforting squeeze.

The others were already laughing as Maisie Redmond shouted out, 'Sorry about that. I'm having a Hollywood, Mark, that's what the f . . .'

He turned to his mother. 'A Hollywood?' he echoed, mystified.

Gina pointed south.

'Totally bald,' Michelle added for the sheer pleasure of it.

His eyes dilated as the image of stout little Maisie Redmond with a totally bald . . . He backed away. 'OK, too much information,' he protested, and planting a swift kiss on his mother's cheek, and another on Vivi's new hair, he told them he'd see them at home later and beat a hasty retreat.

Deciding for everyone's sake, including her own, that it would spoil the day if she stayed angry with her mother, Vivi accepted Holly's offer of tea and followed Michelle into the area of squishy sofas that filled up one of the salon's deep-bayed front windows. The other bay was a haven for exotic silk palms, a large Tibetan Buddha, an ornate Balinese birdcage and various other Oriental-style *objets* that Gina had collected from fairs and antique shops over the years.

Vivienne had always loved it here, especially as a child when she used to play at being a hairdresser, or manicurist, sometimes even a masseuse (that was usually for NanaBella). It hadn't really changed much since that time, there was still soothing mood music playing on the salon's sound system, while aromatic candles burned in colourful glass dishes and crystalline water flowed through table-top fountains. The place was as elegant and stylish – and mysterious, in Vivi's view – as Gina herself, and had become, over the years, the most popular hairdresser's in town. Some appointments were made months in advance, with most insisting on Gina;

however, Jade's reputation was growing, and Yvonne, the beautician (and Michelle's mother) who'd worked with Gina for the past ten years, had built up an impressive client list of her own.

'So what are you girls doing for the rest of the day?' Gina asked, as she began clearing the island where she'd worked her magic on Vivi's hair.

Michelle turned to Vivi. 'We were thinking about doing some shopping?' she said, making it a question. 'Are you still up for it?'

'Definitely,' Vivi replied, amazed and thrilled that she still had the energy to look forward to it. 'Some new clothes to go with my new look? It has to be done.'

Gina glowed as she said, 'Next thing we know you'll be going out dancing.'

'Don't rule it out,' Vivi warned, though they both knew that dancing was in the same category as champagne. Anything that stimulated her heart rate to that extent had to be off the agenda, at least for the foreseeable future. 'You can even come with us if you fancy it,' she offered.

Gina twinkled and turned round as a curtain at the back of the room swished open and Yvonne emerged, drying her hands on a towel. 'Great idea,' she declared happily. 'Count me in for a good bop.' She broke into a smile as her eyes found Vivi. 'Oh, wow! Will you look at yourself?' she murmured admiringly. 'You're an angel, as pretty as a picture.'

'Don't leave before I come out,' Maisie Redmond called from the hidden depths of the cubicle. 'I want to see it.'

Yvonne came to tilt Vivi's face, keen for a better look. She was a tall, forthright woman, as dark-haired and olive-skinned as Michelle was fair and freckled, and managing to look even better at fifty, according to her wily husband, than she had at twenty. 'Of course he didn't know me when I was twenty,' she'd add whenever he said that, 'so it's no compliment at all.'

'It's not just the hair,' she decided, taking in Vivi's eyes and skin. 'The lights are coming back on,' she pronounced.

Smiling, Vivi said, 'They changed my medication,' and a quick glance at her mother gave her a small rush of pleasure, for Gina was looking as though someone might have improved her medication too.

'So where shall we go for a rave-up?' Yvonne demanded, as though it might really be an option.

'What about a tea dance at the town hall?' Michelle joked.

'You can mock,' Maisie Redmond chided as she emerged freshly waxed and fully clothed – and ever so slightly flushed. 'It's a good place to meet an Internet date,' she informed them knowingly. 'It's safe and fun, and it gets you off to a very good start, provided he can dance, of course. Having said that, it's the ones with the smooth moves you've got to watch. You can tell some of them are rehearsing for moves of another kind, if you get my meaning. Cheeky devils, they can be. Oh, Vivi, you're so gorgeous I could eat you all up, and your brother's right, you do look more like your mother now. So how are you feeling? Am I allowed to ask?'

Having known Maisie for as long as she could

remember, Vivienne found it easy to say, 'I'm trying to forget about it, Maisie, but this is definitely a good day.' Her smile widened. 'So you're still doing the Internet dating?'

'Oh, I love it, so I do. You meet so many interesting characters, and best of all you don't have to go home with them if you don't want to. I only wish I'd got rid of that waste of space I was married to twenty years ago. The fun I could have had! Still, there's nothing stopping me now. Here we go, Vonny,' she said, handing over her payment and loyalty card. 'Book me in again for next week.'

'Blimey, how fast do your pubes grow?' Michelle choked on a laugh.

Maisie's eyes glittered mischievously. 'There are things about me,' she said darkly, 'that defy a lot of science . . . but that isn't one of them.'

Laughing, Yvonne said, 'I've got you down for an eyebrow thread and colour. Is that right?'

'That's right. Make me look nice and surprised, I find the fellas like that. Makes them feel . . . Well, we won't get into that. Oh, there's Gerald come to pick me up,' she said, as someone blasted on a car horn outside. 'My son likes to make himself heard, in case you didn't notice. OK, see you next week, Vonny. You, lovely girls,' she added to Vivi and Michelle, 'go and have yourselves some fun while you still can. You're a long time dead, I always tell myself.' It wasn't until the words were out that she realized what she'd said, and her horror was so great that Vivienne immediately got up to hug her.

'It doesn't matter,' she whispered, as Maisie started

Susan Lewis

to gulp an apology. 'It really doesn't, and what's more I think I'll take your advice.'

Turning to Gina, Maisie said, 'I'm so sorry. I . . . There's a mouth on me and it runs away . . . I didn't mean anything . . .'

'We know you didn't,' Gina assured her. 'Now, I think Gerald's getting a little impatient out there.'

'I shall box his ears, so I will. And my own. Definitely my own. What am I like? Oh dear, oh fuck. Seventy years old and I'm still putting my foot in it . . .'

She continued muttering to herself as she closed the door behind her, leaving Gina to throw out her hands as Vivienne said, 'Is she really seventy?'

Yvonne nodded.

'And getting a Hollywood?'

Yvonne grinned.

'I mean, there's nothing wrong with it,' Vivienne insisted, 'I'm just . . . Actually, I'm probably about to put my foot in it too, so where were we before all this began?'

'About to go dancing,' Yvonne reminded them, 'but more seriously, we need to do something to show you off, so how about we all go out for dinner tonight?'

Gina said, 'Gil's coming.'

Vivienne frowned. Was that an excuse not to go?

'That's perfect,' Yvonne announced. 'With Mark at home as well we can make it a big family outing – at the Crustacean if we can get in. I'll ring them now, if we're all up for it?'

'Some of us have children,' Michelle reminded her.

'And you have babysitters right next door in Sam's parents. I'll call them myself, and if they can have the

160

children are we all up for the Crustacean? We know the men will be, because they're always up for anything to do with food.'

Before her mother could respond, Vivienne said, 'I'm definitely up for it, and I'm sure Gil will be too.'

Yvonne declared, 'That's great! So you girls go and buy yourselves something new for the occasion and I'll make all the arrangements.'

As Vivienne led the way to the door she was about to reach for the handle when a sharp, powerful thud suddenly struck her like a knife in her back. For one bewildering moment she thought her mother or Michelle had hit her, then realizing what had happened she clasped a hand to her chest.

'Are you OK?' Michelle asked worriedly.

Gina turned round.

'I'm fine,' Vivienne insisted.

Paling, Gina said, 'Yvonne, call an ambulance. Her device has gone off.'

'No! Don't,' Vivi protested. 'I'm OK.'

'Did it go off?' Gina pressed, coming to her.

'Yes, but they told us . . .'

'To call an ambulance . . .'

'To assess the situation,' Vivi growled angrily, 'and . . . I'm OK. I'm still on my feet, I haven't passed out and . . .' she paused, 'everything's fine.'

Gina's face was ashen. 'Sit down for a moment,' she instructed shakily. 'Give yourself a few minutes, then you need to contact the clinic to let them know . . .'

'I will,' Vivienne interrupted. 'Just don't fuss.' When she was back on the sofa she said to Yvonne, 'Please . . . book the dinner.'

'Vivi,' her mother said gravely.

Vivi couldn't look at her. She wanted to shout and rage and blame her for the fact that out of nowhere, provoked by nothing at all, her heart had just tried to stop beating. *It's your fault,* she wanted to yell. *You keep stressing me out.* But she knew that was as untrue as it was unfair, so she said nothing, just sat quietly, clenching her hands and feeling the terror of knowing she might have died just now were it not for the device.

'Did it hurt much?' Mark asked her later in the day.

It had hurt like bloody hell, Vivi didn't say, but only for a moment, and thankfully it hadn't knocked her out, or off her feet. Sighing, she put her head back and closed her eyes. They were in her sitting room, where her grandparents' old table and chairs had returned to replace the bed that had been moved upstairs. It was definitely a design clash, but the bed had made her feel like an invalid, as if she couldn't be allowed to go very far from it, or make it up the stairs when, provided she took it slowly, she could.

'If you still feel like it,' Mark said, 'I think we should go out tonight.'

Vivi's eyes remained closed. She wouldn't tell him how she really felt, she didn't want to get into it with him, or even with herself; she just wanted to feel thankful that the implanted defibrillator had shocked her heart back into action, preventing her from dying right then. Presumably it was now performing some of the less violent tasks it was programmed to do, such as storing information of pulse rate, blood flow . . . She couldn't feel anything, no buzzing or burning, just the horrible dread of being struck right through the heart by another brutal electric shock. Trey, at the clinic, had taken a reading from the device as soon as she'd got home and connected to the bedside monitor. To her relief he hadn't told her to come in. He'd simply asked how she was feeling now, had instructed her to visit her GP in the morning for a new prescription and take things easy for the next couple of days.

As if she ever did anything else.

Realizing Mark was waiting for an answer, she said, 'Everyone would feel they couldn't have any wine because I can't, and what fun would that be?'

'They're grown-ups,' he retorted. 'They can make up their own minds – unless you want them to feel bad, of course.'

She eyed him balefully.

'Well, do you?' he prompted, apparently wanting an answer. He was sitting on the floor, his elbows resting on his knees, his handsome, tanned face showing more interest than judgement.

'No, of course not,' she said. 'I just want them . . . I want *me* to stop being like this. I thought the new medication was making a difference . . . It *is* to the way I feel in myself, but then the damned device went off, and now they're bloody well changing things again . . .' The frustration, the helplessness, was so intense she might have screamed if she'd had the energy. She widened her eyes and stared at him challengingly, as if he could somehow make a difference.

He looked back and, seeing how worried he was, she said, 'Sorry, self-pity's not good, is it? I really can't stand it, but getting rid of it . . .' She brightened her smile. 'The blonde thing's working, though. I'm quite liking it.'

Going with the change of subject, he said, 'She did a great job. It was good that you let her. I think it meant something.'

Knowing that it had, she felt a surge of guilt and affection for her mother as she said, 'I wish I could stop being horrible to her. It just seems to happen before I even know it's going to.'

His eyes went down for a moment, giving her the impression that he had something to say, and when he looked at her again she realized she was going to hear it. 'I know I'm probably not meant to say this,' he began, 'but it really upsets her when you're . . . Well, you know, kind of off with her. Not that she ever says anything to me, but she does to Dad. That's why he keeps coming here to make sure you're all right – I mean both of you.'

Feeling shamed, like a bully who'd been called out, she closed her eyes again. She had to try harder, somehow stop the resentment that kept surfacing in such awful ways: ways that didn't always need words because her mother sensed it anyway, and was as hurt by it as if Vivienne had slapped her, or worse.

She could hear the murmur of Gina's voice now, as she and Gil talked in the kitchen. She wondered what they were saying, and decided it was probably best she didn't know. After a while she asked Mark, 'Is it true your dad's met someone?'

He nodded slowly, not looking at her.

Sensing he was no happier about it than she was, she said, 'Have you met her?'

'No, but her name's Emily. I'm not sure how serious it is.'

'I don't suppose coming here so often is helping things much.'

'Probably not.'

'Do you want them to get back together? I mean Mum and Gil.'

'Of course, if it's what they want.'

'I think it is.'

He nodded in agreement.

'Maybe I should make it a dying wish,' she suggested.

As his face became pinched she realized she'd gone too far. He looked so lost and afraid – maybe as afraid as she was, if the truth were told. 'I'm sorry,' she murmured.

'No, don't be. I'm your brother, you can say anything. I just . . . I just wish it wasn't happening.'

'I know,' she responded softly.

'They'll probably find you a heart,' he said after a while.

She nodded, in spite of knowing how unlikely it was. The doctors might not have actually said that the wait could be as long as three years, two more than they'd given her, but she knew because she'd been reading all about it online. However, she wasn't going to get into statistics and chances with Mark, it would only make him feel worse than he already did, so switching the subject back to their mother and Gil, she said, 'If we could find out *why* they broke up, then maybe we'd stand a chance of getting them back together.'

Taking a moment to untangle his thoughts from his

fears, he said, 'All I know is that it was his decision to leave, so despite what they might still feel for one another, I'm not sure he wants to come back.'

Vivi felt quietly stunned by that. She'd always assumed it was her mother who'd ended the marriage. Gil had certainly allowed her to think that, but apparently he'd told Mark something else. 'Did Gil ever say why he left?'

Mark shrugged. 'Not really. We never got into it. He just wanted me to know that it wouldn't make any difference, we'd still be a family, but we'd have two homes.'

This was what Gil had said to her too, without mentioning that it was what he wanted, rather than her mother's decision. Just in case Mark really did know more, she said, 'Has Gil ever said anything to you about my father?'

Mark frowned. 'Like what?'

'Like, is there a chance he might have been behind the break-up?'

Mark was looking perplexed and anxious as he shook his head. 'If he was then it's news to me,' he replied. 'But I don't ever talk to him or Mum about anything like that. It's not really my place to.'

Accepting that was true and feeling bad for putting him in an awkward position, she told herself to let it go and tried to lift the mood again. 'Can you do something for me?' she asked, managing the ghost of a twinkle.

He eyed her warily.

She smiled. 'Can you please go and join your mates in Italy? I know they're already there, because I've seen their posts on Facebook, and going to the Lakes and Venice and Florence would be on my bucket list if I could have a proper one, so I'm relying on you to go for me. And then to FaceTime me at least once a day to show me around and to reassure me that you're having a brilliant time.'

She meant every word, she really did want him to go and have a brilliant time, because sitting around here, worrying about her, wondering how long it would be before someone died so she could have a new heart, or didn't so she died instead, wasn't going to help anyone, least of all him.

'But NanaBella, I don't understand how you can't know who my father is. You said yourself that Mum was living with you when I was born . . .'

'When you were born, Vivi, not when you were conceived.'

'OK, so where was she then?'

'Actually, she was here, in Kesterly, for most of the time. She'd come back from uni during the summer, but she was always out with friends, staying over at parties and concerts, taking off for weekends on the south coast. I didn't know who most of the friends were. She'd met them at uni and they came to stay, or pass through . . .'

'Was there anyone in particular? Someone who might have been my dad?'

With a sigh NanaBella said, 'Your grandpa and I asked ourselves that many times, but neither of us remember there being anyone special. She just seemed to be having fun. She was too young to get involved

167

was what she used to say, and we never had a problem with that, because nineteen was young. She had a bright future ahead of her . . . She had all sorts of plans . . .' NanaBella caught her breath. *'She returned to uni after the summer was over, but then she came home a month or so later and everything . . . changed.'*

'Because she was pregnant?'

NanaBella nodded.

'Were you angry when you found out?'

'Not angry, no. I was more concerned about her and the way she was at the time.'

'What does that mean? How was she?'

NanaBella sighed again and shook her head. *'To be honest, my love, I thought she was going to say she wanted a termination so she could continue her studies, but it turned out that she'd decided to give them up and have her baby instead.'*

Not realizing that her question hadn't actually been answered, Vivi asked hopefully, almost desperately, 'So do you think that means she really loved him?'

NanaBella blinked in bemusement. 'I don't know what it means, my love, because she wouldn't ever talk about him.'

Vivi and Gil were strolling arm in arm along Bay Road, soaking up the evening sun as it sank slowly towards the horizon. There was no one about, just a lot of gulls and faraway surfers, and the occasional glimpse of a car passing the end of the road.

'So no more scares?' he asked, turning off his phone as it rang.

'Not so far,' she replied, thankfully. In truth, she

was becoming increasingly depressed by the suddenness of the shock when she'd been feeling so good, and was afraid she wouldn't be able to snap out of it for a while – by which time it might have happened again, and again. Short, sharp bursts of electricity to restart her heart each time it tried to give up on her. And what was that actually doing to it? Wearing it out even more? The spectre of a Ventricular Assist Device, the pump that would take over her heart completely, tried to appear, but she managed to push it away. She'd promised herself only to deal with that if she had to, for the nightmare of the tubes and batteries, the way it would limit her life to an even greater degree, should only be lived when she had no choice. 'I feel fine now,' she insisted. 'Well, maybe that's overstating it, I wouldn't be up for a marathon or a bungee jump, but I'm out here walking with you and that's good, isn't it?'

He smiled as he squeezed her arm. 'It's a pity it happened,' he commented sadly. 'You seemed to be gaining strength, but I guess it was a reminder for us not to get carried away.'

A horrible reminder, she thought, but she didn't want to discuss it any more. If it was going to happen again it would, and talking about it was hardly a preventive. So moving away from it, she said, 'I know we've had this conversation before, but we haven't had it for a long time and there are a few things I'd like to ask you again, if you don't mind.'

'Fire away,' he invited, his easy tone telling her that he hadn't guessed what was coming.

The big decision now was where to begin. 'It's about

my real father,' she said, deciding to get that bit out first. She waited. He said nothing, just kept walking with his hand over hers, so she continued. 'I know Mum's never told you who he is, but I wondered, since we last spoke about it, if that had changed.'

His eyes remained straight ahead as he said, 'No, it hasn't changed, sweetheart. We never talk about him. We never have.'

'But don't you find that strange? You must.'

He ruminated for a moment. 'Not strange, exactly, more concerning, because obviously something happened back then that was . . . Well, we don't know what it was, because she won't discuss it.'

She climbed up onto the dunes after him, accepting his help in case the effort was too much for her. It wasn't, but there again, after today's shock what did she know?

They tramped through the grassy sand until they reached a public bench offering an uninterrupted view of the bay. She rested her head on his shoulder as they sat watching the distant tide, her hand linked in his, and finally she said, 'Did my father have anything to do with the reason you left?'

He inhaled deeply, letting the question sink in for a while, before he said, 'I'm not sure.'

As surprised by the answer as she was thrown by it, she said, 'What does that mean?'

He drew a breath. 'To be honest,' he replied, 'I think he's the reason she's . . . the way she is, and it's because of the way she is that it became . . . difficult for us to stay together.'

Feeling faintly light-headed as she realized she might

170

actually be getting somewhere at last, she said, 'What do you mean by the way she is?'

It was clear that he didn't really want to answer that, and she felt bad for testing his loyalty to her mother, but she needed to know.

'Please,' she said softly.

In the end he said, 'She's difficult to get close to at times, as you know, and . . . Well, shall we just say that I don't think she's the person she might have been if things had been different.'

'You mean if she hadn't had me?'

He sighed heavily. 'Yes, I do mean that, but it doesn't mean she regrets having you. She's never made me think that.'

'But she has made you think that there's unfinished business with my father?'

Again he took a moment to consider her question before shaking his head. 'I'm not sure I'd put it like that, but who knows, you could be right.'

'Do you think . . . ? This is probably going to sound crazy, but do you think she's afraid of him?'

He frowned doubtfully. 'What I have sometimes thought is that he, or what happened between them, might still be influencing her in some way.'

Feeling certain it was, Vivi said, 'Do you think I have a right to know who he is?'

Resting his head on hers, he said, 'Yes, I think you do, but there's a lot to consider before you start taking any steps in that direction.'

'Like how it might affect her if I do manage to find him?'

'Yes, and there's also how it might affect you.'

171

She realized she hadn't actually given much consideration to that.

'Frankly,' he said, 'if he were a good man I'm sure he'd have been in your life.'

It was a logical assumption. 'Even if he were married to someone else?'

'That makes it less likely, of course, but not impossible.'

'And if he was married,' she said, countering her own argument, 'why wouldn't she at least have told NanaBella, or you, when you came into her life? She wouldn't have been the first girl to fall pregnant by a married man.'

'Indeed,' he agreed.

She hesitated before voicing another suspicion, until deciding there was no point in holding back, she said, 'I've sometimes wondered if she was raped.'

He nodded. 'I've wondered that too.'

'Did you ever ask her?'

'No, but your grandmother did and she said she wasn't.'

So he'd discussed it with NanaBella. 'Did Nana believe it?'

'I don't think she was ever completely sure, but apparently your mother was adamant that it hadn't happened that way.'

'Maybe she doesn't actually know who got her pregnant. There might have been some sort of group sex going on that she doesn't want to admit to.'

He shrugged, showing that he'd considered that possibility too, but how would they ever know?

She wound her fingers through his and brought their hands to her cheek. 'Whoever he is,' she said, 'whether

I find him or not, it'll never change how much you matter to me. I hope you know that.'

He turned to press a kiss to her new blonde waves. 'I'm glad about that,' he smiled.

She smiled too. 'Can I tell you something strange?' she asked after a while.

'Of course.'

'Knowing that I might die without ever finding out who he is . . . It makes me feel . . . unfinished.'

He moved to put an arm around her. 'I think I can understand that,' he said softly.

'So,' she said, 'will you talk to Mum with me? I can't do it on my own. I don't think I'm strong enough, not if it goes the way it did the last time I asked when I was eighteen.'

Gina was incandescent, and looked as though she might actually hit Vivienne if she so much as uttered another word.

'No, your father, as you like to call him, had absolutely nothing to do with me and Gil breaking up. I don't know where you get such ridiculous ideas. What the hell goes on in your head?'

'You pushed Gil away because in your head you're still in love with my father,' Vivienne raged back. 'You always have been, but he doesn't want you, so you take it out on the rest of us, especially me, because I look like him, or sound like him . . .'

'You are nothing like him,' Gina screamed over her. 'And let me tell you this, you don't want to be . . .'

'So you do know who he is?'

'Of course I know who he is . . .'

'*Then tell me.*'

'*This conversation is ending right now. You can stay here tonight, and tomorrow I'll put you on the next train back to university where you'd do well to concentrate on your studies and give up this . . . nonsense you've created for yourself.*'

'*I came here to try and save your marriage, which is more than you seem to be doing.*'

'*My marriage is my business . . .*'

'*And my father is mine. I have a right to know who he is.*'

'*Just stop it, Vivienne. Stop right now.*'

'*Is he dead?*'

'*Oh for God's sake . . .*'

'*Does he know about me?*'

'*What difference does it make?*'

'*All the difference in the world to me.*'

'*But it means nothing to me.*'

'*How can you be so cruel? I don't understand . . .*'

'*It's you who's being cruel, always bringing this up, forcing me to relive a time I've tried so hard to forget, and doing it now, when Gil has just gone . . . Don't you think I'm feeling bad enough? Why did you have to come here and make me feel even worse?*'

They swung round as the door opened and Nana-Bella came in, pale and fiery-eyed. 'I can't let you carry on like this,' she said forcefully. 'You're tearing each other to pieces and nothing good is ever going to come of it.'

'*Then make her tell me the truth,*' *Vivienne implored.*

Gina's eyes flashed in her mother's direction. Turning to Vivienne she said, 'You've heard the phrase, be careful

*what you wish for, well it applies here, young lady. I
am trying to save you from yourself. Remember that
the next time you want to bring this up.'*

'What do you think she meant by that?' Vivienne asked,
as she and Gil got up to meander back to the house.

'I probably think the same as you,' he replied.

Wanting it put into words, she said, 'You mean that
he wasn't a particularly good person so she's trying to
save me from him?'

'It seems the most logical conclusion.'

Of course it was, but there were still other options.
'What if,' she said, 'she was afraid he'd try to take me
away from her? That could be a reason why she never
told him about me.'

He gazed up at the gulls swooping and screeching
about the cliffs as he pondered this. 'That might
account for how she was about him when you were
young,' he said, 'but not for why she still won't discuss
it now.'

Having already come up with the same answer for
that, she said, 'But if we don't get her to talk about it,
how on earth are we ever going to find him when
we have absolutely nothing to go on?'

Coming to a stop, he turned her to face him and put
his hands on her shoulders as he gazed tenderly into her
eyes. 'There can't be a "we" in that scenario, Vivi,' he
said softly. 'I'll be there when you try to talk to her, if
that's what you want, but if she still won't tell you
anything I'm afraid I can't help you to find him.'

Though she'd half expected the answer, Vivi still felt
crushed. 'You feel it would be disloyal,' she said.

'I'm sorry,' he murmured. 'As much as I love you, I love her too and I don't want to do anything that's going to hurt her. I think – I'm certain – that if she knew I was helping you to find your father it would hurt her very much.'

CHAPTER TEN
SHELLEY

Winter 1995

By the time *The Darling Buds of May* was turned into a hit TV series, Jack had been gone for almost two years. None of the family watched it; they were probably the only people in the country who didn't. They simply couldn't. It was too painful a reminder of the evenings he'd read the books aloud to them, and the way they'd teased one another about being just like the characters. Jack had looked nothing like David Jason who played Pop Larkin, though Shelley knew he'd have thoroughly approved of the casting, since Jason had been a favourite of his.

The series was over now, it had run for two years but there were still a thousand and one reminders of Jack all over the place and no one had stopped missing him, even for a minute.

Shelley knew she never would. Even now there were times when the loss was so deep, the grief so wrenching that she had to take herself into the woods to scream and rant as though the noise and the effort would somehow blot out the pain – and the disbelief, and the sickening, senseless tragedy of it all. Such a vital and beautiful man who did so much good in the world, who cared for everyone and brought so much joy into people's lives. It was so wrong, so futile and cruel. What kind of god or fate would do this to someone who was in his prime and who'd still had so much to give?

Shelley was a thinner, even duller version of the woman she'd been six years ago, a woman who spent too much time being afraid for her children, and who was far more cynical now than she'd ever been. However, her heart remained in the farm and her family, the engine that seemed to operate in spite of her, keeping everything going the way Jack would have wanted her to. His heart was still here too; hardly a day went by that she couldn't feel it beating alongside hers; often it was what got her through the day. Other times it was the children, *their* children, who reminded her that life, *they* still mattered. They'd meant everything to their father, and they continued in their different ways to try to make him proud.

'Dad would have really liked that,' Hanna might say for any number of reasons.

'I wish I could tell Dad about my violin lessons,' Zoe would lament. 'I think he'd be pleased.'

'I made the squirrel better all by myself,' Josh told her yesterday, dashing in through the kitchen door, pride and amazement all over his face. 'I can probably put it back in the woods next week.' He'd learned his healing skills from Jack, of course, and it just about broke Shelley's heart to see how brave her young boy was, and how determined to follow in his father's footsteps. He'd grown so tall already, and was so like Jack it caught at her heart in the most painful way, especially when he smiled. There wasn't another smile like it. She loved him so much, probably too much, but they all did. He had the same reckless air about him that Jack had always had, along with an interest in everything, a mischievous humour, and an energy that had a magnetic quality all of its own. Just about everyone seemed to respond to this – his friends, neighbours, teachers, and the many people who came to the farm. Most impressive of all was the way he seemed so effort-lessly to connect with the natural world. Animals never appeared to be as afraid of him as their protective instincts should have made them; Shelley could swear that some even spoke to him, for the way he understood them allowed no other explanation.

'They do,' he would assure her whenever she teased him about it, and he'd look so serious, and surprised she'd even doubt it, that she'd play along and ask what they said. He'd usually tell her that it was a secret between him and the sheep, or pony, or weasel, or whatever was receiving his attention that day. Then he'd break into a grin, not yet able to hold the tease the way his father had, and she'd have to hug him even though he didn't much like being hugged now he was ten.

This morning Shelley was in the kitchen, oblivious to the icy rain spattering the windows outside and to the delicious aroma of a stew rising from the Aga. It was a rare quiet moment that had turned into a reflective one as she'd found herself staring at the bronze figurine in its niche – the female dancer whose flapper elegance and fluid movement had been so exquisitely captured by her creator that she almost seemed to breathe. As always, her right hand was reaching for her partner's, ready to be whirled into the next steps, but her partner, the man with the rakish hat and baggy suit, was no longer there.

Shelley still wasn't sure precisely when she'd noticed the male dancer had gone. She only knew that it had been sometime after Jack's funeral; not the same day, but a few days, maybe a week later. It had baffled and even scared her when she'd first registered the empty space. It was as though the tragedy of Jack's death was being reflected in the separation of the inanimate objects. The man had gone; the woman was alone, unable to continue even the illusion of a dance. How, when exactly, had it disappeared? No one would have moved it, there was no reason to, and yet it wasn't there. She'd questioned everyone, her tone close to accusing, as if someone had deliberately hidden it from her, but no one had. She'd got them to search the house from top to bottom, turning every room and cupboard inside out, even emptying the bins, and ransacking the barns, pens, stables . . . It had felt as though she was looking for Jack, that if she could find the missing male bronze she'd somehow find him.

When it hadn't turned up she'd contacted the police to let them know that something was missing after all, but as she couldn't tell them for certain if it had disappeared the night Jack died, there really hadn't been anything they could do. There was no evidence of an intruder, added to which was the fact that the post-mortem had shown that his death had been caused by a fatal blow to the head resulting from a fall down the stairs. No foul play involved, and how could she argue with that when she'd been right there?

For a while, during the craziest period of her grief, she'd actually wondered if Jack had taken it with him and was waiting to hand it to her when she finally went to join him. She didn't think that now, of course, at least some sanity had prevailed in the past six years, but whenever she paused for a moment to look at the female, alone in the niche, she found the symbolism of it hard to bear.

'Oh, God, not again,' Hanna groaned as she came into the kitchen to find her mother gazing wistfully at the figurine. 'Isn't it about time you put something else there? We're never going to find the other one. I hope you realize that by now.'

Hurt, but not showing it, Shelley turned to look at her elder daughter, thin, scruffy, brittle and not yet sixteen. She had Shelley's light brown hair and pointy chin, Jack's cornflower-blue eyes and her own view of the world. Like most girls – and boys – of her age this view was constantly changing, but one that seemed to have stuck for Hanna lately was the one that had apparently turned her mother into an imbecile.

The saddest part of that, for Shelley, was how Hanna had started to scorn the farm in the same way. Ever since they'd come to Deerwood she had loved the animals, the land, the freedom, the very essence of life here. She'd learned so much from her father, even more than she or Shelley had realized until after he'd gone when, as a family, they'd pulled together to make things work. It was either that, or return to London.

Hanna had never been in any doubt about the way forward.

'The last thing Dad would want,' she'd insisted hotly

back then, sounding far older than her meagre nine years, 'is for us to give up on everything we've built here. I get that it's going to be a struggle, and that it won't be anywhere near as much fun without him, but I think we should at least try to make him proud.'

'I agree with that,' four-year-old Josh had piped up, putting his arms round Dodgy as if speaking for the dog too.

'And me,' Zoe told her mother, red-eyed from crying over the loss of her father.

Shelley would never forget that deputation of three small children who'd believed in themselves and the spirit of their father so intensely that they'd never seemed to entertain the idea that they couldn't keep things going. She'd felt so proud of them that day, and so moved by their determination, that even now the memory of it melted her heart.

'Where have you been all day?' she asked, as Hanna yanked open a cupboard and grabbed a packet of KitKats. 'Zoe and Grandpa waited for you this morning. You said you were going to help at the Farmers' Market.'

'So I had better things to do,' Hanna retorted rudely.

'Such as?'

Hanna scowled. 'What's it to you?'

Shelley tried not to sigh, knowing it would only fan the flames. 'I'd like to know where you keep disappearing off to,' she replied, not for the first time over these past few months. Recently Hanna had become almost unrecognizable from the heroic, hard-working land girl she'd been before teenage hormones had turned her into a budding monster.

'I'm getting what's called a life,' Hanna snorted, 'and

that definitely isn't to be found around here in this godforsaken place.'

Shelley took a breath and let it go slowly. She was aware that on some level Hanna's new and unpleasant attitude was some kind of delayed reaction to her father's death. She hadn't seemed to grieve much at the time, had simply thrown herself into hard work and study; however, to suggest such a thing to her would only result in more rudeness, or outbursts of scorn. So for the time being Shelley was doing her best to back away from confrontations, and told herself that Hanna was going to the gym, or a dance class, maybe even the library where she used to do a Saturday morning story-reading session for under-fives until she'd found other things to occupy her time. However, the next point had to be made, so bracing herself, she said, 'You should be revising. Your exams start next week . . .'

'Tell me something I don't already know,' Hanna cut in tartly. 'God, you're such a nag. Why don't you do us both a favour and just leave me alone?' and spinning on the heel of a tatty trainer she stomped up the stairs to her room, taking the KitKats with her.

Shelley looked around the kitchen and tried to focus on what she should be doing, instead of what she'd like to do, which was sit down and weep. The water troughs were frozen; more hay needed moving into the lambing shed, a dozen or more tree guards needed repair . . . A batch of new fruit trees had arrived yesterday, but the ground was too hard for planting, and it was too late in the day to start any more hedge-trimming or ditch-clearing now.

Hearing the boot-room door open, followed by the

sound of someone kicking off their wellies, she guessed it was her mother, and felt a stir of relief as Patty trudged into the kitchen, red-cheeked and wind-tousled, and carrying a large basket full of empty jars.

'Did I see Hanna just now?' Patty asked, hefting her heavy burden onto the table.

'You did. Are those for preserves, pickles or pesto?'

'Not the season for any of them,' Patty reminded her, dabbing a square of kitchen towel to her wet cheeks. She might be in her mid-sixties now with a slightly arthritic hip and high blood pressure, but she still looked ten years younger, and had the energy of a forty-year-old. Shelley had always loved her dearly, and couldn't remember a time when they'd ever gone through what she was enduring now with Hanna, or certainly not with so much bitterness attached. 'I've brought them over to be washed,' Patty explained. 'Our dishwasher's on the blink, and the plumber can't get here till Monday.'

Since Jack had gone the family had pulled together in a way that had made all the difference to them being able to stay at Deerwood. No matter how strong her children's resolve to keep things going, they'd been too young to take on everything themselves, and besides they were at school. However, unprompted, Nate had given up his job as a firefighter to come and work full-time on the farm, while Kat had opened a crèche in the nearby village to help bring in some extra funds. Meantime, Shelley's parents had sold their London home to come and live at Deerwood, staying in the farmhouse while one of the derelict barns was converted into three parts, a quaint, two-bedroomed cottage for them, a small animal sanctuary for Josh with a loft store above, and the rest of the space for rustic-holiday rentals.

'Plenty of people want to bring their children to farms for a holiday,' her father, George, had insisted when they'd been deciding what to do with the barn, and he'd been proved right, for even before the place was ready to let they'd advertised for the coming summer and received plenty of bookings. Now it provided another small but fairly steady income to add to David's thriving organic fruit and vegetable business, and her mother's popular hampers of everything from home-made jams, to goat and sheep cheeses, elderflower wine and succulent sponge cakes. She even made soaps and rose-scented room sprays these days.

Under George's steady guidance the family had learned how to capitalize on their assets, and though they'd never be rich, they were certainly making ends meet. Jack would have been thrilled to see how innovative they had become. He'd even, knowing him, have been fully supportive of the many other plans Shelley had in mind for Deerwood. However, they were for the future, and if his death had taught her anything, it was to appreciate what they had now before it suddenly wasn't there any more.

'I'm expecting a shipment of Spanish lemons from the wholesaler,' Patty chattered on, as Shelley helped her to load the dishwasher. 'No sign of them, I suppose.'

'Not yet,' Shelley confirmed. 'What are they for?'

'Cheesecakes, possets and tarts. David wants some for his stall next Saturday – they went down very well last week – and I've promised a selection for the WI event on Sunday. Have you seen your father since this morning?'

'He's helping Nate and Josh move the pregnant ewes inside ready for their vaccines. The last thing we need is some God-awful disease getting hold of them. Actually, that reminds me,' and turning to the wall calendar that Zoe and Josh had created as a Christmas gift for her last year, Shelley searched for her blue-coloured entries. It was the first calendar they'd made since Jack had gone – in fact, it had taken over a year for anyone to bring themselves to take down the one that still had all his chocolate-brown entries on it. Shifts at the vet's; renewals of memberships; dental visits, Shelley's birthday surprise . . . In the end, in a fit of rage with the world and more pain than she could bear, Shelley had torn it to pieces and burned it.

Hanna hadn't deigned to get involved with the new one; she hadn't even selected a colour for her crayon, or entered a single commitment to the daily squares.

'When am I supposed to be taking Dodgy to the vet for his shots?' Shelley murmured, searching for the entry. Finding it, she added a note to pick up more pellets for their substantial family of pigs while she was out, and she still needed to talk to Giles about how he wanted to use the top fields this coming year. Maize/graze was what they called their arrangement.

At the sound of more bumps and thumps in the boot room she started to smile, and a moment later Josh burst in through the door. 'Mum! Mum! Guess what!' he shouted excitedly. 'I've found another hedgehog and he wasn't hibernating. He should be, because it's bad for him not to at this time of year, but I've rescued him and put him with the others in the sanctuary. Hello, Grandma. Would you like to see my new hedgehog?'

'Lead me to him,' Patty insisted. 'Do you think he needs anything to eat?'

'It's OK,' Josh assured her, 'I have lots of mealworms, so I think he'll be all right. Mum, can I have a KitKat?'

'I'm afraid Hanna took them,' Shelley replied, 'but there's a slice of fruit cake left in the fridge. You can have it now, or after you've shown Grandma the hedgehog.'

Tearing open the fridge door, he bit into the cake, and was reprimanded for speaking with his mouth full as he tried to say, 'Can you ask Hanna to feed the pigs, because I promised Zoe I'd exercise Madonna before it gets dark.' Hanna had outgrown the pony three or more years ago and had generously turned her over to Zoe, who probably wouldn't be riding her for much longer either. Would they find the heart to sell her? Probably not, knowing them, though they'd had some interest from Bella Shager, the woman at the tourist office whom Jemmie had introduced Shelley and Kat to a few years ago. She'd been looking for a pony for her five-year-old granddaughter, Vicky? Vivienne? but it hadn't come to anything in the end. Shelley wasn't sure why, maybe they'd found one elsewhere.

'Grandma, can you drive me over to Giles's farm?' Josh asked, as they headed for the boot room to put their wellies back on. 'He said he's got some hibernation boxes for me.'

'Of course, sweetheart, I'll just pop into the cottage to get the car keys.'

As Josh explained more about his hedgehog rescue

project – as if they hadn't heard it a dozen times by now – Shelley checked the stew before going to put on her own coat and boots. She'd feed the pigs herself. It would make for an easier life, no arguments or tantrums from Hanna, just her and the snorting, grunting porcine rascals who adored human attention almost as much as they did food.

By the time she came back to the kitchen her mother and Josh had taken off for Giles's farm and she had received five calls on her mobile phone – three from Zoe and David, who were on their way back from town (three because neither of them quite had the hang of leaving messages yet so kept repeating them); one from the mother of Josh's friend, Ben Carter, asking if Ben could come over later; and the last from Giles wanting to know who was going to the livestock market with him on Monday, Shelley or Nate.

Deciding to try her hand at texting, she pressed a few keys on the phone, managed to bring up the right screen and spent five times as long composing a reply as she would have if she'd just made the call. Still, it was all practice, and everyone was texting these days, or so Hanna kept telling her, apart from Hanna, of course, because *she* wasn't allowed to have a mobile phone.

Almost as soon as Shelley had sent the message to Giles, he rang.

'Did you get my text?' she asked, amazed by how speedily it had got there.

'Yes, no. It's not about that.' His voice was dark and grave, and Shelley felt herself starting to stiffen.

'What is it?' she asked. Giles and Cathy had been

through a tough time these last few years, thanks to the Government's appalling mishandling of the BSE crisis. So far Giles's herd had remained unaffected.

'It's Cathy,' he said shakily. 'They think . . . They're saying she might have this CJD, you know, the human form of mad cow disease.'

Shelley sank into a chair. 'But how . . . ? What do . . . ?' Realizing questions were no good, she said, 'I'm on my way,' but before she could hang up he cried, 'No! Don't come. We've got no idea yet if it's contagious. That's why I'm calling, to make sure you all stay away. I'll call when I have more news.'

As the line went dead Shelley remembered that her mother and Josh were on their way to Giles's and she had no way of contacting them to make them turn back.

Dashing outside, she leapt into the tractor and roared off across the fields. If she went this way she might be able to head them off before they got anywhere near Giles's farm and this terrible disease that no one knew anything about, apart from the fact that it had started killing humans as well as cattle.

They learned a few days later that Cathy's virus wasn't connected to CJD after all – so many panicked reactions and diagnoses these days – but whatever it was did take a while to pass. However, the doughty old lady was back on her feet by the time the lambing season was upon them, and was as keen to come over to Deerwood to help as she was every year. Jemmie Bleasdale had begun helping out a lot too, and not just with the lambing, for ever since Jack's death she'd started dropping by regularly, or calling up to invite Shelley to local events, or simply to ask if there was anything she could do. Sometimes her concern, her eagerness to make sure the family was coping, felt almost overbearing, though Shelley would never say so. She was too fond of the woman ever to want to hurt her.

Far more entertaining – and something Jack would have loved – was the way Josh was becoming more like his father every day, not only in looks but in humour. He'd recently asserted that both male and female sheep enjoyed the mating process the way humans did, his dark blue eyes sparkling with mischief the way Jack's always had when trying to get a reaction.

'Well, not quite as much as that,' Josh qualified, astounding Shelley and his grandparents with this apparent knowledge of carnal pleasure. Then he flat-out floored them as he added, 'Actually I think some of them might be gay.'

The wickedness in his eyes as he said it was proof enough that he'd set out to shock; however, he remained adamant that it was true.

Though not yet eleven he was already in year 7 at school, putting him ahead of other kids his age, and the local vet where Jack had once been a part-timer assured the family that Josh was far from a nuisance when he was at the surgery. He was in fact more often an asset, Shelley was told, since he had a remarkable gift for calming animals in distress, and could even diagnose certain conditions that some qualified vets might have found hard to spot.

As time went on, and Josh became increasingly

involved with animals and Deerwood, it seemed his sisters were going in the other direction and distancing themselves, especially Hanna. Even Josh couldn't seem to coax her out of her constant ill humour, and as for Zoe, once she hit her teens her moods turned as irrational and unpredictable as Hanna's. Thankfully they were not as sour or stormy; she was more withdrawn, focused elsewhere, or too often glued to the TV. After trying to engage them Josh would throw up his hands to his mother, as though to say I've done my best, before taking off with his cousin, Perry, to go to school, or to get on with the farm work of the day.

Something else Josh began involving himself in as the year rolled on through summer was the increasingly stressful situation at Giles's farm. Though both Shelley and Giles discouraged him from going there, as Giles's herd were still being regularly inspected for BSE, Josh was determined to walk the cattle, as he called it, and assure them that no one was going to hurt them.

'I know they don't watch telly,' he shouted at Zoe when she pointed this out to him, 'but they can sense that something's happening, just like when they go for slaughter. They're much more intelligent than you realize and I don't want them to be scared.'

How much notice the cows took of his little talks, and how effective they really were, no one could ever say, but what they did know was that Giles's livestock wasn't among the many herds to be condemned.

'Mum, where's Hanna?'

Shelley barely looked up from the computer that lived at one end of the kitchen table as Zoe dutifully planted a kiss on her cheek – a requirement from them all when they left for school in the mornings, and when they came home again later.

'I haven't seen her yet,' Shelley answered, squinting at the screen where she was trying to place an order for hoof-care powder. Had it gone through yet, or was it still checking her credit card? Why was she hearing the dial tone again?

Chiding her mother for swearing, Zoe grabbed a snack from the fridge and wandered through to the sitting room.

Hearing the TV go on, Shelley shouted, 'There are animals to feed and pens to muck out. And Josh could probably use some help with his new hutches.'

Zoe ignored her.

Deciding she had to ring the supplier to make sure her order had gone through, Shelley used her mobile to make the connection. It would have been so much easier to do it this way in the first place. She couldn't see herself ever fully trusting Internet ordering.

After receiving a verbal confirmation that the hoof-care powder would be hers by this time next week, she went to the sitting room to check on Zoe. 'Did you hear me?' she said, and her heart sank to see how glum her fourteen-year-old was looking.

'Yeah, but I've got my period and I don't feel very well,' Zoe complained, her eyes not straying from the latest episode of *Grange Hill*.

Going to sit with her, Shelley slipped an arm round her shoulders and rested her head on hers. 'Do you have any pain?' she asked.

'Yeah, loads. It's horrible. I hate being a girl.'

'It's certainly not one of the best parts,' Shelley agreed. 'I'll get you something for it and you can stay here, nice and snug, once I've lit the fire.'

As she made to get up Zoe said, 'Mum?'

'Yes?'

Zoe fell silent.

Shelley turned to look at her. 'What it is?' she asked, realizing that something more than period pains was troubling her easier daughter.

Zoe shook her head. 'It doesn't matter.'

Certain it did, Shelley tilted up her chin and said, 'This is me you're talking to. You know you can say anything.'

Zoe's eyes went down, but Shelley held gently to her chin and in the end Zoe blurted it out, 'Is it true what they say about Dad?' she demanded.

Thrown, Shelley tried to think what she meant. 'What are they saying?' she asked, genuinely perplexed, since Zoe's tone was suggesting it wasn't good.

'They're saying he had affairs. Well, an affair, anyway.'

Stunned, reeling, Shelley tried to process this, but found she couldn't, not right now. Not ever. It made no sense at all; it simply hadn't happened. In the end she managed to ask, 'Who's saying that?'

'People at school.'

Shelley stared at her daughter and felt she was seeing someone else entirely: a young girl standing in the sunlight at the crematorium watching the funeral, seeming to look straight at her, or was that part of it just her imagination?

It had been with this girl in mind that Shelley, hating herself, had rung the vet in the days after Jack's funeral to enquire after the dogs her husband had treated the night of his fatal fall. To her relief she'd been told they were doing well and that Jack had done a wonderful job with them. 'If he hadn't been so tired by the time he left . . . It was so late and it had been a traumatic few hours . . .'

So he hadn't lied about where he was, and when she thought of the way he'd made love to her that night . . . He could never have done that if he'd been with another woman, not someone like Jack.

And the girl had looked so young, hardly more than a child. That wouldn't have been Jack's style at all; nothing about unfaithfulness was his style.

'Mum? You're scaring me,' Zoe protested.

Pulling herself together, Shelley said, 'It's nonsense, sweetheart. I don't know why people say these things. They just want to make mischief, I suppose. Ignore them. Daddy would never have done anything like that.'

Shelley returned to the kitchen having forgotten all about Zoe's painkillers and addiction to TV; she couldn't even focus on what she was supposed to be doing. She just kept staring at the female dancer in the niche and asking herself over and over what on earth had happened to the male.

She didn't hear Josh come in until he asked where he could find Hanna or Zoe.

'I've managed to put one of the hutches together,' he told her, 'but I need someone to hold the door while I . . .' He broke off as Nate came in and before his uncle could as much as speak, Josh had him by the hand and was marching him out to the barn to act as his assistant.

A few minutes later Shelley found Zoe asleep on the sofa, so she turned the TV down, lit the fire and went back into the kitchen. Five o'clock already, she noticed. Her mother would be over at any minute to start the evening meal; Shelley's next task was to take cups of tea out to the greenhouse for David and her father, who were busy watering their cannabis plants. The crop consisted of several sorts of veg really, but in a light-hearted moment recently Hanna had accused them of growing weed and it had stuck.

Where was Hanna? Shelley couldn't remember her saying she'd be late this evening, and since she still refused to jot her movements onto the calendar there was no point in checking there.

Kat arrived at the same time as Patty, immediately uncorked a bottle of wine and filled three glasses. 'What a day,' she sighed, slumping down in a chair as Patty filled a bowl with peanuts. 'Kids are so much easier than their parents. I had one woman turn up as I was leaving to accuse me of poisoning her son's mind by reading Roald Dahl to him. *Roald Dahl*, I ask you. Of course she's a complete nutter, but I didn't realize that straight away, because it's always the father who brings him . . .' She broke off, frowning as she realized Shelley wasn't listening. 'Shell? Are you all right?' she asked. 'I know I'm boring, but you seem miles away.'

Patty turned from what she was doing as Shelley said bluntly, 'Do you think Jack ever had affairs?'

Neither Patty nor Kat could have looked more shocked. 'No way!' Kat cried, almost choking on her drink.

'What nonsense,' Patty scoffed. 'Where on earth did that come from?'

'Zoe,' Shelley replied. 'Apparently someone's said something at school and . . .'

'For heaven's sake,' Patty interrupted, throwing out her hands. 'You can't take any notice of things kids say at school. They're probably accusing everyone's fathers, or mothers, of affairs. They're that age! Half of them don't even know what it means.'

Grasping the truth of that, Shelley felt it slip through her hands as she said, 'There was a girl at the crematorium, the day of the funeral. Nate saw her too. I pointed her out . . . She was way over the other side of the cemetery, but she seemed . . . I got the feeling . . . Has Nate ever mentioned it?' she asked Kat.

Kat was clearly mystified. 'Never. What makes you think she was there because of Jack?'

Shelley shook her head and shrugged helplessly. She wasn't even sure she did think that, yet the girl kept coming back to her mind.

Patty said, 'She was probably just a passer-by, stopping to have a look in case we were people she knew.'

'Jack loved you with all his heart,' Kat reminded her. 'There was never anyone else for him, the same way there's never been anyone else for you – although I'm not sure that should continue, but that's a subject for another time.'

Coming to cup her hands around Shelley's face, Patty said, 'Listen to me, my girl, grief can do strange things to your mind, even this long after the event, but I'm telling you, here and now, that Jack *never* had an affair with anyone.'

Despite appreciating the reassurance Shelley found her

eyes going back to the female dancer as if there were an answer there, if only the bronze could speak.

By the time they were ready to eat Josh had taken off with his grandfather David and a pack of sandwiches to keep him going through his 'evening shift' at the vet's, and Shelley had finally managed to shake off her unease over Jack. She'd never found a single thing in his papers, or pockets, or even in his business books to indicate that he'd ever been anything but true to his family. He'd been a decent, honest man with no sides to him, no guile, and certainly no lack of integrity. It simply hadn't been in him to deceive or cheat or do anything he knew would hurt those he loved. She'd never doubted him when he was alive – apart from once, which hadn't been a doubt at all, just a moment of ludicrous girlish insecurity – and she wasn't going to start doubting him now.

As her mind cleared she suddenly realized that there was still no sign of Hanna, nor had she rung. She instantly felt a different kind of knot tightening her insides. 'Did Hanna come home on the bus with you earlier?' she asked Zoe, who was bringing dishes of veg to the table.

'Nope,' Zoe replied, still looking pale and fed up with the clawing pains that were getting worse for her as the months went by.

'Did you see her at school?' Shelley persisted.

'I never do. She's in a completely different building to me.'

'Did she get the bus in with you this morning?' Patty asked, clearly picking up on Shelley's concern.

Zoe nodded, and groaned as she clutched theatrically at her stomach.

'OK, Zoe, we all know what you're going through,' Shelley snapped, failing to cover how worried she was becoming. 'Eat up, everyone. I'll go and call some of Hanna's friends. She'll be with one of them somewhere . . .' She broke off as someone knocked on the door. It was such a rare sound, since everyone they knew usually walked right in, that Shelley's throat turned dry as her heartbeat slowed.

'Come in,' Nate called out.

The door didn't open, but whoever it was knocked again.

Nate got up to answer.

'I'm sorry to bother you,' a tall, short-haired woman in her fifties said in a foreign accent, 'but my husband and I, we are walking on the footpath and we see a lamb standing in the stream. We cannot get to it, but I thought I should let you know.'

'Thanks,' Nate responded. 'I'll come and see to it,' and leaving Kat to put his meal in the oven to keep warm, he followed the woman into the murky darkness.

Able to breathe now she knew the police hadn't come calling with terrible news, Shelley turned to her father as he said, 'Have you looked in her room?'

Slapping a hand to her head Shelley raced upstairs, certain now that Hanna had crept in without them noticing – it would have been just like her.

Finding the room empty, she wanted to scream.

'Zoe,' she cried, running back down to the kitchen. 'Who's Hanna been hanging around with lately? Do you know their names?'

Starting to look frightened, Zoe said, 'She never tells me anything.'

Shelley grabbed the phone and began calling everyone they knew. Her parents and father-in-law did the same, while Kat and Zoe carried out a further search of the house and barns.

Fifteen minutes later Shelley was staring at her father, eyes wild with fear, not knowing what to do next. 'I should have let her have a mobile phone,' she said shakily.

'She's always going on about one,' Zoe reminded them.

'Do I call the police?' Shelley asked, feeling sick. 'Is that overreacting?' *Please say yes. Please tell me there's no need to be this afraid.*

'I'll do it,' George said gently, and picking up the landline he connected to the local station.

He was asked so many questions that in the end he had to hand the phone to Shelley. She did her best, struggling to make herself think straight, to say, 'No, she's never run away from home before.' 'No, there haven't been any arguments in the last few days, or none that stood out from the usual bickering.' 'Yes, I've contacted all her friends.' 'Yes, there could be others I don't know about.' 'No, she doesn't have a mobile phone.' 'No, she doesn't take drugs.' *Drugs?* She turned to Zoe.

Zoe threw out her hands as if to say, 'Don't ask me.'

'No, I don't think she's pregnant. She doesn't have a boyfriend.' Her eyes were still on Zoe, begging for answers, but Zoe clearly didn't know any more than she did.

Still more questions.

'No, I haven't checked to see if she's taken anything with her,' Shelley said.

At that her mother and Kat ran upstairs to find out.

They came back shaking their heads. 'Everything seems to be there,' her mother told her.

'Nothing appears to have gone,' Shelley told the officer at the end of the line. *Oh God, she's been taken. Someone's got her. They're holding her somewhere, doing things to her . . .*

'I've got all the details,' the officer was saying, 'but I'm afraid at this stage, given her age and how long it's been . . .'

'You have to find her!' Shelley cried furiously. 'I just told you, she's not someone who runs away. She's never done this before. I'm worried out of my mind . . .'

'I understand, but you've already told me that her friends confirmed she was at school today, so she hasn't been gone for more than twenty-four hours . . .'

'So what are you going to do? Just let her stay out all night? For God's sake. She's only fifteen . . . She's not mature like some girls her age. She's . . . She's . . . Her father died,' she choked desperately.

There was a pause. 'How long ago?' she was asked.

'Six years, but I think . . .'

'Mrs Raynor.' The man's voice was still kind, but firmer now. 'I'm sorry this is happening, I really am. Teenagers are notoriously difficult, and they're giving their families scares all the time, it's like a national sport for some . . .'

'*She's not like that.*' She could hear all parents in her shoes saying the same, and how did she know what Hanna was really like when they hadn't communicated properly in months?

The officer said, 'I'll log your call and ask the beat

guys to keep an eye out for her. If you haven't heard from her by tomorrow morning then please call us again.'

Two days later a full-scale police search was under way. Hanna's pale, serious face was all over the TV and newspapers, the house and farm were turned upside down, all her schoolfriends received visits, the local villages were subjected to door-to-door enquiries and just about everyone they knew was questioned.

Someone said they'd seen her on the notorious Temple Fields Estate, home to gangs and dropouts, but a search of the area and scrutiny of local CCTV proved fruitless.

Someone else claimed to have spotted her boarding a train at the station, but again surveillance cameras showed no sign of her.

Shelley was beside herself, unable to eat, sleep or think of anything else. *Why isn't Jack here? He'd know what to do, where to find her.*

She'd never have left if he were here.

She blamed herself in ways that didn't even make sense. She appeared on TV pleading with Hanna to come home; she joined in an inch-by-inch search of local fields; she went to church and prayed.

Zoe and Josh took to coming into her bed at night, as terrified as she was that something unspeakable had happened to their sister. They had nightmares that Shelley did her best to cope with, but it was mostly left to David and her parents to calm them down.

Two weeks and three days after Hanna had disappeared, the police rang Shelley during the early hours of a Thursday morning. So much terror flooded through her when she realized who was at the end of the line that she couldn't speak or breathe. She was screaming inside, telling them to go away, that whoever the body belonged to it wasn't Hanna's. It couldn't be. She wouldn't let it . . .

'. . . so I'll put her on,' she finally heard the officer saying.

Stunned, and shaking badly, Shelley held her breath as she waited.

'Mum?' Hanna's voice was quiet and hoarse, and Shelley choked on so much relief that her words collided into each other. 'Oh my God, are you all right?' she spluttered. 'I've been so worried. Are you hurt?'

'I'm fine.'

'I'll come and get you . . .'

'It's OK, the police are going to bring me home.'

Shelley started to sob – and sob and sob. *Hanna was coming home. The police were bringing her home.*

'MUM! DAD!' she yelled, dashing outside into the farmyard. Dodgy came shooting out of the barn, barking frenziedly, as the lights went on in her parents' cottage. She grabbed the dog's muzzle and kissed him hard. 'She's coming home,' she cried, almost falling over him. 'Oh my God! Oh my God. She's coming home,' and sinking to her knees in the mud she gave thanks to the Almighty, the Universe, and even Jack, for she couldn't help thinking that on some level he'd kept their girl safe and was now steering her back to where she belonged.

Less than an hour later, cleaned up and slightly calmed down, Shelley ran back into the farmyard as a police car drove in. She'd told just about everyone she knew by now that Hanna was on her way home, she'd even called Jemmie and Humphrey Bleasdale, who'd been in touch every day since Hanna's disappearance, and who'd brought food and joined in the public search of the surrounding countryside.

Though she understood how eager the rest of the family was to see Hanna, they'd all agreed that Shelley should be the only one to welcome her at first. There was no knowing at this stage what frame of mind her daughter might be in, what sort of trauma she'd been through, or even where she'd been all this time, so they needed to tread carefully. Nevertheless, Shelley couldn't hold back as Hanna got out of the car. She ran to her, and wrapped her in the tightest, most loving embrace she'd ever given in her life.

Hanna didn't hug her back, nor did she try to break free. 'Hello, Mum,' she croaked.

'Thank God you're home,' Shelley murmured, over and over. 'I've been so worried. Oh, Hanna. My baby.' She drew back to look at her, needing to be sure she wasn't dreaming. 'Are you all right? You're not hurt?'

Hanna shook her head, but she didn't look at her mother, nor did she seem all right. Her hair was matted and filthy, her eyes were red and shadowed, and her clothes stank worse than the pigpens.

'Come inside,' Shelley urged. 'Let's get you a hot drink and put you in the bath.'

Hanna didn't protest. She simply allowed her mother to take over while her grandparents thanked the female officer who'd brought her home, and went to boil the kettle.

Shelley led her up the stairs, and as though Hanna were still a small child she gently peeled away the foul clothes and hugged her thin, shivering body again.

It wasn't until she was in the bath, thawing out and seeming to gain some colour, that Hanna finally said, 'I'm sorry for what I've put you through, Mum. I didn't mean to . . .'

'We can talk about it when you're feeling stronger,' Shelley told her, somehow managing to hold back all the questions as her eyes searched her daughter's body for any sign of abuse. There was none, apart from a small bruise on her shin and a few faint scratches on her fingers.

Hanna said, 'There's a lot to talk about.' Her eyes finally met Shelley's, bloodshot and haunted with tiredness, but there was a glow in their depths that reminded Shelley of Jack. 'I've had this idea,' she explained. 'It's completely brilliant and I think, no I *know*, that Dad would love it, and I reckon you will too. You just have to keep an open mind, OK?'

CHAPTER ELEVEN
VIVIENNE

Present Day

Vivienne twisted the cap of a small transparent tube back into place and watched a trickle of blue liquid merge with the saliva she'd just deposited inside. When it was done she looked at Michelle and their eyes sparkled, the way they had when they were small and up to no good.

'I'll send it off first thing,' Michelle promised, taking the tube and dropping it into a package already addressed to a laboratory in Ireland. 'This is so cool. I can't wait to find out the results.'

Vivi's nerves fluttered. Having decided to spare Gil – and herself – the ordeal of confronting her mother over her father, at least for the time being, she was now torn between the fascination of having her ancestry traced using her DNA, and the trepidation of what it might bring – if it brought anything at all. The website had asked for as much information on her family as she could provide, which wasn't difficult on her mother's side. On her father's . . .

'Six weeks is a long time to wait,' she sighed. Time had a different meaning to her now. She wanted everything to happen right away, before it was too late, but had to accept she had no control. Reaching for her glass of iced tea, she said, 'I just can't see how they're going to find anything when I've given them next to nothing to go on.'

They were relaxing on the spacious deck of Michelle's house on Westleigh Heights, where cosy wicker chairs and sofas were small islands between all the toys, magazines, kiddie shoes, compost sacks and huge urns of vibrant flowers.

'The thing is,' Michelle responded, tilting her face to the sun, 'we don't know the science of it, so we've got no idea how they go about it. So, we need to have faith – and in the meantime have you ransacked your mother's bedroom yet to see if there are any old letters or photos hanging around, or something that might give us some sort of clue to work with?'

Vivienne had to smile. The idea of them as detectives kept reminding her of when they were young adventure-seekers trying to identify the source of treasures found on the beach, or attempting to discover a new secret pathway that might link their houses. This was before Vivi had also lived on the Heights. When she'd moved here with her mother and Gil they'd simply had to make a hundred and fourteen skips to reach each other's front gates. 'I did the ransacking years ago,' she reminded Michelle, 'but OK, I have looked again, and what I *can* tell you is that she still has the bronze sculpture all wrapped up in the bottom of a drawer. Do you remember how I used to think it was him?'

Michelle laughed. 'I do, and it was a kind of romantic notion, thinking of him as a gangster-dancer, or I thought so at the time. I wonder why she keeps it hidden away. From what I recall it's quite lovely. You'd think she'd want to display it somewhere, if only in her bedroom. Why don't you ask if you can have it in your room?'

Vivi arched an eyebrow. 'Because I'd have to admit I'd been snooping through her things,' she pointed out, 'and because I haven't forgotten how she laid into me the last time I mentioned it.' She sighed and drank more tea. 'There's definitely some sort of mystery surrounding it,' she murmured, 'but the chances of her telling me what it is are about as good as her telling me who my father actually is.'

Michelle looked thoughtful. 'Which is why we keep connecting the two,' she declared. 'The sculpture and your father.'

It was true, Vivienne did feel there was a connection, though she could offer no good reason why. 'Maybe she stole it,' she ventured.

Michelle pondered this before shaking her head. 'I reckon it was a gift to her from him, but that's about as far as I can get with it, because it doesn't answer why she won't display it or tell you where it came from. She's got more secrets than MI5, your mother, which actually makes her quite interesting in a wholly maddening sort of way.'

'Tell me about it,' Vivi muttered.

Glancing at her watch, Michelle stretched and got to her feet. 'It's time Ash was awake or he won't sleep tonight,' she said. 'I'll be right back.'

Resisting a check of her emails since there were rarely any these days, Vivi strolled over to the balustrade and rested her hands on the warm stone as she gazed out at the view. From here it was spectacular, especially on such a clear summer's day. The sky over the bay was a perfect cerulean blue, with only a wisp of white cloud floating across the far horizon, and the mesmerizing rise and fall of the birds as they soared through the air and dived into the glittering mass of waves. She envied their freedom with a longing that seemed to burn; she even wondered how possible it would be for her to fly from the cliffs and look down on the coast in one of the hang-gliders that had just come into view.

She guessed not possible at all.

She inhaled deeply, felt nothing unusual in the region of her heart, no tightness in her lungs or stirrings of dizziness, and let the breath go. Bizarrely, in spite of two more shocks over the past couple of weeks, she'd been feeling less fatigued, even slightly more positive and engaged, so it seemed the recent change in her medication was working on one level, while the ICD reliably performed on another. She'd get used to the thumps, she'd read on the forums, comments written by those who also had the device. The shocks became less frightening over time, and if she was lucky she might go weeks, even months without experiencing one at all.

She wondered if she actually had that much time, or if a dreaded VAD was even now moving up the calendar towards her, with the end close behind. As though breaking away from the ominous, unseen advance she followed the course of a waterskier winding and speeding across the bay, and remembered the first time she'd been able to do that, taught by Gil. Her mother had been driving the boat, cheering her on, while Mark, also cheering, had impatiently waited his turn.

Something else she wouldn't be doing again.

There were so many things, but what was the point of working herself into a state of useless frustration? It wouldn't change anything; no amount of wishing she could be with Mark in Italy now, or skydiving from a plane in a surge of madness, or living it up in Monte Carlo with the GaLs was going to make it happen.

Earlier, she and Michelle had FaceTimed with Trudy and Shaz. It had been fun; they'd laughed a lot while catching up on each other's news, though Vivienne hadn't had much to report. They'd wanted to know how she was, of course, and she knew they genuinely cared, but she'd simply said 'fine', and tried to move on. No one wanted to talk about her condition, least of all her.

Trudy, however, had asked if her ICD had gone off at all, and Michelle had told her that it had. 'But she's right as rain again within minutes,' she'd added proudly. This was true, that was how it happened, a brutal kick in the chest out of nowhere, a small gasp or groan from her and maybe some nausea or faintness, but not much, and it was over. It shook her up mentally more than physically, but Trey the physiologist was still insisting that there was nothing for her to worry about at this stage. If that changed she'd be returned to hospital for more extensive checks. She couldn't help but panic every time she thought about slipping away. But thankfully she didn't have to torment herself with what that could lead to because Michelle had just returned.

'Here she is,' Michelle sang out to Ash as she carried him onto the deck.

Vivi turned and felt a rush of tenderness as thirteen-month-old Ash broke into a toothy grin and excitedly reached for her.

Once she was seated Michelle handed him over and Vivi buried her face into the heavenly baby smell of him, loving how sturdy and satisfying he felt in her arms and the way he seemed so thrilled to see her. He grabbed her cheeks and her hair, stuffed her fingers into his mouth to give them a good bite and let out a yell of pure joy for no apparent reason at all. Having been a baby who'd screamed for the first seven months of his life, he was now the happiest child, who loved to eat, play, laugh and be fussed, probably in that order, and hardly cried at all.

As Michelle relaxed back in her own chair a piercing little voice suddenly screamed out, 'Mummy! We're home. Where are you?'

'Out here,' Michelle called back. 'There goes peace and quiet,' she murmured to Vivi, and turned to watch as five-year-old Millie in red tutu and ballet pumps came clumsily pirouetting through the kitchen onto the deck.

'Auntie Vivi,' she cried ecstatically. 'I didn't know you were here. Did you see me?'

'I did,' Vivi confirmed, leaning towards her little goddaughter to receive a bruising hug and kiss. 'You were brilliant.'

'My teacher says I might be in the show we do for Christmas. Will you come and watch me?'

'Of course,' Vivienne promised, fleetingly seeing the empty chair where she should be sitting.

'Do I get one of those?' Michelle prompted, tapping a finger to her cheek.

Millie gave a little leap as she laughed. 'Sorry, Mummy, I forgot you,' and running to Michelle she delivered a dutiful adoring hug and nose-bumping kiss.

'Where's Daddy?' Michelle asked. 'Didn't he bring you home?'

'Yes, he went into his office. Can I have a drink, please? And one of the cakes I made with Auntie Vivi?'

'That was over a week ago,' Michelle reminded her, 'and you've eaten them all.'

'But there are some Kinder eggs as a special treat,' Vivi told her. 'Two for you and one for Ash.'

'Because he's too little for two,' Millie said with wise understanding, apparently not guessing that her brother had already eaten one. Then grabbing the baby by the cheeks she blew a raspberry on his lips and giggled as he let out a shriek of delight.

Minutes later Millie was back with a beaker of cold milk and a chocolate egg, which she placed carefully on the table. 'Shall I show you some more of my ballet?' she suggested.

'Yes, please,' Vivi encouraged, enjoying the feel of Ash's head on her shoulder as she stroked his curly blond hair.

'Clear away some of the toys,' Michelle cautioned, 'or you'll have an accident.'

Millie turned to Vivi. 'I don't want to have an accident,' she told her gravely.

'No, you certainly don't.'

Millie's cute little face lit up with a smile. 'I'm on holiday for all of the summer,' she declared, 'and Mummy said you're going to be here too.'

'That's right. So we'll be able to bake lots of cakes and do drawings and go to the beach . . .'

'Shall I get my doctor's set and listen to your heart?' Millie offered, suddenly remembering why Vivi was often there.

'That would be lovely, thank you, but let me see some more of your ballet first.'

Needing no further bidding, Millie hurriedly kicked Ash's toys out of the way and struck an opening pose. 'This is called first position,' she explained, her heels tightly together and toes turned slightly out. 'See my arms are like this, because it's got to be like I'm holding a big beach ball.' She shuffled her feet so that her right heel was against the arch of her left foot and arced one arm over her head while reaching out to the side with the other. 'This is second position,' she announced proudly, then screwed up her face in confusion. 'Um, I think it might be third. Yes, it's definitely third, so we don't need to worry about second.'

Vivi was trying hard not to laugh, while Michelle lost the struggle.

'Don't be rude, Mummy,' Millie chided. 'Daddy, Mummy's laughing at me,' she told him as he came out onto the deck.

'She's a terrible mummy,' he declared sympathetically. 'What shall we do with her? Hello, son,' he laughed as Ash started bouncing around in glee, and sweeping him up in his arms he planted a giant smackeroo on his forehead.

Millie was bursting with a good idea. 'I think we should send her to bed without any supper,' she told him. 'And we'll send the wicked witch to get her if she tries to escape.'

'Let's do it!' he agreed.

Millie squealed with laughter and threw her arms around his legs. 'I'm only joking, Mummy,' she assured Michelle, 'but you shouldn't laugh at me.'

Setting Ash down, Sam embraced Vivi, saying, 'I forgot you were going to be here. You're looking good. Better than good.'

Smiling, Vivi said, 'Mark FaceTimed us earlier from Pompeii. He said to tell you there's quite a lot of rebuilding work needs doing if you're interested.'

Laughing, he said, 'I take it he's having a fantastic time.'

'Oh, I think we can be sure of that, although I'm getting the impression he's a lot more interested in Italian girls than he is in exploring historical sites.'

'And so he should be at his age.' He checked his watch. 'Sorry, I have to pop over to Deerwood for an hour, but you're staying for dinner?'

'That's the plan,' Michelle told him. 'I thought we'd barbecue.'

'OK, I'll do the honours. We'll probably be one extra, by the way, making us six including the kids, unless your parents are coming, in which case we'll be eight.'

After he'd gone Vivi said, 'Deerwood?'

'He does a lot of work out there,' Michelle explained, scooping up Ash. 'The owner's son is an old friend of his going back to schooldays. I expect that's who our extra guest will be.'

CHAPTER TWELVE
SHELLEY

Spring 2004

'So when did you first come up with the idea of using Deerwood Farm this way?' the young reporter was asking Shelley, pencil poised over his notebook with a small tape recorder spinning away on the kitchen table between them for backup.

His name was Martin Coolidge and he was, Shelley gauged, around Hanna's age, twenty-two or twenty-three, and he had the engaging, though comical look of Clark Kent about him. All slicked-down hair, dark-rimmed glasses and intelligent blue eyes. She could tell he was trying to make himself seem older and more experienced than he probably was; however, he must be good if he'd managed to get a job with a national newspaper. *He'd be really bloody good if he went to the loo and came back with his pants over his trousers and suddenly took off over the fields on a rescue mission.*

Since she was getting used to doing these interviews now, mostly with local media, though not exclusively, she could answer his question straight away. 'It was my daughter's idea originally,' she explained, admiring the pastel-coloured tulips he'd so thoughtfully brought with him and she'd already placed in a vase. If he'd done his research before coming here he'd already know about Hanna, but he wouldn't be doing his job if he didn't get the full story from as many sources as possible.

'You have two daughters, is that correct?' he asked.

Shelley nodded towards the family portrait that sat proudly over the sideboard, where much chaos and clutter still reigned and the female bronze dancer continued to wait in her niche for her partner to come home. Though Shelley had long ago accepted that wasn't going to happen, there was still a part of her that hoped they'd be reunited one day – this was the part, she realized, that wanted to believe that she'd be with Jack again when her time came. Hanna and Zoe had commissioned the large portrait a couple of Christmases ago, giving the artist a family photograph to work from. It showed them as young girls of nine and seven, with Josh aged four, all clustered around their parents, Jack at the heart of the group looking so lifelike and *there* that Shelley often felt his eyes following her about the kitchen; sometimes she even sensed him speaking to her in a voice no one else could hear. 'The children are much older now, of course,' she said, wondering where the years had gone, with the girls now in their twenties and Josh not far off joining them. It was Hanna who conceived this project of ours – I'm sorry she's not here for you to interview right now, but she should be back any minute.'

'That would be great,' he confirmed. 'The photographer's due about midday. Do you think she'll be around by then?'

'I'm sure she will. In the meantime, I'm here to do my best for you.'

He smiled in a way that made her feel quite maternal – and willing to be rescued, should he turn out to be an actual superhero. 'Hanna's put a lot of work into getting us to where we are now,' she told him, 'and we've done our best to support her all the way.'

'So what actually gave her the idea?' he prompted.

Shelley sipped her coffee and savoured the moment, for she always enjoyed this part of the story. 'I'm sure she'll tell it better than I can,' she said, 'but here's my version. She was still only fifteen when she decided to give us the fright of our lives by running away from home. She certainly succeeded in that. It was a terrifying time for us all, not knowing where she was, if any harm had come to her, if we'd ever see her again . . . Luckily she came back. The police found her living in a caravan – a squat really – over at Perryman's Cove with a bunch of homeless kids. They were mostly a year or two older than her, but they'd been subjected to some very different life experiences to any that she'd had. By comparison she'd had quite a sheltered upbringing, although it hadn't all been easy. Her father's death when she was eight hit us all very hard. It's not easy to get over a sudden loss like that, and my husband was a wonderful father.' As her voice trailed off for a moment she was thinking of the gossip Zoe had brought home from school all those years ago about him being unfaithful, but she'd never heard anything like it since. She'd probably have made herself forget all about it if the image of the girl at the crematorium didn't still haunt her from time to time. Who was she? Had she even been there because of Jack? It shouldn't have mattered after so long, but sometimes it did.

'Anyway,' she continued, bringing herself back to the present, 'before she took off Hanna had already started staying out for long periods of time and never telling anyone where she was or who she was with . . . It turned out she'd been connecting with kids on the street who were so obviously worse off than she was that she started to feel guilty about her own existence, and resentful in a way she couldn't understand. She was too young, and still too traumatized by her father's death to know how to process things properly. She felt as though she needed to live with these kids, to lose her own pain in theirs and get a proper understanding of what things were really like for them. So she moved into this caravan, watched them drink themselves senseless, take drugs, sell themselves on the street, fail to connect with any sense of self-preservation or dignity . . . Most had lost all contact with their families if they even had one, and many didn't. They'd spent a good deal of their lives in care of one sort or another, residential, fostering, difficult adoptions, and by the time Hanna got to know them they were on their own. Of course social services are supposed to provide some sort of transition process when a child leaves care, a support network, counsellors, help with jobs and finding homes, but what is supposed to happen and what actually does are two different things.'

He wasn't writing now, only listening, intently, as his tape recorder absorbed her words along with the distant sound of clacking and tinny bells that had just started up.

'Hanna was deeply affected by what she witnessed while she was in that caravan,' Shelley continued. 'She told me afterwards that she felt really close to her dad while she was there, as if he was guiding her, keeping her safe and showing her what to do. It was very moving to hear her say that, and to realize how deeply she believed it, because she was right, Jack would have wanted her to help those less fortunate than herself. He'd be so proud of her if he were here now.'

She paused, half expecting Martin to glance at the portrait, or to fire more questions at her, but it seemed he wanted to hear the story in her words, however they came.

'It's quite amazing really,' she said, 'or I think it is, that such a young girl with so little real knowledge of the world could feel such empathy and compassion for those who'd never known what it was to be loved and cared for. She was in no doubt about what she wanted to do when she came back. It took her no time at all to tell me. I put her in the bath and it all just came tumbling out. "We have to do something to help these kids, Mum," she informed me, as if I'd already objected and she was getting ready to fight. "We can't just let them drift into the gutter or prison as if they mean nothing to anyone. They're human beings, for God's sake, and no one's looking out for them."

'Of course I agreed with her that it was appalling, and yes we did have a duty as a society, and as individuals, to do what we could to help. "I think we have to use Deerwood," she told me. "I think we should turn it into a place for them to come when they leave care at sixteen to prepare them for the wider world."' Shelley smiled at the memory of Hanna's skinny body in the bath, pale, thin and seeming so small to be bottling up so much worthy ambition. Yet the fervour in her big blue eyes, the steel and determination that had emanated from her, had made her seem so like Jack that Shelley had taken her seriously from the start.

'It was true,' she told Martin, 'that in my heart of hearts I thought the scheme was crazy, a kind of impulsive, romantic reaction to the tragedies she'd seen. On the other hand I never did anything to try and dampen or criticize her aims. At best she might actually make it work, at worst she would learn some extremely valuable life lessons in trying. What I hadn't expected was how quickly the rest of us would get on board. We were fascinated by her efforts, energized by her, and we all wanted it to work as much as she did. So we helped her to take on the system, invested in various building works here at the farm, raised funds in any way we could and guilt-tripped the authorities into matching it. It was amazing the way the project seemed to take on a life of its own, and it was happening so fast. By the time Hanna finished sixth-form college and announced she was done with education, we weren't far off being ready to take in our first residents.'

She looked up as the door opened and Jemmie Bleasdale came in, laughing and shaking her head in mock despair. She was at Deerwood so often now that she almost felt like family; even Sir Humphrey had managed to morph into a milder, slightly more human form of his irascible self during the years since the tragedy of Jack's accident. Shelley only wished she could say the same for their sons. Though she saw almost nothing of them now that all three lived in London, she was aware of the problems they often brought to their parents' door, even if she didn't always know the details.

'Those lads out there are too hilarious,' Jemmie informed Shelley, picking up the string bag full of fresh produce she'd left on the table. 'You should see them, camping it up like . . . Oh, sorry, I'm interrupting. I just came back to collect this.'

'No problem,' Shelley assured her. 'This is Martin Coolidge, who's come to write about us. Martin, this is Lady Bleasdale, also known as Jemmie.'

With an engaging smile Jemmie shook Martin's hand. 'I'm very pleased to meet you,' she told him, 'and now I'll disappear. Will I see you later, Shelley?'

Remembering her promise to go and help with a seating plan for Matthew Bleasdale's upcoming wedding, Shelley assured her she'd be there and would have returned her attention to Martin as Jemmie left, were it not for the merry shimmy of jingles and a ludicrous kick-up of youthful limbs that came through the door.

'We are totally amazing,' Josh informed her, still making his morris-dancer costume ring like a shop doorbell in a state of excitement. 'We are going to put everyone to shame at that show, you wait and see. You should come,' he told Martin. Then apparently realizing he had no idea who the young man was, he held out a hand to shake. 'Josh Raynor, good to meet you.'

Half rising as he took the hand, the reporter said, 'Martin Coolidge. Good to meet you too. You're Hanna's brother?'

'One of my claims to fame,' Josh replied drily. He

was already six feet tall, and though not as filled out yet as his father had been, he was so like Jack in looks and temperament – even the sound of him – that Shelley often damned the fate that hadn't allowed Jack to see his son grow up.

'If you're wondering about this weird get-up,' Josh was saying to Martin, 'then I should explain that I, along with my mate Sam and cousin, Perry, lost a bet. Well, looking at me, that's probably a given. So we're having to take part in the morris dancing competition at the county fair. We've just had our first lesson, and I've got to tell you, we're demons.'

Laughing, Shelley said, 'Martin's here to write about Deerwood for one of the national papers. Is it the *Guardian*?' she asked him.

'The Saturday magazine section,' he clarified.

'Awesome,' Josh responded, checking his mobile as a text came through.

'I should probably tell you,' Shelley said to Martin, 'in case it's of interest for your article, that Sam, the friend Josh just mentioned, is the son of the builder who's done most of the work on the place. The boys act as labourers to earn some money when they're back from uni for the summer and it was Henry, Sam's dad, who won the bet that's ended them up as morris dancers.'

'So what was the bet?' Martin asked, turning back to Josh.

Grinning, Josh said, 'We reckoned we could construct a four-by-eight-metre drystone wall in a day, which we did, but then it fell down. Anyway, good luck with the article. Let me know if you want to see any of my projects. It's not all about Hanna, you know.'

As the door closed behind him, Shelley was smiling and rolling her eyes in exasperation. 'I'm dreading what's going to happen when he finishes uni,' she confided to Martin, 'it feels empty enough around here already when he's away.' What she didn't add was how afraid she was that it might feel like losing Jack all over again – or that Josh would go out into the world and decide not to come back. *Of course he wouldn't come back, he was a young man with his whole life ahead of him, and she wanted him to live it, just please God don't let it turn out to be the other side of the world.* 'So where were we?' she asked, checking the time and deciding she could spare Martin several more minutes yet.

'We'd got to the point,' he replied, 'where you were more or less ready to take your first residents.'

Shelley nodded and inhaled deeply. 'I'll spare you what we had to go through with the authorities to get that far. Suffice it to say you'd have thought they'd be pleased to have someone willing to help transition these youngsters into a wider society and hopefully better life, but they definitely weren't going out of their way to make it happen. However, in the end it wasn't them who closed us down before we even got started, it was the wretched foot-and-mouth disease.'

Martin blinked, as though the news was a shock, but of course it wasn't: the entire nation had known about it, and many, not only farmers, were still traumatized by the sheer horror and tragedy of it.

'Obviously no one was allowed to come here while that was going on,' she continued. 'We had a D notice slapped on us, meaning we couldn't move any livestock in or out, and it wasn't possible for anyone to come onto our land without going through the whole disinfection and interrogation process. It was a terrible time; more stressful than anything I've known in all my years on this farm. We lived in daily terror of being ordered to destroy our sheep and pigs.' She shook her head, still not quite over the anguish of those times. 'We were lucky to come through unscathed,' she continued. 'Government inspectors were crawling all over the countryside. Many of our friends were made to destroy their herds. It was heartbreaking, ruthless . . . Well, I'm sure you remember. It wasn't so long ago. You'll know about the suicides and bankruptcies. Maybe you even reported on it.'

Martin nodded. 'I did, and it's not something I ever want to see or report on again. Actually, I almost changed career at the time. I'd only just got a job on a national, covering real news, and I thought that if this was how it was going to be, watching blameless and perfectly healthy animals be sent to their deaths . . . Then 9/11 happened and it was like the world had gone into meltdown. 2001 was a terrible year.'

Shelley nodded agreement; those particular nightmares still had the power to subsume all other thoughts, but that wasn't what they were here for, so she quickly moved on. 'It wasn't until the following year,' she said, 'that we were able to look at Hanna's project again. It turned out that we still had the heart for it – maybe we were more eager than ever, given how much we needed something positive to happen. There was a lot of red tape to go through again, but then one day, just over six months ago, we found ourselves with all the necessary permissions, health and safety certificates, criminal record checks, you name it, and miracle of all miracles, we finally welcomed our first transitioners.'

It still did seem like a miracle, in spite of all the problems they'd faced since, but she wasn't about to make them a part of the story. They'd be ironed out one way or another, and talking the project down at this stage was going to serve no one, least of all those they were trying to help.

'And so far it's working?' he said.

She smiled. 'Most days. Kids of that age who've led the kind of lives they have are never going to be easy. However, most of them seem glad to be here. They understand that this can be a new beginning for them, an experience that will help to shape their futures in a way that's far more positive than any they'd have grubbing around on the streets, having nowhere to go and no one to turn to. Sadly we can't take extreme cases, we're not qualified or practised enough yet, but we hope that'll change over time. We'll see.'

'So how do you choose who comes here?'

'It's mainly down to social services, but the police and various charities are also involved. At the moment we're only geared up for eight residents at any one time, but we'll look into expanding if things work out.'

'Where do they live when they're here?'

'You passed it on your way in, just before the footbridge. Henry, the builder I mentioned just now, has constructed a kind of hostel with eight small bedrooms and three bathrooms, a fully equipped kitchen and a large communal living space. Donations of furniture, bed linens, cooking equipment, you name it, came in from all over once word got out. So it really isn't just our family getting behind the project, because a lot of farm families and nearby villages are doing their bit too.'

After jotting this down, he said, 'And how long do you expect your current residents to stay?'

'That will mostly depend on the individual. If all goes well we hope they'll be ready to leave, with jobs and a place to live, within a year or two. Others might want to go on to further education – or go back to get the qualifications they missed out on. Again we're working with the local authority on that.'

'Do you have rules they must stick to while they're here?'

'Oh, we have plenty: a strict no-drugs policy first and foremost; general behaviour has to be acceptable, of course, everyone has to pull their weight around the farm, and we don't house "guests" they might want to bring in from outside. Nor do we allow fighting or sex. The last is extremely hard to police, so we tend to turn a blind eye if we know about it. It's important to remember that Deerwood isn't a prison. The residents are over sixteen and are free to leave if they feel it isn't working for them.'

'And if someone drops out, there are always others to take their place?'

'Indeed.'

Refocusing, he said, 'So how exactly would *you* describe Deerwood and what you're trying to achieve here?'

Shelley checked her phone as it rang and seeing it was someone from Dean Manor, probably looking for Jemmie, she let the call go to messages. Jemmie would be there soon enough. 'I'd describe Deerwood first and foremost as a farm,' she replied, 'because it is still very much that, but in the sense you're meaning it, I've heard it called a halfway house, a rehabilitation centre, a transition project . . . Some of the kids even refer to it as farm-school. I think that's the term Hanna prefers, but you'll have to check with her. Anyway, the important thing is that kids who've lived most of their lives in care and who have nowhere to go when the system spits them out, can come here to learn how to take the next steps. We place much emphasis on social integration, discovering the therapeutic value of nature and animals, basic survival skills, and getting in touch with themselves in a way they've never been encouraged to before.'

Noting this down, he said, 'And you have experts helping you in this?'

'We do, and I'm sure Hanna will put you in touch with them if you want to know more about them. Frankly, without them we'd never have been able to get off the ground, so their support is vital in every way. Thankfully, we are finding more and more experts are interested in helping us. We've even had a few get in touch from other parts of the country, and we've started to hear from university students who want to be involved as part of a degree course in social studies. It'll take quite a bit of coordinating, but between us all I'm sure we'll manage.'

With an ironic smile, he said, 'I can see you having problems getting the residents to leave when the time comes.'

Shelley laughed. 'We have people ready to help with

finding homes and jobs, but again all untested as yet. Now, it sounds as though Hanna and Zoe have just turned up, so I'll let them give you the guided tour. There's quite a bit to see, and you'll probably find the residents will be eager to talk to you. They're enjoying the fame, that's for sure. You probably won't be able to get them to shut up about their ambitions for the place. It can be quite entertaining, if a little unrealistic. However, as we know, "Nothing happens unless first a dream."'

A while later Shelley was driving through the country lanes on her way to Dean Manor, and remembering all the things she'd forgotten to tell Martin Coolidge. She wondered whether she ought to call Hanna or Zoe to make sure they added them in, although, knowing them, they'd cover all bases without prompting. She just hoped they didn't get into how over-friendly some of the girls were being towards Josh. While Hanna and Zoe found it hilarious, Josh really didn't, though he seemed to have it fairly well under control – and hopefully it would stay that way until he left for uni. The last thing any of them wanted was Josh becoming a father at nineteen, or finding himself accused of something he hadn't done. That could turn very messy indeed.

Glancing at her phone as it rang she saw it was Jemmie and clicked on, even though she knew she shouldn't while driving. 'I should be there in less than ten minutes,' she shouted into the speaker.

'Oh Shelley,' Jemmie's voice was shaking. 'You haven't heard? Humphrey rang Deerwood . . .'

'Heard what?' Shelley broke in worriedly.

'Something . . . Something terrible's happened.'

Shelley started to brake. 'What do you mean?' she demanded.

As Jemmie answered, her words were drowned out by the sound of Josh's motorbike zooming up alongside the car. Perry was riding pillion and they were waving frantically for her to pull over.

'What is it?' Shelley cried into the phone and at the boys as she came to a stop.

'Oh, Shelley, Shelley, I don't know what to do,' Jemmie sobbed. 'He's dead. They've killed him . . .'

Shelley was stunned.

'Keep calm, Mum,' Josh cautioned, opening the driver's door. 'Sir Humph just rang Uncle Nate. Matthew Bleasdale's been in an accident . . .'

'He's getting married in less than two weeks,' Shelley shouted, as if it this could make everything stay normal, reinforce the fact that it had to.

The voice of Fiona, the Bleasdales' daughter, came down the line. 'Can you come, Shelley?' she asked shakily.

'I'm on my way,' Shelley told her.

Josh had already handed the bike to Perry, and opening the driver's door he drew Shelley out. 'I'll drive,' he told her.

'What does she mean, they killed him?' Shelley demanded as Josh helped her into the passenger seat. 'Who are *they*?'

'I don't know any details,' Josh replied, 'only that it concerns Matthew,' and returning to the driver's side he restarted the engine.

As he took them the rest of the way Shelley found

herself fixating on how scathing Matthew Bleasdale had been about their social project. His brothers too, but they were hardly ever around. They had been lately, though, as preparations got under way for the upcoming wedding.

Dear God, she was praying inwardly as they sped through the lanes, *please don't let Matthew have got into some kind of altercation with one of our residents. Please, please, don't let that be what's happened here. If it had they could end up having to close the project down, and it did so much good . . .*

'Josh,' she said shakily.

He turned to her, but she didn't know what to say.

As Josh zipped along Dean Manor's tree-lined drive towards the main house, Shelley was already clocking the blue flashing lights up ahead. Two police cars were blocking the front steps, and more vehicles she didn't recognize were haphazardly parked on the forecourt. A group of suited men turned to watch Josh bring the Volvo to a stop.

As they got out Fiona came running out to meet them.

'Shelley. Oh, Shelley,' she cried, dashing straight into Shelley's arms. 'Thank you for coming. It's so awful. Mummy's in the drawing room. She keeps asking for you, but to be honest I don't think she realizes what she's saying. Daddy's even worse.'

Slipping an arm around the girl, Shelley told Josh to explain who they were to the police, and took Fiona inside. Her heart was beating raggedly; her mind was frozen against the dread of what was about to unfold.

They've killed him, Jemmie had sobbed down the phone. *They've killed him.*

Passing another officer at the door of the drawing room, Shelley followed Fiona inside and found Sir Humphrey standing in front of the enormous fireplace, his back to them as he ran trembling hands over the ornate family crest.

'Shelley,' Jemmie exclaimed, and seeming to spring out of the shadows she ran across the room to clutch Shelley's hands. 'Thank you for coming,' she sobbed. 'It's so awful. Matthew's . . . They're saying . . . I don't know what to do.'

Bewildered, Shelley looked to Fiona for an explanation.

It was another voice that spoke. Male, deep and drawling, but not quite steady. 'We're all in shock,' he stated. 'It's . . . The police are saying his car went off the road . . .' It was Charlie, Matthew's twin, a tall, slightly overweight thirty-year-old with ruddy cheeks and bloodshot eyes. The younger brother, Felix, was with him, looking ashen and pinched, and clearly not as relieved to see Shelley as his mother and sister were.

'What's happened?' she pressed, glancing round as Josh came into the room.

The Bleasdale sons looked at the newcomer, then at one another. Charlie said, 'A motorcyclist ran Matthew off the road.' The way he eyed Josh made Shelley's heart turn over. Surely he wasn't trying to imply that Josh was responsible?

'When did it happen?' she asked anxiously.

No one answered. There was such a strange atmosphere in the room now that she was becoming more unnerved by the minute.

Charlie said to Josh, 'Have the police spoken to you?'

Josh's handsome young features darkened. 'Why would they need to speak to me?' he countered, showing no reluctance to stand up to the older man, or much reverence for his recent loss.

Shelley felt so sick, so horrified by what was happening, that she barely heard the next words.

'. . . no doubt thought you could get away with it,' Charlie was saying savagely.

'Stop! Stop!' Fiona jumped in. 'It has nothing to do with Josh and you know it.'

Charlie's tone slapped her down. 'Do we?' he demanded. 'He rides a motorbike, and so does that cousin of his, illegally in his case I might add . . .'

'Leave it, Charlie,' Felix barked. 'I know what you're thinking, but it won't fly.'

Charlie rounded on him, so angrily he might have hit him had Fiona not stepped between them.

'What's going on?' Jemmie cried in confusion. 'What isn't going to fly?'

Felix moved away from his brother and checked his phone.

Knowing they'd just abandoned some hare-brained scheme to land some sort of blame on Josh, Shelley turned to Humphrey as he mumbled, 'We told him it would end badly. We said he needed to stop, to understand he'd never win with people like that.'

'The old fool doesn't know what he's saying,' Charlie growled, as though to distract them.

Felix snapped. 'Pa, come with me. You need to lie down.'

Shelley watched them go, needing to understand what

was happening, while wondering if she really wanted to. 'Where's Matthew now?' she carefully asked Jemmie.

'The police are going to take us to him,' Fiona replied.

'So what's delaying them?'

Fiona shook her head; she seemed to have no idea.

Josh took Shelley's arm and steered her to a far corner of the room. Keeping his voice low he said, 'I think we should go.'

Having a feeling he was right, Shelley said, 'But I can't just leave Jemmie.'

'You have to. If someone really ran Matthew off the road . . . You just saw what Charlie tried to do. If Felix hadn't made him back off . . . Something's going on here, Mum, that we really don't need to be a part of.'

He looked so young and yet resolute, so wise to whatever further dastardliness Jemmie's detestable sons might try to concoct, that Shelley had to agree.

She turned back to Jemmie. There was so much going round in her head, too much. 'I'm truly sorry about Matthew,' she said gently, taking Jemmie's hands, 'but Josh and I have to leave now.' At Jemmie's look of surprise and alarm she pulled her into an embrace. Her eyes met Charlie's over Jemmie's shoulder, and she had the satisfaction of seeing him flush with discomfort. 'I know what you just tried to do to my son,' she said quietly. 'It would never have worked, but the fact that you even attempted it . . .' She let her words trail off, not wanting to say more in front of Jemmie, and with a last apologetic glance in Fiona's direction, she followed Josh out of the room.

* * *

Three days later the police came to Deerwood. They didn't stay long; they were simply collecting statements from anyone who'd been in the vicinity of the 'accident' on the day in question.

Nothing was said about Josh and his motorbike, but rumours of a Honda Gold Wing (not the same model as Josh's) being involved in the incident were spreading about the county like a summer muck spread.

Not long after the police left, Giles turned up.

'Don't tell me,' Shelley quipped as she plonked a coffee in front of him, 'you'll give me the latest gossip for a fee.'

Giles's grey-bearded face remained sober even as he grinned. 'Word has it,' he said, 'that the twins, maybe all three brothers, were into some sort of money-laundering scheme that the Revenue caught up with. Someone who's remaining nameless, if anyone even knows who it is, foreign, I expect, reckoned the Bleasdales were about to do a deal to get themselves off and land everyone else in it. So Matthew was sent to rest under a tree as a warning to the others that the same will happen to them if they don't keep their mouths shut.'

Feeling the bafflement of what went on in other people's families, the secrets and lies, and even the ignorance of what loved ones could be capable of, Shelley thought of Jemmie and Humph with nothing but sadness. How much they'd known before Matthew's death she had no idea, though they'd obviously known something, or why else would Jemmie have said '*they've* killed him'? when she'd called Shelley in a panic. As for Humph, it seemed highly likely that he'd been trying to help his

233

Susan Lewis

sons out of the mess they'd got themselves into, and now he'd learned the hard way that his efforts had been in vain.

'From what you told me about the day you were over there,' Giles went on, 'I've deduced – and my mate at Kesterly nick agrees with me – that Charlie, because he's stupid and always has been, had the grand idea to try and blame Josh for the "accident" because Josh is known to roar about the countryside on that bloody noisy bike of his. Felix was a bit cleverer, I'm told; he made his brother let go of that nonsense before it even got off the ground. Tangling themselves up in false accusations was only going to land them in an even bigger mess than they're already in. Best to play it down, go along with it being a tragic accident and that way their "business partners" might back off and leave them alone.'

Shelley looked up as Josh came in from the boot room, all long limbs and rain-soaked hair. 'Hey, Giles,' he said, helping himself to an apple and a towel. 'You've heard about the money-laundering thing?' He pulled out a couple of chairs, slouching into one and plonking his feet on the other.

Giles nodded. 'Daft buggers. Trouble is, they always thought themselves cleverer than the rest of us, reckoned the world was their playground and they had a right to it all, and look where it's ended them up.'

'Do you reckon Charlie and Felix will go to prison?' Josh asked, biting into the apple, and seeming not in the least bit sympathetic to the fate of the Bleasdale sons, or their wives, since both were already married with kids.

234

Giles shrugged. 'Depends what the Inland Revenue have got on them, but I shouldn't think they'd be squealing on anyone after this, so yes, it's likely one of them at least will carry the can, if not both.'

Feeling again for Jemmie and Humph, and already worrying about how this terrible business was going to affect their future, Shelley looked at Josh as she said, 'When you go off to uni promise me, if you need money, you'll always come to me.'

Josh looked stricken. 'Do I have to wait that long?' he protested, 'because Glastonbury's coming up and they've asked me to play the Pyramid Stage.'

Shelley slapped his feet off the chair and sat down. 'Stop talking nonsense,' she chided, 'and anyway, if they really were inviting you they'd be paying you, not the other way round.'

'This is true, I think, but The Vet Shop Boys – we changed our name again, by the way – have been given a ten-minute slot at midnight in the New Bands Tents and I'm in dire need of a new guitar.'

Chuckling as he got to his feet, Giles said, 'There are a lot of different ways to die, young Josh. Best you choose this one, is what I say.'

Scowling at the inappropriate timing of the remark, Shelley walked outside with him, and was about to ask if he thought she should go to see Jemmie when the phone inside started to ring. A moment later Josh called her back.

'It's Jemmie,' he said quietly, his hand covering the mouthpiece.

With her eyes on his, Shelley took the phone and said, tentatively, 'Hello. How are you?'

'I'm sorry to bother you with this, Shelley,' Jemmie sounded frail but coherent, 'but I thought I should let you know that Charlie and Felix have been arrested and Humphrey's collapsed.'

CHAPTER THIRTEEN
VIVIENNE

Present Day

By the time Sam returned from his mission to Deerwood Farm the children had been bathed and changed into their pyjamas, and Michelle's parents, Yvonne and Paul, had turned up. Although Vivienne had called to invite her mother to the barbecue, Gina apparently already had plans for dinner with friends in town, taking advantage of the fact that Vivienne was going to be out for the evening.

It was balmy and beautiful, with the sun casting a rich golden glow over the distant bay, and the sound of birds tweeting and cawing mingled with the chafe of invisible insects. In spite of being in Kesterly for all the wrong reasons, Vivi couldn't imagine wanting to be anywhere else right now. It felt so important to be with people she'd known all her life, friends who were as dear to her as if they were family, who wanted to be there for her until there was no more they could do. Or until she got a new heart, but the hope for that was as unpredictable and ephemeral as the foam on the waves.

'Right,' Sam declared, clearly meaning business as he

strode onto the deck rubbing his hands, 'have you got the beers on ice, Paul? I'm gasping. OK, OK, Yvie,' as his mother-in-law turned a baleful eye on him, 'I promise I'll have someone come and straighten up your mailbox by the end of the day tomorrow.'

'Just don't send the guy who put it up in the first place,' she admonished as he embraced her. 'It makes me feel drunk every time I look at it. Oh, Josh, hi, good to see you.'

Vivi turned to find a tall, dark-haired man, probably in his early thirties, standing behind her, and for no good reason her heart gave an unsteady beat. He had the tousled look of a Romany about him, or an eighteenth-century poet, or someone who was simply too handsome for his own good. His hair was thick, almost jet-black, his strong jaw unshaven and his smile as he turned it to her was so captivating that it made her own falter. She'd never seen him before, she knew that for certain, but there was something about him that seemed . . . familiar? Maybe he was reminding her of someone, though who it was she couldn't say. She only knew that he didn't feel like a stranger . . .

'Vivi and Josh, I don't think you guys have met,' Sam said, slipping an arm around her.

Josh held out a hand and Vivi felt the physicality of him closing around her like a small force of nature. His eyes were remarkable, almost unsettling in their intensity, for he wasn't just looking at her, she realized, he seemed to be *seeing* or *reading* her in a way that felt . . . It should have felt presumptive or even invasive, but they were too friendly for that.

'Vivi,' he said, holding the gaze with no apparent

self-consciousness. 'Michelle's best friend from your first day at school. It's good to meet you.'

Surprised, and faintly embarrassed, she said, 'You have me at a disadvantage because . . . Well . . .'

He laughed, and she almost blinked without being sure why. 'Don't tell me, no one's ever mentioned me,' he protested. 'I guess I'm just not important enough, but . . .'

'Oh, someone pass me a violin,' Michelle cried. 'I'm sure we have mentioned you.' She looked at Vivi, but Vivi was certain no one had. 'We must have,' Michelle insisted. 'Josh and Sam have been friends for years, and Josh's family are our best clients. Millie, darling, please don't do that with the cat.' Millie was holding the large, long-suffering tabby, Bitsy, in her tiny hands, carrying him awkwardly across the deck.

'I'm taking him to Josh,' Millie explained. 'Please can you make him better?' she implored, holding him up for Josh to inspect.

Going down to her height and smoothing the cat's soft grey fur, Josh said, 'What's the matter with him?'

'He's not very well, because he sleeps all the time.'

'I see,' he said thoughtfully. 'Well, that's what cats do during the day. They mostly sleep, and at night, they go out hunting.'

Millie's eyes dilated. It was clear her mind was whirling around that little revelation and those who loved her, which included everyone present, were waiting to hear what she made of it. 'You mean, when I'm asleep and my toys get up to play so I can't see them, Bitsy goes out . . . What's hunting?'

With a smile, Josh said, 'He goes out looking for mice and birds and even fish if he can catch them.'

Millie was entranced. 'Mummy! Did you hear that? Josh says Bitsy can catch fish. Grandma, maybe it's not the gulls stealing from your pond, it could be Bitsy.' She drew in a sharp breath. 'Bitsy, you bad boy. You mustn't steal Grandma's goldfish, because they're very expensive and it's naughty.'

'OK, seems like I've started something,' Josh said wryly, as he stood up again.

'Thanks for that,' Michelle replied sweetly. 'Now, make yourself useful and pour some wine. Sam, I've put everything for the barbecue on a big plate in the fridge. Dad, could you get it? Ash, that's not a good thing to do with your food, sweetheart.'

As Vivi picked up the bowl Ash had hurled from his high chair, Josh unscrewed the cap from a bottle of wine and began filling glasses. When he handed them around Vivi declined with a simple, 'Thanks, I'm on iced tea.'

Millie followed this up with, 'Auntie Vivi can't have wine because she isn't very well, but I take care of her with my doctor's set, don't I, Auntie Vivi?'

'You do indeed,' Vivi confirmed, aware of Josh's eyes on her.

'I'm going to make her better,' Millie declared. She gave a sudden gasp of excitement and turned back to Josh. 'Can you make her better?'

'Josh is a vet,' Sam reminded her. 'He treats sick animals, not people. Now, have you eaten all your supper, young lady?'

'Yes,' she cried, jumping up and down. 'Grandma, can we go and feed your goldfish?'

'Not right now, sweetheart. It's almost time for bed.'

'I don't want to go. It's not fair, I always have to go to bed. You're really mean . . .'

'Millie, that's enough,' Michelle cut in. 'Go and put a DVD on or learn to let someone else speak for a while.'

Opting for the DVD, Millie hurried off inside, leaving the others to cook and drink, and take Ash and eventually her off to bed, before they sat down to eat.

Vivi listened to the conversation as it ebbed and flowed, joining in at times, laughing in a way that felt . . . how did it feel? Liberating, she decided, because she hadn't felt this relaxed in a while. She was conscious of Josh watching her from time to time, and while wondering what he was thinking she wished he'd talk more, so she'd have an excuse to look at him. She did anyway, because she couldn't help it, and each time their eyes met she found herself feeling, fleetingly, as if they *did* know one another . . .

For a few uneasy moments she found herself wondering if this evening had been planned to get them together, until she realized that Michelle and Sam wouldn't be so insensitive as to try to do that either to her or to Josh.

Nevertheless, she was intrigued by the man, and of course attracted to him; it was impossible not to be when he looked and sounded the way he did. But she stayed mindful of the fact that Michelle had mentioned his family, so he was presumably married, probably with kids, and was no doubt used to women everywhere feeling attracted to him.

It wasn't until the meal was over and they settled

into the more comfy chairs that she got to learn a little more about him.

'So how's everyone at Deerwood?' Paul asked, as Michelle came out with a tray of coffee and chocolates. 'It's been a while since I was out there.'

'Oh, they're all fine,' Josh replied, taking an espresso. 'Crazy and busy as ever. Sam's come up with some great plans for the latest expansion.'

Apparently realizing Vivi was in the dark, Michelle handed her a peppermint tea as she said, 'Josh's family own Deerwood Farm, out on the old Dean Valley Road.'

Vivi said, 'I think I've passed it a couple of times when I've been out that way. I've seen the signs, but I can't say I know it.' She vaguely remembered wanting to stop and buy fruit there, but her mother hadn't wanted to, had even behaved oddly over it, but it was a faint recollection from a time when she'd still been so weak. . . .

Yvonne was saying with a laugh, 'You'll be the only one around here who doesn't know it. His mother's a legend and his sisters are saints.'

Josh immediately protested. 'Not quite how I'd describe them,' he corrected. 'In fact, not at all how I'd describe them.'

Enjoying his humour, Vivi said, 'So how would you describe them?'

After considering the question, he said, 'Actually, I tend not to get into that. It always ends me up in trouble.'

As the others laughed, Yvonne told Vivi, 'They adore him. In their books he can do no wrong . . .'

'Huh,' he scoffed. 'In their books I never do anything right.'

'If you don't know Deerwood,' Michelle put in, 'then we should probably explain that it's a farm *extraordinaire*.'

How could Vivi not be intrigued by that? 'Which means?' she prompted, wanting to hear it from Josh.

'Which means,' he replied, 'that it's time to change the subject and talk about something far more interesting, like what brings you to Kesterley at this time? I know you and Michelle have been friends most of your lives, so I guess . . .' He broke off, and Vivi realized from the sudden darkening of his eyes, that he'd just reconnected with what else he'd heard about her. She tried desperately to think of a way to smooth it over with something humorous, even dismissive, but she was afraid she'd make a fool of herself and embarrass him.

Michelle was there. 'You guessed right,' she was saying. 'She's here to babysit while Sam and I go off to France and Spain for a month to recreate our honeymoon. Sam, that was a hint. Would be lovely, when you can fit it in, my love.'

'But every night's a honeymoon with you, my darling,' Sam countered, refilling his glass.

'Hang on,' Paul protested, 'that's my daughter you're talking about.'

'Oh my God, is that who she is? I've been asking myself for a while, but I kind of like her, she's good to have around and great with the kids . . .'

Throwing a napkin at him, Michelle said, 'Speaking of not knowing who people are, Vivi's about to trace her ancestry using DNA.' Realizing her indiscretion too late, she tried a hasty retreat with, 'I was going to do it too, but you lot are enough for me, can't cope with any more.'

Josh looked fascinated as he turned to Vivi. 'I've seen it promoted on Facebook,' he said. 'They say that most of us who think we're British aren't even close.'

'Speaking personally,' Sam piped up, 'I'm sure I'm from Planet Macho. I kind of feel it in here, you know what I mean,' he said, punching his chest.

'We do indeed,' Michelle responded drily.

As everyone laughed, chocolates were passed around and Vivi found herself relaxing again, even feeling faintly light-headed, as she listened to the banter flowing as effortlessly and randomly as it had before. Josh was clearly as at home here as she was, which made him feel like a friend already, and it wasn't surprising that he should feel so comfortable when Michelle and Sam were such easy-going hosts. She just wondered why Michelle had never mentioned him before – unless she had, and Vivi hadn't really taken it in. Too busy with her own life, her own world . . .

It was almost midnight – the latest Vivi had been up since coming out of hospital – when she received a text from her mother asking if she was still at Michelle's.

She sent a quick message back assuring her she was, but she'd be home soon. No need to wait up.

'I can guess who it was,' Michelle smiled. 'She's worried, but you can stay here tonight if you like.'

Mindful of needing to be next to her home monitor, and of the medication she had to take before going to sleep, Vivi said, 'That would be lovely, but I ought to go. I'll call a taxi if you've got a number.'

'No need for that,' Josh insisted. 'I've only had a couple of glasses and I should be going myself before I outstay my welcome.'

'Not possible,' Michelle protested.

Nevertheless he got to his feet, and to Vivi's surprise he offered a hand to help her to hers. She felt the strength of his grip as she rose, and wondered if he was feeling the size and shape of her hand too. If he did he showed no sign of it, was already turning to the others to start saying goodnight.

He drove an old Land Rover, which made sense for a vet who apparently lived on a farm. It smelled, predictably, of hay and animals and a vague hint of something a little more savoury – and of him.

'You'll have to direct me,' he told her. 'I don't think I'm familiar with your part of town.'

'It's not far,' she assured him. 'I hope it isn't too much out of your way.' She knew it was, for Deerwood Farm was in completely the opposite direction.

'I'm staying in town tonight,' he informed her. 'I've got a flat over by the Botanical Gardens, so definitely not out of the way.'

She wanted to ask about the flat, how long he'd had it, who he lived with there, but afraid it might sound too inquisitive, too personal, she said instead, 'Where do you practise as a vet?'

He smiled. 'All over. I specialize in farm animals, so I tend to go to my patients more often than they come to me. When they do, I've got an office and surgery at Deerwood.'

Intrigued to know more about the farm, she was about to ask when she realized he was going to take a wrong turn.

Hitting the brakes and spinning the wheel with one hand, he threw out the other to hold her in her seat. 'That was fun,' he grinned, when they were safely on the straight and narrow again.

Smiling, she started to pick up where they'd left off, but he said, 'I hope you don't mind me saying this, but you don't look ill.'

Surprised by his bluntness, her eyebrows rose. 'Well there's a blessing,' she commented drily.

He glanced at her quickly. 'Am I wrong to mention it?'

She gave it some thought and shook her head. 'I don't much like talking about it, though. It's starting to define who I am, and I like to think that there's still a bit more to me yet.'

He looked at her again, but she kept her eyes straight ahead.

They drove on quietly, but she was aware of his frequent glances, as though he was trying to get the measure of her. In the end she said, 'Am I allowed to look at you too?'

He laughed in a way that made her laugh too. 'You're going to find this odd,' he told her, 'but I keep feeling as though you're someone I know, someone I haven't seen for a long time . . .'

'Yes, that is odd,' she agreed, her eyes shining with mischief as she turned to him. She wouldn't tell him she understood what he meant because she was feeling it too, but she did say, '*Have* we met before?'

He shook his head. 'I'd remember.'

Certain she would too, she fell silent again. *This is crazy,* she was telling herself. *This can't be happening now. It just can't.* But it was. She was attracted to him in a way that felt both exhilarating and terrifying.

'Do you miss your life in London?' he asked.

She could hardly deny it, and yet would she want to be there now, in her weakened, limited state, struggling to be the person she no longer was? 'I enjoyed it while I was there,' she said, 'and I guess I still would if things hadn't changed the way they have.'

'You had quite a high-powered job, from what I hear.'

She smiled. 'I suppose it could be categorized that way. Bay Lane's about fifty yards along on the left, by the way. It's easy to miss . . .'

A few minutes later he turned the Land Rover round outside number 8 and came to a stop. As they were now talking about their student days, she didn't immediately get out of the car. He was telling her about his time at the Royal Veterinary College, and it turned out that although they hadn't been in London at the same time – he was more than five years older than her – they'd frequented many of the same bars and cafés, and in a more amazing coincidence they'd actually lived on the same street, albeit several years apart.

'So what did you do after you graduated?' she asked, aware of how late it was getting, but he didn't seem keen to get away and, amazingly, she wasn't feeling tired.

'I went to South Africa to work on various animal-conservation projects,' he replied, gazing absently out at the darkness. 'Lions, leopards, rhinos . . . I was there for almost four years. I would have stayed, but . . .' He threw her a look. 'You were just being polite. Sorry . . .'

'No, really, I'm interested. You would have stayed, but . . .'

He inhaled deeply and turned his gaze back to the black expanse of sea that glittered and rippled in the moonlit bay. 'There was a girl,' he said. 'She worked on one of the projects . . . We talked about marriage, but then it didn't seem such a good idea when we realized we wanted different things from life.'

Intrigued, Vivi said, 'How different?'

'Basically, Elena saw her future in her family's business – they own a winery near Franschhoek – and I didn't see mine there at all. So we parted, more or less amicably, and much to my mother's relief I decided to return to Deerwood.'

His eyes were closed now, his hands resting loosely on the base of the steering wheel, and though he was very much present, she could sense that his mind was somewhere far away. 'Do you regret the decision?' she ventured softly.

He seemed surprised, but his eyes remained closed as he said, 'To come back, or not to marry?'

'Either.'

'No to the second. I'm still not sure about the first.'

There was so much more she wanted to ask; in fact she wanted to know everything about him, but that was hardly going to happen tonight.

Or any other night, she reminded herself firmly.

Nevertheless, she said, 'You mentioned your mother just now. What about your father?'

He took a breath, pressed his fingers to his eyes as

though rubbing away tiredness, and said, 'He was killed in a freak accident when I was four.'

She quietly reeled. *Four years old. So young.* 'I'm sorry,' she murmured, truly meaning it. 'Do you remember him?'

'Some things.'

She let a few moments pass, wondering if she should tell him about the situation with her own father, but decided not to. Not knowing who someone was couldn't be compared to losing a parent you'd known and loved with all your heart.

Realizing he'd raised an eyebrow and was watching her with one eye open, she felt a reaction in her heart that she knew very well had nothing to do with her condition.

'Tell me more about you,' he said softly.

His tone was almost intimate, and for a heady, irrational moment a part of her wanted to tell him everything, leaving out nothing, even the terrible, wrenching, cowardly fear of dying. In the end she shook her head. 'I want to hear about Deerwood,' she insisted.

He pushed his hands to the roof of the car in an effort to stretch out his arms. 'Deerwood is a long story,' he replied, 'too long for now, but if you're really interested?' He made it a question.

'I am,' she assured him.

'Then let's save it for another time.'

Vivi let herself quietly in through the front door and stood in the hall, listening to the sound of his car driving away until she could hear it no more.

If she'd met him three months ago she knew exactly

how she'd be feeling now – gloriously alive, breathless with anticipation. She'd be unable to sleep for thinking about him; she'd lie in the moonlight, smiling, dreaming, until she drifted off, waking a few hours later to a renewed rush of wonderful memory.

If it were three months ago she wouldn't even be here, she reminded herself soberly. She'd be in London and would never have met him . . .

Her eyes closed against a surge of misery.

For weeks, ever since she'd known how sick she really was, there had been things she'd tried hard to keep away from, but tonight they were almost overwhelming her. She was a shell of who she used to be, a young woman who could no longer function in a way that was considered normal; she couldn't even think about having a relationship, much less about satisfying the needs of her body, or anyone else's. It seemed cruel, almost perverse, that those needs should still be very much alive, as though they had a pulse, a bloodstream all of their own. She could feel the longing in her body, opening her up in a way only a man could fulfil. Josh Raynor had awakened that longing, had drawn her to him without as much as a single touch . . .

Starting as a light went on upstairs, she blinked the self-pitying tears from her eyes and went through to the kitchen.

'Vivi? Are you all right?' her mother called out.

'I'm fine,' she called back. 'Sorry to wake you. I'm coming up now.'

Apparently satisfied with that, Gina returned to bed, and Vivi felt sadness and despair flooding into her useless heart. She wanted to tell her mother how afraid she was of the future and how pointless her existence seemed. She even wanted to tell her about Josh, how surprised she'd been by him, and the connection she'd felt. She probably wouldn't be able to find the right words to explain him, but it didn't matter because she wasn't going to try. Her mother would only tell her what she already knew, that no matter how hard it might be, she must put him out of her mind. She wasn't strong enough to have the kind of relationship a man like him would need and expect, that was presuming he even wanted a relationship with her, and there was nothing to say that he did. It didn't matter. It couldn't happen and so there was no point putting herself through this. Life for her had changed. She must deal with the truth of that in a way that avoided delusions and false promises, and most of all avoided hurting anyone, including herself.

Vivi ended up paying for the late night at Michelle and Sam's with a spell of weakness and exhaustion that kept her mostly in bed for the next two days, sometimes struggling for breath, or turning her face to the pillow as she wept with despair and frustration. There was even talk of taking her into hospital for a while, but thankfully, on the third morning, when she woke from a night of scattered sleep, it was bizarrely as though she'd pulled some energy from thin air. She was able to shower and dress without her mother's help, and when Gil came to take Gina out for lunch she decided to accept the invitation to join them.

She needed to get out of the house, to feel she was

still alive and able to escape the depression that seemed to lurk in the corners of her room as well as her mind.

They went to the Luttrell Arms in Dunster, a place that was special to Gil and Gina. It was where he'd asked her to marry him, many moons ago, and where they'd come to celebrate the anniversary of that day every year during the time they were together.

And now, here they were celebrating it again – with Vivi as the third wheel, or perhaps she was some kind of chaperone to make sure the day didn't stumble into territory they couldn't find their way back from. That would never do, at least not for Gina, and since Gil had someone else now, Vivi could only wonder what he was doing here.

As she watched them clearly enjoying themselves she made herself laugh at something Gil was saying, not quite sure what it was, but as he and her mother seemed to find it funny, she decided to go along with it. It obviously pleased them to think she was having a good time, and she was, in a way – just not in the same way as they were.

Catching a little boy watching her from a nearby table she smiled, and loved the way he smiled back. He was probably no more than three years old, with a mass of brown curly hair and a bright red birthmark covering one of his baby-soft cheeks. His eyes were bright and happy in spite of being misaligned, and she couldn't be sure but she thought, from the way he walked, that one of his little legs was shorter than the other.

What a sweetheart he was. She wanted to wrap him up in her arms and thank him for smiling at her, because he'd reminded her of how little it took to make someone feel good. It was odd how children could do that so much more successfully than adults. She guessed it was because there was no artifice in their smiles; no motive at all that wasn't born of happiness to be alive and noticed.

'Penny for them,' her mother offered.

Vivi turned to her, and after a moment Gil said, wryly, 'Seems like they might be worth a lot more.'

Gina smiled, but she was clearly concerned as she said, 'Are you all right? Is this too much for you? We can always go . . .'

'I'm fine, Mum,' Vivi interrupted. 'It was a lovely idea to come here. I needed a change of scenery more than I realized.' It was true, she really had, and if she hadn't come she knew she'd have sat at home reading about her condition online, finding out how others were coping, searching for some hope, a way of changing her destiny, and that really wouldn't have been a helpful distraction at all.

What was helping her, strangely, was thinking about Josh Raynor, in spite of her resolve not to do so. During the better moments of the past few days she'd let her mind drift over the short time they'd spent together, their conversation and its many directions, and to her surprise she'd found it more calming than upsetting. She enjoyed picturing his profile in the moonlight, almost lost in shadow, and recalling the sound of his voice as he spoke, the sense of him breathing. Occasionally she'd remind herself that she had no intention of seeing him again, and she meant it, but it didn't seem to stop her from wondering what he might be doing now, who he was with, what he might be saying, or even thinking. He'd promised to tell her about Deerwood, but he hadn't been in touch. She wasn't sure if she'd expected to hear by now; she only knew that she was trying hard not to wait for his call, despite the fact that she was.

'That was one major swoon the other night,' Michelle had teased when they'd finally spoken this morning. 'He's a dreamboat, isn't he? I take it he got you home in one piece.'

'Yes, of course,' Vivi had laughed. 'It was a lovely evening. Thanks very much.'

'I'm glad you came, and the kids loved seeing you, as always.'

They'd talked on for a while, not mentioning Josh again, though Vivi knew very well that Michelle had sensed the chemistry between them; she simply wouldn't try to encourage a situation that had no future.

'So how are you getting on with your plan to accept your lot and try to appreciate every day you have left, without panicking yourself into an early grave?' Gil asked chattily.

Vivi blinked in shock.

He was smiling warmly, so was her mother, until seeming to sense that something was wrong their expressions turned to bewilderment and concern.

'I'm sorry,' Vivi said quickly, realizing it was the voice in her head she'd heard, not Gil's. Of course he hadn't said that, he'd never be so crass or brutal. 'I was miles away, what did you say?'

'I was just asking if you'd like anything else,' Gil replied. 'A dessert, maybe?'

Knowing it would please her mother to see her eat

more than the few mouthfuls of sea bream she'd managed, Vivi said, 'I'd love some fresh fruit with almonds. Thanks.'

She was far too thin, her eyes were sinking into dark hollows, her face was as pale as a winter sky. Josh had said she didn't look ill, but she knew she did. Some days thanks to her failing heart her lips were tinged with blue, and the strain of her condition seemed to sharpen the bones in her cheeks. How could he possibly find her attractive? How could any man?

It would be so much easier to get through this if she could somehow shut off her mind. Even when she was sleeping she was tormented by dreams that could be beautiful and gentle at the start, until they turned into something dark and frightening, even violent. It was a reflection of her life, she thought, the one that had been happy, healthy, fulfilling in every way until suddenly it wasn't any more.

'I can't stand doing nothing,' she told Josh in her mind. 'I want to be someone who uses the time I have left to make a difference in a good way. If I had cancer I'd still be able to do things, raise money for a children's hospice; put on events in support of the British Heart Foundation; help those who are also dying so they don't feel so alone. I'd be able to make love and dance, fly to faraway places, or throw myself into a world full of hopes and dreams.'

What would he say in return, she wondered, and why was she talking to him in her mind when she had her mother, Gil and Michelle to talk to at any time in reality?

'Is there anything in particular you'd like to do this afternoon?' her mother asked as their desserts arrived.

Vivi thought about suggesting they drive past Deerwood Farm on the journey home, but it was out of the way and how would she answer when her mother asked why? Which of course she would.

So she said, with no preamble, 'I'm having my ancestry traced using DNA.'

Gina frowned, seeming confused for a moment, until understanding dawned and her cheeks burned with colour. 'Why?' she asked stiffly, and Vivi almost laughed at the disingenuousness of it.

'Why do you think?' she retorted. 'You won't tell me anything, so I've decided to take matters into my own hands.'

Gina glanced at Gil.

'How exactly do you go about it?' he enquired, making an attempt to keep things calm while they were in public.

She explained about sending off the saliva sample to a place in Ireland. 'Don't worry,' she told her mother, 'it takes six weeks or more for the results to be posted, and I might be dead by then.'

Gil said sharply, 'That was uncalled for, Vivienne. We understand how difficult this is for you, but attacking your mother . . .'

'I'm not attacking her. I'm just saying that there's a good chance her secret will stay safe in spite of my efforts to find out who my father is.' Before Gina could interrupt, she said, angrily, 'Do you know how many people are waiting for donors so they can stay alive? It's not just me, there are thousands of people, and hundreds of them have died in this past year alone. If . . .'

'They're not all waiting for hearts,' Gil pointed out.

'Does it matter what they're waiting for? Do you have any idea how frightening and miserable it is for those who need dialysis every day? You should read some of their stories. I don't know how many healthy organs have been buried or cremated this past month alone, but believe me, it's a lot, and every one of them could have made all the difference to someone's life. If they'd put themselves on the register, or if they'd told their families they want to try and help someone in need, then young men like Jim Lynskey might not be in the position he's in now.'

'Who's Jim Lynskey?' Gina asked quietly.

'He's twenty-one and he's been waiting for a heart since he was nineteen. That's two years, Mum. *Two years*. His story's online, if you want to read it. It's insane the way this country operates over organ donation. OK, they're talking about an opt-out system now, but God knows how long that will take to go through Parliament. It won't be in place in time for me, you can be sure of that . . .'

Stepping in quietly, Gil said, 'We understand what you're saying, sweetheart, but it's not your mother's fault that . . .'

'I'm not saying it is,' Vivi interrupted hotly, though she desperately wanted to blame someone for the frustration and helplessness that she, and everyone like her had to live with every day, never knowing if there would be a happy ending, locked in the fear that there really might not be. Fixing her eyes on her mother, she said, 'I just don't understand why, when you know how things are for me, and how much I want to know the truth, you still won't tell me who my father is. I'm likely to die, for God's sake. Can't you at least tell me *something* about him?'

Clearly agitated, Gina said, 'I can only repeat what I've told you all along. It won't help you to know who or what he is, or even where he is . . .'

'Do you *know* where he is?'

Gina's eyes went down as she shook her head.

'I don't believe you.'

As Gina flinched, Gil said, 'Vivi, this isn't the time or the place.'

'Are you still in touch with him?' Vivienne pressed her mother.

'No, of course not,' Gina replied. To Gil she said, 'We should get the bill.'

As they left the hotel and walked down through the village towards the castle, Vivi said, 'So you're really going to deny me my dying wish?'

'What I'm doing,' Gina said hoarsely, 'is protecting you from something that will only hurt you and . . .' She broke off as Vivi's mobile rang.

As she dug around in her bag Vivi knew her mother was holding her breath, the way she did every time Vivi's mobile rang. Maybe a donor had been found. They should be readying themselves for a mad dash to the transplant centre. Vivi herself felt sick with the dread and the hope of it.

It was a number she didn't recognize.

She clicked on carefully and waited for someone to speak.

'Hi. Vivi? It's Josh Raynor. Is this a good time?'

As the surprise passed she felt suddenly as though

she'd swallowed sunshine. 'Of course,' she said warmly. 'How are you?'

'I'm good. I was hoping to see you again.'

Thrilled and overcome with eagerness, she hardly knew what to say, apart from, 'That would be lovely. I'm free most days.'

There was a wonderful irony in his tone as he said, 'Oh well, if you're going to play hard to get I shall just come over there and beat the door down.'

She laughed, joyfully, and knew that the sensations in her heart had nothing at all to do with anything but pleasure.

As soon as they got home Vivi went into her room and closed the door. To make doubly sure she couldn't be overheard she put on some music, then rang Michelle.

'I've had a call from Josh,' she told her, aware of how ragged her limited breath was making her voice. 'He wants to see me and I want to see him, but . . .'

'I've already spoken to him,' Michelle interrupted. 'He rang to get your number. Please tell me you didn't turn him down.'

Surprised, and suddenly wanting to laugh and embrace her best friend like she never had before, Vivi said, 'I didn't, but . . .'

'Listen,' Michelle said firmly, 'I know what you're thinking, but let's be frank about this, shall we? He knows what's going on with you and he still wants to see you. So what's the point in trying to deny the attraction you feel for one another?'

Vivi's swirl of emotions was so mixed and unsteady that she could hardly connect with even one. 'So you noticed?' Her smile grew to a point where it couldn't get any wider.

'Noticed?' Michelle spluttered. 'We could have lit up the whole town with the chemistry going on between you two the other night.'

Vivi bit her lip, wanting to laugh and cry and heaven only knew what else. 'I've told him to come tomorrow when you're supposed to be with me. Do you mind?'

'Of course I don't mind. I'm guessing that means you're not going to tell your mother?'

'I don't think so. It'll only worry her . . . God knows my heart's already in enough trouble, she won't take kindly to me putting it in the way of even more.'

With tenderness in her voice, Michelle said, 'He's a wonderful man, Vivi. Far too good-looking, of course, and he's got a whole list of flaws that include being impulsive, annoyingly clever and a hopeless timekeeper, but he's different, special in a way that's hard to put into words. The best I can manage is that if we were having this conversation about anyone else I'd be worried. I'd even be trying to talk you out of it. As it's him . . . Well, let's speak again tomorrow after you've seen him.'

CHAPTER FOURTEEN
VIVIENNE

Present Day

It was just after eleven when Josh arrived the following morning, so he was hardly late at all, Vivi noted as she watched him getting out of his Land Rover. She guessed Michelle had told him that Gina didn't like her sick daughter to be alone for long in case something happened, so perhaps that was the reason for his arrival only ten minutes after her mother had left for The Salon.

She was standing at the front door ready to greet him as he came across the drive towards her. Though she was ludicrously pleased to see him, a part of her was nervous, anxious even, and yet she also felt calm and confident in a way she hadn't expected, certainly not for a first date, if that was what this was.

He wore his smile as unselfconsciously as the faded jeans and old grey polo he'd no doubt had for years, and as he came closer she felt the magnetism of him already reaching her. She wondered if he had that effect on everyone, or if it was just her.

'Are you OK?' he asked, holding her eyes in a way that dispensed with the need for a handshake, or a friendly kiss on the cheek. It was an embrace all of its own.

'I'm fine,' she assured him, and stood aside for him to come in.

She showed him through to her room, feeling thankful that the bed was no longer there like a relic from Miss Havisham's world. 'I made some coffee,' she said, gesturing towards the tray on the table.

He went to the open front window, taking in the view and the gentle sea air, dampened by a drift of fine rain. She could feel the masculinity of him in this essentially feminine room, was aware of the hard muscles of his arms and back that filled out his shirt, the length of his legs, the dark hair that curled over his collar. Then he turned and regarded the tray she'd set out, and seemed puzzled for a moment. 'What are you having?' he asked, apparently registering the single mug.

Gesturing to the white china pitcher, she said, 'Iced tea. Strawberry flavour. I don't do much caffeine these days. You're welcome to join me.'

His eyes returned to hers, and the irony in his smile sent her gently to the stars. 'I'll have a manly coffee,' he quipped. 'Black, no sugar.'

Embarrassing herself, she said, 'I might have some manly biscuits to go with it.'

He raised an eyebrow. 'What are manly biscuits?'

'Jammie Dodgers,' she said cautiously, and loved it when he laughed. 'Seriously, I have some digestives. Or I might be able to rustle up a Hobnob or two.'

'Digestives,' he decided, and to her surprise he came to tilt her face up to the light. The feel of his fingers on her chin was as unsettling as the curiosity in his eyes. He nodded and said, 'Yep, I was right. They're the colour of African violets.' Before she could comment that his eyes were also blue, though darker, he let her go and looked around the room. 'Sam told me he'd recreated your London apartment,' he said. 'You have great taste, in that it chimes with my own, I guess. That's the only way we judge these things, isn't it? Would you like me to pour, or just to stop talking?'

Smiling, she said, 'No, please don't stop. If you do I'll have to speak and I'm not sure what I want to say.'

Clearly amused, he sat down in the armchair and took the coffee she handed him. 'Am I allowed to say that I've never met anyone like you before?' he ventured.

Thrown, she almost replied, *You mean someone who's dying?* Stopping herself in time, she said, 'I'm not sure whether to ask you to explain that.'

He took a sip of coffee. 'What I should probably have said is that I don't *think* I've ever met anyone like you before. It's hard to be sure when we don't really know one another, but I do know that I haven't been able to get you out of my mind since the other night – and I've come to see you at eleven o'clock on a workday morning, abandoning all other commitments.'

Though his words were wonderful to hear, so honest and free of the usual games and reticence of first meetings, her eyes widened with as much concern as amusement. 'What are you supposed to be doing?' she probed.

'Treating sick animals. However, I have to admit, if I had an emergency I'd be there. Sorry if that sounds . . .'

'It sounds right,' she interrupted.

'Are you an animal lover?'

'What's not to love? Although I have to admit I don't know much about them.'

He pondered this. 'I guess I don't know your world either.'

Deciding he was referring to her life in London, she said, 'This is my world now, quite different to the one I was used to.'

The interest in his eyes seemed to intensify, and after a moment he surprised her as he said, 'Are you afraid?'

Her first instinct was to pull back from the question, try to make light of her feelings, but she could see that he was expecting a truthful answer, and she realized she wanted to give it. 'Yes,' she admitted, 'I'm afraid, especially when my device kicks in. It's like it's saying, don't get too carried away, Vivienne, you haven't got what it takes to see it through, whatever *it* might be.'

He sat with those words, and she knew he'd heard the subtext she hadn't intentionally included, and was assessing it. 'Tell me what gets you carried away,' he said, making it both a tease and a serious question. 'It would be good to know, so I don't get us into any trouble.'

Enjoying the 'us' as much as the banter, she said, 'If I feel it happening, I'll be sure to let you know. Now, you promised me, the last time we met, that you'd tell me about Deerwood.'

He looked disappointed, but also curious. 'You mean you haven't Googled it since then? I thought everyone Googled everything right away these days.'

'Do you?'

He laughed. 'No, I guess not.'

'I didn't look it up,' she told him, 'because I wanted to hear about it from you.' This was true, but not only because she hadn't wanted to go on a voyeuristic – or perhaps masochistic – journey into a world that she'd been trying to tell herself she could never be a part of. She'd remembered how her mother hadn't wanted to buy fruit there, and though Gina's behaviour that day might have had nothing at all to do with the farm, Vivi simply hadn't wanted to connect with anything negative about it.

She still didn't.

He said, 'I didn't Google you either.'

She had to laugh. 'Because Michelle and Sam had already told you about me,' she pointed out.

'I have to admit it.'

'Which makes me wonder why you're here. However, let's please not get into that. I really, truly, want to know about Deerwood.'

An hour later he was stretched out in a lazy way in the armchair, having finished two coffees and several biscuits, and was seeming as comfortable as if he were here every day. 'So now,' he said, with a luxurious yawn, 'having gone from eight residents when the project started fifteen years ago, we're up to around thirty at the last count and if I know my sisters, it won't stop there.'

Loving everything she'd heard so far about his sisters, his mother, grandparents, aunt and uncle, indeed everything that made up a family and existence so different from her own, she said, 'OK, let me get this straight. Your mother oversees everything, but she's mainly involved with the farm. As is your uncle Nate. Your sister Hanna runs the social integration – or residency – programme; your other sister, Zoe, organizes the health and fitness side of things. Your grand-father is – what did you call him? An organic engineer?'

He laughed. 'His words. He thinks it's witty. What he really is, is a brilliant gardener, but he's in his eighties now – really good for his age, it has to be said – and with half a dozen sizeable greenhouses to take care of, God knows how many raised vegetable beds and a whole orchard of fruit trees, he's quite happy to take all the help he can get. In reality, my cousin, Perry, runs the organic farming, and the kids – residents – do most of the hard labour. As do the university students who keep turning up for work experience or just for the fun of it, as far as I can tell. They come from all over, pitch their tents in one of the fields, or camp out on the floors of the residents' blocks if it's cold or wet, and they actually add a whole other dimension to the experience for the kids who've spent most of their lives in care.'

Entranced by the thought of all that unusual activity and invaluable interaction, Vivi said, 'What sort of other dimension?'

He measured it for a moment. 'Well, to begin with a lot of the students bring music with them and that's a tremendous bonus to any education – at least in my opinion. Everyone joins in the campfire singalongs, even the shyest or most aggressive amongst them, and we've had quite a few kids leave us able to play the guitar, or the recorder, or even a cello, one year. Someone local came in to coach him when he showed real talent. The kids, both privileged and challenged, often bond in a way that they probably wouldn't even come close to in the wider world. There are no class barriers at Deerwood. There's just the work and the learning and the gradual understanding of who they are, where they've come from and, to an extent, where they hope to go next.'

'It sounds wonderful,' she murmured. No wonder he loved it so much, she was thinking, it hardly seemed possible not to.

His voice dipped into irony as he said, 'That's definitely how Hanna would like to paint it, as wonderful, even idyllic, but I'm sure you won't be surprised to hear that it has its problems. There have been times when we've had to call the police to break up fights, or to help remove someone who's threatening to burn the place down, or blow us all up. Drugs are a constant challenge, but Hanna and her team mostly manage to stay on top of it. The hopeless cases have to go, unfortunately – Deerwood isn't a rehab centre – so they're sent to places better equipped to deal with them. I won't get into the couple of suicides we've had, or the attempted murder, but they've happened too. It's never a dull moment on our farm, that's for sure.'

Aware of starting to feel breathless, Vivi made herself push past it and said, 'So what exactly do you do in all this?' Her breathing would sort itself out in a minute or two, it usually did.

Watching her, he slid down to the floor and rested his elbows on his knees, his hands linked loosely together. 'I just muck in where it's needed,' he replied, seeming more focused on her than his words. 'I think I told you I have a surgery and office there, so I take on any of the kids who show an interest in animals. This can range from nature night watches – they're always popular for some reason. Interesting, isn't it, how kids love going out on an adventure at night? I always did when I was young. Some of our residents have never even been to the countryside before they come to us, so identifying birds and their calls, following tracks, or rescuing something that's injured seems to fascinate them. I could get into all sorts of parallels here, but I'll spare myself the embarrassment and just say that there are certain similarities between their own lives and those of creatures in the wild that seem to work very well for them. No one's gone the whole way to becoming a naturalist or a vet yet, but three of our girls are now working as veterinary nurses, two in Bath and the other in Southampton.'

Impressed, she said, 'So it's like a radic . . . radically different kind of sixth-form college?'

He nodded. 'I guess you could say that.' Though he continued to speak she was aware of how closely he was watching her, seeming to know that things weren't right, but unsure as yet what to do about it. 'It's wonderful the way so many professionals are willing to share their time and expertise,' he said, his words forming a bridge over the changing current between them. 'Some, of course, do it for the kudos and publicity, but most get involved because they really want to.' He paused, still watching her, seeming to wait for a cue. Or . . . What was he doing? His thoughts seemed to be . . . seemed not to be on his words.

'Go on,' she prompted.

Still going with it, he said, 'Our friend Sam has worked miracles in all sorts of ways. He gets the kids involved in all the trades from plumbing, to electrics, to roofing . . . Those who're really interested learn how to construct a small dwelling somewhere on the farm, making it as isolated or as close to the main complex as they choose. It's always temporary, so we don't have to apply for planning consent. Some have started renovating old caravans, or repurposing disused shipping containers; last year someone even transformed a boat.'

Enchanted by the amazing opportunities his family had created for so many underprivileged children, Vivi said, 'I can understand . . .' she took a breath, 'why Michelle says it's a very special place.'

'You'll have to come and see it one of these days,' he told her, seeming to mean it.

Knowing she'd love to, she said, 'I'm just wondering what other life experiences you've had besides uni, South Africa and Deerwood.'

Instead of answering, he said, 'Shall we sit quietly for a while?'

She shook her head. 'I'm just . . . It comes and goes.' With a smile she knew was probably tinged with blue, she added, 'I hope you're not avoiding my question?'

He smiled too and proving that he'd read her correctly, he said, 'I'm not married, and I never have been, because I've never met the right woman, although, as you know, I thought I had for a while when I was in Africa. My sister Zoe, on the other hand, has been more successful. She's in California at the moment, on honeymoon with her new wife, and learning even more holistic therapies to bring back to Deerwood.'

'So she lives at Deerwood?'

'One way or another we all do. Maybe not permanently, but Zoe's still got her old bedroom at the farmhouse, and Hanna has the main part of the barn that was first converted into a holiday let by our maternal grandparents aeons ago. Patty and George – said maternal grand-parents – are still in their two-up two-down end of the barn, while Hanna and her husband, Martin – he's a journalist who came to interview her back in the early days and never quite left – they and their three, soon to be four, children rocket around the rest of the barn. Have I lost you yet?'

Smiling past the tiredness that was trying to drown her, she said, 'I think I'm following it all. I was just wondering . . . I notice how you keep changing the subject away from yourself.' Was that what she'd meant to say? She wasn't sure for the moment how well she'd heard everything. Maybe he'd talked about himself more than she realized and she'd failed to take it in. She wanted to stay awake, and to stop him from looking so concerned. He was getting up, coming to . . . She didn't object as he eased her down on the sofa, raised her legs gently and rearranged the pillows . . . It felt good to have him here . . . Really good, as though he was . . . She watched him through blurry eyes as he smoothed a calming hand over her forehead and murmured that it was time to rest for a while. She closed her eyes and put a hand over his, holding it to her cheek as though she might absorb some of his strength.

When she awoke she was still lying in the same place, but it was Michelle on the floor beside her now, playing with Ash. A cool breeze was drifting in through the open windows, toys were scattered about . . .

She blinked, trying to get a sense of the time and how long she'd been out. She took a breath, found it came easily, and took another while trying to decide if she felt dizzy, or lethargic, or even depressed.

There was no sign of Josh and she wasn't sure whether she felt embarrassed that she'd fallen asleep, or disappointed that he'd gone; probably it was a combination of the two.

She smiled as Ash spotted her eyes were open and let out a jubilant shriek. 'Hello, noisy,' she croaked.

Michelle turned to sit facing her, holding an excited Ash back before he launched himself onto the sofa. 'Josh had to go,' she said, 'but he wanted me to tell you that he's never bored anyone off to sleep before.'

Vivi spluttered on a laugh, and eased herself up on one elbow.

'How are you feeling?' Michelle asked.

'OK, I think.' She was definitely breathing easily, and her senses seemed clear. 'My ICD didn't activate, did it?' No, of course not, she'd remember if it had.

'Can I get you anything?' Michelle asked.

Seeing the pitcher of iced tea still on the table, Vivi gestured to it and swung her feet carefully to the floor. 'Well,' she said, as Michelle handed her a glass, 'I guess he can't be in any doubt now that I'm a faint heart. Did he call you to ask you to come?'

'Yes. He had to leave, something to do with a horse, so I said I'd stay with you until your mother gets home.'

Vivi sighed despairingly. 'God, what a burden I am.'

'That's not how he described you,' Michelle assured her. 'Actually, he didn't describe you at all, apart from as someone he'd bored senseless.'

Laughing, Vivi said, 'He told me about Deerwood.

271

It sounds fascinating. I can't believe you've never mentioned it.'

Michelle shrugged. 'It's more Sam's thing than mine, and unless you're in that world . . .'

'Have you been there?'

'A few times. It's a crazy place, or that's how it seems on the surface, but what it's achieving is nothing short of amazing. You'd love his sisters, and his mum, Shelley. Everyone does.'

Remembering how he'd said she should visit Deerwood, Vivi felt sure he wasn't the type to throw out empty invitations or to string her along for the sake of the moment. He'd seemed to enjoy the time they'd spent together, and she couldn't stop herself hoping she'd see him again. To try to resist it would be pointless, she realized. She didn't have the will, and even if she did she could already sense him walking all over it.

Looking at Michelle, she said, 'I don't really understand what's happening. He's . . . I don't know what he is, apart from . . . He said I'm not like anyone he's met before, and that's how I think of him.' Quite suddenly her eyes filled with tears, hot and burning, as the futility of it all swept in to eclipse the dream and bring her harshly back to reality. 'I don't know whether fate's being spectacularly cruel,' she said, as Michelle squeezed her hand, 'or if it's decided to let me have a taste of something truly special before it's too late. Which is spectacularly cruel.' She frowned in confusion, in hope, dismay, and the kind of longing that shouldn't be in her world now. 'Am I overstating things?' she asked softly. 'Reading too much into something that's hardly had the chance to be anything? I'm finding it almost impossible to get a proper perspective on my feelings, or understanding, or anything else that's going on. All I can tell you is that now he's gone he feels like a dream, but when he was here it was as though nothing else was real.' Her eyes went to Michelle's. 'Does that sound weird?' she asked anxiously.

'No,' Michelle smiled, 'it doesn't sound weird at all.'

Josh came again the next day, and the day after that, and the day after that. He stayed only an hour or two, but during that time they talked as easily as if they'd known one another for years. Sometimes they walked on the beach, but mostly they lounged comfortably in her sitting room. They rarely took their eyes from each other, as though if they did one of them might disappear or somehow cease to be real. They shared so many stories about themselves and those they loved that Vivi felt sure they'd run out of words soon, but this never seemed to happen.

If she got tired he sat with her quietly and they listened to music, or watched wildlife videos on YouTube – his favourite, of course, but she was coming to love them too. On the only occasion her device fired – out of the blue, for she'd simply been sitting on the floor beside him browsing a selection of audio books – he'd put the iPad down and lifted her up onto the sofa. He hadn't panicked or fussed, had merely waited for her to tell him what she needed him to do.

She soon recovered, physically, but the reminder of her frailty left her shaken emotionally, and even more fearful of the future now that he was in her life. To try to help his understanding of her situation she showed him Jim Lynskey's blog, not only because she was starting to feel an affinity with the young lad waiting for a heart transplant, but because he was already living with a VAD – the dreaded yet crucial device she had to look forward to unless fate decided to take her a different route. As soon as Josh finished reading Jim's story he suggested they contact him to see if they could help with his campaign for organ donation. They did, right away, but so far they hadn't had a reply.

On the Saturday of their first week together, at Vivi's insistence, he brought his dog with him. She was thrilled to discover that Ellie, the lurcher spaniel cross, was just as he'd described her – minus an ear, vaguely cross-eyed, and willing to do just about anything Josh asked of her. Apparently an old lady from a village near Deerwood had willed her beloved pet to him, certain that no one would take better care of her than a vet.

Ellie clearly adored her new master, and Vivi adored the dog, because it was impossible not to. She was a shaggy mass of champagne-coloured fur with black and white patches around her eyes and a shyly wagging tail that speeded up impressively any time someone showed her affection – or a ball.

As well as the mutt, he brought a large wicker hamper. It contained a flask of iced tea, made from Deerwood strawberries, a small loaf of wholemeal bread, fresh that morning from the oven of a seventeen-year-old resident who'd developed a passion for baking; a summer salad from his grandfather's raised beds; two succulent free-range chicken breasts, a sliver of goat's cheese and an extremely wholesome selection of fresh berries with a blob each of his grandmother's goat's-milk yoghurt.

Vivi had no idea if he'd told his family where he was taking this delicious picnic, nor did she ask. It didn't matter, she told herself. All that did was that he was here.

The day was so warm they decided to wander over to the dunes, where he laid out a blanket, and they sat down to enjoy the sea air, wholesome food and rhythmic hum of the waves. In no time at all he was entertaining her with the latest tales of Deerwood's residents, and as she ate and drank and shared ball-throwing duties for Ellie she felt so at one with the world that she almost missed the name of his very first pet lamb.

'Steven!' she laughed, disbelievingly. 'You had a lamb called *Steven*?'

Looking offended, he said, 'I thought it was a very good name myself, and he always seemed to like it. He answered to it, anyway, and my piglets, Wonka and Bucket, absolutely understood how honoured they were to be named after such iconic characters.'

Loving every minute of this, she said, 'Do you still name all the animals?'

'Well, it's more my nephews' and niece's department these days, however the Border collie – the farm's top dog – is always called Dodgy.'

Vivi eyes sparkled. 'No, you can't,' she protested.

Appearing amazed that she had issue with it, he said, 'The Dodgy we have now is our fifth. His predecessors are all residing in Dodgy Dip, a hallowed spot on the farm where they're buried. Anyone who wants to can go and sit quietly for an hour or two to reflect on whatever they need to reflect on. The Dodgy ghosts have a way of rounding up your troubles and putting them to bed. It's very relaxing, and good for the soul.'

'So you're a regular?'

'No, but everyone tells me I should be.' Taking a couple of raspberries from the bowl he popped one into his mouth, and the other into hers, letting his fingers linger a moment on her lips.

'So why the name Dodgy?' she asked huskily, savouring his touch far more than the fruit.

He smiled. 'Apparently, when my parents took over the farm, they discovered that my great-uncle had named the sheepdog of the time Todger.'

She choked on a laugh.

'So feeling this might not be such a suitable name for children to be yelling around the countryside my father changed it to Dodger, and from there it got shortened to Dodgy. Are you comfortable there?'

'Very, thank you.'

'Good, because your elbow is carving a niche into my thigh.'

Taking the hint, she shifted onto her back and gazed dreamily up at the sky, seeing nothing but happiness.

He gazed down at her and waited for her eyes to come to his. When they did she felt her smile fading as her heartbeat faltered. She wanted him so much, so badly, and she could see that it was the same for him. She imagined him touching and kissing her, fitting the length of himself against her, pulling her in tightly . . .

He was the first to break away, releasing her from the intensity of the moment, picking up Ellie's ball and hurling it down to the beach. Vivi turned to watch the dog run and after a while, when she spotted a small boy and his father trying to fly a kite, she was able to smile.

'It's funny, isn't it,' he remarked, 'how children think their fathers can do anything, even launch a kite when there's no wind? Funnier still is the way fathers still give it a go.'

She was watching him again, and imagining him as a young boy growing up without his dad, and feeling the loneliness of it stealing through her, as it was surely stealing through him. 'Tell me about your father and what you remember of him,' she said softly.

He seemed to consider it for a moment, but in the end he said, 'Why don't you tell me about yours? You never mention him.'

Her throat dried as she closed her eyes, trying to stop his question casting a shadow on the day. But nothing could do that while they were together like this. 'I've no idea who my father is,' she replied frankly. 'My mother won't tell me; she won't even discuss it, so I've decided to try and find him for myself. Hence the DNA test Michelle mentioned at the barbecue.'

He listened quietly, his eyes moving from hers to her mouth and back again as she told him about the terrible arguments she'd had with her mother over the years; about the wondering if her father was a married man, a rapist, or one of many her mother had slept with without bothering to ask for names.

'I'm pretty sure she does know who he is,' she said, wondering what he was thinking. He was lying on his side now, his head propped on one hand as he continued to look at her in a way that seemed to see past her words, to a place she wasn't even sure about herself.

'Do you think he knows about you?' he asked.

She shook her head. 'I've no idea. If he does then he's never tried to get in touch, or not that I know of, and it hasn't actually been difficult since I left home. So maybe I should just accept that he's either dead, or not interested in me, and move on with my life. On the other hand, if he doesn't know about me . . .' She inhaled deeply. 'If he doesn't, there's nothing to say he'd want to, and is it really such a great idea to turn up on his doorstep saying, "Surprise, I'm your daughter, but don't worry I won't be around much longer, just wanted to say hi."'

Reaching out a hand, he smoothed tendrils of hair from her face, and for a moment she thought he might lean forward and kiss her. She wanted it even more than she feared it, but if he did they both knew it wouldn't stop there . . . Though they hadn't actually discussed the dangers of physical intimacy, what the adrenalin rush might do to her heart, she knew he understood and felt as wretched about it as she surely did.

Hearing someone calling her name, she turned to see Michelle wading through the marram grass towards them. 'I hope I haven't chosen a bad moment,' she grimaced, sinking down beside them.

Without looking at Josh, Vivi said, 'It's fine. Where are the children?'

'With my parents. Am I too early? I am, aren't I? We were supposed to be going into town, remember?'

Vivi hadn't forgotten, she'd simply lost track of the time.

'I should go,' Josh said, ruffling Ellie's one ear as he got to his feet. 'I'm due at the Bleasdales in an hour.'

Michelle looked up at him, squinting against the sun. 'Humphrey Bleasdale?' she asked.

He nodded. 'It's time for his horses to have their jabs. Do you know the family?'

Michelle shrugged. 'Only by name, and of course because of what happened to one of their sons. I can't recall the details now, it was quite a long time ago, but I remember it was all over the news. Did you know him?'

Josh nodded grimly. 'Yes, I did,' he replied, and throwing Ellie's ball in the direction of the car he gathered up the remains of the picnic, said a friendly farewell and left.

Michelle turned to Vivi. 'Is everything all right between you guys?' she asked curiously.

Vivi was still watching him, wondering if he'd look back and wave before driving off. 'It's strange and awful and wonderful,' she replied, 'and still so unbearably confusing that I hardly know what to think or do.'

Michelle said, 'I think it's the same for him. Have you talked about your feelings at all?'

Vivi shook her head. 'And I'm not sure that we should. It might make things even more difficult . . . But then I think, what the hell, why don't we just give in to it and be together properly? What's the worst it can do?'

Michelle's eyebrows rose in caution.

'OK, but would one kiss really be the end of me?' Vivi demanded in frustration. 'No, of course not, the trouble is it wouldn't stop there, and we both know it.'

Watching Josh trying to scoot Ellie out of the driver's seat, Michelle said, 'So tell me what you do talk about?'

Vivi was again willing him to look back. 'Everything,' she replied, 'but mostly Deerwood, I guess. Actually, I told him about my father today.'

Michelle looked interested. 'What did he say?'

Vivi shrugged. 'What could he say?' After a beat she said, 'It's odd how on one level we seem able to discuss just about anything, but on another it's like we've created barriers without even trying. I'm not just talking about our relationship and what it really is, or where it can go, there are other things we don't mention.'

'Such as?'

'Well, he knows I haven't told Mum about him, and I'm sure he hasn't discussed me with his family either.' She looked at Michelle. 'Do you know if he has?'

Michelle shook her head.

'He brought a picnic today. It was wonderful. Everything was from the farm; there was even strawberry iced tea. Someone must have wondered where he was going with it; who it was for. They might even have put it together for him.'

'Maybe they asked and he told them.'

Vivi hadn't considered that.

'Do you mind if he didn't tell them?'

Vivi pondered the question. 'I can understand why he wouldn't want to discuss me,' she said. 'I mean, how do you tell your family that you're getting involved with someone who's like me?' And they were involved, she was in no doubt about that, very much involved in fact, in ways too esoteric and even transcendent to grasp with words.

She watched him drive away and felt strangely abandoned and unsettled by his failure to look her way.

After a while Michelle said, 'Have you arranged to see him again?'

'Not yet.' For a moment she felt afraid that it wouldn't happen, that she'd just seen him for the very last time. She turned to Michelle. 'He seemed different when he left just now, or was it my imagination?'

Michelle said, 'Maybe it was my mention of Humphrey Bleasdale. Do you remember what happened? It was a long time ago. We were still at school. One of his twin sons, Matthew, was murdered.'

Vivi did remember it, but so vaguely that there were no details in her mind to give it any sort of substance.

'Maybe he was a friend of Josh's,' Michelle mused. 'They were certainly neighbours, although Matthew Bleasdale must have been at least ten or fifteen years older. Still, that might account for how distracted he seemed when he left. I probably shouldn't have brought it up.'

Vivi got to her feet and enjoyed the luxury of stretching out her limbs. 'I'm sure he'll forgive you,' she said, feeling certain he would, if that was indeed what had seemed to sober his mood. She guessed it would sober her too if she'd just been reminded, out of the blue, about a friend who'd been murdered.

CHAPTER FIFTEEN

VIVIENNE

Present Day

Josh was visibly tired – understandable after being up most of the night saving the lives of a Hereford cow and her calf – but amusement was so alive in his sleepy eyes that Vivienne had to laugh too.

'Tell me what you're finding so funny,' she challenged, as he poured more iced tea into their glasses. Though it was cooler today, they were outside on the back patio at her mother's house, protected from the rain by the tiled roof of the veranda, and enjoying the wonderfully heady scents flowing in from the gardens and nearby cliffs.

'I'm finding it interesting,' he replied, 'that you didn't Google Deerwood, but you did Google the Bleasdales and all that business so many years ago that I can hardly remember now.'

She was surprised. 'So he wasn't a friend of yours?'

He shook his head. 'For a start he was quite a bit older than me, and I'm not sure I actually met him more than a handful of times. On those that I did I never came away liking him much.'

'So do you think he *was* murdered?'

He shrugged. 'Nothing was ever proved, as far as I know, but everyone *knew* it wasn't an accident.'

She sat with that for a moment. 'So why did it seem to upset you when Michelle brought it up at the weekend?' she asked.

He regarded her in confusion. 'Did I seem upset?'

'OK, distracted.'

He shrugged. 'I know I didn't want to leave you,' he said, 'and I guess I wasn't thrilled about having to go to Dean Manor. It isn't my favourite place.' He drank deeply and put his glass down. 'Humphrey's never been the same since Matthew died and his other two sons were carted off to prison,' he explained. 'The grief and the shame were unbearable for the old chap. From what my mother and uncle tell me he was pretty widely detested back when my parents first took over Deerwood, but he changed after my father died. He found some humanity, apparently, but since his own tragedies he's been going into a steady decline. Jemmie, his wife, is . . . What is Jemmie? She's great one day, somewhere else in her head the next. Fiona, their daughter, and her husband more or less run the estate now.'

'Where are the other sons these days? Surely not still in prison?'

He grimaced. 'Not unless they've been sent back for something else since. I don't think they served very long, a couple of years at most. They visit Dean Manor from time to time with wives and children, but our paths don't often cross. I have to admit, I try to make sure they don't. I haven't forgotten the way Charlie, one of the twins, tried to drag me into whatever happened to his brother, just because I rode a motorbike. Felix, the younger brother, put a stop to it, but my mother's sure if they could have got away with it they'd have pinned something on me, to try and divert attention away from the real offender.'

'They sound so charming,' Vivi remarked drily.

His eyes shone with humour. 'Enough about them,' he declared. 'Tell me why you seemed surprised to see me today.'

It was true, she had been surprised, and now she was infuriated with herself for having allowed a horrible sense of insecurity and foreboding to dominate her weekend. 'It was just a feeling I had on Saturday,' she confessed. 'I'm not sure where it came from, but when you drove off it felt as though I was seeing you for the last time. It was so convincing that I . . .' She shrugged. 'I guess I believed it.'

Seeming bemused by that, he said, 'Well, here I am, but you're still looking . . . sad?'

Wondering how he could read her so easily, she shook her head as she said, 'Not sad, exactly, just . . .' She wasn't sure how to put this into words that wouldn't embarrass or even upset her. Maybe she shouldn't try. But with the way things were, was there any point in holding back? What did she have to lose by being as honest with him as she tried to be with herself? So with a sigh, she said, 'I'm feeling frustrated and angry that I can't do more. For your sake, as well as mine. I mean, most days I feel fine, as though I have the energy for just about anything, but every time I speak to the clinic I'm told I'm still in the recovery phase, so no to any kind of sustained physical exertion, and I've no idea how much longer this phase will go on.' Or if I'll ever come out of it, she didn't add, knowing she'd sound self-pitying if she did, which was how she was feeling.

He nodded thoughtfully, clearly taking it all in, and trying to come up with a way around it. This was typical of him, she was learning; he felt compelled to fix things, and maybe if he thought hard enough he'd come up with a way to fix her.

She was about to remind him that she wasn't his responsibility, and suggest that they change the subject, when he said, 'Why don't you tell me what you'd *like* to do?'

Her whole body seemed to open up like a flower at the first thought that came to mind. Apparently sensing it, he said quietly, 'Yeah, that's top of my list too.' He held her eyes, letting the desire build itself to full force as it used their minds to bring their bodies together. She could almost feel him wrapping himself around her, pulling her to him, using his hands, his mouth, all of him to take her to the places she longed to go.

In the end, he said, gruffly, 'So now we've got number one on our bucket lists established, what else is on yours?'

Wanting nothing more than to stay with number one, to make it real and never let go, she somehow made herself turn away and gazed out at the tiered, rock-strewn garden. Trying to put her thoughts in a different order was almost impossible, when making love with him was such a present and overpowering need.

In the end, she said, rashly, to break the mood, 'I'd like to do a sky dive. Or climb Kilimanjaro. Hang-gliding looks fun. Have you ever done it?'

'Not for a long time,' he replied, 'but aren't you being a bit extreme?'

Her eyes sparkled mischievously. 'Are you saying I'm not allowed to dream?'

He broke into a smile. 'OK, if it's dreams you want,' he said, 'let's go for it. The world's your oyster, anything's possible, so apart from ravishing me, what would you really like to do, and where would you like to go?'

Getting tangled up in the ravishing again, she sighed as she looked at him, and laughed to see the way he was watching her. 'I feel like none of my thoughts are private,' she chided. 'You see right through me.'

'If that's true then I'm going to guess that provided you could always spend your nights with me, you'd fill up your days working for world peace, and ending animal cruelty.'

Spend all her nights with him. The words dizzied her, as the idea of it carried her straight into the dreams she didn't dare to have. 'Actually, I hadn't got to those points yet,' she told him, shakily, 'and the second one's definitely yours. However, I have no problem supporting it, or with sharing my list.' She swallowed, and tried to make herself think straight. 'I'd also,' she said, 'like to raise a shedload of money to help Jim Lynskey's organ-donation campaign . . .'

'Have you heard from him?'

She shook her head. 'I messaged again today, but still no word.'

'Then we should up our efforts to find out where he is.'

'I'm hoping it's in hospital receiving a new heart.'

He nodded agreement. 'Let's tell ourselves that, until

we find out otherwise,' he advised. 'So now, go on with your list.'

Picking up again, she said, 'OK, I'd make the whole world understand the psychology of animals the way you do; I'd go waterskiing around Lake Como with my brother, who FaceTimed me from there this morning; I'd persuade you to take me to South Africa for a safari; I'd get to know as much about music as you do . . .'

He laughed.

'What?'

'I hardly know anything,' he protested.

'You know more than me, and you play the guitar, which I've yet to hear, by the way.'

His eyebrows rose. 'Who told you that?'

'Michelle, of course. She says you and Sam are pretty passable when you've had a few, less so when you're taking yourselves seriously.'

He raised a lofty eyebrow. 'I'll have you know I played Glastonbury once.'

She was immediately sceptical. 'Yeah, OK,' she responded, drawing out the words.

'I swear it's true. I was about nineteen, and we played the New Bands Tent. It's called the John Peel Stage now. We didn't get booed off, but we didn't get signed up by a mega producer either, or any producer come to that, nor were we invited back again.'

Wishing that she could have seen it, she said, 'If we're still going to Michelle and Sam's this evening, will you play? For me? Before you say no, it's just gone to the top of my bucket list, so I don't think a negative reply is an option.'

'That's blackmail,' he protested.

'Yep, so I win. You and Sam will play for us this evening and I promise to swoon.'

Looking as though he'd enjoy that, he said, 'It's a deal. Now, back to the rest of your bucket list. Are you sure you've mentioned everything?'

She tried to remember what she'd said. 'I think so, for the moment. Can I add things later if I think they should be on it?'

'You mean like finding your father?'

Her eyes widened in surprise at herself. 'Of course that's on the list too,' she insisted. It was funny, she thought, how the search for her father didn't seem so important now. Or, it did, but it definitely hadn't featured at the top of her list the way it would have a week ago. However, her list was just a random jumble of dreams, most with no hope of ever being fulfilled, and with him sitting right there it was hard for her focus to be reliable.

Later that evening, after a delicious dinner prepared by Michelle, and a hectic bath night with the children that Vivi and Josh somehow directed, Josh and Sam sat down to play their guitars. Josh explained that they were performing some South African jazz and fusion numbers that he'd taught Sam soon after his return. Vivi had never heard any of the songs before, and she didn't always understand the language, but the melodies, the unusual assonance and haunting riffs were so soulful and hypnotic that she felt herself caught up in soothing wave after wave of musical sensation.

The English lyrics came from a Jonathan Butler classic, 'Do You Love Me?' The way Josh didn't take his eyes from hers as he sang the words, as he conveyed the question and the meaning through the very tone of his voice, filled her with more feeling, more love and longing than she could possibly bear. It was as though Michelle and Sam were no longer there. She couldn't even be sure at what point Sam put the track on a speaker and took Michelle off to bed, leaving her and Josh to dance in the moonlight. She only knew that the sensations of his arms around her, his legs hard against hers, his desire as palpable as her own, were making it feel as though his strong heart was somehow capable of beating for them both.

Vivienne was lying on the sofa in her sitting room.

She'd spent the last two days in hospital undergoing an exhaustive reassessment of her condition, following three ICD shocks in quick succession. In the end, to her overwhelming relief, they'd once again decided against implanting a VAD, but she'd been advised that if her heart continued to require such regular electrical stimulus to keep it going they'd be forced to take that next step. Meanwhile, they'd administered a two-day-long infusion of inotropes, and upped the oral medication she could take home with her. It was still too early to know how she was going to cope with their side effects, either mentally or physically. What she did know was that she felt so emotionally shattered by the reminder of her failing state that it was only the thought of Josh and the need to see him that had made her determined to come home.

He'd called and texted regularly since Michelle had told him she'd been taken to hospital, and she knew he'd have come right away if she'd asked him to. But it wouldn't have been the right time to tell her mother about him, not when Gina was so fearful already, so Vivi had asked him to send her funny texts and emails to keep her up to date with the events of his day. He had, and with each message he'd sent he'd made her laugh and gasp and love him more and more.

Now he was here, sitting cross-legged on the floor in front of her and making her feel stronger just by being there.

'Are you hurting?' he asked, seeming to think that she might be.

As she almost smiled she wondered if her blue, dry lips were somehow rosier by now, less alarming than the last time she'd looked. 'Not in the sense you're meaning it,' she replied.

Nothing had happened with her device since she'd come home, no shocks at all, only her doing her best to rescue herself from an encroaching despair and depression. It was hard to see the point of anything when there really wasn't a point, unless it was to make him happy, but being in the state she was, how was she ever going to do that?

'You should go,' she whispered hoarsely.

He didn't answer, simply crooked an eyebrow, as though saying he knew she didn't mean that.

'Josh, we – *I* – have to stop pretending,' she made herself say. 'People wait years for new hearts and I don't have years . . .'

'Are you asking me to give up on the time we do have?' he asked, his tone telling her that he expected more of her.

Her eyes closed, not because she was tired, but

290

because she needed to stop looking at him, it made her want him too much.

'Tell me what you're thinking,' he said softly.

His words floated into her mind, curious and caring and seeming to loosen the innate sense of self-protection that would have prevented her old self from speaking the truth. She was different now. She understood that she needed to say it all while she still could, because in the next hour, the next day, the next month it would be too late, and she wanted him to know everything.

'I'm thinking,' she said, 'that you make me feel happier and more loved than I've ever felt in my life, than I even knew it was possible to feel.' A tear rolled onto her cheek and dropped onto the hand beneath her face. 'You just make me happy,' she added hoarsely.

'This is you being happy?' he teased.

She had to smile. There was more, so much more, and reaching for his hand she drew it to her heart. 'This is the weakest part of me,' she said softly, feeling the warmth of his palm through her shirt, 'but that's only the muscle. You make the rest of it the strongest part of me, and I don't know what to do about it. I only know that this is the heart that loves you, that is glad you've come into my life in spite of the terrible timing, and even if a donor does come along I don't want to lose any part of myself that loves you.'

She saw her words reach him, almost felt their impact as their joined hands absorbed the faint pulsing of her heart, the blood flowing into it carrying all her feelings with it. She took one breath and then another, afraid to let the moment go, afraid to stay with it.

Bringing her hand to his mouth he kissed it, and she

suddenly needed the feel of him against her the way it had happened when they'd danced. But if she gave into it again, if she were to feel that same potency of desire, the build-up of adrenalin that had apparently been too much for her heart the last time . . .

'We should take Ellie for a walk,' she said, needing to distract herself.

'Are you sure?' he asked, frowning.

She nodded. It wasn't her energy that was low as much as her spirits, but being with him was already helping, and she needed to get out.

Minutes later they were strolling hand in hand through the marram grass down to the beach, with Ellie racing on ahead in pursuit of her ball.

'I had a message from Jim Lynskey today,' she told him. 'He's been in hospital too, but it wasn't for a transplant. He developed an infection around the drive-line leading into his heart.'

'How is he?'

'Better, but still in hospital. He's hoping to go home tomorrow.'

They walked on quietly, each with their own thoughts, hers mainly on the twenty-one-year-old whom she'd never met, and yet felt connected to in a way that made her want a new heart for him almost as much as for herself. It was as though he was just a few steps ahead of her, showing her what it was going to be like living with a VAD, the good days and the bad, and the desperate need to make people understand the importance of being a donor – not only for him, but for everyone whose lives could be so dramatically improved or even saved. That was his mission.

'I have something to ask you,' Josh said, breaking into her thoughts.

She tried to rein in her imagination, to keep her mind blank until she'd heard the question, but it wasn't easy when there was so much she wanted to ask him too. In the end, when he didn't go on, she told him, 'You're keeping me in suspense.'

Stopping, he turned to her and said, 'Will you come to Deerwood at the weekend?'

It wasn't what she'd expected, it hadn't even crossed her mind; nevertheless, sensing how very much it meant to him, she found it lighting her up inside. 'I'd love to,' she said, and as he wrapped her in his arms, his lips pressed to her forehead, she felt elated and loved and afraid of how his mother and the rest of his family were going to react to her, for who in their right minds would ever wish someone in her condition onto someone they loved? They would want so much more for him, and the truth was, she did too.

CHAPTER SIXTEEN
SHELLEY

Present Day

Shelley was mucking out stalls in the barn, only half listening to a dozen or so sheep bleating a backing track to 'Isn't She Lovely' on Radio Two as she worked. Her mind was more focused on a couple of newcomers in the residents' block and Hanna's suspicion that they were trying to push drugs. It was a recurring problem, unfortunately. However, Tom Bakerson, a retired DCI from Kesterly, was always willing to come and help out with one of his stern talkings-to when the need arose. They often did the trick, which made Shelley smile, for Tom's stern talkings-to regularly came her way too, but she was less in awe of him than the youngsters. And fond as she was of him, which was actually very fond, she really didn't feel inclined to get married again. Their 'friendship with benefits' as Hanna and Zoe had drolly dubbed it, worked very well the way it was, thank you very much.

If she'd been paying more attention to what was going on around her she'd have registered the ovine accompaniment getting louder and less harmonious, but it wasn't until Josh was in front of her that she picked up on the excitement. Their very own rock star had come to pay a visit, and the silly old girls were falling all over themselves to get noticed.

Smiling as he fed his fans with alfalfa leaves, she said, 'So to what do we owe this pleasure?' They didn't usually see him in the barn on weekdays unless one of the animals was sick, and as far as she knew none was, at the moment.

Before he could answer Bessie the fat-bellied Gloucester Old Spot came snorting and barrelling towards him, four squealing piglets stumbling along after her, and he dutifully fussed the old sow about the ears, sending her into a frenzy of porcine pleasure.

Shelley was about to hand him a tin bowl of peelings for the pigs, when he scooped up one of the piglets to check his hind legs. They'd been splayed at birth, causing some concern, but the tape Josh had carefully wound around his hips certainly seemed to be helping.

'You're doing pretty well,' he told the tiny creature, holding it nose to nose. 'I think we can have that harness off in the next couple of days,' and putting him down, he took the scraps from his mother to stifle Bossy Bessie's demanding grunts for treats.

'So,' Shelley said, still watching him as she pulled off her rubber gloves and enjoyed the feeling of fresh air on her work-worn hands. 'You're here because . . . ?'

'Because,' he said, watching the pigs trot off back to their open-plan sty, 'there's something I need to tell you.'

When his eyes didn't come to hers, Shelley's abiding fear that he was leaving Deerwood again sprang into life. Of course she understood that his ambitions for himself might well take him away from the farm, and she wanted nothing more than to see him happy, but the years he'd spent at uni and then overseas hadn't been easy for her. She'd missed him terribly, almost as much as she'd missed Jack in the early years, and she dreaded going through it again. However, this couldn't be about her, she reminded herself firmly. It had to be about him, and whatever he wanted to do she would find it in herself to support him.

'Don't worry,' he said drily, 'I'm not going back to South Africa.'

She had to smile. He might have a gift for reading minds, as well as sensing her moods, but in this instance he knew very well that his return to the wild was always her biggest dread. 'Well, now we have that out of the way,' she said, relieved beyond measure, 'I'm ready for the good news.'

'What makes you so sure it's good?'

She shrugged. 'It's written all over you,' she replied teasingly. She was making it up, for in truth she couldn't tell what he was thinking – his inscrutability could be doubly annoying considering how easily he read everyone else. 'I'm going to guess you've found a hippo,' she ventured.

He laughed, though she knew he had no recall of the 'sighting' he'd made with his father when he was four, but she'd teased him about it often enough to turn it into a shared memory for them. She plonked herself down on a solid hay bale, wincing at a pain in her hip, and gestured for him to take the bale opposite. 'I'm all yours,' she informed him, loving having him to herself for a few minutes.

As he sat, a particularly devoted ewe rested her face

on his shoulder, and he idly stroked her as he said, in a tone that really got his mother's attention, 'I've met someone.'

She sparkled inside. This was what she'd been hoping to hear for so long, and since the girl was probably local, given the picnics and frequent absences, she was eager for him to continue.

'She's pretty special,' he said softly, 'and I . . . Well, frankly, I haven't felt like this about anyone before.' He flicked a look her way. 'Corny?'

She only smiled.

'She's a lawyer,' he said, 'bright, beautiful, funny . . .' He took a breath and Shelley could tell that he was seeing her in his mind's eye and didn't want to let the image go. 'She's a lot of things that make her different,' he continued, 'and special and someone I want to be with all the time.' Then he added, 'I think if Dad were here he'd understand what I'm saying, because I'm sure that's how he felt about you. You were his everything, and that's what Vivienne is for me.'

Touched that he should feel that way about her and Jack, Shelley might have said so had she not sensed there was more, and that it might not be as straightforward as he'd like it to be. 'Do I get to meet her?' she prompted tentatively.

He nodded. 'I've invited her to come on Saturday, if that's OK?'

Relieved, and delighted, she said, 'Of course it is. I'll look forward to it. We all will.'

He rolled his eyes. 'The *entire* Deerwood clan might be too much for a first meeting, so if we can keep it to family . . .'

'Well, of course family. I'm not suggesting all the residents should come along too. Anyway, most of them have signed up for a coach trip to Salisbury Plain on Saturday, meaning it'll be quieter than usual around here, so your timing is good. Shall we do a barbecue? Lunch? Dinner? What are you thinking?'

'Probably early afternoon and a barbecue will be great, but there's something you need to know about her . . .' He took a breath and held it.

She's married, shot straight to the front of Shelley's mind, but she said nothing, simply waited.

'There's no easy way of saying it,' he decided, 'so I'll come right out with it. She has a terminal heart condition.'

Shelley slowly froze, certain she hadn't heard correctly, while knowing from his expression and his tone that she had. She continued to stare at him, unable for the moment to find any words, or to grasp a full and dreadful understanding of what this was going to mean for him.

'I had to tell you,' he said, 'because of her diet and sometimes her energy . . .'

'How . . . when did you meet her?' Shelley interrupted.

'A few weeks ago at Sam's. She's Michelle's best friend.'

Shelley nodded, though she wasn't really taking it in. Her son, her beautiful, talented, insanely eligible boy who could have anyone he wanted, had fallen in love with a girl who was dying. How could she be happy for that? How could any mother? It was going to break his heart.

Looking at him, she could see now that it already was. His pain, his helplessness, and all the terrible feelings that must go with loving someone he already knew he was going to lose, were etched all over him.

'Oh Josh,' she murmured, and going to him, she took one of his hands in hers and held it tight. 'How long does she have?' she asked.

'We're not sure. Maximum a year, unless they find a new heart for her.'

'And will they?'

'No one knows.'

Realizing he had all his hopes invested in that one terrifyingly unpredictable scenario, she slipped an arm round him and pulled his head to her shoulder.

'I have to ask this,' she said softly, 'as your mother and someone who knows you so well. Are you sure this isn't . . .'

'Don't go there, Mum,' he cautioned. 'I swear, it isn't about rescuing her, though God knows I wish I could. I'm a vet, not a doctor, or a miracle worker. The way I feel about her . . .' He broke off, apparently done with trying to put all his complicated emotions into words.

'Does she feel the same about you?' she asked tenderly.

'Yes, she does.' After a while he said, 'Tell me this, if you'd known at the outset that you were going to lose Dad when he was so young, would you still have married him?'

Shelley's eyes closed as she considered the question, in spite of already knowing the answer. 'Of course,' she whispered. 'The time I had with him would always be better than no time at all.'

He swallowed hard. 'That's how I feel about Vivienne.'

She absorbed the words and their beautiful, but tragic meaning and rested her head against his. 'Then we must do everything in our power, to make her – to make you both – as happy as we can, for as long as we can.'

CHAPTER SEVENTEEN

VIVIENNE

Present Day

'You're looking rather lovely,' Gina commented, as Vivienne came into the kitchen wearing a strappy floral dress that showed her lightly tanned shoulders and floated airily about her skinny knees. She'd also defined her eyes with mascara, coated her lips with a pale pink gloss, and her still-damp blonde locks were drying into random, lively waves.

Glancing up from the text she was reading, Vivi couldn't hold back her smile when she saw the sparkle of a tease in her mother's eyes.

'I'm just wondering when you're going to tell me about him?' Gina prompted wryly.

Though Vivi's impulse was to feign puzzlement, the fact that her mother didn't appear to have an issue with there being someone special made her realize how much she wanted to confide in her. 'He's wonderful,' she tried not to gush, but she felt such a rush of happiness that she almost sobbed on the relief and joy of being able to say it.

Gina came to hug her, saying, 'I wouldn't have expected him to be anything else.' Pulling back, she

301

looked searchingly into Vivi's eyes. 'Does he know about . . . ?'

'Yes, he does. He has from the start and . . .' She took a breath at the feel of an unsteady beat in her heart. *Not now. Please, please not now,* she implored, dreading that her ICD was about to go off. But it had never given a warning before, it just fired volts straight into her, and it wasn't unusual to feel a slight tremor now and again. So she took another breath and made herself move past it. 'I can't say my condition doesn't make a difference,' she admitted, 'because obviously it does, but it's not getting in the way . . . I mean, it is . . . Well, we don't . . . He understands that we can't, but . . .' Her eyes shone with incredulous laughter as she said, 'For some reason that seems to make us even closer.'

Clearly surprised and relieved to hear it, Gina said, 'I'm guessing he's someone you met at Sam and Michelle's?'

Vivi nodded. 'His name's Josh and he's . . . Did I tell you he's wonderful?'

Laughing, Gina returned to the shopping list she'd been making when Vivi came in. 'So do I get to meet him at some point?' she asked.

'Of course. And I know you'll love him every bit as much as I do. In fact, he should be here any minute, so you'll see I'm right. He's taking me to meet his family today.'

Gina looked up. 'Hence the pretty dress and make-up. Well, like I said, you look lovely, better than I've seen you in a while, so he's obviously having a good effect. Where does his family live?'

'They have a farm about fifteen miles inland. Actually, it's more than just a farm, it's a kind of community, really. You might have heard of it, or read about it in the paper. It's called Deerwood.'

Gina went very still, and as the colour began draining from her face she seemed to stop breathing. 'No,' she said shakily. 'No, you can't . . .' She was so agitated she seemed unaware of what she was saying or doing, and Vivi could only stare at her in bemusement.

'Mum? What . . . ?'

Gina was shaking her head, putting a hand to it and saying, 'No. You can't go there. You . . .'

'Don't be ridiculous,' Vivi protested.

'You *can't*.' Gina looked around, seeming distressed and disoriented, as though she'd lost the sense of where she was or what she'd been doing. 'Gil,' she murmured, 'I need to speak to Gil,' and to Vivi's amazement she suddenly snatched up her bag, ran out to the car, and drove away.

By the time Josh arrived ten minutes later, Vivi had received so many texts from the GaLs and Michelle wishing her good luck for today that her mother's odd behaviour was no longer at the front of her mind. She wasn't even going to think about the vague suspicion she'd held for some time that Gina had a problem where Deerwood was concerned, because whatever it was, Vivi had no intention of allowing it to spoil today. Instead, she simply melted into his embrace. Josh's dark, expressive eyes showed how much he was loving the way she looked, and how much today was meaning to him too.

As they drove out of town, heading into the country-side, they kept glancing at one another and smiling, while curling their fingers more tightly together. Even Ellie seemed excited as she whined and panted and grinned for all she was worth in the back.

'I'll introduce everyone when we get there,' he told Vivi, 'but don't worry about remembering all their names. What's important to them, and to me, is that they know who you are.'

Amused by how straightforward it was seeming to him, and determined not to give in to her nerves, she said, 'Have you told them about me? I mean about my heart.'

'Yes, and you don't need to worry. My mother under-stands how I feel about you, and she accepts that whatever time we have together matters far more than anything else.'

Vivi swallowed drily. Was his mother just saying that because she'd realized it was what he wanted to hear, and that he probably wouldn't tolerate any other kind of response? She guessed she'd find out soon enough. 'Have you ever taken anyone to meet them before?' she asked, accepting that she was likely to be weighed up for comparison if he had.

His eyebrows arched. 'Once or twice, but not since I've been back from South Africa.'

'Does that mean you haven't been involved with anyone in all that time?'

'No, it just means that there hasn't been anyone I've wanted to take home.' He laughed. 'I hope you're not going to end up regretting the experience; there are so many of us, and my nieces and nephews can be pretty full on. I include my cousin, Perry's, children in that, because his are probably the noisiest.'

'What about the residents? Will they be there?'

'Some will be around, I'm sure, but most have gone on a day trip to Salisbury Plain.'

'And your sister Zoe is still in California?'

'She is, and my aunt Kat will be running the Farmer's Table, which is what we call the shop, but she's going to close up early today so she won't miss out on meeting you.'

Vivi looked at him again, and as he lifted her fingers to his lips she let go of her nerves and allowed the moment to become all about them. She could feel the most wonderful fluttering sensations in her heart, and knowing they were wholly emotional and nothing to be afraid of she brought his hand to her lips too, and kissed each of his fingertips in turn. The eroticism of this small intimacy was as powerful as anything she'd felt before, maybe even more so, and it almost made her fearful of what it might be like if they really could make love.

Maybe it would happen one day, maybe her recovery would progress far enough for her to risk it, for it even to be approved – certainly it had happened for others. She'd read about it online: in some cases it was recommended as gentle exercise, with the emphasis on gentle, and a reducer of stress, so she wasn't giving up hope. But it wasn't going to happen today, so she turned to watch the passing fields and hedgerows, so vivid and inviting in the summer sunshine that she felt she could drink them in for ever.

'This is where our land begins,' he told her, as he

edged the Land Rover over a narrow crossroads and began driving through a new swathe of meadows that looked very like the ones they'd just passed through.

'Are they your sheep?' she asked, spotting a few fat creamy bundles in a nearby field.

'They are,' he confirmed. 'I'm not sure where all the others are, but they'll be meandering around somewhere.'

'What about the horses? Are they yours?'

He glanced in the direction she was pointing and said, 'Those two are Hanna's, she's a keen showjumper, and there are six more who stable with us. Presumably they're out with their owners, or back at the farm.'

'Along with all the pigs, goats, chickens and . . . What else do you have?'

'Geese, ducks, ponies, guinea pigs, and whatever else my nieces and nephews have recently rescued. They're big on rescue – I guess it runs in the family, because they actively go out looking for any living thing that might be in distress, insects included. Actually, we have a real live Bambi with us at the moment, unless Nate returned him to his mother this morning. She's been waiting in the woods nearby since we brought him in. Poor thing got hit by a car. The woman who ran into him rang the RSPCA, who contacted me, so we were able to get to him in time. OK, here we are,' he announced, and turning in through a gateless entrance with a Deerwood Farm and Shop sign to one side and a table of fresh fruit and veg the other, he waved out to the youngsters manning the stall and started along a narrow winding track.

Aware of her nerves returning, Vivi covered his hand on the gearstick and took several quiet breaths. She couldn't remember ever feeling so apprehensive, or aware of the stark reality of her situation trying to close in on her. There was a fleeting moment recalling her mother's bizarre agitation when she and Vivi had passed through here, but then it was gone again. In its place was only him and this incredible, almost surreal small village they were passing through . . .

'The three red-brick buildings on the left,' Josh explained, 'are where the residents stay, if they're not camping out somewhere else on the farm. Then we have the artisan centre coming up on the right, where just about anything happens from carpentry, to rope-making, to blacksmithing, to pottery . . . Name the trade, it probably goes on in there at some point. There's a small gym on the mezzanine, and a basketball court at the back. Next we have the studio for those who are interested in painting, dancing, singing, basically anything to do with the arts. They put on plays or concerts, attend lectures or debates . . . The stone barn next to it is where my grandparents live, at the far end, and Hanna and her family are spread out around the rest of it. Beyond that is the main barn, with all its attendant coops, sties, pens and sheds – and right ahead of you is the farmhouse.'

As Vivienne looked at it she could feel herself all but melting into its midsummer beauty. It seemed so settled and welcoming in the heart of its full-blooming sunflowers and hollyhocks, with climbing jasmine crowding white window frames and cascades of petunias and fuchsias overflowing their hanging baskets. The rose-covered porch arched over a half-open stable door, and as they drew closer she made out a small sign, written in a child's hand, saying, Granny's House.

'Of course it's at its best right now,' Josh remarked drily as she turned to him, enchantment glowing in her eyes. He grinned and got out of the car, and leaving his door open for Ellie to follow he came around to the other side. 'Are you ready for this?' he murmured, slipping his hands round her waist, apparently wanting to help her down.

Not at all sure she was now they were here, she allowed him to lift her to the ground, and felt strangely as though she was landing in the middle of a dream. She closed her eyes in an effort to centre herself, and felt his hand touch her neck as he said, 'It'll be fine, I promise. They're going to love you.'

For no reason she could think of, she was suddenly afraid and even ashamed of what she was bringing to Josh's life. No matter what his mother had said, she was unlikely to feel happy about it, but for his sake she, and the rest of his family, were going to welcome her to their home and pretend that everything was just as it should be.

Tilting her face up to his, he said, more firmly, 'It's going to be fine.'

She wasn't sure why that gave her courage, but it did, slightly, and as some of her nerves faded the bottom half of the farmhouse door suddenly crashed open and a boisterous Border collie hurled itself at Josh.

Spinning the dog away from Vivi before it knocked her over, he said, 'This is Dodgy. He has unusual manners, but he's very good at doing as he's told,' and holding up a hand he said, 'Dodgy, this is Vivienne. Please say hello.'

To Vivi's amazement Dodgy turned to her, tilted his head to one side and gave a small bark as he raised a paw. Taking it, she shook it politely. 'Hello, Dodgy, I'm very pleased to meet you.'

Dodgy's tongue lolled as he panted with pleasure.

'Please don't let's do any master/owner analogies here,' Josh muttered. To the dog he said, 'Find Ellie,' and Dodgy was instantly shepherding a worried-looking Ellie to Josh's side.

As they walked around the outside of the house to the back garden Vivi could hear voices and was aware of her heart hammering in an unnerving way. Apparently sensing it, Josh's hand tightened on hers and she tried to pull herself together. Her condition didn't make her less of a person, she must remember that, and stop assuming that people would even think it.

At first no one noticed the newcomers, they were all too busy chatting and drinking wine under an enormous vine-covered gazebo where the table was laden with so many dishes and bottles it was barely possible to see the white linen cloth underneath. She glanced about the garden and was instantly charmed by its vivid colours and meandering lawn, by the children playing in a large paddling pool beneath the protective branches of an old cedar tree, while a lamb and a goat slept peacefully beside a rocky outcrop.

'Uncle Josh!' a child's voice suddenly squealed, and Vivi watched as a small boy, as naked as the day he'd been born, raced from under cover of a weeping willow and screamed in protest as Josh pretended to run away.

An older woman with beautiful grey eyes got to her feet and came to join them as Josh swept the boy up and gave him a playful shake. 'Vivienne, how lovely,' she exclaimed throatily, and Vivi knew right away that she was Josh's mother. She was tall and curvy with an abundance of silvery hair tumbling from a loose bun at the nape of her neck, and though she had to be in her sixties the only real telltale sign of her age and occupation showed in her weather-beaten hands. Smiling in welcome, she clasped Vivi into a hug, and when she murmured, 'I'm Shelley, and I promise the only one who bites around here is my son,' Vivi knew instinctively that their shared loved of Josh was all they needed to understand one another.

'Come and meet everyone,' Shelley insisted, and tucking Vivi's hand through her arm she led her to the table, where everyone was starting to get up.

'No, please don't,' Vivi protested.

Sinking back down, a forty-something woman with a shock of reddish-brown hair and blue-grey eyes gave a casual wave as she said, 'Hi, I'm Hanna, Josh's sister. It's lovely to meet you. The noisy offspring are mostly mine, but we try to ignore them so please feel free to do the same. I'm sorry my husband's not here – he's in Brussels this weekend – but he asked me to say hi on his behalf.'

'Hanna's husband is a consultant editor for a weekly news magazine,' Shelley explained. 'They met when Martin first came here to interview us about Deerwood, thirteen years ago, and he never quite left.' Continuing around the table, she said, 'This is my brother-in-law, Nate; my mother, Patty, and dad, George. The handsome devil over there is David, my father-in-law. Next to him is the other handsome devil of the family, Perry, and then we have Perry's wife, Selma, who, as you can see, might just get carted off to the maternity ward before the day is out.'

'Unless, like you,' Perry added, 'she decides to give birth halfway down the drive.'

'That was Josh,' Shelley informed Vivi. 'He never could wait for anything, so his dad was forced to bring him into the world before we could even get to the main road, which is kind of about right for my son, to be birthed by a vet. Now, what would you like to drink? We have some delicious iced tea made from Deerwood summer berries, or you can try our home-made plum and ginger smoothie, ingredients also from Deerwood. There's wine, which you might prefer, but I'll leave that up to you. Do sit down. Anywhere is fine. Josh, pull up a chair.'

In what felt like no time at all Vivi was laughing at the family banter, understanding that much of it was a show especially for her, particularly when it came to embarrassing stories about Josh. Although it was clear he wished they'd stop, she kept squeezing his hand to let him know that nothing, not even his very worst escapades, could make her do anything but love him more.

'Ah, Tom,' Josh announced, getting to his feet as a distinguished-looking, casually dressed older man came out of the kitchen door to join them. 'Vivi, meet Tom Bakerson, my stepfather in waiting.'

'Don't you ever do subtle?' Shelley groaned, as Vivi shook Tom's outstretched hand.

'I'm a patient man,' Tom declared, giving a wave to the table at large as he sat down next to Shelley. 'Are we barbecuing?' he asked.

'About to light up,' Nate assured him, and passing Tom a beer from a cold bucket at his feet, he ambled off to start the honours.

Soon they were eating, and Vivi began to suspect that almost everything had been prepared with her in mind, from the abundance of fresh salads coated in all the right oils, to a luscious avocado and salmon salsa, to the organic burgers and sausages that came from the grill. It was so delicious and wholesome that she wondered if she ought to ask Shelley's mother for a heart-friendly diet to post online.

By now she was on her third berry tea, and close to feeling intoxicated on the atmosphere alone as Shelley said, 'Tell us about your family, Vivienne. Do you have any brothers and sisters?'

'I have a half-brother, Mark,' she replied. 'He's touring Italy with some friends from uni at the moment. My mother is a hairdresser in town.'

'Do we know her?' Selma asked, biting into a chocolate-dipped strawberry. 'Some of us do go on occasion, although you might not believe it looking at us now.'

Laughing, Vivi said, 'She has The Salon on the . . .'

'The Salon?' Shelley exclaimed excitedly. 'Of course we know her. Gina Hamilton. I mean, we don't *know* her, but she donates regularly to our residency programme, and she even sends stylists out to give some free training now and again.'

Surprised that her mother hadn't mentioned this, which made her reaction to the mention of Deerwood this morning even more baffling, Vivi wasn't sure what to say.

'She's the best hairdresser in town,' Patty declared knowledgeably. 'I go to her all the time and look at me. I'm eighty-five and she makes me look like a supermodel.'

As the others laughed, Vivi twinkled as she said, 'I'll be sure to tell her.'

'She's so beautiful herself,' Patty commented, gazing fondly at Vivi. 'And so are you, my dear, *very* beautiful . . .'

'Mum,' Shelley groaned.

'I'm just saying,' Patty retorted.

Josh said, 'So why don't we stop embarrassing her and carry on embarrassing ourselves instead? Hanna, your turn.'

Throwing a napkin at him, Hanna asked, 'Has he told you, Vivi, why he has a flat in town?'

Turning to him, Vivi said, 'No, not really.'

'For God's sake,' Josh protested, throwing out his hands.

'It's because,' Hanna informed her, 'our female residents tend to develop crushes on him. We've even had them breaking into the house when he's here, desperate to get hold of him.'

'It's true,' Selma insisted, clearly enjoying the moment.

'And she needs to know this because?' Josh demanded.

Wading in to the rescue, Patty turned the subject back to Italy, and soon more stories were being told about family holidays around Europe, until the children decided to join in and it became all about them.

Vivi had been there for almost three hours before the first waves of tiredness came over her in a dreamy, restful sort of way. Josh moved in to put an arm around her so she could lean on him, and she thought she might have drifted off for a few minutes, because the next thing she knew the table was being cleared.

'Oh, please, let me help,' she tried to insist, and she would have jumped to her feet had Josh not held her back, seeming to realize that the sudden movement would dizzy her.

'It's OK,' Hanna chided softly, 'we can manage.'

'Unless you'd like to see my new kitchen,' Shelley invited with a playful waggle of her eyebrows.

'You should,' Patty urged. 'It's quite state of the art, circa 1990.'

'That's mean,' Shelley scolded. 'Just because it looks the same doesn't mean it *is* the same. The ovens and worktops are new, so are all the handles, and we now have soft close cupboards and drawers. We didn't have anything like that back in the day.'

Vivi was smiling, thinking still of Josh making his first appearance halfway down the drive, straight into his father's arms . . . Touched by how meaningful that was, she turned to look at him and smiled deeply into his eyes.

'What are you thinking?' he murmured, brushing the hair from her face.

'That this has been a perfect day. I love your family and the farm. I feel I could stay here for ever.'

As his lips touched her forehead, he whispered, 'We're being watched.'

Vivi turned to find Vicky, Hanna's six-year-old, staring at them with frank curiosity. 'Hello,' Vivi said with a smile.

Vicky swung herself from side to side, her big eyes

still fixed on Vivi as her pink ruched swimsuit dripped water onto the patio, and her fair hair ran small rivulets onto her neck. 'You're pretty,' she stated, as if just coming to a conclusion.

Vivi smiled. 'Thank you. So are you.'

Vicky nodded, signalling she already knew that. 'Are you going to marry Uncle Josh?' she asked.

As Josh gulped, Hanna growled from the kitchen, 'Vicky!' Her tone made it clear she'd overheard.

'Are you?' Vicky persisted.

Josh said, 'Tell you what, why don't you let me do the asking?'

Vicky nodded and waited.

Vivi had to laugh.

'Not now!' Josh protested.

Unperturbed, Vicky stayed where she was, apparently fascinated by Vivienne, until her mother reappeared and shoved half a dozen ice lollies into her hands. 'Go and share them out,' Hanna instructed, 'and don't come back for at least half an hour.'

As she watched the little girl skip away, Vivi felt the sadness of all that she and Josh could never share overwhelming her. She swallowed hard on the emotions and stared at her phone, too upset for the moment to look elsewhere.

Josh said, 'Why don't we go for a walk?'

Bolstering herself, she said, 'Good idea. I haven't met all the animals yet.'

As they got to their feet, Patty handed Josh a large empty platter. 'Take this in with you,' she said, 'and help yourselves to an ice cream on your way through. They're in the freezer in the utility room.'

315

Scooping up a handful of plates to clear away, Vivi followed Josh through the open door, and was blinded for a moment as her eyes adjusted to the sudden change of light. When they did she was as impressed by the kitchen, where Shelley was loading the dishwasher, as she was by everything else she'd seen that day. It had everything a self-respecting farmhouse kitchen should have, from the Aga, to the flagstones, to the abundance of dried herbs and battered pans hanging high from a square rack over the table. There were even granite worktops and a hand pump next to the vast inglenook fireplace, to bring water up from the well, Shelley explained.

'You have a well!' Vivi cried, impressed.

'No,' Shelley confessed, and they laughed.

As Josh went for ice cream Vivi put down the plates and looked around again, until her eyes reached the family portrait over the sideboard. The man at the centre of the group was so like Josh it could almost have been him.

'It was done from a photo,' Shelley explained, coming to stand beside her. 'Josh was four at the time it was taken.'

'He's so gorgeous,' Vivi smiled, trying not to think of how their son would look if they could have one. Just like this adorable, curly-headed little boy with wide blue eyes and an impish grin that would light any mother's heart. 'And the image of his dad,' she said.

'He is,' Shelley confirmed, and added with a sigh, 'Jack wasn't much older there than Josh is now. It shocks me sometimes to realize how many years have passed.'

Sensing she still missed her husband, Vivi was about to ask more about him when she noticed a bronze sculpture in a niche to one side of the portrait. For some reason it seemed familiar, so she stepped forward for a closer look. She was sure she'd seen it before. Or no, what she'd seen was something like it, perhaps a piece created by the same sculptor. The way this female's arm was outstretched, the position of her feet and illusory movement of her skirts, the backward tilt of her head . . .

'Beautiful, isn't she?' Shelley murmured. 'She used to have a partner, a male, but he got lost around the time Jack died and we've never found him.'

Vivi was suddenly finding it hard to breathe, or even to think straight. She tried to clear her head, to push away the suspicions that were crowding her, but the worst of them was as immovable as the bronze, and she couldn't escape it. She knew where the partner was, who had it secreted away in a bottom drawer, but it wasn't making any sense. Why would her mother have it? Who had given it to her? Why had she kept it hidden all these years? Vivi's hand went up as though to stop the appalling ambush of understanding that was growing darker and more terrible by the second, but it was already wrenching up the memory of her mother's reaction this morning . . .

It couldn't be what she was thinking. It wasn't possible, and yet it was making the worst, the *very* worst kind of sense.

'Are you OK?' Josh asked, coming up behind her.

She flinched, unable to let him touch her. 'I need to go home,' she said shakily. 'I'm sorry . . . I . . .'

'It's OK. I'll take you.' He clearly thought she was unwell, but didn't make a fuss or draw attention to her. 'Go on out to the car,' he said softly, 'I'll fetch your bag and make your excuses.'

As she moved towards the door Vivi was aware of Shelley's eyes following her, curiously, worriedly. Unable to look at her, Vivi only half turned as she said, 'I'm sorry . . . It's been . . .'

'It's all right,' Shelley insisted. 'We've enjoyed meeting you. Please come again.'

Vivi stumbled outside and started to dry retch as she reached the car. She couldn't be right about this, please God, *please* God, she just couldn't be . . .

After feigning sleep most of the way home, Vivi finally opened her eyes as Josh pulled the Land Rover to a stop at the end of Bay Lane. She felt so devastated, so completely shattered inside that she hardly knew what to say to him.

Aware of his concern, and his arm about to go around her, she pushed open the car door and stumbled out. 'I'm sorry,' she said brokenly. 'I need . . .'

'It's OK,' he assured her. 'I'll come and help you in.'

'No! No, I'm fine. I . . . I'll call you when I've had some rest.'

As she went to the front door she could feel him watching her, and she silently begged her wretched heart to fail now so she could put an end to the monstrous trick fate had played them. Wasn't it enough that it had wrecked everything else by turning her into an invalid, a shadow of who she used to be, making her dependent on someone else dying so she could carry on living?

Why had it done this too? Why bring him into her life and let her believe, *feel* what true love could be like, when it hadn't been *true* love at all?

Hearing voices in the kitchen, she went silently along the hall and upstairs to her room. She couldn't face her mother, not now, maybe not ever. She couldn't even bring herself to speak to Michelle. She simply lay down on the bed, but as the unthinkable nightmare swamped her she swung her feet back to the floor.

She needed to find the male dancer. She had to see it again, to hold it in her hands and be certain . . .

She could hear Gil's voice downstairs, and her mother's. She had no idea if they knew she was home, and didn't care. She wasn't thinking about them, had no interest in them as she moved across the landing and up the three stairs into her mother's room.

The sculpture wasn't where she'd last found it; it wasn't in that chest of drawers. She finally tracked it down to the darkest depths of an old wardrobe in a spare room at the other end of the landing. It was still wrapped in linens and tissue, yellowed with age, which fell apart as she unwound them.

She held the male dancer to the light, registering the one hand raised behind him, the other reaching for his partner's, ready to spin her on into the dance. It was so obvious they were a pair, so clear that they belonged together that she could hardly bear that they'd been parted, much less what the separation meant.

'. . . he got lost around the time Jack died,' Shelley had said, 'and we've never found him.'

* * *

'Vivi! Stop! *Stop!*'

Vivi heard Sam's car braking as she ran from the house, and knew he was coming after her, but she couldn't, wouldn't let him catch her. She was running harder than she ever had, pounding the sand, scrambling over rocks, leaping pools, pressing herself on and on, putting every bit of strain she could on her heart until it could take no more.

'Vivi! For God's sake!'

Her muscles and lungs were burning; blood coursed through her veins like fire. She couldn't let the nightmare catch up, couldn't allow it to be real.

She wanted to die.

Aware of a hand grabbing her arm she tried to break free, but Sam was spinning her round, holding her up as she started to fall.

'It's all right,' he whispered raggedly. 'I've got you.'

'No,' she sobbed. 'Oh God, oh God,' and sinking to her knees she buried her face in her hands as the breath blazed through her body and her wildly beating heart continued to break into a thousand pieces.

'What were you thinking?' he asked, panting as he knelt beside her. 'Why are you doing this?'

She couldn't answer, couldn't even look at him. She turned away, but as his strong arms went round her she fell sobbing helplessly against him.

He held her for a long time, letting her cry, asking no more questions, until, in the end, as her terrible grief began to subside into exhaustion, he eased her to her feet and helped her back across the beach to where her terrified mother was waiting.

* * *

As Gina rushed forward to help, Vivi pushed her away so harshly that Gina almost fell.

Ashen, Gina looked at Sam, then at Michelle as she came out of the house.

'Vivi, what is it?' Michelle implored. 'What the hell made you do that?'

'Leave me alone,' Vivi growled, moving past her. 'I can't speak to you . . . I can't . . . I . . .' As she started to break down again, she was saved by rage. 'I want this thing out of me,' she seethed, thumping a hand against the device in her shoulder. 'I need to get it out now.'

'Vivi, stop,' Michelle cried, grabbing her hands as she began clawing herself.

Vivi fought, but then Gil was holding her, pinning her to him, and urging her to calm down.

'Let me go!' Vivi sobbed. 'Please let me go.'

'Not until you tell us what this is about,' he insisted.

She couldn't. Nothing in her could utter the words.

'Vivi, you have to tell us,' Michelle urged. 'You could have killed yourself out there.'

Vivi rounded on her mother. 'Ask her what it's about!' she shouted, pointing at Gina and shaking so badly that her entire body seemed about to collapse. 'Make her tell you who my father is.'

Gina's face was white; her eyes huge, dark pools of fear. As she started to speak Vivi gave a cry of pain – an electrical charge was shooting through her heart. She clasped her hands to her chest and would have buckled to her knees if Gil hadn't caught her. He took her inside and made her sit down on the sofa in her mother's sitting room.

'Do you need to call the clinic?' Michelle asked, handing her a phone.

Vivi ignored it and clutched her head.

'Vivi,' her mother implored.

Vivi looked up, her eyes burning with a blinding fury. 'Have you told them yet who my father is?' she raged. 'Have you?'

Gina regarded her helplessly.

Gil started to speak, but Vivi cut him off.

'It's Jack Raynor,' she cried savagely. 'Isn't that great?' she shouted at Michelle and Sam. 'Josh and I have the same . . .'

'No!' Gina shouted. 'What . . . ? *No!* He's not your father.'

Vivi stared at her, stunned into silence, until the words reached her and she felt herself coming apart. She was hardly daring to believe her mother, but already the relief was so intense, so consuming that she started to sob and choke.

Going to her, Gina held her as she tried to catch her breath. 'Please try to calm down,' she urged. 'You have to rest after a shock . . .'

Vivi couldn't think about rest, couldn't think about anything apart from what her mother had said, and about Josh who wasn't who she'd feared he was . . . She could have killed herself running like that, she'd meant to . . .

Turning to her mother, she said hoarsely, breathlessly, 'You need to tell me . . . I want to know how you come to have the bronze dancer that belongs at Deerwood here in this house.'

Gina's face was haggard and frightened as she looked

at Gil. She was like a child who'd lost its way and had no idea what to do next.

Putting an arm around her Gil said softly, 'You must do it, Gina.'

Gina nodded. Her eyes came to Vivienne's and at last she murmured, 'Yes, yes, I must.'

CHAPTER EIGHTEEN
GINA

Summer 1989

The vast, sandy curve of Kesterly's main beach was so crowded with music lovers, bands, dancers, all kinds of party animals, that Gina knew as she floated down from the Promenade that she was unlikely to find her friends in the mayhem. She didn't mind. It felt exciting, daring, to be alone in her dreamy, chilled-out state. She was already half in love with all the revellers, who seemed just as dreamy and chilled as she did. Many reached for her as she sauntered aimlessly past, pulling her into a dance, stroking her hair, pressing kisses to her bronzed bare skin.

It was summer, the night was hot, the concert free. Everyone was high; thick, pungent smoke fogged the air, drifted from joints, burning oils and small bonfires. Ecstasy was offered and taken, blues downed like candy, while cocaine was snorted from bare breasts and thighs. In the light of flames faces glowed with euphoria, and inhibitions melted away as everyone gyrated, hummed and thrust to the beat.

Gina had known how it would be; they all knew, it was why they'd come. Concerts like this happened often around universities and beaches; but if she went to one, she always took something. Tonight it had been E, almost an hour ago, with another pill tucked into her bikini top for later.

She smiled vaguely as she walked, letting her head fall back to watch embers floating high into the night like crimson stars. The great black canvas of the sky was so inviting she felt she could fly right up to it. Aware of hands on her legs she closed her eyes, yielding to the erotic charges sweeping through her, raising the hair from her neck as she swayed and laughed and felt the music entering her as though she were a puppet and it her master.

He didn't ask her name, and she didn't ask his, she simply let him pull her down beside him, and when he laughed she laughed too. She was aware of others watching, and stretched out a hand to them. Someone took it, and she moaned softly as he held her to him, protectively, telling everyone she was his. She didn't mind; she was barely listening, she just wanted to be with them, whoever they were, passing spliffs and tipping back wine.

It was a long way into the night that she heard someone mention the police. Joints were extinguished and buried, searches began for abandoned clothes, causing hilarity and tangled limbs. Had she already swallowed the second pill? She couldn't remember.

He took her by the hand and tugged her across the sand. She went willingly, intrigued to know where they were going, where she would end up tonight. Others came, and soon they were in cars, heading out of town into the pitch-black countryside. He drove recklessly, and through the open top she felt the wind whipping through her hair, and over her body like a beautiful, violent storm.

Eventually they stopped in the middle of nowhere. In the moonlight she could make out the shape of tents, pitched in a field.

'The party continues,' he murmured against her lips. 'Just remember you're mine, all mine.'

She laughed and got out of the car, wondering what had happened to her shoes, but not really caring. She was with him; she already loved him, whoever he was, and she wanted him more and more.

Suddenly they were blinded by flashlights. Men, older men, were coming towards them, emerging from the darkness like alien beings. Voices were raised angrily, abusively. Her lover let go of her hand and moved forward aggressively, fists clenched. She drew back with the other girls she'd barely noticed until now.

'What's happening?' she heard one of them whisper.

Nobody knew.

The anger in the air was palpable; the threats became terrible, fraught with violence and murderous intent. This was a different kind of dream. Something had gone wrong.

An explosion suddenly tore through the night like a thunderclap, filling it with deafening sound.

Silence fell like invisible rain.

'Jesus, she's got a gun.'

Gina watched, as though hypnotized, as one of the older men took the gun from a woman with furious eyes and shaking hands. What was the man going to do? Were they all about to be killed?

Her lover was shouting, gesticulating, snarling along with the others.

'We need to get out of here,' a girl whispered in her ear, but Gina was held captive by weakened limbs and bewildered fascination.

The older men closed in on the younger ones, telling them to take the tents down, to move on, get off their land. There was pushing and shoving, more violent threats, until the roar of a vehicle drowned the fracas. It was coming in through a far gate, dazzling them all with its headlights. It came closer, at speed, and the younger men started to run from it. Gina's lover grabbed her, his face taut, white, and handsome in an other-worldly way.

The sudden stench was overpowering. She gasped and gagged.

So did the others.

The older men were laughing; the tents were sagging under the weight of the foul slime that had been dumped on them.

Keeping hold of her hand he dragged her back to the cars, where others were already starting to speed away.

'Back to mine,' he shouted as he revved his engine.

'See you there,' someone shouted back.

Gina closed her eyes as they sped through the night, unsure of what had just happened, or where they were going.

It wasn't until the next morning, after the high had started to wear off, that she registered her surroundings. She was in a high-ceilinged room with large windows overlooking a tree-lined drive and manicured lawns.

He brought her tea, told her his name and said he wanted to fuck her again.

She let him, because she wanted it too.

He was special, she could feel it. She wanted to be with him again and again.

When it was over he rolled off her and said, 'OK, little slut, time to fuck off home and have a good life.'

Autumn 1989

When Gina realized a couple of months later that she was pregnant she felt so sick and ashamed that she could tell no one, was hardly even able to admit it to herself. His parting words kept ringing in her ears. She couldn't forget them; she'd barely heard anything else since. She needed him to take them back, to swear he hadn't meant it, that he knew in his heart she wasn't really that sort of girl.

Sometimes, to buoy herself, she wondered if he might be looking for her. He'd have no idea how to find her. Maybe she should contact him so he could tell her how much he regretted hurting and humiliating her so cruelly. She was sure he'd want to; he must feel so bad about the way he'd treated her; anyone would. Then she could tell him she was pregnant and he'd be so sorry for the way he'd behaved that he'd cry and beg her to forgive him. She would, of course, and then everything would be all right again. She wouldn't have to go on feeling so disgusted with herself that she could hardly bear to look in the mirror, or any of her friends in the eye.

She went home for the weekend, telling her parents that she was in need of some peace and quiet for revision. She was aware of her mother's bemusement

– there were no exams coming up, and there were libraries and other places belonging to the university where she could study.

She rang Dean Manor from a call box in town and asked to speak to him. When he came to the phone she could hear her heartbeat in her ears and felt queasy as she said, 'Hi, it's the girl with no name. Remember me, from the beach in the summer? Do you fancy getting together again?'

There was a short silence before Charlie Bleasdale said in a drawl that was both friendly and intrigued, 'Yeah. Yeah, I remember you, and I do fancy that. In fact your timing's pretty perfect, Ms No Name. Tell me you're free tonight.'

Swallowing, she said, 'I'm free tonight.'

'OK. Do you have a car?'

'Yes.'

'Then come to the Ring o'Bells car park at eleven.'

'Why so late?'

He didn't answer, and she realized he'd already rung off.

VIVIENNE

Present Day

Vivi stared at her mother's ashen face, seeing and feeling every part of her pain and despair, understanding her regrets, her refusal ever to speak of the despicable man who'd hurt and humiliated her so vilely. The shame and self-loathing he'd made her feel had spread through her young mind like a cancer, choking off parts of her so they could no longer function as they should. She'd been afraid to love since then, had felt undeserving of it, had even pushed it away as though it would turn into some kind of punishment for the way she'd behaved.

Vivi wanted desperately to end this ordeal for her mother now, to tell her that she was sorry she'd forced her to relive a single minute of it, but as though sensing what she was about to say Gina touched her fingers to Vivi's lips, quietening her.

Michelle and Sam had left a while ago, feeling it wasn't right for them to be present while Gina opened up, but Gil had stayed. Vivi had wanted him to, and Gina had agreed that he needed to hear the truth too.

Gina drank deeply from the glass of water Gil passed her; Vivi noticed how badly her hands were shaking, and unable to bear it she reached out for her. Her mother seemed almost childlike then as she looked into Vivi's eyes, her expression showing how much she wanted to be forgiven and understood, how sorry she was, how riddled with guilt she felt, and had for years. Behind it all Vivi could see how deeply her mother loved her, and how afraid she was of losing her.

'I know there's more,' Vivi said softly, 'but I want to tell you now that nothing you can say will ever change how much I love you.'

Gina's voice caught on a sob as she said, 'Thank you. Oh, Vivi,' and gathering her into her arms she held her so close that they could feel the beat of each other's hearts. 'I wish he wasn't your father,' she gasped. 'I wish with every part of me that I could erase him from both our lives as though he'd never existed, but holding back, never telling you about him was all I could do. I'm sorry for all the pain it's caused you . . . Do you understand that I needed to keep you away from him, because I was afraid of how much he might hurt you too?'

'Of course I understand,' Vivi whispered. 'And I'm sorry for all the pain I caused you.'

'I should have been truthful,' Gina insisted, 'I know that, but I just couldn't bear to think of him, much less speak of him. Every time I tried I felt as though I was going to inject some sort of poison into our lives, a poison I'd never be able to get rid of . . . Maybe that doesn't make any sense to you, but it felt so real to me, and even now I hate the fact that his name has been spoken in this room.'

Vivi hated it too for what it was doing to her mother, and had done for so many years. She looked at Gil as he sat beside them, his head down, his elbows resting on his knees. Sliding a hand into his, she brought it to her lips and kissed it. This must explain so much for him. 'Are you OK?' she asked him.

His smile was wry, his eyes shining with tears as he turned them to her. 'Everything that's beautiful about you,' he said hoarsely, 'and there's so much, is down to your mother. You're her daughter, not his.'

'And you're my father,' she said, understanding it was what he needed to hear, and feeling the truth of it as though it was cleansing away the stains of reality.

Gil swallowed hard, tried to speak and found the words blocked by emotion. 'This thing that's happening to you . . .' he said wretchedly. 'You have so much to live for, so many people who love and need you . . .'

Breaking in gently, Vivi said, 'We mustn't talk about me now.' She didn't want her condition to be a part of this, wasn't even going to allow herself to consider that she might have inherited the defect from that pig of a man. As far as she was concerned it was all hers, and would stay that way unless, until, she could find a new heart.

She turned back to her mother and smoothed a hand over Gina's tear-ravaged face. 'Do you want to go on?' she asked softly.

There was a long moment before Gina said, 'You must be tired . . .'

'I'm fine,' Vivi lied. Her mother needed to finish her story, and she, Vivi, needed to hear it.

Gina's head went down, and her breathing sounded unsteady as she drew in air and quietly exhaled it. There was clearly still some distance to go and she needed all her reserves.

Eventually she looked at Vivi, and at the same time reached for Gil's hand. She started to speak, slowly at first, but as the words came more easily Vivi could feel the bond they shared tightening around them as though to keep them safe. It had always been there, she realized, throughout everything it had never let her down, and she knew it never would.

It was gone midnight by the time they finally went to bed, Vivi and Gina to their rooms, Gil to Mark's. They were all emotionally drained and exhausted, Gina most of all.

Vivi slept badly, her bruised and battered body aching and throbbing through the night, the cuts she'd sustained on the beach stinging like hot needles and the fear of what further damage she'd done to herself burning the edges of her pain. Mostly though, her mind raced and reeled with all that her mother had told her.

She knew the whole story now.

Gina had held nothing back, had revealed everything that had happened the night Jack Raynor died, and Vivi had felt her mother's heart drowning in a bottomless well of grief and sorrow. Gina had spared herself nothing, had spoken almost as if in a trance, as though telling a story about someone she used to know.

It was how Vivi had felt as she'd listened, that the reckless free-spirited nineteen-year-old her mother had described was someone who'd stopped existing the night she'd gone to the beach and met the man who'd shamed, humiliated and impregnated her.

By the time her mother had finished Vivi had felt as devastated and beaten by the events of that night as Gina clearly had while it was happening. She'd also known what they needed to do next, and Gina, in spite of how afraid she was, hadn't argued.

'You have to tell Shelley,' Vivi had said quietly. 'She deserves to hear it from you.'

Gina had nodded, looked at Gil and, as though sensing his support, nodded again.

So now here they were on their way to Deerwood, Gil driving with Gina beside him and Vivi in the back. Vivi gazed out of the car window, barely registering the countryside that she and Josh had passed through the day before.

It felt like a lifetime ago.

'My mother would like to meet yours,' she'd told him when he'd called this morning. 'Can we come today?'

He'd laughed in surprise. 'Of course. I'll tell her.'

Because she had to, she said, 'It's not going to be easy, I'm afraid. It concerns your father.'

He fell silent, clearly bewildered and waiting for her to explain.

'There's a history,' Vivi said, thanking God that he knew nothing of the terrible suspicion that had driven her into an insane attempt last night to stop herself facing it. 'Gil's coming too. It would be good if we could talk somewhere we won't be interrupted.'

To disguise how badly she'd injured herself on the rocks as she'd run, she was wearing long sleeves and ankle-length jeans. Josh might notice her fingers, scratched and swollen, but she'd try to keep them hidden inside the cuffs of her shirt. The exhaustion she felt, the swirling light-headedness and raw ache in her chest was making everything seem slightly surreal, yet she knew with clarity that if he felt he couldn't love her after this she would understand – and then she would want to run and run again . . .

When they arrived at Deerwood, pulling up beside his Land Rover in the farmyard, the place was teeming with activity. Teenagers seemed to be everywhere, working with the pigs and goats, clearing the barn, leading ponies into a field, piling boxes onto a forklift, or pushing wheelbarrows along a track signed to the vegetable gardens. No one paid them any particular attention, until Ellie came to greet them, followed by Josh.

In spite of looking perplexed and worried, he shook hands warmly with Gil and told Gina he was glad to meet her at last. When he looked at Vivi a shadow darkened his eyes, telling her he was aware she wasn't herself, that he was worried, but he only said, 'My mother's inside. The kitchen is always busy, so she's in the far sitting room.'

They found Shelley standing with her back to the large empty fireplace, her lovely face anxious and bewildered as she looked from Vivienne to Gina and back again, though her natural warmth made her greet them kindly.

When they were seated, Shelley on one sofa, Gina between Vivienne and Gil on another, Josh closed the door and went to stand where his mother had been when they'd come in. Vivi was glad to know that he'd be there for his mother when this was over; she would need him then.

Gil began, his solemn gaze moving between Josh and Shelley as he explained that Gina wanted to tell them what had happened the night Jack had died.

Though Shelley's eyes widened with shock, she said nothing, simply turned her gaze to Gina and waited for her to begin.

GINA

Autumn 1989

Gina was sitting in her car watching people spilling out of the pub laughing, promising to see one another soon, and shouting playful insults as they drove off into the night. Though she was certain she knew no one, she kept her head down in case someone recognized her. She couldn't seem to think straight. She had no idea now why she'd come. She wished she'd never called him, had never met him, could wipe away the summer as though it had never happened.

Her foot tapped up and down so fast it was like a drill; she began biting her nails, and muttering to herself. She didn't want to see him. She hated and despised him in a way she'd never even known it was possible to hate and despise anyone, apart from herself. That was what he had done to her; his sneering, cold-hearted cruelty, his rich-boy disdain had made it almost impossible for her to live her life. Last year she'd loved being at uni, she'd had dozens of friends, a social life that was fun, bordering on wild, but everyone was doing it so why shouldn't she? Now, she could hardly make herself go out at all.

OK, little slut, time to fuck off home and have a good life.

She was here, she reminded herself, because she needed him to take those words back, to understand that she was a decent person, from a loving family, not a nobody who deserved no respect.

She felt so confused and agitated that she couldn't make herself think straight. She was afraid, and suddenly knew that she had to get out of here. She should never have come. All she had to do was start the car and drive away. He'd never know she'd turned up, and she wouldn't ever need to speak to him again.

She turned the keys in the ignition, but suddenly the back doors of her car were wrenched open by unseen hands at the same time as *he*, Charlie Bleasdale, slipped into the passenger seat.

'Good *girl*,' he drawled proudly, and she felt sickened to her soul by the reminder of that unforgettable goodbye.

She had no idea who the others were, getting in behind her. She couldn't see their faces in the darkness, could only hear them laughing and snorting, telling one another to 'fuck off', or 'suck my balls'. Their voices were like *his*, plummy and guttural, and he slapped his thighs in mirth as his companions' comments became cruder and drunker. She was suddenly so certain they were going to rape her, that *he* had told them she was easy, was theirs as many times as they wanted that night, that she started to scramble from the car.

'No, don't go,' he laughed, dragging her back, and grabbing her by the jaw he turned her to face him.

'Get out,' she muttered. 'You . . .'

'Oh, now don't be like that,' he admonished. 'I've been looking forward to seeing you.'

'I – please,' she stammered. 'I want to go home.'

'Sure, when we're done you can go wherever you like. First, though, we're going for a little drive. It shouldn't take long. All you have to do is what you're told, and everyone will be happy.'

The others seemed to think that was hilarious, and so did he.

She was shaking so violently she couldn't even speak.

'OK, start her up,' he instructed.

She tried to push open her door again, to throw herself onto the tarmac, but someone grabbed her from the back and locked an arm round her throat as he growled, 'Drive,' in her ear.

Bleasdale leaned across her, turned the engine on, and gestured for her to move the car forward. With her head still pinned to the headrest it was hard to reach the pedals, but she made herself, telling herself that she could drive into town, stop at the police station, or even a traffic light, and scream.

She could barely see where they were going as she was directed along narrow, winding roads, so dark it was hard to make out anything beyond the hedgerows and one or two signs. Crawley Common; Footpath; Kesterly-on-Sea; Deerwood Farm.

Bleasdale half turned to the others. 'One of you'll have to stay in the car with her,' he said. 'M J, you come with me.'

'Why him and not me?' the other protested.

'Because you're an arse,' Charlie retorted, and they all howled with laughter.

'Tell me again what I've got to do,' someone said.

'Just follow me,' Charlie answered. 'We'll be in and out of there faster than you can say the bastard had it coming.'

'So who is he? I know you told me, but I was stoned at the time so you'll have to give it up again.'

'It doesn't matter. He's just someone who owes my family, so we're collecting.'

'What if he doesn't have any cash in the place?'

'For God's sake, M J. All we have to do is grab something he'll know is his, then we get out of there. He'll piss his shitty pants when we send him photos and he realizes we've been in his house while his wife and kids were sleeping. He'll think if we can do it once, we can do it again.'

'But he's not going to know it's us, is he?'

'He'll know, but he won't be able to prove it. OK, whatever your name is,' he said to Gina, 'there's a gate up ahead, on the right. Pull in there and turn off the engine.'

She did as she was told, still in a headlock and rigid with fear, but taking some heart from what she'd overheard. It seemed raping her wasn't what they were about – at least not yet.

Bleasdale was becoming more hyper by the second, practically leaping up and down in his seat as they passed around a bottle, burping and panting as they downed the neat vodka.

It was pitch-dark all around them, no cars were passing, and as far as Gina could make out there was no sign of a house or any other building.

If she could get out and run, maybe hide in a hedge . . .

'OK, little slut,' Bleasdale murmured, 'just so we're clear. You're the driver tonight. If there's any trouble, if anyone sees a car it's going to be yours, so you'll be the one with the explaining to do.'

She didn't answer, couldn't. She had no idea what he was talking about and she was still being held so tightly she was struggling to breathe.

He got out, leaving the passenger door open, and cold air rushed in, followed by more as someone clambered out of the back. She was still unable to turn her head; her legs were trapped by the steering wheel.

Charlie said, 'If you want some sport with her while we're gone, be my guest, just make sure you're here when we get back.'

Blind terror slaked through her as he closed the door,

339

leaving her to the mercy of the man who wouldn't let her go.

Several excruciating moments followed. She could hear him breathing close to her ear; she could smell him, sweat, aftershave and booze.

'Give me the keys,' he growled.

She couldn't make herself move.

'Get the keys,' he barked, and grabbing her hair he shoved her forward.

She took them from the ignition and put them into the hand he was holding out.

As he closed his fist around them he let her go, and the next instant he was at the driver's door, locking her in. Then he was around the other side getting in next to her.

'No, please,' she begged, pressing herself to the door and fumbling for the handle. 'Pease don't hurt me,' she sobbed.

'I'm not going to hurt you,' he said, sounding bored with her now. 'I might be a lot of things, but I'm not a fucking rapist. So just keep quiet, be a good girl, and before you know it we'll be on our way home.' He looked her up and down. 'You're not my type anyway,' he grunted, and tipping back his head he emptied the vodka bottle into his throat.

Gina had no idea how much time passed before the others came back. It felt like hours, but maybe it was only minutes. She heard an owl, saw a fox cross the road and turn back again. Their breath fogged the windows, she shivered with cold and fear, tried to think how to persuade him to let her go, but then he was saying, 'Here they are,' and giving her the keys he told her to start the car.

As the headlights came on she saw two figures leaping over the gate. They tore open the back doors and Bleasdale was shouting, 'Drive, fucking drive.'

In a panic she stalled the engine.

'*Fucking drive*,' he yelled, thumping the roof.

As she steered jerkily onto the road, someone growled, 'What the fuck happened?'

Silence.

'Charlie! What happened?'

'You were there,' Bleasdale growled.

'Yah, and you fucking killed him.'

'Don't be a moron,' Bleasdale spat, grabbing his throat. 'Don't ever fucking say that, all right?' He let him go, pushed him back and clasped his hands to his head. 'You don't know he's dead,' he hissed. 'You don't know . . .'

'I'm telling you, he's fucking dead.'

Gina kept driving, following the passengers' directions, praying they'd let her go as soon as they were ready to be dropped off.

A horrible silence dragged on. She didn't dare to glance in the rear-view mirror, she didn't want Bleasdale or anyone to catch her looking at them. She just wanted them to forget she was there.

Eventually she was told to stop and she realized they were outside the lodge at Dean Manor. As the others got out, Bleasdale leaned forward and thrust something hard and heavy into her hands.

'What – what is it?' she gulped, trying to drop it.

'Call it a memento,' he snarled. 'Your fingerprints are on it now. If anyone asks we'll say it was you who took us to the farmhouse, because you wanted to pull a train with us and Jack Raynor. You're that kind of a girl, aren't you? One who pulls trains. We'll tell them you've been shagging Raynor since the night he threw us off his land.'

She was shaking her head violently. She didn't understand. 'But I don't . . .'

'Shut up, *shut up*.' He stared at the object in her hands, but she could tell he wasn't seeing it. 'He might not be dead,' he said raggedly, 'but whether he is or isn't, you need to keep your mouth shut about tonight and for fuck's sake hide that away. If you don't, it won't be us who suffers, it'll be you. Do you get that? You, and your family, and anyone you care for, because you go talking about this, I'll come for you and you don't want that, slut girl, I promise you, you really don't want it.'

By the time Gina got home she'd wet herself in fear. Her face was so ravaged by terror and tears that she knew she couldn't let her parents see her. Thankfully, they were asleep in bed and didn't hear her stumble and creep past their door into her room. She was still carrying the heavy object he'd thrust at her, and turning on the bedside light she made herself check it for blood, certain she'd find some, that this was what he'd used . . . But there was none. It was a dark, solid, unstained bronze. She sank down on the bed, shaking with a horror she wasn't even close to controlling.

You fucking killed him.

You don't know he's dead.

We'll tell everyone it was your idea . . .

Hours passed, or maybe it was minutes, before she

was able to peel off her soiled clothes, wrap herself in a robe and get into bed. She pulled the covers over her head as if total darkness and near-suffocation could somehow obliterate the nightmare. She was too traumatized even to cry.

She stayed in bed all the next day and the next. She couldn't go back to uni, she couldn't face the world; she couldn't even leave her room. Her mother wanted to call the doctor, but Gina begged her not to.

'I'll be fine, Mum, honestly, please don't fuss.'

She made herself listen to the radio and when she heard the news that Jack Raynor had died in a tragic accident at his home she almost screamed out loud. It couldn't be true, she didn't want it to be true, but it was.

There was no mention of a break-in, or a fight, or a bronze sculpture going missing . . .

But the sculpture was here, in her room, wrapped in a towel and stuffed to the back of the wardrobe.

Jack Raynor was dead.

She was tormented by thoughts of his wife and children, of what they must be going through, of all they didn't know . . . She told herself she had to speak up, to make clear what had happened, but she didn't know for certain what had, because she hadn't been there, and they were saying it was a freak accident, and if she went to the police Charlie Bleasdale would tell them things about her and Jack Raynor that weren't true, but Jack Raynor was no longer alive to confirm or deny it. It would be her word against Bleasdale's and his friends'.

* * *

As the days passed and Gina still wouldn't or couldn't get out of bed, and continued to refuse to see a doctor, her mother called one anyway.

By the time he arrived Gina had slipped out of the house. She'd been planning to go anyway – not planning exactly, she just knew that she had to go to Jack Raynor's funeral. She needed to speak to his wife, to explain that it hadn't been an accident. She would give back the bronze and tell her about Charlie Bleasdale. It wasn't until she got to the crematorium that she realized she'd forgotten, in her distraught state, to bring it with her.

She parked a long way from the entrance gates and walked along a narrow track to get to the far side of the gardens. She stood in the sunlight, next to a child's memorial stone, and watched the mourners who were there for Jack Raynor. She didn't know any of them; she could barely make out their faces from where she was standing. Then she saw Charlie Bleasdale, dressed in black, and she was so terrified of him spotting her that she ran back to her car and drove and drove until eventually she arrived home.

A week or more went by and she was still too afraid to leave her room. Her parents called the doctor again, and after he'd examined her Gina sat shivering at the top of the stairs listening to what he told them. She didn't understand post-trauma stress, hadn't really heard of it before, but he was certain that she was bottling up a bad experience and needed some help to make her let it go.

Jack Raynor hadn't deserved to die and she didn't deserve to live. That was all she knew, and she'd never be able to let that go.

'Gina,' her mother said softly one morning, 'you know you can't go on like this. You're wasting away, look at you, and Dad and I are worried out of our minds . . . Please tell me what's happened. Let us help you.'

Gina said, 'I'm pregnant,' and as the words left her lips she started to sob and sob and couldn't make herself stop.

Holding her close, soothing her as best she could, her mother said, 'Yes, I know that, sweetheart, so now tell me . . .' She took a breath. 'Gina, did someone force themselves on you? Is that why you're so scared?'

Gina couldn't answer. She could only cling to her mother as if she'd drown without her.

'If someone attacked you we can go to the police.'

'No! No one forced me,' Gina choked. 'I didn't . . . He . . .'

Her mother waited a moment, then said, 'Is it someone we know?'

Gina shook her head.

'Are you sure?'

'Yes, I'm sure.'

'So whoever it is, have you told him? Is that what's wrong? You told him and he doesn't want to know?'

'I don't want him ever to know,' Gina cried. 'I never want to see him again. He's . . . He's . . .'

'Ssh, it's all right,' her mother whispered as Gina started to retch. 'We'll work this out. It'll be fine. Just tell me how far along you are.'

'Four – four months.'

Her mother nodded. 'It's not too late for a termination. Is that what you want?'

Gina nodded, but then shook her head. She couldn't

go out, couldn't leave the house ever again, not even for that.

Lying down on the bed next to her, her mother continued to hold her, stroking her hair and waiting for the tears to stop. In the end she said, 'If you change your mind we can see a doctor.'

Gina had no idea what to do. Everything was so jumbled in her mind, so twisted by the horror of who she was and what she'd made happen that she couldn't make any sense of her thoughts.

'If you decide to keep it,' her mother said, 'then of course Dad and I will be here for you.'

How could she keep it? How could she not keep it? If she didn't she'd be responsible for another death, and that would make her an even worse slut than she already was.

VIVIENNE

Present Day

Shelley's cracked and worn hands were pressed to her cheeks, her grey eyes glassy with shock. She was staring hard at Gina, though whether she was seeing her was hard to tell. Vivienne could hardly begin to imagine how she was feeling, but the distress of the past coming back like this, the effort to take it all in was palpable.

Josh's hand was on his mother's shoulder, comforting,

strengthening. His eyes were down; his mouth set in a harsh, thin line. It wasn't possible to gauge what he was thinking, but Vivi knew that concern for his mother would come before anything he was feeling for himself, or anyone else.

As Gina and Gil rose to their feet, Vivi got up too. They had no place here now. Gina had said what she'd come to say; it was time for them to leave.

'I'm sorry,' Gina whispered shakily. 'I'm so sorry.'

Vivi glanced at Josh again, but he still didn't look up. Beside him his mother remained trapped in the past, seeing only she knew what, as she struggled to come to terms with what she'd heard.

Vivi followed her mother and Gil across the room.

As they reached the door, Shelley said, 'I saw you.'

Gina turned round, and she looked so fragile that Vivi wanted to wrap her in her arms.

'At the crematorium,' Shelley explained. 'I've always wondered who you were. I thought . . . There were times I thought you were someone Jack had . . . known . . .'

Gina shook her head. 'I never met him,' she said.

Shelley looked up at Josh and began speaking quietly, reminding him of how she'd always known someone had been in the house that night, that it was what had woken her. 'No one would believe me,' she said. 'There wasn't any sign of a break-in . . . But now we know, it was Charlie Bleasdale, so Jemmie must have lied about them being in New York . . .'

Though Vivi vaguely recognized the name Jemmie, she wasn't sure from where, and her concern right now was for her mother. The trauma Gina had suffered as a result of knowing Charlie Bleasdale had drastically altered, in some ways ruined, her life. She'd never been the same since then. She'd become a victim of so much fear and guilt that she'd seen every bad thing that had happened in her life as a form of punishment. It had even broken her marriage to Gil, for she'd been unable to accept that she deserved to be loved.

Shelley rose to her feet, and as she came to take Gina in her arms Gina started to break down. 'There, there,' Shelley soothed gently, pulling her in close. 'Sssh, it'll be all right. You must stop blaming yourself . . . You did nothing wrong . . .'

Vivi had to swallow as Gina clung to Shelley like a child. She felt Gil beside her, and put her head on his shoulder as his arm went round her. He was the only father she'd ever known, and God knew he was the only one she wanted.

'I brought the bronze,' Gina told Shelley. 'Vivienne said there's another.'

Shelley managed a smile. 'Yes,' she whispered hoarsely, 'yes there is.'

As Gil went to get the male figurine Josh followed him outside, while Shelley led Gina into the kitchen to show her the female. The instant Gina saw it she gasped. There could be no doubt at all that the two figures belonged together.

When Gil returned and placed the male dancer in the niche with his partner, Shelley slipped a hand into Gina's. 'I've waited a long time for this,' she murmured.

Sensing how special the moment was, perhaps more meaningful than she could understand, Gina said, 'Will you tell me about them?'

'Of course,' Shelley replied. She couldn't take her eyes off the bronzes.

'Maybe this is enough for today, Mum,' Vivi said quietly.

Accepting that it was, Gina allowed Vivi and Gil to take her to the car. Vivi looked around for Josh, but there was no sign of him.

Before they drove off Shelley came out after them, her eyes still shiny with tears. 'I think I met your mother once,' she said to Gina.

Gina looked surprised.

'Bella?'

Gina smiled and nodded.

Shelley smiled too. 'She seemed . . . like a lovely woman.'

Swallowing a lump in her throat, Gina said, 'Thank you. She was.'

Shelley held her eyes. 'I'll tell you another time about the bronzes.'

'I'll look forward to it.'

'I'll call,' Shelley promised, and Vivi was in no doubt that she would.

CHAPTER NINETEEN
VIVIENNE

Present Day

Three days had passed since Gina's meeting with Shelley and in that time the two women had spent many more hours together, mostly at Deerwood, but once at Bay Lane. Though Vivienne hadn't been party to their lengthy chats, she knew they were drawing a lot of comfort from one another, and seeing her mother finally breaking free of all the guilt and self-loathing she'd carried for so long was almost as uplifting as if it were happening to her. Gina looked younger, lighter, and a new confidence was already starting to bloom in a way that was clearly giving her the courage to draw closer to Gil again.

The effect that the friendship was having on Shelley Vivienne learned from her mother, for she hadn't heard from Josh since the day they'd visited the farm.

Though it upset her, and on a deeper level even frightened her, for she was constantly aware of how limited her time might be, she understood his silence. She knew too that she needed to respect it, but she missed him so much and wanted desperately to know what he was thinking. The fact that her father was responsible for the death of his would be weighing heavily with him; God knew it weighed heavily with her. In fact it made her sick to her stomach to know that the blood of a man such as Charlie Bleasdale ran through her veins.

Now, as she got to her feet, Vivi took a moment to steady herself, and went outside. The air felt cooler, fresher, this morning, and she inhaled deeply as if its elixir might in some way strengthen her. Though she'd received no more shocks from her device since the day she'd run out to the beach, she lacked energy, and had been informed by the clinic that their nightly monitorings were showing some unusual activity in her heart. That was the word they'd used, unusual, which she knew was a euphemism for worrying, perhaps even alarming.

She hadn't told anyone; she didn't want to turn everyone's attention to her when so much else was happening for them.

Her gaze skimmed lightly over the glistening sweep of the bay, taking in the small white fins of sailboats, and a hang-glider swooping in from the cliffs. She was willing Josh to come. The need to ring him was overwhelming, but she knew instinctively, painfully, that he needed this space. He had much to think about, and to process, not least of all how they were to go forward after this. She had no clear idea herself, nevertheless the ache for him never left her. Her mind was full of the words she wanted to say to him, and her eyes could see him even though he wasn't there.

And then he was.

She gave a low moan of relief as the Land Rover

came along the lane and drew to a stop at the gates. She watched him get out and come towards her, and then she was going to him, walking straight into his arms.

He wrapped her up more tightly than he ever had before, pushing a hand into her hair and, as she inhaled the earthy, familiar scent of him she could feel his strength flowing into her like a drug.

'I'm sorry,' he murmured harshly. 'I should have rung . . .'

'It's OK,' she whispered. 'I knew you'd come when you were ready.' She pulled back to look at him, and seeing the strain in his face, the burning light in his eyes, she put her lips to his.

He kissed her back, gently, tenderly, cupping her face in his hands as though it were the most precious thing in the world. This was the first time their mouths had touched, and she yearned so much for the kiss to deepen, to lead them to all the places they longed to go, but he was already drawing away.

'Are you all right?' he asked gruffly.

Vivi nodded, but he probably knew she wasn't. He had a way of knowing that she'd never quite understood. 'I'm sorry,' she said.

'For what?'

'For being the daughter of the man who brought about the death of your father. He might not have actually killed him, but if he hadn't gone to your house that night . . . You wouldn't have had to grow up without . . .'

'You can't blame yourself,' he interrupted, 'or your mother for what happened. It was no one's fault but his.' She'd never heard bitterness in his voice before, or hatred, but it was there now and she knew instinctively that what he felt for Charlie Bleasdale ran even deeper than that.

Taking his hand, she led him into the kitchen and put her arms around him again. He looked down at her, their mouths so close, their eyes drinking each other in, but then he was holding her at a distance as he said, 'What do you want to do?'

She frowned, not quite following.

'Do you want to see him?' he asked.

She baulked in shock. 'No! Never,' she insisted. 'I'm ashamed even to know I'm related to him.'

He looked both angry and anguished. 'No one should ever have to say that about their own father,' he muttered, 'but where Charlie Bleasdale is concerned . . .'

'What do *you* want to do?' she asked.

His eyes flicked to hers and away again. 'I can't just let it go,' he said. 'Do you understand that?'

'Of course.' How could she not? His father had died unnecessarily and as a young man, thanks to Bleasdale's vengeful prank. Josh and his sisters had grown up without a father because of it, and Shelley had been forced to live without the only man she'd ever really love. 'So what have you decided?' she asked gently, understanding that this was what his absence over the last few days had been about.

The bones and muscles in his face seemed to clench as he said, 'If it weren't for you and your mother I'd be finding out if it's possible to bring some sort of charges, but I can't let him do any more damage to your lives. My mother doesn't want that either, and not only for your sakes, for Humphrey and Jemmie's too. She says she can't forgive the way Jemmie lied to her at the time of my father's funeral, but the Bleasdales are old now, and frail, and punishing them wouldn't serve any purpose.' He looked questioningly into her eyes. 'They're your grandparents, of course. Maybe you want . . .'

She was already shaking her head. 'I don't want to meet them,' she assured him. 'I'm not going to do anything that might hurt or upset my mother, and contacting them would certainly do that. Besides, I don't want to explain to them why they've never heard of me, and why I've never been in touch before.'

Josh nodded, as though it was the answer he'd expected.

'You still haven't told me what you're going to do,' she prompted.

'I'm going to see Charlie,' he replied. 'He lives in west Wiltshire. I got his address from his sister, Fiona, and I've already been in touch to tell him to expect me.'

Though she wasn't surprised, she was immediately concerned. 'Did you tell him what it's about?'

'No, but he'll probably assume it has something to do with his father's horses.'

She continued to look at him, trying to read, even to feel all that was going on inside him. She understood the anger and the need for justice, even if it was the sort he had to exact himself. 'I'm coming with you,' she told him.

His eyes widened in protest, but before he could speak she said, 'Please don't argue. There's a very good reason why I should be there, and once I've told you what it is I know you'll agree.'

* * *

The following morning was wet and grey as Josh drove them around the outskirts of Bath into Wiltshire, and on towards the quaint, touristy village of Castle Combe. It was where a number of movies and TV series had been filmed over the years, due to its fourteenth-century market cross and abiding olde worlde charm. It was also, Vivi remembered, where Sam and Michelle had spent the first night of their honeymoon, at the magnificent Manor House hotel, set back from the village at the heart of a billowing cluster of landscaped gardens.

Charlie Bleasdale's ivy-clad, former rectory was about half a mile past the upper village, fronted by tall iron gates that stood open to the main road. They drove straight in, tyres crunching on the gravel, and came to a stop between a moss-covered wall and a sleek silver Jaguar. Vivi looked up at the trees hanging over the house, rich with foliage, and darkening the upper storey in a way that made it seem vaguely chilling.

Realizing she'd probably be seeing the house in a more flattering light if it had a different owner, she turned to Josh, anxious herself, but knowing that his feelings were running much deeper. 'Are you OK?' she asked.

'I'm fine,' he replied, not sounding it. 'I'm more concerned about you.'

'Let's get it over with,' she said, and sliding down from the car she waited for him to come and join her.

As they reached the front door it opened before they could press the bell, and a plump fifty-something woman in a tight tweed jacket and jodhpurs barely took her eyes from her phone as she told them to come in.

'Through there,' she said, pointing to an open door off the shadowy entrance hall. 'I'll tell Charlie you're here.'

Vivi watched her disappear to the back of the house and felt Josh's hand on her arm, as though he'd sensed her annoyance at the lack of manners. He gave a shake of his head, telling her to let it go, it wasn't why they were here, and led the way into a grand, though shabby sitting room. It was cluttered with brown antique furniture and carpeted with faded and threadbare rugs. The fireplace was empty and dusted with old ash, the mirror above it seeming as weary as the ancient paintings and wallpaper it reflected. Through a tall casement window she spotted the woman crossing a neatly mowed lawn, with a crop under her arm and her mobile phone pressed to one ear.

'I guess that's the wife,' she said to Josh.

As he agreed, the sound of footsteps carried in from the hall and Vivi felt her mouth turn dry. She was about to come face to face with the man she'd longed to know, had pictured in so many ways, had even romanticized and turned into the victim of her mother's selfishness. Now he was someone she'd never, *ever* think of as a father. After today he would be dead to her.

She glanced at Josh, and seeing the purposeful set of his jaw she knew that the instinct to come with him had been a good one. His need to make Bleasdale pay was only just shy of murderous.

She turned back to the door and as Charlie Bleasdale appeared, tall, eagle-eyed, with thinning brown hair, pitted cheeks and a faded handsomeness that she suspected he continued to play on with half-drunk ladies, she felt herself become rigid with tension.

His coldness, his air of arrogance and disdain were in no way masked by his attempt at an affable welcome. 'Young Raynor,' he drawled, his tone somewhere between jovial and supercilious. He held out a hand to shake, and looked surprised, affronted when Josh didn't take it. 'So what brings you all this way?' he asked, tucking the hand into his jacket pocket. His eyes slanted to Vivi with a glint of confusion. 'You brought the girlfriend, I see?' he said, looking her up and down. 'Nice. Don't see any problem with that.'

Somehow keeping his loathing in check, Josh said, 'This is Vivienne Shager. She's a lawyer and she's here to bear witness to what takes place between us today.'

Bleasdale's eyes bulged with astonishment. 'What *takes place*?' he repeated incredulously. 'What are you talking about, man? I thought we were going to discuss my father's stables. It's high time he put the old nags out to grass. I keep telling him that . . .'

'I'm here,' Josh cut across him, 'to discuss the part you played in my father's death.'

Bleasdale froze, then blanched. His eyes shifted to Vivi and back again. He clearly knew he was on thin ice, and was scrabbling for a way to get off it. '*What?*' he hissed. 'Have you lost your mind? I had nothing . . .'

'If you hadn't been in the farmhouse that night,' Josh continued, keeping a tight rein on his fury, 'my father would still be here.'

Bleasdale blustered, 'Look here, I don't know where . . .'

Josh growled at him to shut up. 'It was a joke for you,' he snarled, 'a way of getting back at him for throwing

357

you off our land. You took the bronze, a *trophy*, to prove you'd got in and out while the family was sleeping. It was meant to unnerve him, make him worried for his children, afraid of what you might do next and when you might do it. Only it didn't work out that way, did it?'

Clearly shocked at having his plan so accurately described, Bleasdale put up his hands in defence. 'Listen to me . . .'

'*You* are listening to me,' Josh gritted his teeth. 'The only reason I haven't gone to the police with what I know . . .'

'I didn't do anything . . .'

'*You were there.*'

'It was an accident.'

'That wouldn't have happened if you . . .'

'It's the girl, isn't it?' Bleasdale blurted. 'After all these years . . . You've been talking to the slut who . . .'

Enraged, Vivi started forward, but Josh was faster. His fist slammed into Bleasdale's face so hard it sent the man sprawling backwards onto the floor. Josh went to stand over him, white with loathing, his hands still clenched, and for a moment Vivi thought he was going to kick him. Instead, he hauled him up by his shirtfront and spoke savagely into his face. 'That was from *the nameless girl*,' he spat, 'and *this* is from me and my father.' He drove another blow into the side of Bleasdale's head, and another. When he made to do it again Vivi stepped forward, needing to stop him before he went too far.

'It's all right,' Josh panted, letting Bleasdale drop heavily to the floor and standing back. He glared down

358

at his victim with all the repugnance it was possible for one man to muster for another. 'Remember, there's a witness to what just happened,' he told him, 'so before you try spinning this into some sort of unprovoked attack, you might want to think about the consequences of the real story coming out. There's no legal time limit to manslaughter, and don't rule out a murder charge . . .'

'Josh,' Vivi murmured softly. 'We should go.'

He didn't argue, just wiped the back of his bruised and shaking hand across his mouth, and turned away from the groaning specimen on the floor.

Had Vivi been able to drive she would have done so, but her licence had been taken away, so she returned to the passenger side of the Land Rover and buckled up as Josh sped away. He was still seething with rage, she suspected he was barely even seeing the road, and was no doubt bitterly regretting pulling back from Bleasdale when he had. She didn't blame him, she despised the man just as much, but it had been time for them to leave. There had simply been no knowing how far Josh would go, and the last thing they needed was Bleasdale ending up in A & E. Too many questions would be asked, accusations would start flying, and the next thing they knew it would come out that he was her father and she'd rather die than have anyone know that, most of all him.

Eventually, to her relief, Josh swerved the Land Rover off the road and drove into a deserted picnic area where he came to an abrupt stop.

Several long moments passed as he struggled to regain control of his emotions. His face was taut and pale; his knuckles white as he gripped the wheel and stared blindly out at the glorious view of Bath. At any other time it would have captivated them; today they were barely seeing it. 'I wanted to kill him,' he said savagely, and she knew he meant it.

She put a hand over his, letting him know that she understood.

His voice was strangled when he spoke. 'Neither of our mothers needs to know about this.'

'Not yet, anyway,' she agreed. There might come a time when it would be satisfying for them to learn that Bleasdale had been on the wrong end of Josh's fist, but it wasn't today.

He took a breath, as though it might help control the turmoil of fury still roiling inside him. Then he threw open the car door and strode to the edge of the clearing, his hands over his face, his shoulders hunched against the onslaught of his grief.

Vivi stayed where she was, understanding that the loss of his father, the whole pointless deprivation of the centre of his world, was overwhelming him. He needed these moments alone as the memories he treasured, the dreams of what might have been, the longing he'd always had for his beloved dad came vividly, painfully to life. Jack Raynor should never have died, wouldn't have died, were it not for Charlie Bleasdale and his mindless, vindictive need for revenge. She knew now that it had all started over Jack's refusal to let the Bleasdales hunt on Deerwood land. To teach him a lesson, Bleasdale's sons had trespassed with their tents, inviting a showdown and getting one. The fact that Jack had humiliated them that night was an offence the Bleasdale sons had been unable to let go unpunished. Pride had to be restored, and it was for that that Jack had died.

Thinking of her mother and the effect Bleasdale's cruelty had had on the young girl whose name he still didn't know, Vivi suddenly wished she'd let Josh finish what he'd started. The man deserved to be beaten to a pulp; he needed to know that he hadn't got away with it; that nothing had been forgotten and would never be forgiven.

She watched Josh turn his face to the sky and wondered if he was talking to his father in his mind, trying in any way he could to reach him. What would he say, and if Jack were able to answer, what words of comfort would he use?

Slipping from the car she went to stand with him, and as they gazed out at the view, hazed by rain, he pulled her into the circle of one arm.

Minutes passed. Everything was so still and silent around them that it was as though they were alone in the world, standing on the edge of it and trying to decide where to go next.

In the end, he said, gruffly, 'I should get you home.'

Stepping round in front of him, she cupped his face in her hands and looked into his still moist eyes. 'There's somewhere I'd rather go,' she told him softly.

He regarded her curiously.

Saying no more, she took his hand and led him back to the car.

The sun was a golden orange orb on the bay's horizon by the time they drove into Kesterly and turned into the leafy streets of the Garden District behind the Promenade. For much of the journey Vivi had sat with her head resting on the seat back, her eyes turned to Josh's profile, and each time he'd glanced at her her insides had fluttered with an intense and beautiful anticipation.

She could sense that he was calmer now, that he'd finally let go of the anger that had consumed him and was focusing on them, refusing to allow anything or anyone to come between them. Their shared understanding of what they needed to do next excluded everything else.

He came to a stop in the parking recess of a recently renovated Victorian-style house with large bay windows either side of a porticoed front door, and two small strips of garden edging the surrounding walls.

They took an old-fashioned cage lift to the second floor, and his expression became sardonic, even uncertain, as they emerged onto the landing. 'I want you to know,' he said, taking out his keys, 'that interior design is something I admire more than practise.'

Laughing, she waited for him to open the door, and as she stepped inside the flat the scent of him immediately assailed her, as though he was already there to welcome her. She turned to look at him, and loved how perplexed he seemed.

The sitting room with its pale oak floorboards and whitewashed walls was bathed in a crimson sunset glow. Twin casement windows overlooked the garden square below. The kitchen was a part of the room with a small bar sectioning it off, and she guessed the door opposite to the one they'd entered through led into the bedroom.

The only furniture, looking vaguely lonely in the spacious surroundings, was a large brown leather sofa, probably donated by Josh's mother or someone else in the family, and a retro entertainment centre containing a flatscreen TV and an untidy collection of DVDs, CDs and various games, no doubt for his nieces and nephews to play when they came.

'I guess you'd call it more of a crash pad than an apartment,' he said drolly. 'As you can see, I haven't really got round to furnishing it yet.'

With a playful twinkle, she said, 'Perhaps I can help you with that.'

Clearly liking the idea, he pulled her round to face him and long minutes ticked by as he regarded her questioningly, seeming for a moment to have lost the ability to read her – or perhaps he needed to be sure that he understood her correctly.

'Do you have a bed?' she whispered.

Though his eyes darkened with understanding, she could tell that he was still unsure.

'I want you to make love to me,' she said huskily.

She felt desire rush through them both as his eyes closed and his forehead dropped to hers. 'Vivi, you know how much . . .'

'Please,' she murmured.

'But what if . . .'

'It won't, but even if it does, I don't want to leave this world without knowing how it feels to be with you, in every way.'

Seeming to sense the inevitability of it, he gently lifted her into his arms and carried her into the bedroom.

It was almost as sparingly furnished as the sitting

room, just a large, unframed bed, a wardrobe and two mismatched nightstands with his guitar resting against one and a reading lamp on the other. As he laid her down on the navy-blue quilt his eyes gazed deeply into hers and she held them, touching her hands to his face and telling him without words that she was yielding herself to him completely.

When they were undressed and in each other's arms the feel of his skin, the hardness of his body all over hers was the most potent and transcending sensation she'd ever known. She murmured and gasped as he kissed and caressed her; and when he entered her, tenderly and powerfully, she cried out and held him, circling him with her arms and legs, moving with him as they journeyed slowly, blissfully all the way to the stars.

Later, long after darkness had settled over the town, they drove to Bay Lane so Vivi could collect the home monitor and the medication she'd need in the morning. After being together so intimately they weren't ready to be parted, even for a few hours. And the fact that she'd experienced no shocks, at least not yet, or even the wrong sort of breathlessness while they were making love, had been almost as great a relief to them both as the exquisite release of so much pent-up desire. She felt tired now, but was glowing inside and out. She wasn't going to allow herself to be afraid, or to spend this precious time dreading a shock that she had no way of controlling. She'd rather tell herself that they could make love again and again, and maybe they would.

When they got to the house her mother wasn't at home; she'd texted earlier to say that she and Gil had been invited to Deerwood for the evening. *I expect we'll see you there,* she'd said. Both families were probably wondering where they were by now, but the certainty that they'd be together would stop them from worrying.

Because Vivi had to go everywhere with an overnight bag in case a call came from the transplant centre, she had no need to pack any clothes or toiletries, but she wanted to anyway. 'Maybe I can stay for more than one night?' she said playfully against his lips, while handing him the fourteen different sorts of medication that she had to take each day.

'Maybe,' Josh said, 'we could turn my flat into our home.'

She stood back to look at him. Did he mean what she thought . . . ? Seeing from his expression that she'd understood him completely, she felt suddenly so emotional that she could find no words.

'We don't have to make love every night, if that's worrying you,' he told her.

'But I want to,' she insisted, turning her mouth to his hand as he wiped away her tears. 'And I want to make your flat our home.' What was the point in denying themselves? The call might never come, and if there was no new heart for her, then surely they should be spending every minute of every hour that they could together.

CHAPTER TWENTY

VIVIENNE

Present Day

Jim Lynskey had gone silent again. Neither his vlog nor his blog had been updated for over a week, nor had he responded to the many messages Vivi had sent. She checked her account three or four times a day, and tried hard to think positively, but inside she couldn't stop herself fearing the worst. She knew it made no sense to believe that she was being shown her future through him, that everything he'd experienced she was going to experience too, but she could think of no other reason for the way she'd connected with him when there were so many others who shared their need for a new heart.

If he was back in hospital then something must have happened to put him there – another infection? A serious deterioration? A fault with his Ventricular Assist Device? Or maybe, by now, he was recovering from a life-saving transplant and would soon be ready to sit up and sing at the top of his voice. He loved music, she knew that from his vlogs, and he was passionate about football too, although of course he never played.

Maybe he'd been invited to train with West Brom, his favourite team, and was too busy experiencing the exhilarating adrenalin rushes to his new, healthy heart to bother with his old life any more. Of course that wouldn't be the case, the recovery period after the transplant was far too long to allow for it, but she liked to imagine it nonetheless.

'Do you know how to contact his family?' Josh asked from the kitchen, where he was taking the heavy dish of mushroom bourguignon, made by Vivi, from the oven.

'I've found his mother and sister on Facebook,' she replied, 'but they're not posting anything either. If I could private message them I'd ask how he is, but we're not connected and I don't feel right about just crashing in on them.'

As the entryphone sounded, alerting them to Sam and Michelle's arrival, Josh placed the hot dish on the hob and went to buzz them in while Vivi closed her laptop and told herself firmly that Jim was OK. He'd be back online again any day now and she'd be FaceTiming, or at least messaging him, to congratulate him on his successful transplant.

By the time Sam and Michelle came into the flat their hosts were standing at the centre of the sitting room, ready to welcome their best friends to their very first dinner party in their new, shared home. The fact that both Sam and Michelle had helped to move Josh's old furniture out and replace it with Vivi's far more elegant, and in some cases whimsical, pieces, was a minor detail. They hadn't seen the place since it was properly finished, in part because Vivi had wanted to wow them with how cosy yet glamorous it now was, but also because she'd had to spend the last few days in bed recovering from too much activity.

Fortunately she was up again now, and her lungs were no longer struggling quite so hard to take in air, due to the reduced blood flow that had caused the problem in the first place. Best of all was that she hadn't suffered any shocks since the night she'd run onto the beach, apart from the one that had happened at the time. Not a single one had struck her since then, which was as amazing to her as it was to everyone else, including her cardiac team. She'd fessed up to them after deciding it was probably best they knew, so they'd have a full picture should something happen further down the road. So it would seem that in spite of the strain she'd put on her heart by running like that, she hadn't, as far as they could tell, hastened herself to the next stage of treatment: to bypass surgery for the fitting of a Ventricular Assist Device. Nor had the frequency with which she and Josh were making love, albeit gently, caused a problem yet, although she knew from her chats with the clinic that the scrutiny of her overnight readings had begun to show a few anomalies lately.

'Are you concerned?' she'd asked the cardiac physiologist, Trey, when he'd told her. She'd felt sick with nerves and fear, feeling her time with Josh shortening as if someone were pressing a delete key.

'Let's just say we're interested,' he'd replied tactfully, and clutching at what sounded to her like a mild concern she'd been happy to leave it at that.

'This place is amazing,' Michelle declared, throwing out her arms, then wrapping them round Vivi. 'You've made it so . . . so . . . what's the word?' she asked Sam.

'Feminine?' he suggested.

'You should see the bedroom,' Josh muttered, though Vivi knew he loved it almost as much as she did, for the sight of him lying naked in a sea of frost-blue linens and gossamer voile, flagrantly and uncompromisingly male amongst all this femininity, was so erotic that she simply couldn't keep her hands off him. He was nothing if not an exhibitionist, she'd discovered, and it seemed the trait was rubbing off on her, for they loved being naked together whether in bed, in the bath, or in each other's arms.

'It's stunning,' Michelle told her decisively. 'Your things fit in here beautifully, and you are looking so scrumptious we might have to eat you for dinner.'

'Don't worry, we have something much tastier,' Vivi assured her as she hugged Sam hello, 'but with even less meat. In fact no meat at all.'

Catching Sam's worried expression, Josh handed him a beer and Michelle a glass of wine as he said, 'We've become reducetarians.'

Sam blinked. 'What's that when it's at home?' he demanded.

'It means we still eat meat,' Vivi explained, 'but a lot less of it, which is good for our health, the planet and animals. There's a book about it. I'll send you a link if you like.'

'Yes please,' Michelle responded.

Sam's alarm showed as he looked at Josh for help.

'Actually, I'm on board for this one,' Josh told him. 'Stopping animal cruelty is my thing, you know that, and if it has positive side effects for health and the planet, why wouldn't we do it?'

'My husband's such a Neanderthal,' Michelle teased,

rubbing Sam's arm, 'but don't worry, darling, your Sunday roasts and burger barbies are safe. They'll just be ethically sourced, the same as they've always been.'

Enjoying the relief on Sam's face, Vivi went round to the kitchen to check on things, while Josh lit candles and turned down the lights. 'Tonight's recipe is one of Josh's grandmother's,' she informed them, 'and all the ingredients have come from Deerwood, including the mushrooms.'

'Oh, magic,' Sam joked, rubbing his hands and making his wife and Josh groan.

Looking up as her phone rang, Vivi was aware, as Josh went to get it, that he, like her, was daring to hope that it might be the call they were waiting for. The need to hear from the transplant centre had all but dominated their days since they'd moved in together, and they couldn't be sure whether willing it to happen would bring it about, or was it in some way jinxing it?

It wasn't the centre, and she wondered whose disappointment was the greater, hers or his. The fact that every day was giving her more and more reasons to live made no difference at all to where she came on the transplant list – or to the fate that would ultimately decide whether she should die before a donor could be found. It was such a horrible thought that she could never allow herself to stay with it for long.

It was later in the evening, after they'd finished eating and were sprawled on the sofas and new floor cushions, that Vivi said to Michelle, 'By the way, I got the results of my DNA ancestry search.'

Michelle's eyes widened with interest.

Vivi grimaced. 'Unfortunately it didn't come up with

a replacement for the pig,' which was how she now referred to Charlie Bleasdale, if she had to refer to him at all, and she tried not to. 'Not that I was expecting it, and thank God there was no mention of him – of course I wasn't expecting that either.'

'In fact,' Josh added teasingly, 'all it did come up with was a possible fourth cousin somewhere in Dublin, and the fact that she's forty-nine per cent British, thirty-nine per cent Western European and twelve per cent other. It's the twelve per cent other that's intriguing me the most – I haven't quite decided yet whether or not to be scared.'

As the others laughed, Vivi said, 'I gave them so little to go on, it's a miracle they came up with anything at all. Anyway, I'm far more interested in Josh's ancestry these days, or I would be if I could get him to engage. Is he hiding some skeletons that you know of, Sam?'

Grinning, Sam said, 'Don't worry, mate, they're safe with me.'

Josh was about to respond when Vivi's phone rang again.

It was awful the way everyone's hopes sharpened as she reached for it, and then how deflated they all seemed when she signalled that it still wasn't the call they were waiting for. However, while she was confirming her yoga class with Josh's sister Zoe at Deerwood the next morning an iMessage arrived from Jim Lynskey.

Having to find out immediately what it said, she quickly clicked on.

Hey, sorry I haven't been in touch. I was cruising the fjords in Norway with my dad. Have you ever been? It's something else. How are you? Jim.

As she passed the phone to Josh she was torn between an overwhelming relief that Jim was OK, not in hospital and not suffering any sort of decline, and despondency that he still hadn't found a new heart.

'Save9Lives,' Vivienne read aloud from the screen.

'Mm, it's got a good ring,' Josh responded approvingly. 'I like the logo too.'

They were sitting in front of her laptop assessing the various visuals that Jim Lynskey had sent over for his proposed donor campaign. He'd promised them a couple of days ago, but Vivi knew how difficult it was to meet promises when your heart conspired against you, and apparently Jim's was currently causing him a lot of pain. She only knew that because he'd admitted it after not being in touch for a couple of days, though the tone of his messages and eagerness for her and Josh to critique his ideas and hopefully support them would never have given him away.

'Can one donor save nine lives?' Josh asked curiously. 'I thought it was eight.'

'It depends how you look at it,' Vivienne replied. 'Yes, it is eight, but the extra one is meant to symbolize all the other lives that can be vastly improved, even transformed by one person's organs. As many as fifty people can be helped in this way.'

He nodded understanding. 'OK, so the main aim of the campaign isn't only to persuade more people to sign up to the register, it's to make them understand the importance of telling their families.'

'So that a next of kin,' Vivi continued, 'doesn't refuse to let organs go. That happens quite a lot, apparently.'

Josh clicked through to a page of donor statistics and after taking a while to study it, he said, 'It doesn't tell us here how many people die in the UK each year waiting for transplants, but it's obviously a whole lot more than eight hundred and twenty-nine, which is apparently how many donors saved lives in the past twelve months.'

'So less than a thousand,' she said glumly, 'and there are six and half thousand on the organ transplant waiting list.'

'So what I'm asking myself,' Josh continued, 'is how many healthy organs are cremated or buried every *day* that could have been used to make a massive difference to someone's life? I guess we'll never know the answer to that.' He clicked through to an NHS page titled Cardiothoracic Activity, wanting, for obvious reasons, to focus more closely on heart donation. 'So,' he said, after reading it through, 'there have been one hundred and ninety-eight heart transplants this past year, which is more than I'd expected, but only forty of them were non-urgent, which is the category you currently fall into.'

After working it out, she said, 'That means I have a twenty per cent chance of receiving a new heart, the same as Jim, because he's not on the super-urgent list either.' The prospects were so gloomy that she might have regretted getting into it, were Jim's proactive efforts to find himself a heart not so energizing and admirable. She wanted to be on his team, to share his optimism and altruism by doing what she could for everyone on the transplant waiting list, which would be so much shorter if more people were willing to sign up to it.

'Ah, here he is,' Josh said, as the FaceTime ringer sounded.

As Jim Lynskey's young, handsome face came onto the screen Vivi felt the tragedy of his situation mix with a flood of affection. He reminded her a lot of her brother with his short dark hair, unshaven chin and engaging smile. He had the sassy look of a young musician or a sportsman, the kind the girls went for in numbers. There was nothing about him at all to suggest that he was entirely dependent on a VAD to stay alive.

'Hey,' he said, chirpily. 'How are you?'

Smiling, Vivi said, 'I'm OK. It's good to see you. This is Josh.'

Raising a hand, Josh said, 'We were glad to learn you were on holiday when we didn't hear from you.'

'Yeah, right. It was cool. You should go sometime, if you've never been.'

Thinking of how much they'd enjoy it, Vivi said, 'We've been looking at your Save9Lives campaign and we like the logo a lot. And the wording. We're wondering if there's a website yet?'

Jim grimaced. 'I'm trying to get funding for it,' he replied. 'It's difficult to get anyone to sponsor it when it's not a charity; people want to be sure of where their money's going, and if they can get a tax break on it, all the better.'

Understanding that, she said, 'How much are you looking for?'

He shrugged and glanced away from the camera, apparently uncomfortable with mentioning a figure. 'I've got a friend who's a really good designer,' he said.

'He wouldn't cost much. He's a student, like me, so he's trying to earn some money.'

'There are many ways of raising funds,' Josh told him, 'but what we need to sort out first is the content you want to include in the website. I've seen the videos you sent Vivi of you talking about your condition, what it's like to be on the transplant list, and why it's important to get the message out about organ donation. You're good on camera, you're also young, good-looking and articulate, so I think you should be the primary contributor, but we also need footage of more people on the waiting list.'

Jim nodded agreement. 'There's quite a bit of education needed too,' he continued. 'Can you believe some people refuse to go on the list because they think that if doctors or paramedics know they're on it they won't try to save them?'

'Oh God,' Vivi groaned, knowing the ignorance existed but having no clear idea yet how to tackle it.

'A lot of people cherry-pick,' Jim went on. 'They'll sign up to donate a kidney and maybe a lung, or a heart, which is fine, they have the right to do that, but the reasons they hold back on other organs aren't always sound.'

'Go on,' Josh prompted.

'They say things like, "No one would want my liver if they knew how much I drank", when they've got no idea what kind of condition their liver is in. It might be perfectly OK, but they're just not giving it a chance. Then there are those who say, "I don't want anyone having my eyes, what if I can still see through them? It would be so weird looking in the mirror and seeing someone else's face."'

That might have been funny if it weren't so ludicrous.

'What other kinds of objections are there?' Josh asked.

'Religious, but that's because a lot of people don't understand what their religion actually says about donation. In fact, no religion is actively against it that I can find. Receiving someone else's organs is a different story, but giving up your own isn't a problem.'

'So it's basically a lack of information and understanding that we're up against,' Josh said.

Jim nodded. 'There was a girl in the news today, did you see it? She was thirteen and she died of a brain aneurysm. They've just worked out that she saved a total of eight lives with her organs.'

Thinking of the girl's parents and how brave and selfless they'd been at what must have been the worst time of their lives, Vivi said, 'It would be good to have an interview with her family if they'll agree to it. Can you send me a link to the news item?'

'I've already been in touch,' Jim told her. 'I'm waiting to hear back, but I'll send the link anyway and I'll put you in touch with Sarah, who's also waiting for a heart. I know she'll agree to be interviewed.'

Impressed by how focused he was, Vivi said, 'That's great. Meantime, we'll carry out some more research at our end, and put it together with yours to start shaping up the website content.' Even if the campaign didn't end up helping her and Jim, it could make all the difference to others, and why wouldn't they want to do that? 'Before you go,' she said, her tone taking on a more affectionate note, 'how's the pain?'

Looking royally fed up, he shrugged. 'I'm on codeine,' he replied flatly.

A nut to crack a sledgehammer? 'Do you know exactly what's causing it?' she asked.

He shook his head and though he didn't say *sometimes knowing is too hard,* she knew it was what he was thinking.

Feeling worried and a little dispirited as they rang off, she turned to Josh and rested her head on his shoulder.

'It's important that we do this,' he said, putting an arm around her. 'I realize it won't necessarily give us what we want for you, but the alternative is to do nothing and that's not going to work for either of us.'

Knowing that was true, she kissed him and got up to answer the entryphone. After buzzing her mother in she went to put on the kettle. There was a lot going round in her mind, mostly about Jim, and how she felt as though they were being sucked towards a cliff edge. He was ahead of her, getting closer and closer, but she was clinging tightly to the rope, trying to haul him back before he went over. If he did, he'd take her with him, not right away, but soon after.

Or maybe he wouldn't go over, a new heart would be found at the last minute, and then she'd be on the cliff edge alone.

Gina had already visited the flat several times by now, so she was perfectly familiar with it, and was always happy to see Josh, even though Vivi knew that she worried about the obvious strain on the relationship. Vivi worried about it too, especially when she considered how selfish she was being. She couldn't give him what he deserved, what she knew he wanted more than anything, the chance of a long life together, and children.

'Are you OK?' Gina asked, taking the tea Vivi was passing her. 'You seem . . . distracted.'

Vivi put on a smile. 'I'm fine,' she assured her mother. 'How are you?'

Gina's eyebrows rose. 'We've already been through that,' she told her, 'we've moved on, but you haven't heard a word I've said, have you?'

Vivi glanced at Josh, and seeing amusement in his eyes she relaxed a little. Apparently it hadn't been anything serious. 'Sorry,' she said to her mother, 'what were you saying?'

Gina waved a dismissive hand. 'Oh, nothing important,' she replied airily, 'I was just asking how you'd feel if Gil turned the main sitting room into his office.'

It took a moment for understanding to dawn; when it did Vivi's eyes flew open with delight. 'Gil's moving back to Kesterly?' she cried, overcome with happiness for her mother. 'That's fantastic. You two should never have split up in the first place.'

'No, probably not,' Gina admitted, 'but I'm handling things a bit differently now.'

Going to hug her, Vivi looked at Josh and wondered if he was feeling suddenly trapped by this new turn of events. It wasn't what his expression was saying; nevertheless, she should probably assure him later that it didn't mean she couldn't go back to Bay Lane, it just meant she wouldn't have her own sitting room any more.

'Are you crazy?' he laughed, when she got round to trying out the reassurance. 'As far as I'm concerned Gil moving in with your mother is the best news I've had since you agreed to move in here. I don't want you going anywhere without me, ever – apart from to yoga and meditation and maybe the bathroom once in a while.'

Biting on her smile, she walked into his arms and felt the power of him enfolding her the way it always did.

'Where is all this insecurity suddenly coming from?' he asked gently. 'You don't really doubt me, surely?'

She shook her head, no she didn't, and she knew the clouds would soon pass to make way for more sunshine; it was just that the really dark times were lurking, and there was simply no knowing when they would come to stay.

CHAPTER TWENTY-ONE
VIVIENNE

Present Day

Days soon began turning into weeks, and though Vivi suffered several challenging spells, both mentally and physically, she had periods when she felt almost as normal and strong as she had before her life in London had come to an end. During those times it was hard not to hope that the prognosis for her life expectancy had been wrong, that she was going to defy them all and stage a miraculous recovery. In more difficult and pragmatic moments she understood that her perceived improvement had far more to do with the drugs she was taking to help stabilize her wait for a new heart.

Her wait for someone to die.

She found it so hard to get her head around that, in spite of how often Josh and her mother – everyone she loved – reminded her that no one was giving up their lives willingly so she could live. They were on their own journey, and what happened to them was as random, or preordained, as what was happening to her.

Only to herself did she ever admit how much loving so wholeheartedly unnerved her, making her fear there would be a price to pay for the physical exertion, never mind the hope that came with it. But apart from the unavoidable side effects of the drugs – numbing fatigue, violent headaches and nausea – she hadn't yet been called to account. Nor had she been able to tell Josh that perhaps they shouldn't make love so often. She knew if she did he'd stop right away, and that wasn't what she wanted at all.

She spent most days accompanying him on his rounds and emergency call-outs and soon became so involved with the animals, and with the hectic social project that was Deerwood, that she could hardly remember the life she'd had before. She felt no yearning for it – if she thought about it at all it felt strangely distant, even vague, as though it had happened to somebody else. What mattered much more to her now was being able to lie down in the hay with an elderly ram, smoothing his tired face as Josh quietly sent him on his way. Or she'd dab tears from the eyes of distressed cows whose calves had been taken to market – she'd had no idea until now that cows could cry, much less that they could pine for their young. She'd even lent a hand, up to the elbow, to bring a tiny donkey foal into the world. A sight she'd never forget was Josh's skilful extraction of a rotten tooth from the mouth of a fully-grown lioness at Kesterly Zoo. As large as his hands were, they'd appeared almost fragile between the vast, powerful jaws of the heavily anaesthetized beast.

There was so much to do, and to learn about his world, not only for her, but for the junior vet, Aaron, whom Josh took on to help with the load.

When they weren't at Deerwood or visiting the many farms, stables, sanctuaries and kennels that fell into his area, they were usually at home relaxing, or working on Save9Lives. They'd gathered a lot of information by now, and since Vivi had already received assurances from the GaLs that they were happy to fund the website – and would give even more if it was needed – they'd soon be ready to engage a professional designer. It wasn't that they were cutting out Jim's student friend, it was simply that he'd decided the project was going to be too big for him now that his final year was underway.

Jim himself, with all the courage and optimism they admired so much, was working hard to gain awareness for his campaign, and listening to him, talking to him over FaceTime, Vivi could almost believe there was nothing wrong with him. Outwardly there was no sign of the pump that kept his heart going, for he wore the cumbersome batteries under his shirt, and the bulk of them was always out of frame.

'Are you still in pain?' she asked him one day.

He nodded almost wryly. 'I'm getting used to it,' he told her. 'I won't let it hold me back.'

Moved by his determination, she said, 'What sort of drugs are you on?'

He named them all, and the list was so long that they both ended up laughing. What else could they do? 'Do you ever pray?' she ventured to ask.

His eyes drifted as he said, 'I used to, but I've kind of lost my faith since the wait . . .' He shrugged, as if to say the wait had been so long.

Having discovered from reading other people's stories that many experienced a move closer to God as the prospect of death became an encroaching reality, the doubt in his beliefs interested her more than it surprised her. Did he want to talk about it, she wondered. Had he believed before?

'Yes, I did,' he replied when she asked. 'Or I thought I did. This kind of changes things, or it has for me. How about you?'

Since she'd never attended church as a child, or even thought much about God before, she shook her head. 'I'm not sure I know how to pray,' she admitted. 'But even if I did would it really make a difference?'

Though he looked unconvinced, he said, 'It does for some people.' He shrugged again. 'I say, whatever works. Does Josh believe?'

Knowing that Josh's ambivalence was much the same as her own, she said, 'We both think that when you're in this position you're ready to grab at anything, and if turning to God helps then that's what you should do. Maybe we will if, when, things get worse. It's hard to say.' She sighed shakily at the thought of that time. 'God takes care of his own, is what some people say,' she added.

He nodded. 'Except, you've only got to look at all the things happening around the world to people – to children – who worship all the time to know that's not true. It's hard to trust in a God who repays his followers with war and famine . . .'

She regarded him carefully, his image as clear and real as if he were with her, not on a screen. 'Jim, you're not giving up hope, are you?' she asked softly.

After a moment he broke into his boyish smile. 'Not me,' he assured her, assuming his familiar brave face. 'I just get a bit down when I think about God, that's all, but don't let that stop you and Josh from praying if you want to. Like I said, whatever works.' Then, changing the subject, 'Remember Sarah who I told you about? She's on the transplant list? Well, she's confirmed that she's OK with being interviewed for the website, provided you and Josh think she's right for it. Is there a good time for her to FaceTime you?'

After promising to message him as soon as she'd spoken to Josh, Vivi rang off and sat quietly for a while thinking about Jim and God and faith and miracles – and the fact that maybe she'd used up her quota with having survived her heart attack and cardiac arrests so she could have Josh in her life before she went.

They'd have FaceTimed Sarah sooner if Vivi hadn't developed a sudden intolerance to one of her drugs. To her relief she wasn't hospitalized, but she was restricted to bed for over a week with severe migraines and nausea, and the growing fear of what would happen if she continued to reject the medication . . .

She couldn't go any further with that thought, it would only lead her into panic or depression and for Josh's sake, as well as her own, she mustn't allow that to happen.

So, on the first day that she was able to sit up for a while without feeling queasy or faint, and Sarah was able to make it too, Josh set up the laptop and they met the young mother via FaceTime.

She was impossible not to love right away; with her wild auburn curls, sky-blue eyes and rosebud mouth she looked so playful and sweet-natured that it was hard to believe she was both sick, and in her thirties.

The only suggestion that she wasn't as healthy as she at first appeared was in the purplish hue of her lips and the faintly bruised sockets of her eyes.

'How long have you been on the transplant list?' Josh asked, after they'd introduced themselves.

'This time just a couple of months,' she replied. 'I was on it for about a year before I had the VAD fitted, but then I had to come off while I recovered from the surgery.'

Understanding that she'd have been too sick for another major procedure during that time, Vivi said, 'Have things improved on an everyday basis since you've had the VAD?'

Sarah smiled and grimaced. 'Not especially,' she replied, 'it takes some getting used to: not having a pulse is kind of weird. But it's still early days, so I'll probably get used to it.'

Wanting to ask exactly how it impacted life with her husband, whether the bulky battery and controller, and the driveline – an external umbilical connecting the pump to her heart – prevented or impeded their intimacy, Vivi tried to form the words, but found she couldn't. Anyway, it was a question for when Josh wasn't there, since it would probably embarrass Sarah this early in their acquaintance. It might also have an answer that she'd rather think about alone for a while.

Josh was about to continue when Sarah excused herself, and leaned out of frame. They could hear a child's voice, urgent and pleading, and when Sarah reappeared on the screen the dearest little boy with a bright red buzz cut and cornflake freckles was on her lap.

'This is Ben,' she told them, settling him down. 'You can only stay if you behave yourself,' she informed him. 'Are you going to say hello?'

Though Ben's blue eyes didn't leave the screen, he leaned back hard into his mother.

'Oh, this is all show,' Sarah chided. 'You're not shy really.'

'How old are you?' Josh asked him.

Ben said, 'Ten!'

Everyone laughed, since it was patently not true. 'I think you're four, aren't you?' Sarah prompted.

'I had a birthday,' he informed Josh and Vivi, 'and all my friends came.'

'Cool,' Josh responded. 'Did you play games?'

He nodded. 'We played rugby on the grass. I'm good at rugby. Grandpa says I'll be prof . . .' He looked up at his mother. 'Professional,' she whispered. 'Fessional one day,' he declared. 'Can you play rugby?'

Josh said, 'I used to when I was at school, but I don't think I was as good as you.'

Ben seemed to take that as a given. 'Grandpa and me go to watch our team sometimes, but Mummy doesn't come because she's a girl.'

As though reading the question in Vivi's mind, Sarah said, 'I'm a single parent, but my dad is great with him.'

Leaning towards the camera, Ben said to Josh, 'I had a PlayStation for my birthday.'

'Wow,' Josh responded, suitably impressed.

'We got it on eBay and it came with a game of Yooka-Laylee.'

'Is that your favourite?' Josh asked.

Ben put a finger to his lips as he tried to remember. 'I think so,' he said. 'Do you know how to play it?'

'I'm afraid I don't,' Josh admitted.

Ben seemed to consider whether or not this was a problem. 'Do you have any children?' he asked.

As Vivi's longing flared into a knot of discomfort, for this was something she and Josh had never discussed – they couldn't – Sarah said, 'You're not supposed to ask questions like that.'

'No, I don't have any children,' Josh told him kindly. 'But I have nieces and nephews.'

Apparently deciding that made him OK, Ben said, 'I can beat Mummy at most of our games. She's not very good, are you, Mummy?'

With a laugh, Sarah pressed a kiss to his head. 'Not as good as you,' she assured him. 'Now, would you like to get down?'

He shook his head, and looked up at her as he whispered, 'Are they going to find you a new heart?'

Sarah's smile was sad as she said, 'Not today, sweetheart.'

Seeming just as sad, he leaned into her as he turned back to the screen. 'Do you know where my mummy can find a heart?' he asked hopefully.

'I wish we did,' Vivi replied, wanting to hug him, 'but we're doing our best.'

He gave that some thought, then said, 'Have *you* got any children?'

Feeling Josh's arm go around her, Vivi said, 'No, but if I did I'd like to have a little boy just like you.'

Ben nodded, clearly understanding that.

Pulling him tighter into her arms, Sarah said,

'Obviously, finding a new heart would make all the difference in the world to us.' She didn't have to add that it would mean she could watch her precious son grow up, and no longer have to live with the constant fear of what would happen to him if a donor wasn't found, it was there in her eyes.

'Doesn't having a small child put you on the super-urgent list?' Vivi asked.

Sarah shook her head as she smoothed Ben's hair. 'It doesn't work like that,' she replied. 'At the moment I'm able to function with the VAD. It's only if a problem develops with it that things might change. Then you've got to hope that the problems don't put you into the category of being too sick for a transplant. Anyway, we try to look on the bright side, don't we, Ben? It's not like no one on the non-urgent list ever gets a heart, because they do. I even got called in for one a while back, before the VAD, but by the time I got there they'd discovered there was a problem with the donor heart so it couldn't go ahead.'

Understanding how crushing that blow must have been, Vivi had to shut her mind down to the horror and frustration of it before it crushed her too.

Josh said, 'If you're willing to repeat all this on camera, it would make you one of our most powerful contributors to the website.'

'I'm happy to do it,' she assured him. 'Anything to get the message home about organ donation. You don't know what it's like, waiting, until it's happening to you.'

After they'd rung off Vivi leaned back against Josh and closed her eyes. Small children, healthy hearts, carefree hopes and dreams, none of it a part of life for them. But at least she and Sarah were amongst the lucky ones who could wait at home; so many were hospital-bound, some miles from their families. Vivi knew she couldn't bear that: the praying and hoping every minute of every day that the right heart could be found to set her free.

Seeming to know what she was thinking, Josh wrapped her in close and pressed his lips to her head.

'If we do go to church and pray,' she said, bringing up a discussion from the night before, 'we have to include Sarah and Ben. And Jim, of course.'

'I agree,' he murmured.

'And I think,' she added, putting her hands over his, 'just in case a chat with God might work, we should go sooner rather than later.'

Vivi wasn't so much surprised, when she received a call from the cardiac clinic asking her to go in, as she was struck with dread, for she'd sensed it was coming, how could she not? Her increasing exhaustion, combined with continued nausea and dizziness, clearly meant that she was rejecting her medication again. This time they weren't simply going to change her prescription, they were probably going to carry out a right-heart cathet-erization, the procedure that helped them decide if she was eligible for a VAD. If she was, the implantation would require extremely delicate open-heart surgery and up to a three-week stay in hospital. After that she'd have to live with the cumbersome apparatus strung about her neck, packed around her body, knowing that if it failed she very probably wouldn't survive.

She knew crying wouldn't change anything, that it

was no more effective than praying, but what else could she do? There was no clearer sign than this that time was running out, and that the quality of the life she had left was going into a steep decline.

'But you're always talking about Jim Lynskey and how well he's coping with a VAD,' Michelle pointed out when she brought in lunch later.

Vivi looked at the food so kindly prepared by Michelle and had to fight down another wave of nausea. 'We're all different,' she explained, 'but you're right, it's supposed to improve everything from my breathing to my blood flow, which is great, but it doesn't get us away from the fact that it's a final bridge to a transplant that might never happen.'

Though Michelle's face was pale with worry, she was trying to stay positive. 'Did the cardiologist's secretary actually say that's why you're being called in?' she asked.

'No, of course not, it wouldn't be her place to. I just know that it's the next step, and with the way I've been feeling lately . . .' She looked at the food and once again felt her stomach rise.

Apparently realizing the problem, Michelle quickly cleared the salads away. 'So when's the appointment?' she asked, coming back from the kitchen.

'Next Monday. So they're not hanging around.' That alone was alarming, but she had to remind herself that it was better than being left until it was too late.

'Have you told Josh about it yet?'

Vivi shook her head. 'He's got several surgeries on the agenda today, so I don't want to call him. I just need to try and get my head round what it's going to be like to have two brick-size devices in the bed with us, attached to a driveline planted under my diaphragm.'

Frowning, Michelle said, 'I can't see it making a difference to him . . .'

'But it would to me,' Vivi cried in frustration. 'I don't want it there, even if it is supposed to make me feel better, keep me alive even. It'll be a constant reminder of everything I'd rather forget, and the fact that my condition is worsening is my own fault. The adrenalin rush of making love has put added pressure on my heart and brought the end closer . . .' She clasped her hands to her face, hating herself for the tears that wouldn't stop, and the self-pity that was no more effective than crying or praying, but still unstoppable.

'Making love when you have an ICD isn't forbidden,' Michelle said. 'You told me that yourself . . .'

'But I didn't allow enough time for my heart to build up the strength it needed to cope. They warned me about it right after the ICD was implanted. OK, they didn't put a time on it, but they were clear that intimate relations weren't a good idea until I was stronger. And yes, there have been times when I've felt stronger, but I've lost count of how often my medication's had to be changed since, and I've never admitted to the physiologists that I'm making love. They haven't known what they're dealing with, and now here I am, reaping the results of my deception . . . Oh God, I'm sorry, I'm sorry, I need to pull myself together. I don't want Josh seeing me like this.'

Going to her, Michelle said, 'Don't apologize to me. I understand how horrible this is for you; I just wish there was something I could do.'

Vivi sobbed, 'The only person who can do that is the one who has to die to make a heart available, and how can I wish for that when whoever it is will have a family and friends who love them just as much as mine love me?'

Holding her closer, Michelle said, 'You can't allow yourself to think that way. You have no more control over fate than the rest of us, so there's nothing wrong with putting all our hopes into finding a new heart for you.'

'We can do that,' Vivi agreed, 'but then we have to remember that there are a hundred or more people also waiting who are more likely to get it than me.'

The following Monday it was bright but cold as Josh drove them to the clinic. He'd insisted on taking her, and she was glad, because having him close was strengthening her determination to cope with whatever was in store. Her mother and Gil came too, but when she was called through for the ECG, echogram, X-rays, angiogram, blood and respiratory tests and numerous further scans and assessments, she went alone.

They were there for virtually the entire day, with Josh, Gina and Gil haunting the corridors and coffee shops as they waited, and Vivi sending occasional texts to update them on what was happening. No mention of a catheterization yet, she told them, and she hadn't asked for fear of seeming to make the suggestion.

How absurd she was.

Eventually she came to join them in the waiting room and sat with her head on Josh's shoulder and a hand in her mother's until she was called back in. Rather than dread the results of her tests, she made herself think only of how she and Josh had spent the evening before. It was so much more calming to project her mind back instead of forward, especially when she had something so wonderful to look back on.

In a way, knowing everything would probably change from tomorrow, it had felt as though they were going to a last supper at Michelle and Sam's. However, before they'd left the flat Josh had done something that had made her happier – although in a way sadder – than she'd ever felt in her life.

'When this next stage is over,' he'd said, holding her hands in his and gazing far into her eyes, 'and you're feeling strong again, do you think you might like to marry me?'

As yet more tears flooded her eyes and she started to sob, he folded her into his arms.

'Can I take that as a yes?' he murmured.

'Yes,' she choked, 'it's a yes. Oh God, I love you so much. I didn't know it was even possible to love someone so much.'

'Me neither,' he responded huskily, 'and I could question why it's making you cry, but then you might feel you have to answer and right now I'd rather kiss you.'

So that was how he'd managed to turn dinner last night into a celebration instead of some kind of depressing meal that had to be got through, and when they'd returned home later and made love, he'd shown her exactly how it could be done with two bricks in the bed.

Now, smiling at the idiocy of it, she snuggled more

closely into him and checked her phone as a text arrived. It was from Jim Lynskey.

Just to say thinking of you. Hope it's going all right. Don't forget to let me know what they say. Jx

A few minutes later her phone buzzed again; this time it was a message from Sarah Barker whom she hadn't told about today, but apparently Jim had. *Have you received the results yet? VAD not as bad as you might think, promise. Sx*

Vivi hadn't been tested for one, but maybe that was still to come.

What if they carried it out and decided she wasn't eligible? What then?

More long, dreadful minutes ticked by as they continued to wait. Gina received a text from Mark asking for an update, and a while after that Josh took a call from his mother.

'No news yet,' Vivi heard him say, and then her insides tightened with unease as his face paled. 'Don't worry, I'm at the hospital,' he said, sitting forward. 'I'll find him when he comes in. Are you on your way? OK, I'll see you when you get here.' As he rang off he turned to Vivi. 'They think my grandfather has had a stroke. The paramedics are bringing him into A & E . . .'

'You have to go and find him,' she insisted. 'I'll be fine, honestly. Mum will come in with me and if I'm admitted for some reason she or Gil will let you know where I am.'

Seeing he was as reluctant to leave her as she was to let him go, she whispered in his ear, 'Tell David that I'm counting on him being at our wedding.'

He touched a hand to her face and as he kissed her

he said, 'I love you, Vivienne Shager, and whatever they say in there, just remember, nothing's ever going to change that.'

At last Vivi and her mother were seated opposite the cardiologist, Saanvi Sharvelle, the softly-spoken Canadian whom they'd last seen several months ago during Vivi's first visit to the clinic. Since then Dr Sharvelle had presumably overseen the monitoring of Vivi's progress, and from the way her sharp grey eyes were fixed on the computer screen in front of her now she was still assimilating and assessing the results of today.

'OK,' she said finally, turning to them. She didn't smile, or change the tone of her voice as she apologized for making them wait so long, she simply linked her long fingers together and rested them on the desk in front of her.

'I've been in regular contact with your team at the transplant centre,' she told Vivi, 'and we are all of the same opinion, which is why you've been called in today to undergo more tests.'

Vivi's mouth was dry; her nerves were so tight that she had no idea how hard she was squeezing her mother's hand until Gina was forced to ease herself free.

'First of all,' Dr Sharvelle said evenly, 'there is a . . . *complication* that we weren't expecting . . .'

Vivi reeled and missed the next few words.

'. . . but before we get into the detail,' Sharvelle was saying, 'you need to understand that your decision will affect whether or not you remain on the transplant list.'

Vivi swallowed drily and glanced at her mother. She knew she'd have to come off the list if she had a VAD, at least for a while; she also knew that some people refused them.

'You'll continue with the ICD,' Dr Sharvelle informed her, 'and the medication, of course . . .'

Vivi was finding it impossible to focus. She kept missing words, misunderstanding their meaning, then her mother suddenly gulped on a sob, clasping her hands to her face.

Vivi stared at the doctor. What had she said? What did all this mean? *Oh God, oh God, it was obviously really bad.*

Apparently realizing Vivi hadn't connected with what she'd been told the doctor began again, this time spelling it out more clearly.

Vivi was already at the flat by the time Josh came in from the hospital looking tired, but relieved, for David's suspected stroke had turned out to be a much less serious TIA.

'They've decided to keep him in overnight,' he said, pulling her into his arms, 'and Nate will collect him in the morning. Now I want to hear about you.'

She gazed up at him, and wondered if he really was even more handsome than she'd realized, or perhaps it was just that her news was making her see him in a clearer light.

'What?' he prompted, when she continued to look at him.

She found herself turning away. Right up until the time he'd come through the door she'd been rehearsing how to tell him what the doctor had said, but she still wasn't sure that she'd found the right words.

Taking her arm, he turned her back. 'What is it?' he asked darkly, and tilting her chin up so he could see her expression, his own tightened with more unease. 'Tell me what it is,' he said urgently.

She swallowed hard, bracing herself. 'We're . . . we're going to have a baby,' she whispered raggedly.

He stared at her in shock, appearing to have no idea how it could have happened, which might have been funny if the situation weren't so serious. A beat later she could almost see, even hear, the questions blazing around in his head.

Answering them before he could ask, she said, 'They can't tell me for certain yet if my medication has already caused any damage to the foetus. I have to see an obstetrician tomorrow. We might know more then, but it'll probably be a few more weeks before they can tell us anything for certain.'

Taking that in, he swallowed drily as he said, 'So they're not saying that you shouldn't have it?'

She shook her head. 'In fact, they've already taken me off the warfarin and put me on unfractionated heparin instead – anticoagulants can be a big problem during pregnancy, apparently. A lot will depend on the results of the ultrasound tomorrow. If the obstetrician is happy for things to continue, then they'll keep a close eye on me throughout. It'll probably mean having to spend a lot of the time with my feet up, and maybe I'll even have to stay in hospital until it's born. It'll also mean coming off the transplant list, but I want this baby so much, Josh. Tell me you do too.'

Wrapping her tightly in his arms, he said, 'Don't ever doubt it. Not for a single minute. I want it as much as you do, but if it's going to put you at risk . . .'

'I'll be fine,' she assured him, willing it to be true. It had to be, it just did.

He drew back to look at her again, and began shaking his head in a way she couldn't quite understand. 'This is so not what we expected when we left here this morning,' he said hoarsely. 'I thought . . . I was afraid . . .'

'I know,' she whispered, and seeing the tears in his eyes she pulled his mouth to hers. 'I only wish I could tell you that my heart is healing, but this news . . . Maybe it's even better.'

He seemed unable to answer that, so he simply kissed her again. 'Does your mother know?' he asked.

'She was there when Dr Sharvelle told me. Gil knows too, and I'll have to tell Michelle and Sam, your mother too, but outside our immediate circle I think it's best not to say anything until we're more sure of what's going to happen. If we really can continue with it.'

He nodded agreement. 'Do you know how far along you are?'

'About six weeks.' Her eyes twinkled. 'It's what all the increased nausea and tiredness has been about lately. I should have realized. I would have, if it weren't for everything else.'

Pulling her to him again, he said, 'Tell me what you want to do about a wedding. If you'd rather wait until everything's more certain . . .'

With tearful laughter in her voice, she said, 'I'm

not sure. I can hardly think about anything at the moment.'

Understanding, he lowered his mouth to hers and kissed her deeply. 'Let's make a decision after tomorrow,' he said gruffly. 'I love you so much. I hope you know that.'

'I love you too, more than I can put into words.'

They stood together for a long time, feeling the currents of hope and belonging and dread enveloping them. They couldn't lose this baby, they just couldn't, but if her drugs had already damaged it, or if it turned into a choice between its life and hers, she knew there probably wouldn't be a choice at all.

CHAPTER TWENTY-TWO
VIVIENNE

Two Months Later

The church bells of St Jude's-on-the-Lake were ringing out over the countryside, sounding joyous and all-embracing the way they always did at Christmas and Easter and other significant times of the year. The weather was mild and breezy, with occasional rays of bright sunlight breaking from the clouds to paint the surrounding countryside in a fine, sparkling mist.

A chauffeur-driven car decorated with white ribbons pulled up at the stone-arched gate to the churchyard, the driver got out and then came to open the back door. Vivi stepped out into a flurry of autumn leaves, and paused to look up at the steeple, tall and grey against a milky-white sky. She put a hand to her hair as though to secure the small pearls her mother had carefully laced into the riotous waves, and found herself fighting back a surging ambush of emotion. This was a day that wasn't supposed to happen, that since her heart had gone into failure she hadn't dared even dream about, and now here she was, and here it was, and every precious minute of it was real. She had so much to be thankful for, maybe too much . . .

'Are you OK?' Gil asked, coming round the car to join her. He looked so distinguished and handsome in his dark grey morning suit, blue paisley waistcoat and cream cravat. A father any daughter could love and feel proud of.

She nodded and took a steadying breath.

She knew Josh was already inside, waiting at the altar for her to join him. She pictured him backlit by a towering stained-glass window, dashing and romantic in his dark grey morning suit and bright white shirt, and then she had to stop picturing him for it was bringing tears to her eyes.

As she and Gil walked along the church path, lined by Deerwood's residents and neighbours, all oohing and aahing and wishing her well, her eyes went to her goddaughter, Millie, waiting all alone at the door. Dear little Millie with her golden curls and turquoise-blue eyes, she'd insisted she could do this without her mother's help and it would appear she'd got her way. Vivi smiled and gave her the cue they'd rehearsed. With great importance Millie, in her azure satin dress and princess tiara, turned, went in through the church door and began tossing flowers from her basket as she strode too fast down the aisle.

Seeing her, the organist ceased his sprightly version of 'Hey Jude', presumably a nod to the church's patron saint, and a moment later the ancient building was filled with a rousing recording of the Trumpet Voluntary, performed by Diane Bish on four organs at Münster Cathedral. Gina and Shelley had found it online, and Josh and Vivi had been happy to indulge them. The detail of the ceremony didn't matter to them anywhere near as much as what it actually meant.

As the congregation rose to their feet, every one of them turned to watch Vivi enter on her stepfather's arm. She was wearing an ivory silk sheath dress to the knee swathed in glistening chiffon, with crystals around the neck and hemline and the small diamond studs Josh had given her last night in her ears. Her bouquet of creamy hellebores and frosted foliage was matched in the larger arrangements throughout the church, and had been created by two of Deerwood's budding florists.

The first person Vivi saw as she started forward was Jim Lynskey, sitting in a back pew with his mother and sister, who'd brought him today. He was watching her with a typical young man's sanguine smile, and she felt an overwhelming affection for him and yet more admiration for how genuinely happy he'd seemed for her when she'd told him her news. She wished with all her fragile heart that she could make a very special miracle happen for him.

As she walked slowly forward, carried along by the music and feeling as though she was floating in a dream, she saw each of the GaLs, smiling, tearful and glamorous in their designer dresses and stylish hats. Michelle, stunning in a lilac wool two-piece and twenties-style silk boudoir cap, was in front of them with her parents and Sam's. Gina was at the end of that pew strikingly elegant in a rose-pink lace dress and matching pillbox hat. As she watched Vivi and Gil coming towards her, Vivi could see that she was trying hard not to sob. Beside her Mark was grinning in a way Vivi knew was meant to be comedy cheesy, but was actually an attempt to cover his own tears.

On the other side of the aisle was Josh's entire family,

all four generations of them, from David the eldest, fully recovered from his TIA, right down to Perry and Selma's three-month-old baby, Bobby. Even Dodgy the Border collie was there in a smart bow tie, sitting with Nate at the end of a brand-new lead, a peculiarity that Dodgy hadn't experienced before, but appeared to be suffering with dignity. It seemed Michelle and Sam's sixteen-month-old, Ash, had gone to join the Raynors, for Vivi spotted him standing on the seat beside Shelley, presumably to get a better view of his father, the best man.

Then she saw Josh, and as their eyes met her heart seemed to expand and glow and beat only for him. She had never felt more beautiful or happy or loved in her life. He watched her until the moment Gil handed her to him, looking so romantic and smart in his expensively tailored suit, and so much the man she wanted to spend every single minute of the rest of her life with, that she actually sobbed as they turned to the rector.

The ceremony passed too quickly, a melodious, yet muted chorus of voices, laughter, song and prayer. To her relief she repeated the vows without fault, and smiled when Josh tripped over his own name, and gasped when Sam almost dropped the rings. Their mothers, Gil and Nate came with them to sign the register, and afterwards, as they walked back down the aisle as husband and wife to the very traditional Mendelssohn's Wedding March, she could only thank the fate that had so dramatically stopped her previous life in order to bring her to this one.

* * *

Later, at Deerwood's studio barn, as the banqueting tables were cleared and shoes and hats started coming off, the residents' band began to play Van Morrison's 'Days Like This'. Vivi and Josh took the floor with a dance that felt as intimate and exclusive as the look in his eyes. The lyrics were perfect, said everything in words they might not have found themselves, and added even more meaning to what they had already said.

As the music changed and others joined them, Vivi tried to persuade Jim to his feet. He didn't want to, though whether he was too shy, or not feeling so good, she couldn't be sure. She sat with him and his family for a while, holding his hand and thinking of how shocked most of the guests would be if they knew about the apparatus hidden beneath his clothes that was keeping him alive. People rarely knew about those waiting for transplant, it wasn't displayed in a sign over their heads; it didn't even show in their faces, or the way they walked or talked.

'Did you try praying?' Jim asked quietly, during the few moments they were left alone together. He was the only person outside the family that she'd told about the baby, and she was glad that she had. She didn't want secrets between them; their connection was too special.

'Yes, we did,' she admitted, 'but this wasn't the answer we expected.' She put a hand over the soft mound of her belly, not visible to anyone yet, apart from her and Josh.

'Do you feel worried about coming off the transplant list?' Jim queried.

She sighed shakily. 'Yes and no. Everything's so unpredictable, so precarious it could change again in a heartbeat.'

They both smiled at the lame joke.

'I guess the important thing for me to remember,' she continued, 'is to be thankful for what I have, and to take nothing for granted.'

Looking up as Josh came to join them, she took his hand as he said to Jim, 'Thanks for coming. It's meant a lot to us.'

'To me too,' Jim replied, and because of the way he said it, with so much sincerity and gratitude, Vivi wondered if it would be too gushing to tell him that he felt like family.

'We'll be in touch next week,' Josh promised, 'and if you're going partying in town tonight with Vivi's brother, remember . . .'

'Not to drink?' Jim cut in helpfully. 'It's OK, I don't risk it. I need my wits about me to read the batteries in case something goes wrong. But I'm looking forward to a night out.'

Josh nodded, and Vivi knew that, like her, he was thinking of how different this young man's life should be, could be . . . 'What I was going to say,' Josh continued, 'is that you're welcome to crash at our place.'

Surprised, Jim said, 'You won't be there? No, of course, you're going on honeymoon.'

'We'll be here, at the farm,' Josh told him. After such a long and emotional day they'd decided that a walk across the farmyard at the end of it would be as far as Vivi needed to go.

They turned as the GaLs began calling for them to cut the cake, which turned out to be a spectacular creation courtesy of Deerwood's amateur bakers, not in the shape of a heart, as Vivi had feared since they had to cut into it, but in the shape of something that resembled a sheep, or was it a horse? Whatever it was, it was beautiful, and different, and looked so scrumptious with all its white-chocolate slopes, toppings and sprinklings that it deserved all the photos people were taking.

Putting his hand over hers on the knife, Josh waited for the cameras to finish capturing the image and said, 'Mrs Raynor and I would like to thank . . .' He got no further, and laughed as everyone cheered and stamped their feet in approval. Vivi looked up at him, and as he looked back at her the room erupted again.

'Thank you, everyone, for coming,' he continued when quiet was restored. 'There isn't anyone here today who isn't very special to us, whether friend or family . . .'

'I'm *like* family,' Millie reminded him.

As everyone laughed, he said, 'You are indeed, and you are also the most beautiful flower girl I've ever seen.'

Millie glowed.

Looking around at the expectant faces again, he said, 'We promised no long speeches so this won't be one, but I want to single out both our mothers, Gina and Shelley, and also our friends Michelle and Sam, to tell them how much we love them, and to say how grateful we are for everything they've done to make this such a special day.'

When the applause died down, Vivi took her turn to speak. 'We also want to thank my wonderful stepfather, Gil, for being one of the most special people on earth.' She smiled as he took an extravagant bow, and everyone cheered. 'My brother, Mark, for being just too darned gorgeous and everything anyone could want in a brother.' Another cheer, with some banging of tables and wolf whistles. 'Also my dear, glamorous friends, the GaLs, for coming all this way today. I want to tell you how much all our memories mean to me. When we were at uni, and after, when we were all caught up in ambition and career and more craziness than I should probably go into in front of my new husband and his family, I never imagined for a moment that life had other plans for me. I could wish, of course, that it had chosen another way to throw me in a completely different direction, but how can I be anything but glad now that it did?' She turned her face up to Josh, and to everyone's delight he touched his lips to hers. 'I guess, what I'm trying to say,' she continued, 'is that fate has a very peculiar way of doing things, and though I don't claim to begin to understand it, I do know that while I've experienced some of the very worst moments of my life over the past months, I've also, thanks to my wonderful husband, experienced the very happiest.' She swallowed hard as rising emotions tried to steal her voice – and then they won. She could say no more, her throat was too tight and her heart too full.

Wrapping an arm around her, Josh raised a hand to yet more cheering and applause as he said, 'Thanks, everyone. Please carry on enjoying yourselves, and those of you who are still here in the morning, I guess we'll see you then. On the other hand, we might not.'

A few minutes later, having escaped a lengthy round of goodnights, they were in Josh's room inside the farmhouse, where candles had already been lit by his sisters and the bed strewn with petals. Barely hearing the wind howling outside, or the music that still thumped in the barn, he took Vivi's face in his hands and tried to kiss away the tears. It was hard when he was so close to the edge himself.

'It'll be all right,' he whispered shakily. 'I promise, we'll get through these next months and everything will be fine.'

Josh and Vivi left the Land Rover beside the road at Deerwood's entry layby to stroll along the drive recently transformed into a rambling, glittering Christmas market. Everything was on offer, from hot food and mulled wine, to handcrafted tree ornaments and jewellery, to watercolours of the local landscape, and quirky ceramic pots. The residents had been working up to the event for weeks, building the stalls, stringing lights, sorting music and borrowing braziers, barbecues, a candyfloss machine and even a carousel. The atmosphere was so festive that it was impossible for spirits to be anything but high, and as Josh and Vivi, bundled up in scarves and woollen hats, strolled through the small crowd of eager shoppers they felt themselves becoming as infected by the good cheer as everyone else. These youngsters, still in their teens, had known more hardship and heartache in their short lives than most people could begin to imagine, yet looking at them now, red-cheeked, laughing and loving this seasonal build-up, it was hard to see them as anything other than the hard-working, hopeful and go-getting achievers that Deerwood was helping them to become.

After stopping to buy cookies and hot chocolate from

the Great Deerwood Bake Off stall, they walked on, intoxicated by the aromas of spicy punch and roasting chestnuts. It seemed incredible to Vivi that this was going to be their first Christmas together, and that they'd only been married for a matter of weeks, when it felt as though they'd been in each other's lives for ever. She understood now what it meant to have found her soulmate, the way Shelley and Jack had found theirs, and her mother and Gil. Michelle and Sam, too. She realized it didn't happen for everyone, and that it had happened for her and Josh was yet another miracle amongst the many that had so radically changed their lives in so short a time.

'Hello, Josh.'

Vivi looked up from a tray of handmade chocolates she was inspecting to find an older woman, tall and rangy, staring right at her, not Josh. Her grey eyes were watery and seemed faintly troubled; her fine white hair, topped by a navy beret, fell lankly to the collar of her quilted coat. For all that, she was a lovely-looking woman with a quiet air of gentility and grace about her. Beside her was a slightly stooped man of around the same age, who seemed shaky on his legs and vaguely baffled by where he was.

'Jemmie,' Josh said, in a tone that was both warm and elusive.

As Vivi registered the name she felt a spasm of nervous tension clench her insides. Or was it the baby trying to land its first kick?

'Is this your new wife, dear?' the woman asked, still looking at Vivi in a curious, not unfriendly way.

Josh said, 'Vivi, this is Sir Humphrey Bleasdale and his wife, Lady . . .'

'Oh no, you're to call me Jemmie,' she insisted, 'everyone does,' and reaching for Vivi's hand she clasped it between her thick woolly mittens. 'You're very lovely,' she told her, seeming oddly satisfied with having noticed this. 'Isn't she lovely, Humphrey?'

The old man blinked.

'Thank you,' Vivi replied, momentarily lost for more words. *These people are my grandparents. I am descended from them and they have no idea. Should they mean something to me? Is there an unspoken connection happening between us that I'm not yet aware of?* Her eyes went to Humphrey, the foolish man whose bluster and arrogance had started a silly feud over the hunt all those years ago, and back to the woman who'd lied to Shelley to protect her sons. These were the parents of the insufferably arrogant twin whose cruelty and threats had blighted her mother's life.

She would never think of him as her father.

'You must come for Christmas drinks,' Jemmie was saying, her eyes no longer on Vivi or Josh. She was looking past them now, not at the stalls or anyone else, it seemed, but at something indeterminate, for her expression had turned vague and slightly sad.

'Is Fiona here?' Josh asked, looking around.

'Oh, I think so,' Jemmie replied.

Realizing that Fiona was her aunt, Vivi glanced about too, bracing herself to meet another member of the family she had no desire to know.

'Ah, there you are.' It was a middle-aged woman, bouncy and slight and puffing small clouds of breath into the cold air. She resembled Jemmie so closely that there could be no mistaking their relationship. 'I told you not to wander off,' she chided, and going up on tiptoe she pressed a kiss to Josh's cheek. 'It's good to see you,' she told him warmly. 'And this must be Vivienne.' She took Vivi's hand the way her mother had, between two similar mittens. 'I've been longing to meet you,' she declared with an engaging smile. 'Congratulations on your wedding. We're very happy for Josh that he's met someone special.'

Slightly thrown by the effusiveness, Vivi murmured a thank you as Fiona said, 'Aren't we, Mum? I said we're very happy for Josh . . .'

'Yes, oh yes,' Jemmie agreed.

'You must bring her to the manor for drinks,' Fiona told him. 'The rest of the clan are going to be away skiing or doing other things for Christmas, but we'll be there, and we'd love to see you.'

'Bring Shelley,' Jemmie added. 'We don't see enough of her these days. We miss her, don't we, Humph?'

Apparently aware he'd been spoken to, the old man grunted and shuffled his feet, but he still didn't seem to know where he was.

Vivi's feelings were so tangled and conflicted as she looked at them, pitying their frailty, and yet unable to forget all that had gone before. It was left to Josh to say, 'We'll give you a ring,' and after wishing them a merry Christmas he led Vivi on through the throng.

'Are you OK?' he asked, linking her arm through his.

Was she? She guessed so, but it had felt unsettling to meet her aunt and grandparents for the first time like that, especially when they had no idea who she was. 'I think,' she said, 'if things were different, I could probably get to like Fiona, but I wouldn't do it to my mother.

As for her parents, I don't think they'd understand who I am even if we told them.'

Agreeing, he said, 'We can always be polite, but keeping a distance is the way my mother's decided to handle things.'

Understanding why Shelley had never taken Jemmie to task over the lie – Jemmie was too emotionally fragile to handle it after all these years, and whatever anyone said or did now, it was never going to bring Jack back – Vivi sighed softly, and rested her face against the waxy sleeve of Josh's jacket. In a way she understood the instinct that had made Jemmie want to protect her son. It would be natural for any mother to feel that way. However, the fact that it might have been from a charge of murder, or at least manslaughter, was never going to sit comfortably with anyone, least of all Shelley.

As they left the market stalls and crossed the stone bridge over the frozen ditch the farmhouse came into view, and Vivi broke into a laugh. It looked like an overdone Christmas card with its abundant festoons of coloured lights, window-panes covered in spray snow and enormous holly and mistletoe wreath on the door. Six reindeers hauling a sleigh were on the roof and a jolly Santa was giving them a wave, as if he were about to dive down the chimney.

Josh groaned as Vivi laughed again. None of the barns or pens or sties had escaped the enthusiastic decor; even some of the animals were wearing tinsel collars and fake furry antlers.

'How many children live here?' she asked, making it a reminder that this was what his nephews and nieces would have demanded.

Conceding, he said, 'Six if you don't include the residents, and I'm sure they had a hand in it all.'

Her eyes were alive with merriment as she looked up at him. 'And you didn't?' she asked.

It was his turn to laugh, caught out, although he hadn't known it was going turn into something so . . . spectacular.

Unsurprised to see Gil's car parked next to Sam's, and several others that they recognized too, they wound their way through the haphazard vehicles towards the front door. It was Christmas Eve and tomorrow would be all about the children, which was why they had announced that they would break their news tonight.

The kitchen was full of family scoffing mince pies and downing mulled wine while the little ones updated lists for Santa, or were helped to hang more stockings from the mantelpiece. It was such a magical scene to walk into that Vivi had to pinch herself to make sure it was really happening. She loved her mother, had adored NanaBella and Grandpa, but they'd never had anything like this.

Gina was the first to spot them, and came quickly to embrace them, her face flushed as much from the wine, Vivi suspected, as from the happiness that glowed in her eyes. Gil was close behind, bringing succulent sausages on sticks and cubes of cheese, but before Vivi and Josh could accept or decline Hanna was banging the table to announce their arrival.

'Merry Christmas, you two,' she cried, raising her glass high.

'Merry Christmas,' everyone echoed.

As they were drawn into the group no one urged

them to get on with their news, and Vivi understood it was because they were afraid it wasn't going to be good. Every day was lived on a knife-edge, it seemed, but somehow the two of them were getting through it – in many ways it seemed to be bringing them closer together.

She squeezed Josh's hand and knew he was thinking the same as her right now – with so many people willing her to get through her pregnancy, and with so much love on their side, how could they fail?

Josh tapped a spoon to a glass to gather everyone's attention, and once all eyes were on him, he slipped an arm around Vivi.

'First of all,' he began, 'we both want to thank you all for registering as organ donors – and for getting the residents to do the same. You know how much the cause means to us, and Vivi is keen to spend what time she can helping Jim Lynskey's Save9Lives campaign.'

'We're going to be right behind you on that,' Hanna piped up, as everyone cheered. 'We've got all sorts of things planned for publicity and . . .'

'Let him continue,' Zoe interrupted.

'I'm just saying,' Hanna protested.

'Vivi knows we're all on board . . .'

'So what's wrong with pointing it . . .'

Josh said, 'Will you two either shut up, or take it outside.'

Even they laughed, though Hanna couldn't stop herself reminding him that he was the youngest, whatever difference that made, but she seemed to enjoy saying it.

'I really appreciate everything you've already done,' Vivi told them earnestly, 'not only for the campaign, but for me personally. If we didn't know the value of family before – we did,' she looked meaningfully at her mother – 'we've really come to know it over these last few months. I honestly believe I wouldn't have got this far without you – in truth, I might not have got here at all.' She glanced up at Josh, her eyes shining as her mouth trembled with emotion. 'There have been times when I've felt as though your heart was beating for both of us,' she said to him quietly, 'and I've no doubt that it's strong enough to do the same for the three of us.'

As the silence took on a new quality, one of hope and joyful expectation, she said to the room at large, 'We were told yesterday that the baby's doing fine, and that . . .' She swallowed hard and felt Josh tighten the hold on her hand. 'We were also told that . . . it's . . . a boy.' As her voice faltered on the last words, applause and delight broke out, and after waiting for it to die down her eyes found Shelley's. 'We're going to call him Jack,' she said softly, as if only she and Shelley were in the room.

Shelley's hands flew to her cheeks, and as she started to flood with tears Vivi and Josh went to fold her into their arms. Gina came too, joining in the embrace and the joy. They'd told her and Gil their news last night, not wanting them to get lost in what they'd known would be an overwhelming response from Josh's family today.

Finally, linking both their arms, Shelley turned them to the family portrait, where Jack seemed to be watching them with an overflow of paternal joy. 'I know how proud he'd be of you, Josh,' she said thickly, 'and I know that you're going to be just as proud of your son.'

Josh pressed a kiss to her head and then he was laughing along with everyone else, as she said, 'And I expect, when he's four, you'll take him down to the river and he'll do his very best to keep you safe from the hippo.'

CHAPTER TWENTY-THREE

Jack Gilmore Raynor arrived in the world via C-section three weeks before his due date, and one year to the day after Vivi's heart had changed the direction of her life. Or, put another way, on her twenty-eighth birthday. Though he was taken straight to neonatal care, his lusty cries, even at a few minutes old, gave everyone confidence that he was going to pull through.

'He's a fighter,' the midwife informed Josh and Vivi when she came back from settling him with the specialist care team, 'and I've seen enough early birds to know.'

Vivi was a fighter too, but the birth had taken its toll. Hours after Jack's arrival she was transferred to the cardiac ward where she remained for over a month, too weak to go home, sometimes even to stay awake for long when Josh brought the baby. However, seeing them and registering how well Jack was doing always gave her a boost, could even get her sitting up and holding him for a while. It was the best feeling in the world, her tiny son's healthy body pressed against hers, his navy eyes blinking wide and curious, his comical shock of jet-black hair and creamy cheeks making him nothing less than perfect. He was just like his father at that age, Shelley proudly told her, alert, inquisitive, loud,

Susan Lewis

and always hungry. Vivi loved to hear he was like Josh, it was what she'd hoped for, and all early tests on his heart showed it to be as strong as every other part of him.

The increase and change in her medication rendered her unable to breastfeed, but Josh brought bottles of formula with him so she could play a part in satisfying the bottomless appetite of their precious son. If she didn't feel strong enough she'd lie quietly and watch the two of them, Josh's hands seeming so large as he held the baby's tiny body, with Jack's strengthening limbs kicking and waving as he sucked hard on the teat his father was offering. They were her special men, the best and most powerful reason for her to get well.

Finally, as the new medication began to work, her energy levels started to rise. She spent longer periods awake, was even able to get out of bed and walk slowly along the corridor, wheeling her small trolley of medical equipment ahead of her. She visited the coffee shop or the garden if the weather was fine, aware of the pressure on her lungs as her heart struggled to pump blood through her veins. Eventually her breathing became easier, and her limbs stronger, until a month after the birth it was decided that she could go back onto the transplant list. There was no talk at that time of implanting a VAD, but she knew it was coming, unless, please God, they found a new heart for her first.

In the end, thanks to all the expert medical care combined with a new mother's determination to be at home with her husband and son, she was prepared for discharge. There were so many rules she had to follow, cautions and advice to be noted, but it was clear that everyone's goal was for her to lead as normal a life as she could with her family.

On the day Josh came to collect her from the hospital Jack Junior was already weighing in at almost four kilos, and though Vivi couldn't lift him herself, when Josh put him into her lap in the back of the car she felt such an overwhelming rush of emotion that she sobbed with joy, and fear – *please God let me always be here for him*. She just about melted when he looked up at her with his stern, navy eyes, tiny eyebrows arching before he grabbed a foot and let out a gurgle of what sounded to her like elation. He had both his mummy and daddy now, so what more could he want?

Another bottle, of course.

They'd moved over to Deerwood two months before the birth, settling into the east wing of the farmhouse as soon as its conversion into an independent dwelling was complete, so Vivi knew they would never be short of help when it was needed. It was the reason they'd agreed to Shelley's invitation to make the farm their home, knowing how vital the backup would be while the baby was young and she was still recovering. They quickly discovered that there would be more than enough doting carers, for they were so inundated by visitors over the first few days she was home that Josh kept threatening to charge. He also kept the visits short and banned them altogether the instant Vivi started to look overwhelmed.

Another new development at Deerwood during the early part of the year had been Gina's pop-up salon, where she or Jade trained the residents interested in the art of hairdressing. Together Gina and Shelley came up with the idea of staging a Deerwood Come Dancing contest, with Vivi as head judge. By the time Vivi returned home rehearsals for the show were already under way, with a handful of teachers coming from all over to provide their services for the fun of it.

Vivi soon found, to her relief, that being at home was absolutely what she'd needed, for it was proving more energizing than exhausting. She could feel it most of all on the days she woke to find herself able to get out of bed without Josh's help, and even to shower on her own. There was always something going on around her, successes to celebrate, dramas to defuse, animals to tend, children to enjoy, competitions to judge . . . Though she might not always have been up to the many demands, she did her best, but it often led to squabbles with Josh about her overdoing things. Of course she appreciated his protectiveness, and understood it, but she saw no reason not to liaise with Deerwood's lawyers when the need arose. After all, she was a lawyer herself, and sometimes it was useful for Hanna to have someone to explain things in plainer English, and to help her decide on what action might need to be taken, if any.

Vivi was also keen to receive regular updates on Jim Lynskey's Save9Lives website, for it was almost ready, she was told by Jim and the designers, to go live.

However, most of her time was taken up by Jack, who was passing all the usual baby checks with flying colours, and who'd clearly inherited his father's charm, for he had more fans in his little world than most could boast in a wider one. In fact everything was going perfectly, for the cardiac team were pleased with her progress – there had been no activity from the ICD since the early days following the birth, when her heart had stopped several times and had to be shocked back to life.

When the decision was taken to return her to the transplant list it caused as much hope as it did dread, for she was warned that should it happen she'd be unable to spend time with children under five for at least a year in order to lessen the risk of infection.

It was something they'd have to deal with when, if, the time ever came.

It was a sunny evening in late June when Josh returned from his rounds of the local farms, hot, tired and smelling richly of livestock, to find himself navigating through a rowdy outdoor tango class. Declining all offers to join in, he let Ellie out of the car and went into the farmhouse kitchen in search of Vivi, who was generally there at this time of day.

Surprised to find no one around, he glanced out of the open stable door that led to the garden, and the vision of his wife reclining on a chair with their son on a blanket beside her brought him to a stop. It was the most beautiful sight in the world for him, seeing them relaxing in a halo of sunshine, the blooming garden providing a frame of colour. Opening up his phone, he captured the image to add to the hundreds of others they'd already stored. After smiling down at the result, he looked out to the garden again and decided that the baby, lying on his back under a parasol planted in the grass, must be sleeping, and Vivi, one hand trailing close to her son, was staring into space, apparently miles away.

He'd have gone out to them then, were it not for the unexpected unease that suddenly knotted his insides.

Something was wrong, he could feel it, sense it as it clawed its way into him. He felt a harsh flare of frustration and anger. She'd been doing so well, had almost fully regained her strength since the birth, and there had been no calls, or none that he knew of, from the clinic.

He didn't need to be thinking the worst, he told himself sharply, there was no reason to . . .

Careful to hide his misgivings he went out to join her, and hearing him coming she turned to look up at him. She was wearing sunglasses and nasal specs attached to the oxygen supply close by, but when she tried to smile it didn't quite happen.

'What is it?' he asked, wanting to drop down beside her, but staying upright as if holding back from her would somehow dilute or even dispel the bad news.

She swallowed hard as she said, 'I've just heard that Jim has been taken into hospital.' Her mouth trembled as sorrow welled up in her throat. 'I keep thinking about him and how frightened he must be . . .'

Moving past the swamping relief that this wasn't about her, at least not today, Josh felt a new surge of concern as he sat down beside her. 'What happened?' he asked softly, taking her hand.

Vivi said, 'There's a problem with his VAD. It's stopped functioning properly.'

Knowing that was the biggest fear for anyone with a VAD, he said, 'I'm guessing his mother called.'

She nodded. 'She did, but I spoke to him a few minutes ago. He sounds fine, but I know he's afraid. Terrified, more like; who wouldn't be in his shoes?'

'Where is he?'

'Queen Elizabeth's in Birmingham.'

'But can they repair the device?'

'He thinks it has to be a new one, which'll mean more open-heart surgery.'

Feeling deeply for the lad, Josh said, 'I'll call him myself after I've showered.'

Her eyes came to his and after a moment he saw her move away from her fear for Jim, tucking it into a place where she would care and pray for him inwardly until his next ordeal was over. Managing a mischievous smile, she said, 'Oh, it's you who pongs. I thought it was your son.'

Enjoying the tease, he looked down at the baby and found he was watching them with his big navy eyes. Apparently realizing he now had his parents' attention, he blew a happy little raspberry.

Laughing, Josh lifted him onto one shoulder, and held out a hand to pull Vivi to her feet. 'I've been thinking,' he said, as they went into the kitchen, bringing the oxygen supply with them, but he got no further as Jack grabbed his lower lip and tugged down hard. Groaning a protest, he prised open the little fist and promptly found his finger clamped between two hungry gums.

Enjoying the spectacle, Vivi said, 'You were thinking?'

Deciding a chew on his fingers might be best after he'd showered, he popped the baby into his bouncy seat and was about to start revealing his thoughts again, when her mobile rang.

She clicked on without checking who it was, and her eyes danced as he threw up his hands in mock despair.

'A honeymoon,' he said, undeterred. 'I think we should have a honeymoon.'

Clearly delighted by the suggestion she blew him a

kiss, and said into the phone, 'Sorry who did you say it is?'

As the woman at the other end introduced herself again, Vivi felt her mind starting to spin and her eyes flew in panic to Josh.

His own darkened, and seeing she was shaking he put a hand out to steady her. 'What is it?' he demanded urgently.

'I see,' Vivi murmured to the caller. 'Yes, yes of course.' She listened some more, still looking at Josh. Tears were filling her eyes now and her breath was short and ragged.

'What is it?' he repeated, making to take the phone. *Dear God don't let this be bad news about Jim.*

She pulled away. 'We'll be there as soon as we can,' she said, and ringing off she clasped her icy hands to his face.

'Vivi, for heaven's sake,' he growled. 'What the hell . . .'

'It was the transplant coordinator,' she whispered hoarsely. 'They have a heart . . . They want me to get there as soon as I can.'

He stared at her, muted by shock. 'To Queen Elizabeth's?'

'No, no, I'm not with them. I'm . . .'

Knowing full well who she was with, he pulled himself together and sent her to their room to collect the bag she kept packed in readiness for this. Meanwhile he alerted the local ambulance service, and went in search of his mother so she could take charge of the baby. He called Gina and Michelle, and tried the ambulance service again, needing to be sure they were on their way. There was such a small window between donation and transplant that they couldn't afford to lose any time. It would take at least two hours to get to the hospital, and he had no idea right now where the heart was or when it had become available . . .

Thirty minutes later, deciding they couldn't wait any longer for an ambulance, Josh drove them out of Deerwood and headed for the motorway. If he got pulled over for speeding he felt certain the police, once they realized the urgency, would put on their blue lights and escort them.

As they raced along the country lanes Vivi clung to the edges of her seat, knowing they were both, to some degree, still in shock. It wasn't that they'd stopped hoping this would happen, they'd never be able to do that, but they had stopped thinking that every call might be the one they were waiting for.

And now it had come.

It was almost unbelievable, and yet it was real.

They were in good time, she assured herself. The drive should take no more than a couple of hours. The new heart could survive for up to six hours once it had been taken from the donor, and as far as they were aware that hadn't happened yet, or perhaps it was under way.

She closed her eyes and tried to still her thoughts. They were spinning around her head in a crazy circus of dread and hope, collecting up everything she'd learned about transplants, the chances of survival, the intricacy of the surgery, the chances of bleeds and infections, the immunosuppressant drugs that could cause cancer . . . Perhaps worst of all was the warning that she shouldn't be around children under five for the first year, given how frequently they picked up and passed on infections. She couldn't imagine being without Jack for all that time. It was starting to panic her. They hadn't even considered how they'd manage it . . .

She felt Josh's hand take hers, as though he sensed the commotion going on inside her. She clung to him tightly, as much to still herself as to remind them both that what lay ahead was necessary, vital and exactly what they'd hoped and prayed for. Provided the transplant was a success, it was going to make all the difference in the world to their lives. She'd be able, after time, to pick up her baby, play with him, run on the beach with him and make love to Josh as she never had before. More than that, she'd be able to watch her son grow up, be there for birthdays and sports days, to cheer him on and kiss him better. She'd be a part of his life the way a mother should be; the way she'd hardly dared allow herself to think of until now.

She took a call from her mother. They sobbed with relief and terror, laughed almost deliriously, and she felt glad to know that Gina and Gil were already on their way.

She called Jim, worried about how he'd take the news when his need right now was so much greater than hers. He sounded genuinely pleased for her, and guilt immediately flared through her conscience.

'It won't be the right match for me,' he reminded her. 'We have different blood types.'

This was true. Nevertheless . . .

'Yours will be an inspirational story for the Save9Lives website,' he told her, 'so promise to be in touch as soon as you can.'

'I will, you can count on it. And don't forget to let Josh know how your surgery goes.'

With a smile in his voice he said, 'You bet.' Adding softly, 'See you on the other side.'

The other side of two surgeries that were going to save their lives, albeit in different ways, and for her it would, please God, turn her back into a normal, healthy young woman, or as near to it as she would ever get now – a young woman who was a wife and a mother, and who had so very much to live for.

She found herself thinking about the family who'd just lost a loved one, and felt more guilt flood through her that she was benefiting from their loss.

She crossed her fingers so tightly they turned white, and closing her eyes she prayed silently, desperately, *please let this surgery be a success. Please, please, please let me have this second chance.*

They were almost halfway to the hospital when the transplant coordinator rang again.

'Hi, Vivienne, it's Ruth O'Donnell.' The voice was soft and Irish-sounding, and Vivi felt a ludicrous surge of affection for her.

'Hi,' Vivi replied. 'We're about an hour away. We weren't sure the ambulance was going to turn up, so my husband's driving us.'

'Vivi,' Ruth said gently, 'I'm really sorry to tell you this, but we've just heard from the donor team, and I'm afraid the family have decided that they don't want to let their daughter's heart go.'

Vivi reeled; the whole world seemed to tilt and sway, to come crashing to a terrible, juddering halt and then shatter into a thousand pieces. She couldn't have heard

427

that right, she just couldn't. So much preparation, anticipation, the struggle to control her fear, the daring to let her hopes fly . . . She put out a hand to grasp Josh's arm.

'What is it?' he asked worriedly.

Vivi swallowed hard and heard herself say, 'It's not going to happen. We . . . We can turn back.'

He glanced at her in disbelief, but she knew it would only take a moment for him to understand. This had always been a possibility, but it wasn't one they'd even begun to prepare for.

His face was pinched and pale as he reduced speed and steered the car into the slow lane. 'Is there something wrong with the heart?' he asked, trying to understand.

'The donor's family don't want to go through with it,' she explained, sounding strangely calm when all she wanted to do was scream and cry in protest and despair and grief. To Ruth she said, 'I take it the girl wasn't a registered donor?'

'No, she wasn't,' Ruth confirmed. 'You know, I'm sure,' she continued, 'that whenever death occurs suddenly, mostly through accident, the organ donation centre is immediately alerted. There's almost no time to lose, especially for a heart, so they, we, have to start preparing in the hope that the victim is either a registered donor, or their family will be willing to make a positive decision for them. I'm so sorry, Vivienne, that in this case it's gone against us.'

Hearing the tears in Ruth O'Donnell's voice Vivi almost tried to comfort her, but the words wouldn't come, so she simply rang off and let her own tears slide unchecked down her cheeks.

She didn't want to feel angry with the family, whom she'd never know. It wouldn't do any good. It hadn't been their intention to thwart or hurt anyone; their only thoughts would have been for themselves and the precious daughter they'd lost. Allowing her beautiful healthy organs to be taken and given away to strangers, people they'd never know and might not even like, was too much at this time.

Maybe that was what they thought, how they felt. Vivi had no idea. All she knew for certain was that she and Josh, and their family, were left to deal with the fact that there was a perfect heart out there for her, one that could transform their lives and help at least some of their dreams to come true.

But the girl wasn't a registered donor, so they had no right to it.

All they could do now was leave the motorway at the next junction and return home.

CHAPTER TWENTY-FOUR

The only surprise for Vivi over the next few weeks was that it took her cardiac team so long to begin the conversations about implanting a Ventricular Assist Device. She was weakening by the day; she knew it, so they must surely be picking it up in her nightly monitorings. They'd also have registered the fact that she was getting more shocks from the ICD than usual, shocks that she wasn't coming back from as quickly as she once had.

Knowing that her heart was frequently stopping frightened her far more than she was allowing anyone to see, although she was aware of how easily Josh could read her. She knew that it was frightening him too, but he was better at hiding it, at least from everyone else. Together they put on a valiant front, not allowing the others to know how serious things were becoming; there would be time enough for that when they couldn't hide it any more. In the privacy of their bedroom, with Jack lying between them, they talked about the future in ways that often became too difficult to put into words, that made them both cry harsh, desperate tears and cling to one another as though their love alone had the power to change things.

Was time really running out? They kept trying to believe that it wasn't, that they were only reacting to the shocking, wrenching disappointment of losing out on a heart. Having to turn back that day had been devastating, had made it almost impossible for them to believe the gods were ever going to be on their side. Vivi was determined not to dwell on the fact that the family had apparently regretted their decision twenty-four hours later. It had already been too late by then; she had to let it go. Instead she tried to focus her mind on the beautiful moments of each day, and how truly blessed she was to have Jack and Josh when only a year ago she'd had no hope of ever being a wife and mother.

Another heart would come along, she assured herself, assured Josh, and he often said the same. In the meantime, with a VAD she was going to survive much better than she was managing right now. She might not want to have a mechanical pump implanted inside her heart to make the blood flow through her veins and other organs, or a driveline as thick as a pencil coming out through her skin to connect with two brick-sized batteries and a slightly smaller computer device. She abhorred the thought of going about the place looking like a mobile ICU, worse still was having to plug herself into the mains at night, but then she'd remind herself that if Jim Lynskey could live with it, so could she. She tried not to think about the fact that his surgery to replace the faulty VAD had turned out to be so complicated that it had gone on for over twelve hours and taken him far closer to the end than he'd ever been. This was something she'd have to worry about in the future, should her own device start to fail and need to be replaced. The point for now was that Jim was recovering, albeit slowly, and the alternative of not having the device wasn't one any of them was going to explore.

Her cardiac team had made the decision anyway. She was going to be implanted with a VAD, so this was what all the discussions were about as she and Josh went back and forth to the hospital seeing one specialist after another, and more dedicated nurses than they could count. They were plied with all sorts of information, from possible surgical complications, to device function, right down to how much the VAD cost – seventy thousand pounds – and the fact that the NHS would cover it. Though she felt slightly awkward about that, she wasn't going to refuse it. Instead, she was going to count herself fortunate that she was able to have one at all, because not everyone with a failing heart could.

Just, please God, don't let her heart give up before they had a chance to give it the help it needed.

When the day came for her to check into the hospital Josh drove them along the now familiar route from home to the centre, going at a far less hectic pace than he had the first time they'd made the journey. Vivi couldn't help recalling how much hope they'd had then, how it hadn't even crossed their minds that a transplant wouldn't happen, until they'd been told to stop and turn back. The same wouldn't happen with a VAD. The inanimate, innocuous-looking pump made of metal and plastic was no doubt already at the centre waiting for her. It was a miraculous invention, designed to act as a bridge to transplant. A bridge to nowhere, was how someone had described it online, for once the VAD was implanted the chances of qualifying for a new heart all but disappeared.

She gazed blindly out at the passing scenery, unaware of how tightly her hands were clenched, feeling only the huge knot of anxiety in her chest, tightening harshly as her thoughts moved ahead to what lay in store, loosening for the few moments she was able to think of something else. She tried desperately to obliterate the feeling she'd had on leaving Deerwood that she was seeing it for the last time. She understood that nerves had taken hold of her instincts, and fear was painting false and terrifying scenarios in her head. It was to be expected: she was very sick, so of course she'd be torn between an awful, clawing dread and random surges of hope; anyone would, in her position.

Right at this moment she could feel every living part of her being pulled back to the farm, as though something tangible was stretching and straining over the increasing distance, trying to stop her from going any further. It felt hard to breathe, not just because of the heightened pressure in her lungs, but because of the panic she was trying so hard to control.

I'm going to die. I know it and I have to face it, but I can't. I don't want to leave my beautiful baby. I want to watch him grow up and I want to stay with Josh for ever.

As her throat locked around the intensity of her fears, and tears stung her eyes, she tried hard to centre herself; to detach from the overwhelming sense of dread and reach for calm and hope.

Feeling Josh's hand cover hers, she brought his palm

433

to her cheek and rested against it. He always seemed to understand when she needed physical contact, how important it was for her to draw strength from him. She thought of the song 'You Raise Me Up' and how perfectly the words captured everything he did for her. Yes, she could stand on mountains with him, and she could walk on stormy seas, because he made her more than she could ever be without him.

Now she must be strong for him, and for their precious son who was sleeping quietly in the back.

Both their mothers, Gil, Mark and David, were following on behind in Gil's car. Michelle and Sam were coming tomorrow so they could be there too during the surgery, and afterwards when she was brought round. Gina had already booked everyone into a nearby hotel where they'd be staying for the next few days, possibly a week, until Vivi was ready to go home again.

I will go home. I will, so I must stop thinking I won't.

Her emotions brimmed each time she thought of how lucky she was to have so many people around her who cared. It wouldn't be true for everyone, although she wished it were. Jim had family who loved and cared for him, who had been there to will him through his surgery and the terrifying time after when it had taken so long to bring him round. She wouldn't think about the complications he'd endured, they weren't relevant to her, he kept reminding her, because she didn't already have a VAD that had to be removed from the tissue that had grown around it.

It was the middle of the afternoon by the time Josh brought his grandfather's new Volvo to a halt outside the hospital's main entrance, and while David came to take over the driver's seat Josh went inside to fetch a wheelchair for Vivi. She didn't need one, she insisted, but Josh's expression made her sit into it anyway, and she was grateful to feel it taking her weight. She watched her mother go to lift the still sleeping baby out of the back seat and bring him over for a kiss. Vivi knew he was going to be thoroughly spoiled while she was here, which was fine, just as long as they brought him to see her every day, and of course they would.

So there really was no need for the tears burning her eyes, or the sobs that were trying so hard to tear themselves free from her chest. She was going to see Jack again in no time at all, and before she knew it they'd all be on their way home.

Feeling Josh's hand on her shoulder, she put her own over it and looked up at him. 'Ready?' she said with a smile that was meant to bolster them both.

'Ready,' he said, matching her tone.

They were welcomed in reception by Angela, the VAD nurse they'd met several times already, a plump, energetic woman with a no-nonsense manner and kindly eyes. As she led the way through to the ward, glancing over her shoulder as she spoke, she was explaining once again that either she, or one of her team, would be on call through the night to answer any questions Vivi might have, or to help in any way she needed.

The room that was to be hers for the next few days, apart from when she was in theatre, of course, and during the immediate recovery period in ICU, was on the second floor of the west wing. It was a private room that Gil had insisted on paying for, with a large window looking out to the gardens where other people with heart conditions, young and old, were taking slow walks with their loved ones, while small children who didn't understand what was happening played catch.

While Angela went off to organize some tea, Josh helped Vivi out of the wheelchair and pulled her gently into his arms. She looked around the room. There was a TV on the wall, a small bathroom in one corner and a complicated-looking adjustable bed.

'OK?' he whispered.

She smiled and tilted her mouth up for a kiss. 'Do you think I should get undressed already?' she asked. Then added wryly, 'That's the trouble when I'm around you and there's a bed nearby, I can't wait to get my kit off.'

Laughing, he said, 'Why don't you just lie down for a while? You're probably tired after the journey.'

She was, and yes she wanted to lie down, so she let him help her onto the bed and watched him draw up a leather chair with wooden arms to be close to her.

'It feels vaguely surreal being here,' she said, 'even though we knew it was coming.'

He nodded agreement, as if he too wasn't properly connecting to reality. 'The good part of it is,' he said, 'we could be on our way home again in a couple of days.'

Liking the sound of that she clasped his hand and gave it a squeeze, glad he'd decided to forecast the shortest time she was likely to be here. The longest was about a week, maybe a few more days if something didn't go as planned. 'Matias Velez should be here to talk to us soon,' she said, referring to the surgeon they'd spoken to at length during their preparatory visits. He'd promised to come and see her the day before the surgery and now that day was here. As her insides churned with a sickening onslaught of nerves she said, 'Can you think of anything else to ask him?'

Josh shook his head. 'Nothing we haven't asked already, but it won't hurt if we need to ask it again.'

Vivi looked up as another familiar face – Rosamie, one of two Filipinos on Angela's team – came in with a tray of tea and set it down on a table beside the bed. After greeting Vivi with a hug and a kiss, the same for Josh, she said, 'I'll be back shortly to start filling in the pre-op forms. They're pretty standard, so nothing to worry about. Is there anything you'd like to ask now?'

'Will my family be allowed to come in later?' Vivi said. 'Our little boy is with them, and I'd like to see him before he goes to bed.'

The nurse broke into a smile. 'We've all been looking forward to meeting him, so of course he can come.'

Wryly, Vivi said, 'Provided he's not hungry or sleepy he'll be happy to meet you too. He's very sociable, just like his daddy.'

Josh gave a comical shrug, as if to say *is it my fault it's in the genes?*, and began to pour the tea.

'No more solids after these biscuits,' Rosamie cautioned. 'Remember, your surgery's scheduled for eight tomorrow morning.'

Although Vivi already knew that, she felt her mouth turn dry. A bolt of fear surged through her as though to rip every last shred of hope and confidence from her failing spirits. She wouldn't be able to eat even if she wanted to; she could barely even breathe as she struggled to stop the panic doing its worst.

* * *

After Rosamie had gone Vivi said, 'I think we've had enough now. Can you get me out of here?'

Smiling, Josh said, 'I will, just as soon as . . .'

'OK, I know what you're going to say, that it can happen as soon as everything's . . .' She took a breath. 'I don't want to have the op, Josh, I just want to go home – I'm sorry, I know it doesn't help to hear me say that, but can you at least get me some Valium? I'm tearing myself to pieces here.'

After going outside to talk to the nurses, he returned with two white pills and helped her to sit up while she washed them down. Their effect seemed to be almost instant, although she realized that was more psychological than physical.

As she lay back against the pillow Josh held her hands and coaxed her through some breathing exercises, taking air in slowly, counting to five and gently releasing it. She looked around the room, holding tightly to him, and began to feel weirdly as though she was caught in a dream. Reality was fading again, just like when they'd arrived, only now it was going too far away.

Realizing the tranquillizers were making her light-headed, she pointed to her oxygen supply and lay still as Josh connected it to her nasal specs. It took only a few minutes for her senses to stabilize, and to her relief there was less panic charging around her system now.

She wasn't going to die. She'd get through this like everyone else, and by the time Jack took his first steps she'd have forgotten all about how afraid she was on this day that she'd never see them.

They looked up as Matias Velez came in. He was a

slight, swarthy man of around fifty with short silver hair and hawkish eyes – and hands that Vivi had decided on first meeting were reassuringly as she'd want a surgeon's to be, clean, strong, not too big, and lean.

'Hi, you guys,' he said cheerfully, shaking hands with Josh and coming to perch on the end of the bed. His manner was so casual and friendly he might have been an old friend dropping in for a chat while passing, rather than someone who was going to break open her chest tomorrow and perform a major surgery on the most vital part of her body.

He didn't seem worried, so she shouldn't be either.

'How was the journey here?' he asked, and grimaced before she could answer. 'Don't tell me, it was awful and you spent every minute of it wishing you could turn around and go home. Well, don't worry, you'll be making that trip soon enough. Luckily for you we're a lot more experienced at carrying out the VAD ops now than we were a few years ago, so you shouldn't be here for long. Also good to know is I'll have one of the top teams working with me so you're going to be in very safe hands.' He smiled as he turned his over as if to prove it.

Vivi smiled too, appreciating his understanding of her nerves and the way he was trying to calm them.

Then he said, 'We've already talked about possible complications – stroke, bleeds, cognitive impairment, so we don't need to go there again. Today is all about thinking positively and focusing on how much better your other organs will function once the VAD is in place, and how much stronger you'll feel.'

Wishing he hadn't mentioned the complications, Vivi said, 'The operation will take four hours, is that right?'

'It could be longer,' he replied. 'It all depends what we find when we go in, but, as you haven't had any previous surgeries on this leaky valve of yours, I'm not expecting any surprises.' He smiled and continued, 'The main issue with you right now, as you know, is your pulmonary artery pressure; it's far too high and we need to get it down. I had a guy just a couple of weeks ago whose reading was around sixty, slightly lower than yours, and by the time he was lifted from the operating table with the VAD in place it had already dropped to thirty. So it's not only effective, it's fast.'

Josh said, 'How old was this man?'

'A lot older than Vivienne,' Velez replied, 'so we'll expect to see similar, if not even better results by the time she's in recovery tomorrow.'

Taking courage from that, Vivi said, 'I've read . . . Actually, I think I asked this before, but will the VAD prevent me from having a transplant in the future?'

His answer was swift and frank. 'Yes, if it performs well for you. As you know, we get very few hearts for transplant, so you'll inevitably go to the bottom of the list if the VAD is doing its job. This isn't to say a transplant can't happen; if it's the right heart for you and it isn't suitable for someone on the urgent list it could be yours. It's a bit of a lottery, I'm afraid.' His expression sobered as he said, 'What happened to you, when you were called for transplant and it didn't work out, was very unfortunate. It's not so unusual. Some people have even got as far as being anaesthetized ready to receive a new heart before it's discovered that for one reason or another it can't happen. It's very frustrating and distressing. Of course, if that heart had been made available we wouldn't be sitting here having this conversation, and you'd already be some weeks into recovery with no device, drivelines, or batteries to worry about. However, this is where we are – which isn't bad, it just isn't what you'd hoped for.'

Swallowing drily, Vivi said, 'And I can live for ten years with a VAD?'

Velez shrugged. 'Ten, fifteen, maybe longer. There's a lot of progress being made with this technology, especially in the States, so I'd say, by the time you're ready for a new pump, several years down the line, something even better will be available. Which isn't to say there's any reason to lack confidence in the Heartmate III – this is what we're giving you tomorrow – because it's bang up to date, and has performed excellently in all clinical trials, as well as for the people who currently have them.'

Vivi nodded slowly, knowing this was what Jim had now, and willing herself to feel pleased, or at least reassured.

Josh said, 'And device maintenance?'

'Everything will be explained to you before you leave the hospital, but you can take it from me that your iPhone is way more complicated. An important factor will be keeping the driveline clean so it doesn't become infected. How you carry all the paraphernalia that goes with it, the batteries and computer, will be up to you. Most women use a kind of backpack, which makes the weight easier to deal with, and it doesn't get so much in the way.'

'What about charging the batteries?' Josh asked.

Vivi knew he was confident about this procedure,

and had read up on it more times than she had, so going over it with the surgeon again was no doubt his way of drumming it into her.

As Velez answered, she felt her mind drifting, needing to break free of the words in search of a place that had no definition, no contact at all with what was being said, or what was going to happen tomorrow. She knew Josh would continue to listen, and because he was a surgeon himself he'd understand it all far better than she could. He was merely double-checking what to do if the pump failed, how possible it was for a blood clot to occur before, during or after surgery . . .

There were so many dangers, and he needed to prepare for them all. She did too, and she guessed she'd get used to having to connect to the mains each night, keeping a constant check on the heavy batteries, and to the pain that no one had discussed much, but she knew about it because Jim had told her.

She must have fallen asleep, because when she opened her eyes Velez had gone and only Josh was there. She thought he was sleeping too, until she realized he was watching her, and they both smiled and reached for each other's hands.

'They'll be here soon to start your pre-surgery checks,' he told her. 'Apparently it's nothing you haven't experienced before, all quite painless, and after that the family will be able to visit. Do you think you're up to it?'

'Of course,' she replied. 'I want to see my boy.'

His eyes shone with love and concern as he regarded her carefully. She looked at him too, taking in how handsome and strong he was, how steadfast and brave. He deserved so much more than this: someone who could properly share his life and his dreams, someone whose heart was able to beat as freely and passionately as his. She wondered if he had any regrets, if deep down he wished they'd never met . . .

He said, 'Tell me what you're thinking.'

She felt her insides clench as she pulled away from the truth, for she didn't want to admit that the fear was back, the dreaded certainty that something would go wrong tomorrow. Nor did she want to ask about regrets; he'd never admit to them if he had any, and if she weren't feeling so sorry for herself she'd know that the only one he had was that she had to go through this.

In the end, she said, 'I want you to know that the most important thing this pump will do to my heart is make it strong enough for me to love you even more than I do already.'

His eyebrows rose sardonically. 'I wouldn't have thought that was possible,' he teased.

Tightening the hold on his hand, she said, 'No, maybe it isn't.'

Everyone visited that night, grouping around the bed and making a fuss of Jack, who enjoyed every moment of the limelight. It was an easy way to avoid discussing tomorrow's surgery, for Josh had already warned them that Vivi didn't want to think about it while they were with her. There would be plenty of time when they'd gone – and early tomorrow, before she was taken to theatre. This was provided she slept; more likely she'd be awake all night, worrying and crying and trying desperately to rid herself of the fear that she'd seen her family for the last time.

She didn't want to leave them. She didn't want to imagine their grief, or the empty space she'd create in their lives, or how it would close as the years passed and they carried on without her.

When it was time for the visit to end Josh came to take the baby from her, and as he lifted him up in his arms she knew that if she'd had the strength she'd have tried to take him back. Jack's face was rosy, his dark eyes bright with interest and excitement as his little head flopped onto his father's shoulder and his fist remained clamped around her finger.

Please don't go, please, please, she was crying inside.

Somehow she kept smiling as her brother came to hug her, his young, shadowy eyes heavy with misgiving, his mouth twisting slightly as he made a try for humour.

'Brought you some box sets,' he told her, 'none of them any longer than six episodes, because we don't want you hanging around in here to find out what happens next.'

Vivi's laugh was half strangled by a sob as he folded her into his arms.

'Love you, sis,' he whispered in her ear. 'It's going to be fine, OK?'

She swallowed and nodded, and smoothed a hand around his cheek, having to bite her lips to keep her tears in check.

Her mother was the last to come and hug her, and as their eyes met Vivi wanted to tell her how much she loved her, and how sorry she was to be putting everyone through this, but the words wouldn't come.

'I love you,' Gina whispered brokenly, 'and I don't

want you to worry. We're all here for you, you know that, don't you?'

Vivi nodded, but she still didn't speak. She knew if she opened her lips only sobs would escape, choked and desperate and full of fear.

Gina pressed a kiss to her forehead, and taking the baby from Josh she followed the others out of the room.

After closing the door, Josh came back to the bed and held her eyes as he sat down beside her. She couldn't get enough of looking at him, would never be able to get enough of it, and she knew he was feeling the same. Understanding moved soundlessly between them, a connection that was intangible and powerful, and as the minutes ticked quietly by tears began to slide down her cheeks, dropping to the pillow as she imagined him finding everything she'd left for him. She realized he already knew it was there, but he'd never pressed her to tell him, had understood that it would be too hard. She could feel his grief, his loss and their love stealing through her, filling her up, and breaking every part of her heart.

In the end, she said, 'If I don't make it . . .'

'You'll make it,' he told her firmly.

Her tired spirits moved towards his words, needing to hold onto them. 'But if I don't,' she said, 'you know what to do . . .'

'Yes, so we don't need to have the conversation.'

She thought about it and decided he was right, they didn't.

They didn't talk again, simply lay quietly in the semi-light holding one another, listening to the sounds outside the room, and echoes from the times they'd shared during this past magical year, as they resonated softly between them. So much laughter and music, words spoken in tenderness and joy, fear, hope, determination, endless support and of course love. She recalled the first time she'd seen him at Sam and Michelle's, how deeply he'd affected her right away, how they hadn't wanted to say goodnight when he'd taken her home. She pictured his face when he'd told her for the first time that he loved her, and remembered how often he'd made her laugh when she'd felt so afraid she'd almost been unable to breathe. She thought of the night he'd asked her to marry him, and their beautiful wedding that had meant so much to them, but nothing would ever mean more than their boy.

She inhaled the musky, male scent of him, as though to keep it with her when he'd gone; she tightened her arms around him and felt his tightening around her as the indomitable power of their love made them one.

When it came time for him to leave she could see how hard it was for him to tear himself away, and she wished so much that he could stay. He kissed her on the mouth lingeringly, and with so much tenderness that he didn't have to speak the words in his heart, she could feel them.

She watched him walk to the door and gave him a smile when he turned back. There was so much more she wanted to give him, so many years she longed to spend with him, precious moments she wished they could share.

'Thank you,' she said softly through her tears.

He blew her a kiss, and raising a hand to catch it she placed it over her heart.

* * *

Josh knew even before he saw Matias Velez's face the next day that something had gone wrong. It wasn't only that the surgery had been going on for too long, or that there had been no news for the past two hours, it was that a short while ago a kind of hush had stolen into his heart. It circled it with warmth and tenderness, with words he couldn't hear or discern, only feel. He'd held it quietly to himself, keeping his head down so the others couldn't see his face, as the sense of her going trailed a gentle path around each and every heartbeat, until it disappeared like a mist that might never have been there.

It was the moment she'd gone. He'd known it, but had said nothing, for in the less spiritual depths of himself he couldn't let go of the hope he was wrong.

Now, as the others listened to the surgeon's words, desperate for them not to mean what he was saying, Josh was aware of a sweet scent of air moving past him. He felt strong hands grasp his shoulders, his grandfather and Sam. Gina cried out wretchedly; Michelle and Shelley caught her as Gil drew Mark into his arms.

Josh's voice was quiet as he said to Velez, 'You know what you have to do?'

Velez nodded. He looked as haggard and exhausted as any man ever could, after the kind of battle he'd just fought, but Josh wasn't seeing him. All he could see was his darling, beautiful wife and the way she'd looked last night when she'd caught his kiss and pressed it to her heart.

447

EPILOGUE

The air was warm and still, the sky over the bay a mass of pale grey cloud, showing not a glimpse of blue. Gulls swooped and fluttered around the jagged cliffs at the end of the beach, where a churning sea crashed and fanned in wild and ceaseless waves. Down at the water's edge, as though distancing itself from the stormy performance nearby, the incoming tide lapped lazily onto the shingle, drifting over seaweed and debris before sinking into the gritty sand.

Josh was sitting on a blanket close to the dunes, elbows resting on his knees as he gazed absently towards the distant horizon. Beside him Jack wobbled and gurgled as he chewed his fists, proud of his new achievement – sitting up on his own.

A month had somehow passed since Vivi had left them, although time had lost meaning for Josh and he wasn't even sure he wanted it to come back. Nothing could have prepared him for what it would be like to lose her, how empty even the busy days would feel, how pointless everything important seemed. It was almost impossible to get a grip on this new reality, this place in his life that was the start of a future without her.

No one had wanted to think about a fatal stroke taking her during the surgery, not the doctors, nor the medical team, nor anyone else in the family, although they'd all known it could happen. There had been no sense in discussing it, for it would only make the stress of it all even worse than it already was. It was something they'd held at a distance, allowing it no more presence than a faint shadow at the edges of their hope and urgency for her to make it. And yet he and Vivi, on a level that only they shared, had sensed during those final days that their time together was drawing to an end. They hadn't mentioned it, they hadn't wanted to believe it, much less put it into words, and now he kept asking himself if they should have done so.

Some days anger swelled through him as powerfully as the longing that never released him. In many ways it felt as though his whole life had been leading him to her, and hers to him; that their chance to love, to share, to create a beautiful child was all they had ever been about, and all that would ever matter. Jack *was* all that mattered, but Josh needed to find a way to continue without her, to start feeling nothing but thankful that he was the man she'd loved, and that he'd been able to give her all that he had. He knew that if he had his time over he wouldn't change a thing, apart from her condition, of course. No matter how raw and wrenching the loss he was feeling now, he would never regret what they'd had, would always treasure it and know that he was far richer and more human because of it.

But God, it was hard getting through each day without her.

Aware of Jack toppling softly onto his back he lay down beside him, propping himself on one elbow to watch the joyful leg kicks and tiny punches, as though his growing son was trying out new yoga moves. Achieving something like a Happy Baby Pose with a foot in each hand, Jack gave full voice to a jubilant shriek and turned wide and mischievous-seeming eyes to his father. They were the same colour as Josh's, even the same shape, and yet the looks his son often gave him, particularly the wicked ones, were entirely his mother's.

They'd stroll back over the dunes soon to join a family barbecue at Nana Gina's, but Josh had received a call on the way here that had made him want to bring Jack to this quiet spot where he and Vivi had spent so much time together. It was here that they'd come to realize just how much they meant to one another, and it was during moments like this, when it was only him and Jack, that he could feel her all around them, watching and listening, loving them with all her beautiful heart. She even spoke to them at times, but that was often what he found the hardest, the sound of her voice coming to him in the silence, and also in the letters she'd left them.

There were so many. She hadn't forgotten anyone, but he'd only read a few of those she'd left for him and Jack. She'd written a card for each of their son's birthdays until he was eighteen; she'd put together an album of photographs so he'd be able to see how very precious he'd been to her as a baby. She'd told him, in letters she'd left open so Josh could read them, about the night she'd met his daddy and how she'd known right away that she was falling in love. She explained about her condition, and how sorry she was that her heart hadn't managed to last any longer than it had. She urged him to understand that it had never had the power to make her love him less, only to make her love him more. She wanted him to be as much like his daddy as he looked, and always to remember just how much happiness he had brought to their lives.

'*You are our miracle,*' she told him, '*you are my real heart.*'

To Josh she'd written more pages than he'd been able to face for a while, but recently he'd started to go through them. It was like spending time with her, just the two of them, reliving their love, feeling its truth and depth as more private tears were shed.

Today he'd read, '. . . my darling, thank you so much for everything you've brought to my life, the fun, the laughter, the friendship, the caring . . . There's so much, but most of all it's because of you that I know what it means to be a mother and to be truly loved. I hope you know it too, because you are truly loved, Josh, in so many ways and so deeply that I can't believe anyone has felt this much for someone before.

'I know our beautiful boy will have the best daddy in the world, surrounded by a family who loves him dearly. Maybe one day, when the pain of our separation has passed, you will find someone special to share your life with, someone who will love you and be a good mother to Jack. I want you to try to do this, my darling, please, for both your sakes.

'So many thank yous are coming to me needing to be said, and I'm sure I'll think of many more before this letter ends, but the biggest one of all for now is thank you for being you.'

Josh swallowed hard. His eyes were blurred by tears as he recalled the words, and watched Jack scowling at him as though trying to figure him out.

'One day,' Josh said, touching a finger to Jack's baby-soft cheek, 'you'll understand that your mummy wasn't just any mummy, because she was a real live angel, and shall I tell you why?'

Jack made a grab for his father's finger, trying to bite it with his four ferocious teeth. Hauling him up Josh settled him on his knee, facing him out to sea, and loving the way his small body sank so easily into him. 'This morning,' he said, pressing a kiss to Jack's riot of dark curls, 'I had a phone call from someone who's alive because of your mummy. It's . . .' He paused, taking in the inexpressible wonder of it, still unsure exactly how he felt about it. 'It's true,' he said softly. 'They really are alive because of her.' How could he feel anything but good about that? It was what she'd wanted, and if he had to lose her it was what he wanted too.

Jack's head turned so he could look up at his father, his expression seeming faintly puzzled.

'Just after she left us,' Josh explained, brushing a finger under the baby's chin, 'she gave away the most precious gifts in the world to people who needed them the most, people she didn't even know. And those gifts made the biggest and most important difference anyone can make to someone else's life. She did it for *eight* people. Can you believe that?'

Jack frowned, and suddenly arched his back, letting

it be known that he wanted to stand up. Josh raised him to his feet and put his cheek against his so that together they could gaze out at the bay. A gentle breeze stirred the grasses behind them, and a small patch of blue opened briefly in the clouds. 'Those people won't ever know her,' Josh said softly, 'and we won't know them, but we don't have to know them. All that matters to us is that she gave me the most beautiful gift of all, and that, my son, is you.'

ACKNOWLEDGEMENTS

It's an absolute truth that I could never have written this book without Jim Lynskey's willingness to share his extraordinary experiences. Yes, he is a real person who very generously allowed me to weave some of his story with Vivi's to bring a greater sense of drama and reality to this vital issue. Knowing Jim has made me more aware than ever of the importance of organ donation. It would have changed his young life immeasurably if the right heart could have been found for him, but I'm afraid it wasn't. Between the hardback and paperback publication of this book his wait came to an end. He died on May 13th 2019 at the age of 23.

I will never forget him, and will always be in awe of how much he did to help others. I know he will also live on in the hearts and memories of everyone who knew him, including those who met him at the hardback launch of *One Minute Later*. I am so grateful that he was able to be there, and seeing what a kick he got out of being a character in a book was funny and endearing in equal measures. Everyone present was enchanted by him and impressed by how frankly and eloquently he discussed his condition. He even signed copies of the book for them. I'd also like to thank everyone who follows my page on Facebook for the outpouring of kindness and affection that was so beautifully and generously expressed when we were willing him to pull through his latest setback. Although he left us in the end, this compassion and caring was a wonderful support for his family, and continues to be as your condolences pour in. Rest in peace, Jim and thank you for all you did to help those who need new organs, and for all your efforts to make the rest of us understand the importance of donation.

I would also like to thank Dr Robin Martin, Consultant Paediatric and Adult Congenital Cardiologist at the Bristol Royal Hospital for Children and Bristol Heart Institute, for so much guidance and enthusiasm for the story. Any anomalies or shortcuts in the telling are wholly my responsibility. Sometimes it is more expedient in a dramatic sense to move things along more quickly than might otherwise happen.

My thanks also go to Mr Ash Pawade, retired paediatric cardiac surgeon, Bristol, for pointing me in the right direction at the outset.

Then we come to Shelley's part of the story and for that I warmly thank our local sheep farmer, Ruth Dixon. Ruth's tales of farm life are many and varied, hilarious and inspiring, and in some cases nothing short of tragic. It was quite an eye-opener for me to discover that so much is going on just across the road from us. I should stress however that Deerwood is purely fictional.

I'd like to thank everyone at my new publishers HarperCollins for the incredibly warm welcome I've received since joining. The camaraderie is intoxicating – I use the word with feeling – and being included in the Harper family is a privilege. It's been a tremendous pleasure working with Kimberley Young and her team in the UK on this book and with Liz Stein and her team in the US. I thank Charlie and Annabel Redmayne, Kate Elton, and Roger Cazalet for making the transition so enjoyable.

In a special category all of his own is my wonderful agent, Luigi Bonomi, who I thank with all my heart for so much enthusiasm, advice, support, laughter and fab lunches at The Ivy.

Susan Lewis is proud to support 'Save9Lives', an organ donation campaign founded by NHS Organ Donation Ambassador, Jim Lynskey. To find out more about the campaign and how you can help, please visit www.save9lives.com.

Reading Group Questions

- What was your initial impression of Vivi? Did it change as the book progressed? If so, how and why?

- Discuss how the novel explores relationships between mothers and daughters.

- How does the story explore the subjects of guilt and blame?

- Discuss how Susan Lewis structures the novel to create tension.

- Who is your favourite character and why?

- How do the two timeframes in the story complement each other? Do they work together successfully?

- How did you feel about the ending?

- What have you taken away from the story?

Read on for a sneak peek
of Susan's new novel,

home truths

On sale August 2019

'Don't go! Please... Oh God, no, please don't...'

'I can't take any more, Angie. I swear... If you'd seen what I just have...'

'Whatever it is...'

'Our five-year-old son had a syringe in his hand,' he raged, almost choking on the words.

'Oh my God. Oh Steve...'

'I need to find Liam, and when I do I'm turning him in to the police along with every other one of those lowlife bastards...'

'No! *No!*'

He could still hear his wife screaming down the phone, begging him to stop as he tossed his mobile on to the passenger seat and steered the van, almost on two wheels, out of the street.

He'd had enough. He didn't care about the danger he was putting himself in, or what might happen after, he was too enraged for that. *You bastard! How dare you... He's a child, for God's sake...* The words circled endlessly through his head.

It took a while to get across town. He barely even saw the traffic, or the red lights that tried to delay him, as though giving him some time to think. He didn't want it. He was past thinking, past caring about anything other than the need to make this stop.

When he reached the hellish streets, the sore at the heart of the sprawling estate, he screeched to a halt on the infamous Colemead Lane and leapt out. He was so pumped with fury that his fists were already clenched, his muscles tensed for attack. His rationale had fled, along with his temper and sense of self-preservation.

He looked around, his eyes fierce. The mostly destitute houses with boarded-up windows and padlocked doors were as silent as graves. The tower blocks at the end with graffitied walls and urine-soaked stairwells rose drearily towards a patched grey sky. Even the pub looked deserted, its sign dangling from one hinge, its barred windows telling their own story.

'I know you're here,' he roared at the top of his lungs. 'Liam Watts! Get out here now!'

His rage echoed around the silence like useless gunshot scattering over a ghost town.

'*Liam Watts!* Show your face.'

Everything remained still.

Seconds ticked by as though the world was holding its breath, waiting to see what would happen next. He sensed he wasn't alone, that he was being watched, that this was a charged hiatus before the storm broke.

He was ready for it. His whole body was primed to take it.

There was a scuffling behind him, sharp yet muffled, and he spun round, heart thudding thickly with fury and fear, eyes blazing.

'Go home,' a wretched young woman hissed from a nearby doorway. She was thin, shaking, her eyes seeming to bleed in their sockets. She waved feebly in no particular direction before stumbling into a side alley and disappearing.

He didn't see them coming at first, he only heard them: faint, deliberate footsteps crunching, pounding, almost military in their pace. He peered around, trying to get a sense of where they were. How many they were.

'*Liam Watts!*' he roared again.

The sun slipped its cover of cloud, dazzling him, throwing a rich golden glow over the street, as though to paint this purgatory into something glorious.

He listened, hearing his heartbeat, hectic, scared; the sound of a dog barking, a scream cut suddenly short.

Then he saw them emerging from the shadows like ghouls, closing on him from each end of the street, slowly, purposefully, faces wrapped in black balaclavas, baseball bats and iron bars slapping into palms, chains rattling through brutal fingers.

As his survival instinct kicked in he turned to run. He couldn't take on this many. He'd be a fool to try. 'Liam,' he shouted, more panicked than angry now.

He reached the van, tore open the door, but it was too late. A flying brick hit his back, sending him sprawling into the dust.

He tried to scramble up.

A crippling blow to the backs of his knees buckled his legs under him.

'Liam,' he cried raggedly as he hit the ground.

A steel toe-capped boot slammed into his head.

He rolled on to his back, dazed, blood in his eyes. He could make out the faces gathered over him in a blur, laughing, as blind to his humanity as to their own.

He crossed his arms over his head to protect it. He tried in the chaos to spot Liam, to beg him to put a stop to this.

Time, reality, slipped to another dimension as his hearing faded and vicious blows continued pummelling his body. He thought of his other children, Grace and Zac, as more blood swilled around his eyes and his teeth were crunched from their roots.

He thought of his wife, his beautiful wife whom he loved with all his heart.

The thudding of boots and weapons grew worse, more frenzied, unstoppable; pain exploded through his body with a thousand jagged edges as bloodied vomit choked from his mouth. Darkness loomed, shrank away then tried to swallow him again. Dimly he heard screaming, a distant siren, and somewhere inside the mayhem he was murmuring his son's name, 'Liam, Liam,' until he could murmur no more.

With Susan Lewis, you always need one page more . . .
If you're desperate to find out what happens to
Angie and Steve, *Home Truths* is available
to buy from August 2019.

Keep up to date with

Susan

 @susanlewisbooks

/SusanLewisBooks

www.susanlewis.com

Sign up to Susan's newsletter to receive the latest news about her books, events and competitions

www.susanlewis.com/newsletter